IT seemed more than three days that I had spent in the attic. It was like a dream. Dickon felt it too—so he told me afterward.

It was on the fourth day that he came to see me, and I knew that something was wrong right away. He was paler than usual and his hair was ruffled.

I went swiftly to him and put my hands on his shoulders. It was the first time I had ever touched him. His reaction was immediate. He put his arms about me and held me close to him. He did not speak for a few moments and I did not ask him to. I was savoring the wonder of being close to him.

At length he broke away from me. "You must get away from here," he said. "My uncle will be back soon . . . and I fear he will kill you."

"We shall have to say goodbye," I murmured.

He turned his head aside and nodded. A terrible desolation came over me. "I should never see you again."

"No—no— That must not be," he whispered. Then he held me against him and kissed me.

Will You Love Me in September

A NOVEL BY

Philippa Carr

FAWCETT CREST · NEW YORK

WILL YOU LOVE ME IN SEPTEMBER

THIS BOOK CONTAINS THE COMPLETE TEXT OF THE
ORIGINAL HARDCOVER EDITION.

Published by Fawcett Crest Books, CBS Educational and
Professional Publishing, a division of CBS Inc., by arrangement with G.P. Putnam's Sons.

ISBN: 0-449-24506-3

Printed in the United States of America

First Fawcett Crest Printing: June 1982

10 9 8 7 6 5 4 3 2 1

Will you love me in December as you do in May?
—Old Song

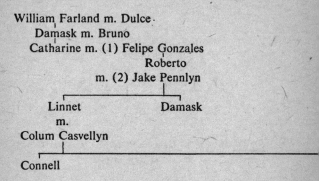

William Farland m. Dulce
Damask m. Bruno
Catharine m. (1) Felipe Gonzales
Roberto
m. (2) Jake Pennlyn

Linnet   Damask
m.
Colum Casvellyn

Connell

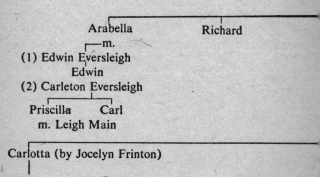

Arabella   Richard
m.
(1) Edwin Eversleigh
Edwin
(2) Carleton Eversleigh

Priscilla   Carl
m. Leigh Main

Carlotta (by Jocelyn Frinton)

Clarissa (by John Field)

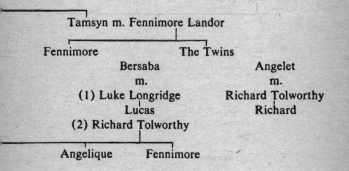

Tamsyn m. Fennimore Landor

Fennimore   The Twins

Bersaba   Angelet
m.   m.
(1) Luke Longridge   Richard Tolworthy
Lucas   Richard
(2) Richard Tolworthy

Angelique   Fennimore

Damaris
m. Jeremy Granthorn
Sabrina

In the Heart of the Family

It is one of the perversities of human nature that when something which has been passionately wanted is acquired, it loses its desirability and there can come a time when the need to escape from it becomes an obsession. Thus it was with me. What I had desperately needed as a child—obviously because of what had happened to me—was security. By the time I was thirteen in that fateful year of 1715, I longed to escape from the cozy cocoon in which my family had wrapped me, and when the opportunity came I seized it.

I must have been about four years old when I was brought to England by my aunt Damaris and my uncle Jeremy. Those first four years of my life had been lived most dramatically, though I did not realize that at the time. I suppose I thought it was the most natural thing for a girl to be kidnapped by her father, taken across the sea to live most luxuriously with her parents, and then suddenly find herself plunged into the poverty of the back streets of Paris, from which she was rescued and whisked over the sea again to an English home. I accepted all that with the philosophical endurance of a child.

One of the events which stands out in my memory is that homecoming. Vividly I recall getting off the boat and standing on the shingle. I shall never forget the ecstatic look in my Aunt Damaris' eyes. I loved her dearly. I always had from the time I met her, when she had been ill, lying on a couch, unable to walk more than a few steps. I had been bewildered as I stood there. I knew that I had no mother, for she had died mysteriously at the same time as my father had, and I was very anxious, for it seemed to me that everyone ought to have a mother—and a father as well.

I had said, "Aunt Damaris, are you going to be my mother now?" and she had answered, "Yes, Clarissa, I am." I still remember the great comfort those words brought me.

I had noticed that Uncle Jeremy was looking at her intently, and I decided that as I had lost my handsome, incomparable father, he would do very well as a substitute, so I asked him if he would be my father. He had said it would depend on Damaris.

I know now what had happened. They had been two unhappy people, hurt by life, each of them watchful so as not to be hurt again. Damaris was gentle and loving, eager to be loved. Jeremy was different. He was on his guard, suspicious of people's motives. His was a dark nature; Damaris' should have been a sunny one.

When I was a child I had not understood this. I had merely realized that I was looking for security and these were the two who could offer it to me. Young as I was, in that moment on the beach I could see that I must cling to them. Damaris understood my feelings. For all her seeming innocence she was very wise—far wiser, in truth, than people like Carlotta, my brilliant, worldly mother.

Those days in England were a joyous revelation to me. I discovered I had a family, and that they were all waiting to greet me, ready to draw me into their magic circle. I was one of them, I was loved, and because of my mother's tragedy I was a consolation to them all. During those days I felt as though I were floating on a cloud of love. I reveled in it. At the same time I kept thinking of that moment when Damaris had come into the cellarlike room where I was with Jeanne's mother and grandmother, and I could smell the odor of dampness and decaying foliage which always seemed to hang about the place and which came from the cans of water in which the unsold flowers were kept in the hope of preserving them for sale the next day. It had been her voice I recognized first when she had said, "Where is the child?" I had flung myself into her arms and she had held me tightly saying, "Thank you, God. Oh, thank you" under her breath, which impressed me even at such a time, for it occurred to me that she must be on very familiar terms with God to speak to him like that.

I remember how she held me as though she were afraid I would run away. I was not likely to do that. I was so glad to get away from that cellar, for although Jeanne was good to me, I was always afraid of Maman, who always took the few sous Jeanne brought in from the sale of flowers and feverishly counted them, muttering as she did so. I had always been aware that she grudged my being there and but for Jeanne would have turned me into the streets. Even more terrifying than Maman was the Grand'mère, who was always dressed in musty black and had hairs growing out of a great wart on her chin, which both fascinated and repelled me. I had quickly realized that they were not my true friends, and Jeanne always had to protect me from them. Sometimes I had gone out with Jeanne, and I was not sure whether I disliked that as much as staying in. It was good to get away from the cellar and Maman and Grand'mère, of course, but I was usually so cold standing in the streets beside Jeanne, holding out bunches of violets or whatever flowers were in season; they were always wet, too, because they had to be kept in water, and my hands grew red and chapped.

It had been a dramatic homecoming and I remember every moment of it. We passed near the great house called Eversleigh Court where, Damaris told me, my great-grandparents lived, and we stopped at the Dower House, the home of Damaris and my grandparents. They were so excited to see us. My grandmother ran out of the house, and when she saw Damaris she gave a cry of joy and ran to her and hugged her as though she would never let her go. Then she turned to me, and as she picked me up she was crying.

A man came out and kept kissing Damaris and then me. After that we went into the house and everyone seemed to be talking at once. Jeremy stood by awkwardly, and as it seemed the others had forgotten him, I went over and took his hand, which seemed to remind them that he was there. My grandmother said we must be hungry and she would give orders.

Damaris declared that she was too happy to think of food, but I told them that I could be happy and hungry at the same time, at which they all laughed.

We were soon sitting at a table eating. It was a lovely room—so different from Jeanne's cellar—and a warm and happy feeling seemed to wrap itself around me. This was going to be my home for a while, I gathered. I asked Damaris and she said, "Until . . . ," and looked very happy.

"Yes, of course," said my grandmother. "It is wonderful to have you back, my darling. And Clarissa too. My little love, you are going to stay with us for a while."

"Until . . . ," I said uneasily.

Damaris knelt beside me and said, "Your Uncle Jeremy

and I are going to be married soon, and when we are, you will come to our home and live with us there."

That satisfied me, and I knew that all of them were glad I was here.

Jeremy rode back to his house and I was left at the Eversleigh Dower House. I had a little room next to that of Damaris. "So that we can be close together," she said, which was comforting because I did dream now and then that I was back in Jeanne's cellar and that the old Grand'mère turned into a witch and the hairs growing out of her wart turned into a forest in which I was lost.

Then I would go into Damaris' bed and tell her about the forest with trees which had faces like old Grand'mère's and their branches were like brown fingers which kept counting money.

"Only a dream, darling," Damaris would say. "Dreams can't hurt you."

It was a great relief to get into Damaris' bed when the dreams came.

I was taken to Eversleigh Court, where there were more relations. These were very old. There was my great-grandmother Arabella and my great-grandfather Carleton, a fierce old man with bushy eyebrows. He liked me, though. He looked at me in a rather frightening way, but I planted my feet firmly together, and putting my hands behind my back, stared at him to show I was not going to let him scare me, because, after all, he was not nearly so alarming as old Grand'mère, and I knew that if he wanted to turn me away, Damaris, Jeremy and the others would stop him. "You're like your mother," he said. "One of the fighting Eversleighs."

"Yes, I am," I answered, trying to look as fierce as he did, at which everyone laughed, and my great-grandmother said, "Clarissa has made a conquest of Carleton!"

There was another branch of the family. They came to Eversleigh to visit from a place called Ayot Abbas. I vaguely remembered Benjie because he had been my father before Hessenfield. It was bewildering and I could not understand it at all. I had had one father, and then Hessenfield had come and said he was going to be my father; now he was dead and Jeremy was going to be. Surely such a surfeit of fathers was most unusual.

Poor Benjie, he looked very sad, but when he saw me his eyes lighted up; he picked me up and gave me one of those emotional hugs.

12

Vaguely I remembered his mother, Harriet, who had the bluest eyes I had ever seen; then there was Benjie's father, Gregory, a quiet, kind man. They had been another set of grandparents. I was surrounded by relations, and I quickly realized that there was a controversy in the family and it was all about me. Benjie wanted me to go home with him. He said he was my father in a way and had a greater claim than Damaris. Grandmother Priscilla said it would break Damaris' heart if I was taken away from her, and, after all, she was the one who had brought me home.

I was very gratified to be so wanted and sad when Benjie went away. Before he went he said to me, "Dear Clarissa, Ayot Abbas will always be your home when you want it. Will you remember that?" I promised I would, and Harriet said, "You must come and stay with us often, Clarissa. That is the only thing that will satisfy us."

I said I would, and they went away. Soon after that Damaris and Jeremy were married and Enderby Hall became my home.

Jeremy had lived there by himself, and when Damaris married him she was determined to change it a great deal. In the days before the wedding she would take me there. The place fascinated me. There was a man called Smith who had a face like a relief map with rivers and mountains on it—there were lines everywhere and little warty lumps—and his skin was as brown as the earth. When he saw me his face would crinkle up and his mouth went up at one side. I couldn't stop looking at him. I realized I was seeing Smith's smile.

Then there was Damon. He was a great Newfoundland dog that stood as tall as I was. He had curly hair, lots of it, half black, half white, with a bushy tail which turned up at the end. We took one look and loved each other.

"Careful," said Damaris, "he can be fierce."

But not with me—never with me. He knew I loved him immediately. We had had no dogs in the *hôtel*, and certainly not in Jeanne's cellar. And I was so happy because I was going to live in the same house as Damon, Damaris, Jeremy and Smith. Smith said, "I've never seen him take to anyone like that before." I just put my arms round Damon's neck and kissed the tip of his damp nose. They all watched with trepidation, but Damon and I knew how it was between us.

Jeremy was very pleased that we liked each other. Everybody was very pleased about most things at that time, except

13

of course when they thought of Carlotta, and when I thought of her and dear handsome Hessenfield I was sad too. Damaris assured me that they would be happy in the place they had gone to, and that made me feel that I could be happy where I had come to—so I started to be.

Enderby Hall was a dark house at first, until they cut down some of the bushes which were all around it and made lawns and flower beds. Damaris took down some of the heavy furnishings and replaced them with lighter colors. The hall was magnificent; it had a vaulted roof and beautiful paneling. At one end were the screens, beyond which were the kitchens, and at the other a lovely staircase, which led to the minstrels' gallery.

"When we entertain we shall have musicians to play there, Clarissa," Damaris told me.

I listened with awe, taking in every detail of my new life and savoring it all with complete delight.

There was one bedroom which Damaris hated to go into. I soon sensed that, and with the directness of a child asked her why. She looked astonished. I think that was because she knew she had betrayed her reluctance.

She merely said, "I'm going to change it all, Clarissa. I'm going to make it unrecognizable."

"I like it," I said. "It's pretty." And I went to the bed and stroked the velvet hangings. But she looked at it with loathing, as though she were seeing something I could not. I understood later . . . much later . . . what that room meant to her.

Well, she changed it, and it certainly looked different. The red velvet was replaced by white-and-gold damask, with curtains to match. She even changed the carpet. She was right. It did look different, but she did not use it as her and Jeremy's room, although it was the best in the house. The door was always shut. I believe she rarely went there.

So this was my new home—Enderby Hall, about ten minutes' ride from the Dower House and an equal distance from Eversleigh Court, so I was surrounded by my family.

That Damaris and Jeremy were happy together there could be no doubt; as for myself, I was so pleased to have escaped from that Paris cellar that I lived in a state of joyful appreciation of everything for those first few months. I used to stand in the middle of the great hall and look up at the minstrels' gallery and say, "I'm here." And I tried to remember the cellar with the cold stone floor and the rats that came at night and looked at me with their baleful eyes that seemed yellowish in the darkness. I did this to remind myself that I had escaped and told myself I would never, never go back there again. I did not like to see cut flowers in pots because they reminded me. Damaris loved them and gathered basketfuls from the garden. She had a special room called the flower room and she used to arrange them there. She would say, "Come on, Clarissa, we'll go and get some roses." She quickly noticed, though, that I grew quiet and mournful and I often had a nightmare the following night. So she stopped cutting flowers. Damaris was very perceptive. More so than Jeremy. I think he was too concerned with the way life had treated him before he met Damaris to think much about how it had treated others. Damaris thought of others all the time, and believed that what had gone wrong in her life was largely her own fault rather than fate's.

When the violets came out she took me to the hedgerows and we gathered wild ones. She said, "It was violets, you remember, that brought us together. So I shall always love violets. Will you?"

I said I would, and it seemed different picking them after that; and in time I didn't mind about the flowers. To show Damaris this I went into the garden to pick some roses for her. She understood at once and hugged me tightly, hiding her face so that I should not see the tears in her eyes.

In those early days they were always talking about me not only at Enderby but at the Dower House, and there were conferences at Eversleigh Court. I often heard someone say, "But what would be best for the child?"

The cocoon was being woven very tightly round me. I had had an unusual start. Therefore I needed very special care.

Perhaps that was why I felt very much at ease with Smith. I used to watch him doing the garden or cleaning the silver. Before Damaris became mistress of the house he used to do everything, but now servants from Eversleigh Court used to be sent over by Great-grandmother Arabella. Jeremy did not really like that; Smith didn't like it either.

Smith treated me, as he would say, "rough." "Don't stand there idle," he would say. "Satan finds mischief for idle hands to do." And I would have to arrange the forks and knives in their cubbyholes, as he called them, or pick up branches and dead flowers and put them in the wheelbarrow. Damaris was often present and the three of us would be very happy together. With Smith I felt completely at ease, not the child whose welfare had to be continually considered—sometimes at some inconvenience to others, I feared—but a fellow worker of very little importance. It seemed strange to want to be of no importance, but I really did. It was an indication, of course, that I was already beginning to feel the bounds of security tightening around me.

There was a discussion in the family as to whether or not I should have a governess. Damaris said she would teach me.

"Perhaps you are doing too much," said Grandmother Priscilla anxiously.

"Dear mother," smiled Damaris, "this will be a great pleasure, and I'll be sitting down all the time!"

Great-grandmother Arabella wondered whether I should have a governess—a French one. I could speak French because I had learned it side by side with English in the *hôtel* with my parents, and later, in the cellar, no one had spoken anything but French.

"It would be a pity to lose that," said Arabella.

"They never do," was Great-grandfather Carleton's comment. "Not once they have acquired it. The child would only need a little practice at any time in her life. And you could not get a French governess now, with a war between our countries."

So it was decided that for the time being Damaris should teach me, and the idea of a governess was shelved.

All the talk of French reminded me of Jeanne. I had loved her very much in those days of trial. She had been a bulwark between me and the harsh Paris streets. If anyone had ever represented security to me, she had. I often wondered about her. I knew that Damaris had offered to bring her back to England with us, but how could she leave Maman and the old Grand'mère? They would have starved without her.

Damaris had said, "If ever you felt free to come to us, you would always be welcome."

I was glad she had said that and I knew she had rewarded Jeanne for what she had done for me. Jeanne was a clever manager and would make what had been given her last a very long time.

So the year began to pass. I had my pony and Smith taught me to ride and I had never been happier in my life than when I was riding round the paddock, with Smith holding a leading rein and Damon running after us barking with excitement. It was better even than riding on Hessenfield's shoulders.

There were long summer days sitting at the table in the

schoolroom learning with Aunt Damaris and then going out to ride—off the leading rein now—walking with Damon, lying in the grass with Damon, going to Eversleigh Court or the Dower House to drink lemonade and eat fancy cakes in summer or steaming mulled wine and pies straight from the oven in winter. I loved all the seasons: Ash Wednesday and the beginning of Lent; the interminable service and the sadness of Good Friday alleviated by hot cross buns; Easter with daffodils everywhere and the delights of simnel cake; sitting in church close to Damaris and counting the blues and reds in the stained-glass windows; the number of people I could see without turning my head; and how many ah's, er's and well's Parson Renton uttered during the sermon. There was Harvest Festival, with all the fruit and vegetables decorating the church; and best of all Christmas, with the crib in the manger, ivy holly, mistletoe, carols, presents and excitement. It was all wonderful and I was at the heart of it. They were always questioning themselves and each other about "the child."

"The child should see more children." Children were invited. There were not many in the neighborhood and I did not greatly care for any of them; I liked best to be with Damaris, Smith and Damon. But I was very content to be "the child" in the midst of all this concern.

As I grew older I began to learn certain things. This was mainly from the servants who came from the Court. They didn't like coming to Enderby, and yet in a way it was an adventure and I think they acquired a little merit from their fellow servants for having come. They would go back to Eversleigh Court and for a while be the center of attraction. I was enormously interested in people and I had an avid curiosity to discover what was in their minds. I had quickly discovered that people rarely meant what they said and that very often words veiled meanings rather than expressed them. I used to listen to the servants talking. I would unashamedly eavesdrop. In defense of myself I must say that I had been made aware that I had had an unusual upbringing and that there were certain facts which had been kept from me; and of course the person I wished to know most about was myself.

Once I heard two servants talking together in the great hall. I was in the minstrels' gallery. Sounds floated up to me while I remained unseen.

"That Jeremy . . . he was always a queer customer."

There were grunts of agreement.

"Lived by himself with one man servant. Just that Smith and himself . . . and that dog keeping everyone away."

"Well, all that's changed now Miss Damaris is here."

"And then her going to France like that."

"It was a brave thing to do."

"I'll grant her that. She's a little baggage, that Miss Clarissa."

My excitement grew. So I was a baggage!

"It wouldn't surprise me if she went the way of her mother. That Miss Carlotta was a Regular One. She was so good-looking they say no man could resist her."

"Go on!"

"Yes, and wasn't it shameful the way she went on and left poor Mr. Benjie. Abducted! Abducted my foot!"

"Well, it's over now and she's dead, ain't she?"

"Wages of sin you might say."

"And Madame Clarissa will be such another. You mark my words."

"They say the sins of the father and all that."

"You'll see. We'll have sparks there. Just you wait till she gets a bit older. You going to do the minstrels'?"

"I suppose so. Gives me the creeps that place."

"It's the part that was haunted. You can change the curtains and things but what good does that do? New curtains ain't going to drive ghosts away."

"A haunted house is always a haunted house, they say."

"That's true. This is a house for trouble. It'll come again—lawns and flower beds, new curtains and carpets notwithstanding. I'll come up the gallery with you if you like. I know you don't want to go up there alone. Let's finish down here first."

That gave me a chance to escape.

So my beautiful mother had acted shamefully. She had left Benjie for my father, Lord Hessenfield. Vague memories came back to me . . . of a night in the shrubbery, being lifted in strong arms . . . the smell of the sea and the excitement of being on a ship. Yes, I was deeply involved in that shameful adventure; in fact I was a result of it.

It was later that I learned the story. In those days I was piecing it together from what I could pick up from gossip and what I could remember.

There were tensions in the household. Jeremy had what were known as "moods," from which even Damaris could not always rouse him. Then he appeared to be very sad and it had something to do with his bad leg, which had been hurt in battle and gave him pain at times. Then Damaris herself had days when she was not well. She tried to hide the fact, but I could see that behind the brightness it was there.

She longed for a child.

One day when we were sitting together she told me she was going to have a baby. I had known something tremendous had happened because even Jeremy looked as though he was never going to have a mood again and Smith kept chuckling to himself.

I looked forward to the coming of the baby. I would look after it, I said. I would sing it some French songs which Jeanne used to sing to me. The household buzzed with preparations. Grandmother Priscilla was constantly fussing over Damaris and Grandfather Leigh behaved as though she were made of china. Great-grandmother Arabella was always giving advice and Great-grandfather Carleton kept muttering "Women!"

It struck me that when there was a baby I should no longer be "the child," and Damaris' own would be more dear to her than I, the adopted one, who was only her niece. That was a faintly depressing thought, but I put it aside and threw myself into the general excitement.

I shall never forget that day. Damaris started to have pains in the middle of the night. Grandmother Priscilla was at Enderby and the midwife was there too. Some of the servants from the Court had been sent over.

I heard the commotion and got out of bed and ran to Damaris' room. I was met by a worried Priscilla. "Go back to your room at once," she said, more sternly than she had ever spoken to me before. I obeyed, and when I went again I was told by one of the servants, "Get out from under our feet. This is no place for you."

So I went back and waited in my room. I was terribly frightened, for I sensed all was not well. It was like being back in the cellar again. What was happening could mean change. I was still at that time clinging to my security.

The waiting seemed to go on and on, and when it was finally over, all the joyous expectancy had gone from the house. It was dreary and sad. The baby was stillborn and Damaris was very ill. Nobody seemed to notice me. There were talks between the grandparents. This time I was not mentioned. It was all "poor Damaris" and what this would mean to her. And she was desperately ill. Jeremy was sunk in gloom; there was a bitter twist to his mouth. I was sure he believed Damaris was going to die as well as the baby.

Grandmother Priscilla was going to stay at Enderby for a while to look after her daughter. Benjie came over. He said he would take me back to Ayot Abbas, and to my chagrin no attempt was made to dissuade him from doing so.

So I went to Ayot Abbas, there to find that loving concentration of affection which I had known at Enderby.

Benjie loved me dearly. He would have liked me to stay there and be his daughter. Oddly enough, when I was at Ayot Abbas, memories came flooding back to me. I remembered being there and how I used to play in the gardens with my nurse in attendance. And most of all I remembered the day when Hessenfield took me away to the excitement of the ship and the *hôtel*, which culminated in the cold and menacing cellar, with Jeanne as my only protector.

I could not help being intrigued by Harriet. Since her husband Gregory was so gentle and kind I could be very happy at the Abbas if it had not meant leaving Damaris, with whom I had a very special relationship.

This must have happened about the year 1710, for I was eight years old. But I suppose what had happened to me had made me somewhat precocious. Harriet thought so anyway.

Harriet and I were alike in a way. We were both enormously interested in people, and that meant that we learned a good deal about them.

She was an amazing woman; she had an indestructible beauty. She must have been very old—she would never tell us how old—but the years seemed to have left her untouched. She dismissed them, and try as they might, they could not encroach on her with any real effect. Her hair was dark still. "I will pass on the secret before I go, Clarissa," she said with a smile which was as mischievous as it must have been when she was my age. In addition to this dark rippling hair she had the bluest of eyes, and if they were embedded in wrinkles, they were alive with the spirit of eternal youth.

She took me in hand and spent a lot of time with me. She probed me, asking many questions, all about the past.

"You're old enough to know the truth about yourself," she said. "I reckon you have your eyes and ears wide open for what you can pick up, eh?"

I admitted it. One could admit to peccadilloes with Harriet because one could be sure she would have committed them in the same position . . . perhaps more daring ones. Although she was old and must be respected, she was different from my family. When I was with her I felt that I was with someone who was as young as I was in spirit but with a vast experience of life which could be useful to me.

"Yes," she said, "it's better for you to know the whole truth. I reckon your dear grandmother would never whisper a word of it. I know my Priscilla, and Damaris—dear, good girl—would do as her mother told her. Even your great-grandmother would never tell you, I'm sure. Dear me! It is left to poor old Harriet."

Then she told me that my mother had fallen in with some Jacobites at an inn, the leader of whom had been Lord Hessenfield. They fell in love, and I was the result. But they were not married. There had not been time and Hessenfield had had to make a speedy escape to France. I was born, and Benjie had said he would be my father, so my mother was married to him. But later on Hessenfield came for my mother and me and took us to France, so poor Benjie, who had thought of himself as my father, was left lonely.

"You must be particularly kind to Benjie," said Harriet.

"I will," I assured her.

"Poor Benjie. He must marry again and forget your mother. But she was so beautiful, Clarissa."

"I know."

"Of course you know. But she brought little happiness to herself or to others."

"She did to Hessenfield."

"Ah . . . two of a kind. Your parents, dear Clarissa, were unusual people. They were rare people. How fortunate you are to have had such parents. I wonder if you will grow up like them. If you do, you will have to take care. You must curb your recklessness. You must think before you act. I always did, and look what it has brought me—this lovely house, a good man, the dearest son in the world. What a lovely way to spend one's old age! But I wasn't born to it, Clarissa. I worked for it . . . I worked every inch of the way. It's the best in the end. Dearest child, you have every chance of a good life. You have lost your parents but you have a family to love you. And now you know the truth about yourself, you must be happy. I was. Be bold but not reckless. Take adventure when it comes but be sure that you never act rashly. I know. I have lived a long time and proved how to be happy. That's the best thing in the world, Clarissa. Happiness."

I used to sit with her and listen to her talking, which was fascinating. She told me a great deal about the past and her stage life and how she had first met my great-grandmother Arabella in the days just before the Restoration of Charles the Second. She could talk so vividly—acting as she went along—and told me more about my family during that brief visit than I had ever heard before.

She was right. It was good for me to know. I think in a way it was a beginning of the slackening of my need for security. When I heard what had happened to members of my mother's family—there was nothing much Harriet could tell me of my father—that craving for security began to leave me.

I was already feeling out for independence. But, of course, I was only eight years old at this time.

One day Harriet called to me. There was a letter in her hand.

"A message from your grandmother," she said. "She wants you back at Enderby. Damaris is recovering and missing you. Your little visit is at an end. We cannot ignore this, much as we should like to. It has made me very happy to have you here, my dear, and Benjie has been delighted. He will be sad when you go, but as your grandmother—and also your great-grandmother—has reminded me on several occasions, it was Damaris who brought you from France and Damaris who has first claims. How does it feel, Clarissa, to be in such demand? Never mind. Don't tell me. I know. And you hate to leave us, but you want to see your dear Damaris . . . and what is most important, Damaris wants you."

So the visit was over. I did want to see Damaris of course, but I was loath to leave Harriet, Gregory and Benjie. I loved the Abbas too, and I was sadly thinking that there would be no more trips to the island which I could see from my bedroom window. I was torn between Enderby and Ayot Abbas. Once again I was conscious of that surfeit of affection.

Harriet said, "Gregory, Benjie and I will take you back. We'll take the coach. It will give us a little more time together."

The thought of a journey in Gregory's coach delighted me. It was such a splendid vehicle. It had four wheels and a door on either side. Our baggage was carried in saddlebags on horses, as there was no room for it in the coach. Two grooms would accompany us, one to drive the horses and the other to ride behind; they changed places every now and then to share the driving.

22

It was a leisurely journey and very enjoyable, with stops at the inns on the way. It stirred vague memories in me. I had ridden in this coach before. That was when I was very young. It was the first time I had seen Hessenfield. He had played at being a highwayman and stopped the coach. As I sat looking out of the window while we jogged along, pictures flashed in and out of my mind: Hessenfield in a mask, stopping the coach, ordering us to get out, kissing my mother and then kissing me. I had not been afraid. I sensed that my mother was not either. I had given the highwayman the tail of my sugar mouse. Then he had ridden off, and it was not until he carried me away from Ayot Abbas and out to the ship that I saw him again.

I felt drowsy in the coach. Harriet and Gregory were dozing too. Next to Gregory sat Benjie. Every now and then he would catch my eye and smile. He looked very sad, which was because I was going. I thought then, if you were Hessenfield, you would not let me go. He carried me away to a big ship. . . .

I did compare everyone with Hessenfield. He had been taller in stature than anyone else. He had towered above everyone in every way. I was sure that if he had lived he would have put King James on the throne.

We were traveling slowly because the roads were dangerous. There had been heavy rain recently and every now and then we would splash through the puddles of water. I thought it was amusing to see the water splashing out and I laughed.

"Not so pleasant for poor old Merry," said Benjie. Merry was driving at that moment. He had a lugubrious face, rather like a bloodhound's. I thought it funny that he had a name like Merry and laughed whenever I heard it. "One of nature's little jokes," said Harriet.

Suddenly there was a jolt. The coach stopped. Gregory opened his eyes with a start and Harriet said, "What's happened?"

The two men got out. I looked out of the window and saw them staring down at the wheels. Gregory put his head inside the coach. "We're stuck in a gully at the side of the road," he said. "It'll take a little time to get us out."

"I hope not too long," replied Harriet. "In an hour or so it will be dark."

"We'll get to work on it," Gregory told her. He was so proud of his coach and hated anything to go wrong with it. "It's this weather," he went on. "The roads are in a dreadful state."

Harriet looked at me and shrugged her shoulders. "We must settle down to wait," she said. "Not too long, I hope. Are you looking forward to a nice warm inn parlor? What would you like to eat? Hot soup first? The sucking pig? The partridge pie?"

Harriet always made you feel you were doing what she was talking about. I could taste the sweet syllabub and the heart-shaped marchpane.

She said, "You rode in this coach long ago, remember, Clarissa?"

I nodded.

"There was a highwayman," she went on.

"It was Hessenfield. He was playing a joke. He wasn't a highwayman really."

I felt the tears in my eyes because he was gone forever and I should never see him again.

"He was a *man*, wasn't he?" said Harriet quietly.

I knew what she meant and I thought, There will never be anyone like Hessenfield. Then it occurred to me that it was a pity there had to be such wonderful people in the world, because compared with them everyone else seemed lacking. Of course it would not be a pity if they did not die and go away forever.

Harriet leaned toward me and said quietly, "When people die they sometimes seem so much better than when they were alive."

I was pondering this when Gregory put his head inside the coach again. "Another ten minutes and we should be on our way," he said.

"Good," cried Harriet. "Then we'll reach the Boar's Head before it's really dark."

"We're lucky to get clear. The roads are in a shocking state," replied Gregory.

A little later he and Benjie were taking their seats in the coach, and the horses, after their little rest, were quite frisky and soon bowling along at a good pace.

The sun was setting. It had almost disappeared. It had been a dark and cloudy day and there was rain about. It was growing darker rapidly. We came to the wood. I had a strange feeling that I had been there before; then I guessed it was the place where Hessenfield had stopped this very coach all those years ago.

We turned into the wood and had not gone very far when

24

two figures stepped out. They rode along by the window and I saw one of them clearly. He was masked and carried a gun.

Highwaymen! The place was notorious for them. My immediate thought was, It's not Hessenfield. This is a real one. Hessenfield is dead.

Gregory had seen. He was reaching for the blunderbuss under our seat. Harriet took my hand and gripped it tightly. Merry was shouting something. He had whipped up the horses and we were swaying from one side of the coach to the other as they galloped through the wood.

Benjie took out the sword which was kept in the coach for such an emergency as this.

"Merry seems to think we can outride them," muttered Gregory.

"Best thing if we can," replied Benjie. He was looking at Harriet and me, and I knew he meant he did not want a fight which might put us in danger.

The coach rattled on. We were swaying furiously—and then suddenly it happened. I was thrown up in my seat. I remember hitting the top of the coach, which seemed to rise as high as the trees.

I heard Harriet whisper, "O God, help us."

And then I was enveloped in darkness.

When I regained consciousness I was in a strange bed and Damaris was on one side of it, Jeremy on the other.

I heard Damaris say, "I think she's awake now."

I opened my eyes and said, "We were in the coach. . . ." as memory flooded back.

"Yes, darling. You're safe now."

"What happened?"

"There was an accident . . . but don't worry about that now."

"Where am I?"

"We're in the Boar's Head. We are going home very soon now. As soon as you are well enough to travel."

"Are you staying here, then?"

"Yes, and we shall be here until we take you back."

It was one of those occasions when I could feel happy to be wrapped in such loving care.

I recovered rapidly. I had a broken leg, it seemed, and many bruises.

"Young bones mend quickly," they said.

I was at the Boar's Head for another two days, and gradually the news was broken to me. The coach would never be on the road again. The horses had been so badly injured that they had had to be shot.

"It was the best way," Damaris told me with a catch in her voice. She loved all animals.

"It was the highwaymen," I said. "Were they real highwaymen?"

"Yes," answered Damaris. "They made off. They did stay when it happened. It was because of them. It was their fault. Merry and Keller whipped up the horses, hoping to escape the robbers. They didn't see the fallen tree trunk. That was how it happened."

"Are Benjie and Harriet and Gregory here at the inn?"

There was a silence, and a sudden fear came to me.

"Clarissa," said Damaris slowly, "it was a very bad accident. You were lucky. Benjie was lucky. . . ."

"What do you mean?" I asked faintly.

Damaris looked at Jeremy and he nodded. He meant: Tell her. There is no point in holding back the truth.

"Harriet and Gregory . . . were killed, Clarissa."

I was silent. I did not know what to say. I was numbed. Here was death again. It sprang up and took people when you least expected it. My beautiful parents . . . dead. Dear, kind Gregory . . . beautiful Harriet with the blue eyes and curly black hair . . . dead.

I stammered, "I shan't see them anymore."

I just wanted to close my eyes and go to sleep and forget. They left me. I heard them whispering outside my door.

"Perhaps we shouldn't have told her. She's only a child."

"No," answered Jeremy. "She's got to grow up. She's got to learn what life is."

So I lay thinking and remembering those who had been so intensely alive—my mother, my father and Harriet . . . now dead . . . filled with sorrow.

I felt I was no longer a child on that day.

It was true that young bones healed quickly, and young bodies could withstand such shocks and throw off the physical effects.

Poor Benjie! He looked like a ghost. How cruel life was to Benjie who was so good and, I was sure, had never harmed anyone in the whole of his life. . . . Yet he had lost my mother to Hessenfield, he had lost me to Damaris, and now he had lost his parents, whom I knew he had loved with that rare tender selfless emotion which only people like Benjie are capable of giving.

He came back with us to Eversleigh. Damaris and Jeremy insisted that he should.

Jeremy carried me into Enderby Hall and Smith and Damon were waiting to greet me. Smith's face was wrinkled up with pleasure to see me safe so that the rivers in his face seemed more deeply embedded than ever, and Damon kept jumping up and making odd little whinnying noises to show how pleased he was that I was back.

Jeremy carried me up and down stairs every day until my bones healed; and Arabella, Carleton and Leigh were always coming to see me.

Arabella was very sad about Harriet.

"She was an adventuress," she said, "but there was no one else quite like her. She has been in my life for a very long time. I feel that I have lost part of myself." They wanted Benjie to stay, but he had the estate to look after. He would be better working, he said.

He did not ask me to come to Ayot Abbas to see him, and I knew it was because he felt it would be too sad a place for me without Harriet.

I made up my mind that I would go often. I would do my best to comfort Benjie.

A Visitor from France

It was about a year after the accident when it was decided that my education must be attended to, and it was arranged that I should have a governess.

Grandmother Priscilla set about the task of finding one. Recommendations were always the best way, she decided, and when the Eversleigh rector, who knew we were looking for someone, rode over to the Dower House to tell my grandmother that he knew of the very person for the post, she was delighted.

Anita Harley came for an interview in due course and was immediately approved.

She was about thirty years of age, an impoverished parson's daughter who had looked after her father until his death, on which occasion she had found it necessary to earn a living. She was well educated; her father had given lessons to the local aristocracy in which Anita had shared, and as her aptitude for learning far outstripped that of her fellow students, she had, at the age of twenty-two, assisted her father in teaching local children. So she was well experienced to have charge of my education.

I liked her. She was dignified without being pompous and her learning sat lightly upon her; she had a pleasant sense of fun; she enjoyed teaching English and history and was not so keen in mathematics—so our tastes coincided. She also had some French and we could read stories together in that language. My accent was better than hers, for I had chattered away to servants at the *hôtel* like a native. Since I had learned it when I was also learning my native English, my intonation as well as accent was entirely French.

We were very happy together. We rode, played chess and conversed constantly; she was indeed a happy addition to our household.

Damaris was delighted.

"She'll teach you more than I ever could," she said.

Anita was treated like a member of the family. She dined with us and accompanied us when we visited the Dower House or Eversleigh Court.

"A thoroughly charming girl," was Arabella's comment.

"So good for the child," added Priscilla.

"The child" by this time was growing up, learning fast. I knew of my origins; I had heard myself referred to as precocious, and the servants who came from Eversleigh Court whispered together that I was a "Regular One" and it would not take a Gypsy with a crystal ball to see that I was going to turn out just like my mother.

I kept up my intention to visit Benjie often. Damaris approved of what she called my thoughtfulness. She said that she would have to come with me, for she would never have a moment's peace thinking of me on the roads after what had haapened.

We went to Ayot Abbas and always made sure that we passed through Wokey's Wood, which was the scene of the accident, in daylight, and there was always a well-armed party with us. I enjoyed the adventure of going through those woods, though my memories of Hessenfield were now overshadowed by what had happened. I would think sadly not only of my exciting father but of dear Harriet and Gregory as well.

Anita accompanied us, for Damaris thought I should continue with lessons. I was glad to have her. We had become great friends. Alas, Ayot Abbas seemed quite different without Harriet, and it was depressing because there was evidence of her all over the house.

Damaris said that Benjie should change everything. It was always wise to do so when something had happened which was best forgotten. She looked very serious when she said that, and I thought of the bedroom at Enderby.

"Perhaps we can advise him," said Damaris. "You might have some suggestions, Anita."

Anita had proved herself to be very good with flower arranging and matching colors. She told me she had longed to be able to furnish the old rectory where she had lived, but there had never been enough money to do it.

So we went to Ayot Abbas, and Benjie was delighted to see us—especially me—but, oh, how sad he was!

He did say that he was almost glad his father had gone with his mother, because he would have been so utterly desolate without her. Benjie implied that he was utterly desolate himself.

"You must do everything you can to cheer him," Damaris had said to me. "You can do more than anyone."

"Perhaps I should go and live with him," I had said.

Damaris had looked at me steadily. "Is that . . . what you want?" she asked.

I flung my arms about her neck then. "No . . . no. It is you I want to be with."

She had been tremendously relieved, and I couldn't help thinking how important I was. Then it occurred to me that all these people wanted me as a sort of substitute—Damaris because she had no child and poor Jeremy had his moods; Benjie wanted me because he had lost Carlotta and now his parents. I was flattered in a way, but I had to face the fact that I was wanted because what all of them really wanted was someone else. I was becoming introspective. It might be because of my talks with Anita.

We rode a good deal—Anita, Benjie and I. Damaris accompanied us sometimes, but she grew tired if she was too long in the saddle, so the three of us went alone. I think Benjie was happier on those rides than at any other time. He was interested in forestry and taught me a great deal. Anita was quite knowledgeable on the subject already. I started to distinguish between the different species. Benjie waxed enthusiastic about the oaks, which were truly magnificent.

"It's a real English tree," he said. "It has been here since history began. Did you know that the Druids had a very special respect for it? They used to perform their religious rites under it, and courts of justice were held beneath its branches."

"I believe," said Anita, "that some of these trees live for two thousand years."

"That's so," answered Benjie. "And our ships are made from the rough timber of these trees. Hearts of oak, they say our ships have."

I was sure that while he talked of the trees he loved he forgot his sorrow.

Anita wondered why the willow wept and told us that the aspen shivered because from its wood Christ's cross had been made and it had never been able to rest in peace since. She talked of the mistletoe, which was the only tree which had not promised not to harm Balder, the most beautiful of all the northern gods, so that the mischievous Loki had been able to slay him with it.

"I can see, Miss Harley," said Benjie, "that you have a romantic approach to nature."

"And I can see no harm in that," replied Anita.

Benjie laughed, I think for the first time since the accident.

We stopped at inns and drank cider and ate hot bread with ripe cheeses and pies straight from the oven. Benjie talked about the estate, which was his sole responsibility now. I could see that he was seeking something which would absorb his interest and help him to get over his bereavement.

I talked about him to Anita.

"He's different from Jeremy," I said. "Jeremy nurses his troubles, and although he is happy about being married to Damaris, it isn't enough to make him forget that he was wounded in the war."

"The pain is always there to remind him of that," replied Anita.

"Yes, whereas Benjie's pain is in remembering and seeing the rooms where they used to live. People can get away from things like that. Whereas Jeremy can't get away from the pain in his leg. It's always there."

I thought then that we ought to get back, because poor Jeremy would be very unhappy without Damaris. I wanted to see him, to give him the comfort my presence brought to him. I knew it did, for I often saw him look at me, remembering, I was sure, his adventure with Damaris when they had brought me out of Jeanne's cellar. Damaris could never have done that without his help, and every time Jeremy remembered that, it lifted his spirits.

"Benjie," I said, "why don't you come back to Enderby with us?"

"I would enjoy coming," he replied, "but, you see, there is the estate." I knew he meant it was no use to run away. He had to stay and face his lonely life.

We went back, and arrived at the end of September when the leaves were turning to bronze and the fruit was ripening on the trees. Anita and I went to the orchards and climbed ladders to gather it, while Smith helped us load the barrows, and the dog Damon sat watching us with his head on one side, bounding about now and then to show his joy because we were all together.

Priscilla came over and she and Damaris made jam and preserves. It was a normal autumn apart from the lingering sadness. Arabella missed Harriet so much, which was strange because she had often been sharp with her in their encounters, and I had always had the impression that there was a great deal she resented about Harriet.

Even Great-grandfather Carleton seemed to regret her loss, and he had always openly disliked her. As for Priscilla, she was very sad. I learned later how Harriet had helped her when Carlotta was born.

"We all have to go in time," said Arabella. "Sooner or later . . . and sooner for some of us."

Damaris hated to hear her talk like that. She said it was nonsense and she was going to see that her grandmother lived as long as Methuselah.

Another year passed. I was now ten years old. There was a great deal of talk about the armistice, which was going to put an end to the war.

Priscilla said it was about time too. Why we should concern ourselves with who sat on the throne of Spain was past her understanding.

Great-grandfather Carleton just looked at her, shaking his head, and uttered his favorite condemnation, which was "Women!"

"If they really come to peace," said Damaris, "there will be free traffic between the two countries." She looked at Jeremy. "I should like to go to Paris. I'd like to retrace our footsteps."

"A sentimental journey," said Jeremy, smiling at her in a way I loved to see him smile. I knew that the pain wasn't troubling him when he looked like that and he was rather pleased with life temporarily and not resentful at all.

"I wonder what became of Jeanne," mused Damaris. "I hope she was all right."

"She's the sort who can look after herself," Jeremy reminded her.

"Oh, yes. I shall never forget how she looked after Clarissa."

"I am not likely to either," replied Jeremy.

Damaris was very happy. She was pregnant again. "This time," she said, "I shall take the utmost care."

The doctor said she must rest a good deal and remember that her health had never been quite what it should have been ever since she had had fever years ago, and childbearing was an arduous matter even for the healthy.

Damaris was radiant. So was Jeremy. The shadows were lifting. This baby was of the greatest importance. If they could have a baby, my responsibility toward them would be lifted. Strange that I should come to think of it as a responsibility, but I did, for I now knew that the journey to France to bring me home had been the beginning of a new relationship between them. Before that they had been two unhappy people. I was glad to have played such a part in their lives, but the deep responsibility which I felt toward them seemed to grow with every passing day. Now I felt I must look after Benjie too. Long ago I had left him—not that I had had any choice in the matter, but if I had, I should have gone willingly with Hessenfield; and thus I had deprived Benjie of a daughter.

Christmas was at hand. Arabella insisted that we should all go to Eversleigh Court. Benjie must come, she said, and he promised to do so.

Damaris said we must do all we could to cheer him, for Christmas was a time when those who were lost were remembered with particular poignancy. I sensed that everyone was a little too bright, trying to pretend that this was going to be a Christmas like any other.

Anita and I went into the woods to gather holly and ivy. We hunted for mistletoe, and even Smith helped bring in the Yule log. Dear old Damon seemed to be extra excited about it. He had his dear ones safe—Jeremy, Damaris, Smith and myself—and as long as we were there he was happy.

Arabella said we must stay at the Court and not think of going home until Twelfth Night, even though we were so close, and that applied to Priscilla and Leigh.

We had decorated Enderby Hall even though we were not going to be there. I heard one of the maids say, "What'll the ghosts think, I wonder?"

"They won't like it," prophesied another.

They would not believe that there was not something malevolent lurking in Enderby.

"It's a shame to leave it," I said to Damaris. "It looks so lovely."

"Your great-grandmother wouldn't hear of it," she said. "It'll be nice to come home to, and Smith will be here to enjoy it."

"Smith and Damon with him," I said. "I shall ride over on Christmas morning to give them their presents."

"Dear Clarissa," said Damaris. "You're a good girl."

It wasn't really goodness, I pointed out. I would want to see Smith and Damon. And I thought that the atmosphere at Eversleigh might be a little oppressive without Harriet and Gregory.

"You're getting too introspective," laughed Damaris. Then she ruffled my hair and went on, "Just think. Next Christmas I shall have my baby. I find it hard to wait until April."

"I hope it's a girl," I said. "I want a girl."

"Jeremy wants a boy."

"Men always want boys. They want to see themselves born again."

"Dear Clarissa, you have been such a joy to me and Jeremy."

"I know."

She laughed again. "You always say what you mean, don't you?" she said.

I thought for a moment and answered, "Not always."

So we went to Eversleigh and there were the usual Christmas celebrations. Benjie came on Christmas Eve and was delighted to see me.

On Christmas Eve we went, as we always did, to Eversleigh Church for the midnight service. That had always been to me one of the best parts of Christmas—singing the Christmas hymns and carols and then walking across the fields to the Court, where there would be hot soup and toasted bread and mulled wine and plum cake waiting for us. We would discuss the service and compare it with the previous year's and everyone would be merry and wide awake. In the past we had all discussed the parts we would play in Harriet's charade. She had always arranged them and given us our parts and presided over them. We would all remember that.

In our bedrooms, fires would be blazing in the grates and there would be warming pans in our beds. Anita and I had to share a room, for although there were numerous rooms, the east wing of the house was shut up and dust-sheeted.

We didn't mind that in the least. We lay awake on the night of Christmas Eve, late as we were, because the day had been too stimulating to induce sleep. Anita told me of Christmases in the rectory with an old aunt who had come to stay with them, and how there was so much cheeseparing that she did enjoy being in a household where there was plenty. She had been terrified when she had thought she might have to go and live with the old aunt, and had chosen to attempt to earn a living instead.

"Dear Anita," I said, "you will always have a home here."

She replied that it was kind of me to console her, but her position was precarious, as it must necessarily be, and if she were to offend certain people, she could be dismissed.

"Damaris would not easily be offended," I reassured her,

34

"and she would never turn you away if you had nowhere to go. You're creating a situation which might never arise."

Anita laughed because that was what she had once told me I was doing.

So we talked of pleasant things, but I did realize that fear was lurking in Anita's mind. I wished there was something I could do to comfort her.

Christmas morning was bright and sparkling, with the frost glistening on the grass and branches of the beech and oak trees making it like a fairy-tale scene. The ponds were frozen, but as the sun was rising, that would soon be altered. The carol singers came in the morning and there was the traditional custom of inviting them in while they sang especially for us, and afterward they ate plum cake and drank punch brewed for the purpose in the great punch bowl. Anita and I were set to fill goblets, and it was just like other Christmases which I remembered since I came to England.

Then there was the great Christmas dinner, with various meats—turkey, chicken, ham and beef—with so many pies, made in all sorts of shapes, that the table was weighed down with food. There was plum pudding and plum porridge—this last I had not seen before. It was like a soup made with raisins and spices.

Afterward we played all sorts of games, including hide-and-seek, all over the house. We did charades too, but that was a mistake because it reminded us of Harriet. Priscilla quickly suggested another game. We danced to the fiddlers and some of us sang. Several of our neighbors had joined us and we were a large party, but I was sure some of the family were greatly relieved when the day was over.

"Christmases after a bereavement must necessarily be shadowed by sadness," said Anita.

We lay awake again that night and I told her more about Harriet.

"She was an unusual person," I said. "People like her can't go through life without having a marked effect on others."

I was thinking of people like my mother and Hessenfield—the beautiful people—and I wondered if I would be one of them when I grew up.

At last we slept, and rose fairly late on Boxing morning. The household was already astir, and when we went down to breakfast it was nine o'clock.

One of the servants told us that Damaris had gone over to Enderby. She wanted to see that all was well and she wanted to tell Smith that we had been persuaded to stay on for a while.

Anita and I were still at breakfast when Benjie came in. We told him that we were going to ride over to Enderby that morning and that Damaris had gone already. She had walked, for she did not ride nowadays. She was taking great care. But she enjoyed walking, even though the doctor had said she must not go too far.

Benjie chatted with us for a while, and later we all rode out together to Enderby. We tethered our horses and went into the house. The door was open, but there was nothing unusual about that as we knew Damaris was inside.

I was struck immediately by the quietness of the place. Usually when I came in Damon would bark and come bounding toward me, or Damaris would call, or Jeremy, or Smith perhaps. But the silence sent a pricking horror down my spine. I couldn't say why. The house seemed to have changed. It was as though I were seeing it as the servants saw it—a house in which evil things could happen, a house haunted by the spirits of those who had lived violently and unhappily in it.

It was a passing feeling. Obviously Smith was out. He often was. He took Damon for long walks through the lanes and over the fields.

"Aunt Damaris!" I called.

There was no answer. She must be upstairs and could not hear, I told myself.

I said, "Come on. We'll find her."

I looked at the other two. It was clear that they had not felt that frisson of fear which had come to me. I started up the stairs ahead of them and saw Damaris' shoe lying at the top of the stairs.

"Something has happened," I said.

Then I saw her. She was lying there in the minstrel's gallery; her face was white and her legs were twisted under her.

Anita was on her knees first. "She's breathing," she said.

I knelt too, looking at my beloved Damaris. She gave a little moan.

Benjie said, "We must get her out of here."

"Let's get her to one of the rooms," said Anita, and Benjie picked her up. She moaned and I guess that something had gone wrong about the baby. It was far, far too early for it to be born yet. Oh, no, I prayed. Not this one too.

Benjie carried her very gently. I opened a door and he laid her on a bed. It was the room which she had recently had refurnished, replacing the velvet with the damask.

"I'll go off at once and get the doctor," said Anita.

"No," interrupted Benjie. "I'll do that. You stay with her ... you two. Look after her until I come back with the doctor."

Anita had had some experience of nursing, for she had looked after her father for several years before his death. She covered Damaris with blankets and told me to get warming pans. I hurried down to the kitchen. A fire was burning there. Oh, where was Smith! If only he would come back he would be a great help. But I knew he walked for miles with Damon and it could be an hour before he returned.

I took up the warming pans and Anita laid them beside Damaris.

Anita looked at me sadly. "I'm afraid she will lose the child," she said.

Damaris opened her eyes. She looked bewildered. Then she saw me and Anita.

"We came over and found you in the gallery," I said.

"I fell," she replied. Then she looked up and saw the damask hangings round the bed.

"Oh, no, no," she moaned. "Not ... here. ... Never ... never. ..."

Anita touched her forehead, and although Damaris closed her eyes, her expression was disturbed.

It seemed a long time before Benjie came back with the doctor.

When he saw Damaris he said, "She will lose the child."

Those were sad days at Enderby. Damaris recovered but she was in despair.

"It seems I shall never have my own child," she said.

Priscilla came over constantly to see her, but it was Anita who nursed her and made herself indispensable in the household. Benjie stayed on. He would not go until he knew that Damaris was out of danger.

I heard the servants whispering.

"It's this house," they said. "It's full of ghosts. How did the mistress come to fall? I reckon it was someone ... some*thing* that pushed her."

"There's never going to be no luck in this house. There's tales about it that go right back into the past."

I began to wonder whether there was anything in it. When it was quiet in the house I would stand below the minstrels' gallery and fancy that the shadows up there took shape and turned into people who had lived long ago.

Benjie rode over often during that spring and summer, and during one of his visits Anita came to me in the schoolroom looking radiant.

"I have news for you, Clarissa," she told me. "I'm going to be married."

I stared at her in amazement and then suddenly the truth dawned on me. "Benjie!" I cried.

She nodded. "He has asked me and I have said yes. Oh, most joyously have I said it. He is the kindest man I ever knew. In fact he is a wonderful man and I can't believe my good luck."

I hugged her. "I am so pleased . . . so happy. You and Benjie. It's obvious . . . and absolutely right."

I felt that a great responsibility had been lifted from my shoulders. This concentration on responsibility was becoming an obsession. Benjie was no longer someone to whom I owed something. He had lost Carlotta and myself—well, now he would have Anita.

Arabella's comment was, "Harriet would have been pleased."

They all agreed that it was the best thing possible for the pair of them.

"Of course," said Priscilla, "we shall have to think of getting a new governess for Clarissa."

"We shall never get anyone like Anita," sighed Arabella.

Damaris said she would teach me in the meantime and added that Anita must be married from Enderby, which was, after all, her home.

So the wedding took place. The preparations absorbed Damaris, for she was determined that Anita should feel that she was one of the family. I think we were all especially happy for Benjie's sake. He had changed; his melancholy had dropped away from him. It was wonderful to have something happy taking place.

So they were married, and Anita left Enderby Hall to set up house with Benjie at Ayot Abbas.

I had passed my eleventh birthday when the Treaty of Utrecht was signed. There was a great deal of relief about that because it meant that the war was over. Great-grandfather Carleton discussed it constantly, and at the dinner table at

Eversleigh Court we heard little else. He would bang the table and expound on the iniquities of the Jacobites and how this was their *coup de grâce*.

"Best thing that could have happened," he said. "This will teach those traitors a lesson. Louis will have to turn them out of France now. There's no help for it. We shall have them sneaking back to England."

"Everyone has a right to his or her views, Father," Priscilla reminded him.

He looked at her from under his bushy eyebrows and growled, "Not when they're treacherous Jacobite ones."

"Whatever they are," insisted Priscilla.

"Women!" muttered Great-grandfather Carleton.

We were all glad that the war was at an end, and as Philip of Anjou was now King of Spain, it all seemed pointless that it had ever taken place. Priscilla's brother Carl would probably be home now, for he held a high position in the army, and that would be a source of delight for Arabella and Carleton.

The year passed peacefully. I went in the summer to Ayot Abbas and was delighted with the change since my last visit. There was no doubt that Anita and Benjie were happy. The house was more as it had been when Harriet was alive.

It was September, a rather chilly day, for the mists had continued through the afternoon and we had not seen the sun. I had ridden over to Eversleigh Court as it was a Sunday and it became a habit for us to dine there on that day. Grandmother Priscilla was insistent that we keep up the habit. It cheered Arabella, she said, who had never really recovered from Harriet's death and whose health was not as robust as it had been.

Even I could see the change in both great-grandparents. Arabella looked very sad sometimes, as though she were looking back into the past, and her eyes took on a misty look as she remembered. My great-grandfather made a show of being more irascible than before, but at times he was a little unconvincing.

I remember we had dined and were sitting back sipping elderberry wine which had come from Arabella's stillroom, and she and Priscilla were assessing its quality and comparing it with the last brew. Carleton was rambling on about his favorite topic—Jacobites. The fact that my father had been one of the leaders made no difference. Whenever he thought of them his face would grow a shade more purple and his eyebrows would quiver with indignation.

I always felt a need to defend them, because whenever he talked in this way it brought back vivid memories of Hessenfield. Sometimes I wondered whether Carleton knew this. He had a mischievous streak in his nature, and when he was interested in young people he would tease them more persistently than if he liked them less. I would often find those bright eyes peering out from the bushy brows, which seemed to have sprouted more hairs every time I saw him.

Even now, although he was supposed to be talking to Leigh and Jeremy, his eyes were on me. He had probably noticed my rising color and a certain flash in my eyes.

"Ha, ha!" he was saying. " 'Get out,' said the King of France. Court of Saint-Germain! What right has James to set up a court of his own when he's been drummed out of the only one he could lay claim to!"

"He had the permission of the King of France to do so," Jeremy reminded him.

"The King of France! The enemy of this country! Of course *he* would do everything he could to irritate England."

"Naturally," put in Leigh. "Since he was at war with us."

"Was! Ah . . . was!" cried Carleton. "Now what will happen to our little Jacobites, eh?"

I could not bear any more. I thought of Hessenfield—brave, strong, tall. He became taller in my mind's picture as time passed, and so had I magnified his virtues, so diminished his faults, that he had become the perfect man. There was none like him, and if he had been a Jacobite, then a Jacobite was a wonderful thing to be.

"They are not little," I burst out. "They are tall . . . taller than you are."

Carleton stared at me. "Oh, are they indeed? So these traitors are a race of giants, are they?"

"Yes, they are," I cried defiantly. "And they are brave and . . ."

"Just listen to this," cried Carleton. His eyes opened wide so that the bushy brows shot upward, and his jaw twitched, which usually meant he was suppressing amusement. He looked fierce, though, as he banged the table. "We've got a *little* Jacobite in our midst. Now, my girl, do you know what happens to Jacobites? They are hanged by the neck until they are dead. And they deserve it."

"Stop it, Carleton," said Arabella. "You're frightening the child."

"He is not!" I cried. "He just said Jacobites are little, and they are not."

Carleton was not going to be deprived of his teasing.

"We shall have to be watchful, I can see. We must make sure that she does not start a conspiracy here in Eversleigh. Why, she'll be raising a rebellion, that's what she'll be doing."

"Don't talk such nonsense," said Arabella. "Try some of these sweetmeats, Clarissa. Jenny made them specially for you. She said they were your favorites."

"You talk of sweetmeats when our country is being put to risk," cried Carleton. But I knew he was only amusing himself at my expense, and I was satisfied, because I had made my point about the height of Jacobites and had stood by Hessenfield, so I turned to the sweetmeats and selected one which had a flavor of almonds, which I particularly liked.

Carleton's attention had strayed from me but he was still with the Jacobites.

"They say the Queen favors her brother. That's what comes of women's reasoning."

I looked at him sharply and said, "That's treason against the Queen. It's worse than saying Jacobites are tall."

I saw his chin twitch and he was putting on the fierce look again.

"You see, she will betray us all."

"It's you who do that," I reminded him, "by speaking against the Queen."

"That's enough, Clarissa," said Priscilla, who was always nervous about political issues. "Now I am tired of this talk, and we will leave the men if they want to fight out their silly battles on the table. I should have thought the recent peace, and all the losses we have suffered to reach it, would have been sufficient answer to all their theories."

Sometimes Priscilla, who was of a somewhat meek nature, could subdue Carleton as no one else could, not even Arabella. My grandmother was an unusual woman. She must have been to have borne my mother in secret in Venice. I was to discover how it had happened in due course, because it was the custom of members of our family to keep a journal, and in this they usually put down frankly and honestly what happened to them. It was a point of honor with them that they should do so, and when we were eighteen—or before that if the moment was ripe—we were allowed to read our ancestresses' versions of their lives.

We were just about to rise and leave the men at the table when one of the servants came in looking bewildered.

Arabella said, "What is it, Jess?"

Jess said, "Oh, my lady, there's a person at the door. She's foreign . . . don't seem to be able to talk. She just stands there and gibbers, saying, 'Miss Clarissa' . . . and 'Miss Damaris.' . . . That's all she seems to say that makes sense, please, my lady. The rest is all nonsense . . . like."

Damaris had risen. "We'd better see what it's about. She mentioned me, you say?"

"Yes, mistress. She said, 'Miss Damaris'—plain as that. And 'Miss Clarissa' . . . too."

I followed Damaris into the hall. Arabella and Priscilla were close behind. The great oak door was open and on the threshold stood a figure in black.

It was a woman and she was clutching a bag. She was talking rapidly in French. It came back to me as I listened and I ran to her.

She looked at me disbelievingly. I had changed a great deal in five years, but I recognized her.

"Jeanne!" I cried.

She was delighted. She held out her arms and I ran into them.

Then Damaris was there. Jeanne released me and looked at her rather fearfully and began to explain rapidly and incoherently, but I could understand quite easily what she was telling us.

We had always said that she would be welcome. We had asked her to come, but she could not leave her mother and grandmother, so she had not gone with us when we left. But we had said she might come, and she remembered. Grand'mère was dead, her mother had married, and Jeanne was free. So she had come back to her little Clarissa, whom she had saved when there was no one to look after her. And she wanted to be with her again. . . .

Damaris cried out in her very English French that Jeanne was very welcome.

Arabella spoke French tolerably well because before the Restoration she had lived in a château there waiting for King Charles the Second to regain his throne. She said that she had heard all about what Jeanne had done for me and she would be very welcome here.

Damaris kept saying, "Of course. Of course."

And I, who was suddenly transported back to that damp

42

cellar, with the hostile Grand'mère and Maman, and only Jeanne to protect me from the harsh Paris streets and from life, cried out, "Do you understand what they are saying, Jeanne? You are to stay with us. You have come to us, and your home is here now."

Jeanne wept and embraced me again, looking at me with wonder, as though I had done something very clever by growing up.

We brought her to the table, where she opened her eyes wide at the sight of so much food. Damaris explained who she was, and Great-grandfather Carleton rose rather ponderously—for as I have said, he was getting stiff in the limbs, though he wouldn't admit it—and he told her in very anglicized French that anyone who had served a member of his family well should never regret it. Jeanne was well aware of the warmth of her welcome.

Hot soup was brought for her, which she attacked ravenously, and then she was given a slice of beef. She told us how she had wanted to come to England but that it had been impossible during the war. But now that there was this treaty and the fighting had stopped, she had at last found a boat to bring her across. It had cost her a great deal, but she had saved when she did not have to keep her grandmother and her mother, so she had a little more money. She was ready when the peace was signed—and here she was.

So that was how Jeanne came to England.

Sir Lancelot

It is amazing how great events which seem so remote from us can play such a big part in deciding the course of our lives. But for the great revolution when Catholic James had been driven from the throne and replaced by Protestant William and Mary, I should never have been born. And then my adventures in France were all part of the same situation. But the peaceful years I had spent at Eversleigh had made me forget such impressive conflicts. It was only when Great-grandfather Carleton talked so fiercely of Jacobites that I remembered there was a struggle still going on.

Because of the peace, Jeanne was with us, and something of even greater importance was to follow—and all because of the peace.

Jeanne had settled happily into our household; she seemed to be in a perpetual state of delight. She said it was like being in the *hôtel* and serving Lord and Lady Hessenfield again. To be ensured of enough to eat was, during those first weeks, like a miracle to Jeanne. She talked volubly, and I found I could chat easily with her and my early grounding in her language enabled me to pick it up again with speed. Jeanne had a smattering of English, learned from my mother and from me, and we had no difficulty in communicating.

She told me how sad she had been when I left, although she knew it was the best thing for me and great good fortune that my Aunt Damaris had found me.

"We suffered much in the winter when there was little to sell," she told me. "Then I must go out to wash floors . . . if I can get the work . . . and what did it bring? Nothing but a few sous. There was Maman and Grand'mère to keep. In the spring and summer I could manage with the flowers. I like that. It gave me freedom. But to work for tradesmen . . . oh, *ma chérie* . . . you have no idea. Those days in the *hôtel*

44

working for milord and milady—ah, that was heaven . . . or near it. But this was different. . . ."

She told me that she must work, work, work all the time, and never a moment to be lost or they would take off sous for wasted time.

"I worked for the druggist and grocer one winter. I liked the smells, though the work was hard. But I did it . . . and sometimes when there were many customers . . . I served in the shop. I loved the smell of that shop. *Parfum* in the air. I learned too how to weigh out the cinnamon, the sugar, the ground pepper . . . arsenic too. That was sold to the fashionable ladies. It did something for their complexions. . . . But they must take care, they were always told. An overdose of that . . . *Mon Dieu*, it could give you more than a good complexion. It could give you a coffin and six feet of earth to cover you."

Jeanne's conversation—delivered half in French, half in English—was racy. It took me right back to my life in Paris—not only to the days in the dark, damp cellar but to the glorious time when Jeanne was in attendance and my beautiful mother paying me fleeting visits to my nursery and my wonderful Hessenfield coming even more rarely.

Jeanne brought a new atmosphere into Enderby. She showed me what the new hairdressing was like. She herself had a beautiful head of hair and had once or twice earned a few sous by being practiced on by a hairdresser. She would laugh hilariously at the recollection. She had emerged bowed down by the weight of two or three pounds of flour and a considerable helping of pomade, looking like a lady of high fashion on the top and a poor flower seller everywhere else. But it was one way of earning a few sous, although she had a hard task getting the stuff out of her hair.

But her greatest stroke of luck was with the druggist. She had done well there and was offered the opportunity to stay, which she did. And it was thus that she had been able to save enough money to make her journey to England.

It was amusing to hear her talk of the ladies of Paris. She would prance about the room in imitation of their elegance. They drank vinegar to make them thin, while they took arsenic in the right doses to give them a delicately tinted skin. The druggist's wife had aspired to be a lady. She had her arsenic at hand for her skin and she drank a pint of vinegar every day. Her coiffure was a sight for wonder, and at night the astonishing creation was wrapped in what looked

45

like bandages, which made the whole contraption twice its normal size. And she would go to bed supporting false hair, flour and pomade on a kind of wooden pillow in which a place had been cut out for her neck to fit into, and which, for all the discomfort, gave the lady immense satisfaction.

Jeanne communicated her happiness to me and we would laugh and chat together for hours. Damaris was delighted to see us together. So Jeanne's coming had been a very happy event.

One day a servant from Eversleigh Court rode over to Enderby with a special message from Arabella. A visitor had called on them; he came from the Field family of Hessenfield Castle in the north of England. It appeared that the present Lord Hessenfield was eager to make the acquaintance of his niece.

It was a moment of great excitement for me. Damaris, however, was a little apprehensive. I think she believed my father's family would try to take me away from her.

We rode over to Eversleigh at once. Arabella was waiting for us, looking rather concerned.

"This man is a sort of cousin of the present lord," she whispered to us when we arrived. "I gather he has been sent to see us."

My heart was beating wildly with excitement as I went into the house. Arabella laid a hand on my arm. "He may make suggestions," she went on. "We shall have to discuss whatever it is all together. Don't make any rash promises."

I scarcely heard her. I could only think that I was going to discover more about my father's family.

He was tall, like Hessenfield; his hair was light with a touch of red in it. He had the clear-cut features which I remembered my father had had; and he had very piercing blue eyes.

"This is Clarissa," said Arabella, propelling me forward.

He came to me swiftly and took both my hands.

"Yes," he said. "I see the resemblance. You're a Field, my dear—Clarissa, isn't it?"

"Yes, that's my name. What is yours?"

"Charles Field," he answered. "My uncle, Lord Hessenfield, knows of your existence and he wants to meet you."

"He is . . . my father's brother?"

"Exactly. He says it is not right that there should be such a close relationship and that you should not have met."

"Oh." I turned to look at Damaris.

Her face had puckered a little. I knew she was apprehensive because this man had come looking for me.

"We feel that such a state of affairs should be rectified without delay," he went on. "You must want to meet your family."

I tried not to look at Damaris. "Oh, yes . . . of course."

"I was hoping that I could take you back with me."

"You mean for a visit?"

"I mean just that."

Damaris said quickly, "We should need time to get Clarissa ready for such a visit. And the north . . . it is a long way."

"The whole length of the country, one might say—your being in the extreme south and we in the north . . . right on the border."

"Is it rather lawless country up there?"

He laughed. "No more than the rest, I trow. You can be assured that the Fields know how to take care of their own."

"I am sure they do. But for a child. . . ."

I felt a faint irritation. When were they going to stop referring to me as "the child." It was at moments like this that I felt more intensely than ever the suffocation of this love they wrapped me in. It was like a great blanket—warm, soft and smothering.

"Aunt Damaris," I said firmly. "I *should* see my father's family."

I wished I hadn't spoken, for she looked so hurt, so I went to her and took her hand.

"It would only be for a little while," I reminded her.

Arabella said briskly, "I think this needs time and thought. Perhaps in a year or so. . . ."

"We are all impatience to meet our kinswoman. Her father was head of the family. It was a great shock to us when he died so suddenly . . . in his prime."

"It was such a long time ago," said Damaris.

"That does not make it any less tragic for us, madam. We want to know his daughter. Lord Hessenfield is very anxious that she should visit us for a time."

Damaris and Arabella exchanged glances. "We will think about it," said Arabella. "Now, you will be tired after your journey. I will have a room prepared for you. You will not want to start the journey back today, I am sure."

"My dear lady, you are so good. I shall take advantage of your hospitality. Perhaps I can persuade Clarissa to come back with me. I am sure if she knew how much we are longing to see her she would agree right away."

"She is a little young to make such decisions," said Arabella.

And again that insistence on my youth irritated me, and I think in that moment I determined to go to see my father's family.

Poor Damaris! She was most distressed. I was sure she thought that if I went to the north I should never come back.

There were family conferences. Great-grandfather Carleton was all against my going. "Damned Jacobites," he growled, growing red in the face. "There's peace now, but they haven't given up. They're still drinking to the King over the water. No, she shall not go."

But Great-grandfather Carleton was not the power he had once been and Arabella finally decided that there was no harm in my going. It would only be a visit.

Priscilla was dubious and said I was too young to make such a journey.

"She would not be on her own," persisted Arabella. "She would have a considerable bodyguard. Jeanne could go with her as her maid. It will keep her French up to standard. I always thought she shouldn't lose that."

"And what of Damaris?" demanded Priscilla. "She will be so wretched without her."

"My dear Priscilla," said Arabella, "she will miss the child, of course. We shall all miss her. We shall be delighted when she comes back. But Damaris cannot expect to keep her with her forever—just for her own comfort. She'll have to remember that Clarissa has her own life to lead."

Priscilla retorted hotly, "You are not suggesting that Damaris is selfish, are you, Mother? Damaris is the sweetest-natured. . . ."

"I know. I know. But she sets such store by Clarissa. I know what she did for Clarissa . . . and what Clarissa has done for her. But that does not mean she can stop the child seeing her father's relations just because she is going to miss her sadly."

Priscilla was silent then. But the argument was continued later. Leigh thought that I should go. They were, after all, my relations. "And it is only for a visit," he said.

Jeremy was against my going. But that was mainly because it upset Damaris.

This was when I really felt closed in by them all, and I decided that I had a right to choose my own future.

I said to Damaris, "Aunt Damaris, I *am* going to see my father's people, I must."

She looked sad for a moment, then she sat down and drew me to her. She looked at me very earnestly and said, "You shall go, my dear. You are right. You should go. It is just that I shall hate to be without you. I want to tell you something. I am going to have a child."

"Oh . . . Aunt Damaris!"

"You will pray for me, won't you? You'll pray this time that I shall succeed."

All my animosity had left me. I threw my arms about her neck.

"I won't go, Aunt Damaris. No, I won't go. I couldn't. I should be so worried about you. I tell you what I'll do. I'll wait until you have the little baby . . . and then I'll go and see my father's brother."

"No, dear, you must not think of me."

"How could I stop doing that! I couldn't be happy if I were not here. I want to be here with you. I want to make some of the baby clothes. I want to make sure that you are all right."

That settled it. I should in time visit the north, but it would have to be later. It would be several months before I could set out.

Grandmother Priscilla was very pleased with the decision. She kissed me tenderly. "It could not have been better," she said. "Damaris is so delighted that you want to stay with her. Pray God this time she will have a healthy child."

So Charles Field went back with the promise that I should visit my relations in a few months' time.

We gave ourselves up to the preparations for the baby's arrival. At first Damaris was too much afraid of losing it to talk very much about it. But I soon put a stop to that. I had a feeling that to imagine the worst might in some mystical way bring it about, and I insisted on believing that this time the baby would live. I watched over Damaris with a care and tenderness which was greater because of what I thought of as my recent disloyalty.

Jeanne was very useful at this time. I was amazed at the change in her. When I had known her in France she had been obsessed first by the need to please in the *hôtel* and later by an even greater need to exist when she was in the cellar. She had been careworn with these necessities, and they had suppressed her natural volatile nature.

Once she had realized she was safe in this comfortable

household, from which she would not be ejected unless she committed some terrible crime, her character reverted to what nature had intended it to be. Her rendering of our language was a continual source of amusement to us all, and she was delighted to see our smiles and hear our laughter. Sometimes I think she deliberately sought to arouse our mirth. She made herself very useful. I was a little old for the services of a nursemaid, so she became my lady's maid. She dressed my hair, saw to my clothes and was with me constantly.

"Clarissa is becoming elegant," commented Arabella.

"We don't want any of those fancy French fashions here," growled Great-grandfather Carleton.

But everyone was pleased that Jeanne had come. They all realized what a service she had done me. We were a family that did not like accepting favors, and when we had them bestowed on us, it was a point of honor that we repaid them a hundredfold.

Jeanne, of course, was delighted at the prospect of a new baby. She loved little babies and she knew a great deal about them. She was full of advice, and as she was very handy with her needle, she provided some exquisite garments.

It was not surprising that with such events looming in the family we should not pay a great deal of attention to what was happening in the world.

Carleton, of course, was aware of it and extremely anxious. Old as he was, he was still interested in the country's politics. Leigh and Jeremy were too. I was aware of this because I was amused by the different reactions of them all. Carleton was staunchly anti-Catholic, and his hatred of the Jacobites was the more intense because he would no longer be of an age to tackle them if ever they attempted to take over the country. Leigh believed that everything would settle down, and he was ready to accept whatever monarch came. Jeremy feared the worst and expressed the opinion that if the Jacobites attempted to put James on the throne, there would be war between the Catholic faction and the Protestant supporters of the Electress of Hanover.

"The Queen is for her half brother," declared Carleton. "She is bemused by family feeling. State affairs should be above sentimentality."

"The people will never accept James," said Jeremy. "There'll be war if he lands."

"The mood of the country is for the Hanoverian branch," said Leigh. "It is because it is Protestant."

"They say the Queen won't invite the Electress to come to England," said Jeremy.

"But," pointed out Leigh, "there are some members of the government who are threatening to do just that."

And so it went on.

The year passed uneasily, and all this talk about the succession seemed very boring to those of us who were thinking only of Damaris.

We watched over her with care, and our spirits were lifted when Priscilla declared she was sure Damaris was stronger than she had been during her previous pregnancies. We were longing for July to come and yet dreading it.

We became indifferent to the talk going on around us. Vaguely we heard mention of the Queen's state of health. She was full of gout and could not walk. Names like Harley and Bolingbroke were often spoken of. I gathered there was some feud between them. Carleton stormed about that besom Abigail Hill, who, it seemed, ruled the country, for the Queen did everything that lady told her to.

"She's as bad as Sarah Churchill was," said Carleton. "*Women* . . . that's what it is. Petticoat government never did a country any good at all."

Arabella reminded us that under the reign of Elizabeth the country had been at peace, and consequently more prosperous than at any other time. "Women have always ruled," continued Arabella, "though sometimes they are obliged to do it through men. But you may be sure that they have always had a hand in government."

Then he abused her and her sex in that way which showed clearly how much he admired her, and we all knew that he had a special fondness for the feminine members of society, so all this added a lighter note to the general brooding on what trials the future might hold.

On the twenty-eighth of July Damaris' pains started. It was a long and arduous confinement, and the child was born on the thirtieth. How great was our joy to find that it was a healthy girl. Damaris was exhausted and there was some concern for her, but even that soon passed.

"This will do her all the good in the world," said Priscilla. Jeremy sat by Damaris' bed and held her hand. I was there too, and I shall never forget the exalted look in Damaris' eyes when the baby was put into her arms.

The child was alive, breathing, healthy. At last she had achieved her goal.

There was a great deal of discussion in the family as to what this precious and most important little girl should be called. Carleton wanted her to be Arabella, and Arabella said that if she was going to be named after one of the family, why not Priscilla? Leigh said that was an excellent idea, but Jeremy thought there was confusion in families when the same name appeared even after a lapse of generations.

Damaris suddenly decided that she would call the baby Sabrina. The name just came to her as suitable, and Jeremy said that Damaris was certainly the one who should have the final say in the matter, and in any case he supported her entirely, for he thought it was a suitable name.

So she was to be Sabrina—and we added Anne, after the Queen.

A few days after her birth an event occurred which was of great significance. The dropsy which had plagued the Queen for so long, went to her brain, so it was said. Queen Anne died.

In spite of the fact that she had been more or less an invalid for some time, her death was a shock. She had scarcely been a clever woman, but the country had increased its importance under her rule. She had been surrounded by wily politicians and had had one of the most successful generals of all time in John Churchill, Duke of Marlborough. None could say she had failed in her duty to produce an heir, for she had had seventeen children, of whom only one survived infancy, and he—the poor little Duke of Gloucester—had died at eleven years of age. Thus she had plunged the country into a crisis by her death.

Only two months before, the Electress Sophia, the daughter of Elizabeth, herself the daughter of James the First which was why Sophia had a claim to the throne, had died. She had collapsed when walking in the gardens of her palace. Some said her death was due to apoplexy brought on by her concern over the controversy aroused by the state of affairs in England.

However, that left her son George as the Protestant heir. Anne had hated what she had heard of George and always had referred to him as the "German boor," which was one of the reasons why she had been in favor of calling her half brother James Stuart back from France.

It was this state of affairs which set the men of the family arguing together and the women praying that the foolish men would not bring about a war over whether German George or James Stuart should be their next King.

"Why we cannot live together in peace is past my understanding," declared Priscilla angrily. "Their wars only cause misery to people who are ready to live contentedly side by side."

Carleton was gleeful at the turn affairs took. Bolingbroke, that arch Jacobite, was taken by surprise when the Queen died. He had thought he would have longer to make arrangements with his Jacobite friends. He was too late. The Whigs were better prepared; they secured the persons of leading Jacobites in high places and simply proclaimed George of Hanover George the First of England.

Sabrina Anne was christened in September. They did not want to leave it until later because of the approaching winter. So toward the end of the month, when the weather was still mellow and there were bronze-tinted leaves on the trees, the ceremony was performed in Eversleigh Church, with all the family present.

It was wonderful to see the radiance of Damaris with her own child at last. She looked pale, but happiness had set a glow upon her, and her delicacy could not hide her great satisfaction. I had never seen Jeremy look so pleased with life since the early days of his marriage. I felt a warm glow of happiness myself and, perhaps above all ... relief. I no longer felt the need to care for them, to repay them all the time for what they had done for me. Fate had done that for me.

After the ceremony we all went back to Eversleigh Court, where such family gatherings were always held.

I heard Arabella warning Carleton, "Let's keep the Jacobites out of this for once."

"My dear wife," replied Carleton, "you can't keep out what is creeping up like a menacing cloud over you, threatening to ruin us all."

"It's no use," groaned Arabella. "I can't part him from his Jacobites."

It was a very happy occasion. The baby was good throughout. Indeed Sabrina was a contented baby and cried only when suffering from some discomfort or wanting food, so it was easy to placate her. She was wearing the beautiful Eversleigh christening robes of white satin and Brussels lace, the same robe which so many babies had worn before

53

her and which, after this ceremony, would be laundered and put away for the next christening. I wondered whose that would be. My own child's perhaps. I was twelve years old. In another four or even perhaps three years ... I could be married.

My thoughts were wandering. They would try to find a husband for me. Oh, no! I would not have that. I should choose my husband.

When we arrived back at Enderby the baby was taken by Jeanne to the nursery and Damaris said she would lie down and asked me to go up with her as there was something she wanted to say to me.

When we were in her room she looked at me very seriously and said, "There is something you will have to know, Clarissa, and now that you are proposing to visit your Hessenfield relations I and your Uncle Jeremy think it is time to tell you. Your mother was a wealthy woman. You are her heiress. We did not tell you this before but we had many consultations in the family and we came to the conclusion that it is not good for young people to know they have money."

I was astounded. I was rich. It was something which had never occurred to me.

"Yes," went on Damáris, "your mother inherited money through her father's family. It has accumulated over the years, as money does. When you are eighteen years of age it will come to you. We had planned to tell you on your seventeenth birthday, but in view of what has happened we thought it best that you should know now."

"Am I .... very rich?"

Damaris looked uneasy. "It is difficult to know exactly how much there is for you to inherit. It will be in bonds and such like. Your great-uncle was a very good businessman and a cautious one. He had arranged for everything to be well taken care of. There is something else too. When your kinsman from the north came here he told us that your father had left you money. A great deal of this was in France, for he had managed to shift some of his assets over there when he was resident at the Court of Saint-Germain and in Paris. The fact is that you are a considerable heiress."

"How strange!" I said. "I don't feel any different."

"My dear child, your grandmothers and I have been a little worried. You see, you are going away from us, and there are fortune hunters. ... You are so young as yet. But your mother, when she was about your age, was deceived by an adventurer. We thought you should know of this. Dear Clarissa, don't look so alarmed. It would be considered good news by most people, you know."

"I'm surprised really. Fancy me . . . an heiress!"

Damaris put her arms round me and kissed me tenderly. "It won't make any difference, will it . . . not to us?"

"How could it?" I asked; bewildered.

"Well, now you know. You will be going away very soon. We shall have to start thinking about that. Clarissa, it was good of you to stay until Sabrina was born."

"I had to. I should have been so desperately worried if I hadn't been with you."

She looked at me earnestly and then she said, "Will you promise me something?"

"Of course . . . if I can."

"If anything should happen to me and Jeremy . . . would you look after Sabrina?"

"Anything happen? What do you mean?"

"We live in a dangerous world. People are killed on the roads. I heard only yesterday of a family who were traveling in their coach and were set on by footpads. There was resistance and the wife was shot. There were Harriet and Gregory. . . . It has set me thinking. If anything should happen to us while Sabrina needs to be cared for. . . . Would you look after her . . . for me?"

"Oh, dearest Aunt Damaris, of course I would." I felt suddenly uplifted. For the first time since I arrived in England I had been made to feel I was not a child. I was someone capable of accepting responsibility and they realized it.

Was that what being an heiress meant?

My great-uncle Carl, of whom I had seen very little, had come home. He had been abroad fighting during the war and had distinguished himself in the service of the Duke of Marlborough and won honors at Blenheim, Oudenarde and Malplaquet. He was something of a hero and Great-grandfather Carleton was clearly very proud of him.

I heard my grandmother Priscilla say to Damaris, "Your grandfather always loved Carl best. I can tell you that when I was a young girl I always took second place. No, not even that. He hardly noticed my existence."

"He does now," said Damaris, and Priscilla just looked thoughtful.

So here was Uncle Carl—bronzed and handsome, a hero

returned from the wars. He must have been in his mid-forties; he was four years or so younger than Priscilla. He was still in the army, of course, and had a great deal to think about.

He did not come alone but brought with him Sir Lance Clavering, who was much younger than he was and who had also returned from the war. Uncle Carl had been his commanding officer and clearly had some respect for him. Lance Clavering was, according to Arabella, nothing more than a boy. I suppose he seemed so to her, but he was quite mature to me. He was in fact twenty years old, nearly eight years older than I was, and that made him seem very grown up. I thought him outstandingly handsome. His clothes were exquisite. He was not in uniform like Uncle Carl, because he had merely been a soldier during the war. Uncle Carl was General Eversleigh and a regular soldier.

But it was Lance who held my attention. His fresh complexion was accentuated by the whiteness of his Ramillies wig, which was drawn back from his brow and puffed out full over the ears. At the back it was made into a plait which was tied at the bottom and at the nape of his neck with black satin bows. The cuffs of his elegantly cut full-skirted coat were trimmed with exquisite lace. This coat came down to his knees so that his breeches were not visible, but I could glimpse a beautifully embroidered waistcoat. His stockings were white and his black shoes had silver buckles. On one of the gold buttons on his coat hung a cane. I had never seen such a picture of elegance and I was greatly impressed.

I was presented to him by my great-uncle Carl, who seemed fond of him in an amused sort of way. He was to stay with us for a while, I learned, until he went with Carl to York. Their business there was secret. I was warned not to ask anything about it.

They both stayed at Eversleigh Court.

At Enderby we discussed Lance at length. Jeremy thought him a fop, but Damaris was inclined to be more tolerant.

"Uncle Carl seems to think something of him," she said. "After all, he's traveling to York with him on what appears to be important business."

"I can't understand that," muttered Jeremy.

"He is only a young man," Damaris pointed out. "He must have been only a boy when he joined the army. That shows some strength of character surely, when he might have been at home having a good time in London. I believe he comes of a rich family."

Jeremy grunted. Of course he would not like Lance Clavering. If ever two men were the exact opposites, these two were. Lance was in constant good humor. He seemed to find life a great joke. He was extremely gallant and expressed interest in whatever interested other people. He even discussed the making of country wines with Priscilla; with Damaris he talked of dogs and horses, and with the men he discussed the battles of the war with a knowledge that almost equaled that of Great-uncle Carl himself. Even Great-grandfather Carleton was amused by him. Lance and I rode together on one or two occasions, and he made a great effort to discover what interested me and then talked about it with such enthusiasm that one would have believed the subject was the one nearest his heart. He had charm, grace, elegance and, above all, that overwhelming desire to please.

"He is a great asset to any gathering," was Arabella's comment.

Jeanne said, "Oh, but what a pretty gentleman!" And when I told him what she had said he was not in the least offended. He burst out laughing and said he must make sure to remain pretty for Jeanne.

His imperturbable good humor was catching and there was a great deal of laughter when he was present. Life seemed a joke to him. When the men were hunting, one of our neighbors—a "country boor," Carleton called him—made a point of splashing through a muddy stream so that the dirty water spattered Lance's pearl-gray riding habit. Lance brushed it aside, I heard, with nonchalance and made the perpetrator of the so-called joke more uncomfortable than he was.

He was always wagering something. It was a favorite expression of his: "I'll wager this . . ." or "I'll wager that . . ."

One day when we were all at Eversleigh Court round the dinner table the talk turned to the arrival of the new King, and Great-grandfather Carleton was saying that it was a pity we had to call on a German to give us the sort of rule we wanted.

All the family was staunchly Protestant. I was the only one who wavered, and that was solely because Hessenfield had been a Jacobite. I did realize that I knew very little about the controversy, and I had heard so much at Eversleigh about the errors of Catholicism that I was ready to accept the fact that the Protestant succession was best for the country.

"But even with our staunch Protestants the new King is not popular," said Arabella.

"Anne called him the 'German boor,' and it is a fitting description," said Great-uncle Carl.

"But we don't want the Jacobites back," cried Carleton. "And George seems the only alternative."

"At least he is in the line of succession," put in Arabella. "I remember hearing about his grandmother . . . oh, long ago, when I was a girl. She was the sister of King Charles, who lost his head, and a very beautiful Princess, they said. She married the Elector Palatine. Sophia was her daughter, and as George was Sophia's son he had a claim to the throne."

"The Jacks wouldn't say that while we have the son of James panting to take the crown," said Lance, laughing as though it were a great joke. "They'll never put him back. The people don't want it. But they'll have a good try."

Uncle Carl flashed a look at him which might have been a warning.

Lance tapped the side of his nose exaggeratedly to show that the point was taken, and he was still smiling as he went on: "Old George is not so bad, I hear. He's a good friend . . . to his friends—and he's quick to forget an injury. He's good-tempered, and as mean as a man can be. He regrets spending a groat. He's completely ignorant of literature and art and doesn't want to be otherwise. 'Boetry' "—Lance made what I guessed to be a good imitation of a German accent—" 'boetry . . . vat ist not vor shenthemans.' But of course his English is not nearly as clear as that. Poor old George—I believe he did not want to come here one little bit."

"People won't like a German," said Arabella.

"They'll get used to him," added Priscilla.

"I believe people get used to anything in time," went on Lance, "even Mesdemoiselles Kielmansegge and Schulemberg."

"And who are they?" I asked.

"Do have some more of this roast beef," cut in Priscilla.

"We thought the sloe gin was particularly good this year," added Arabella.

This was another instance of their protection. I knew at once that there was something shocking to be learned about the ladies Lance had mentioned and that I was being shielded once more, so I repeated, looking directly at Lance, "Who are they?"

"They are the King's mistresses," he answered, smiling at me.

"Clarissa is . . .er . . ." began Damaris, blushing a little.

"The lady Clarissa is more worldly than you give her credit for," said Lance, and I think he won my heart at that moment. He turned to me and went on: "They are German ladies . . . one incredibly fat, the other amazingly lean. You see, his Germanic Majesty likes variety. They speak very little English, like himself, and they are two of the most unattractive women in Europe. It is considered something of a joke that they should be the first German imports to show the country."

"It all sounds a bit of a joke," I said.

"It is. I always thought so much in life is. Do you agree?"

So we bantered and talked and the family watched, and I really believe that at last they realized I was not the baby they had been imagining I was. Lance had made them see that I was almost grown up, and I loved him for that.

It transpired that my great-uncle Carl and Lance would shortly be leaving for York. They were on some mission for the army.

Damaris said, "Clarissa is going north to stay with her father's relations. Perhaps she could accompany you as far as York. That is surely on the way. It would be a great relief to know that she had your protection . . . even so far."

Lance immediately cried out that it was a capital idea, and after a few moments' reflection Carl said he was sure it could be managed. It would mean my setting out a little before I had intended, but Damaris was reconciled to that because she thought it would be good for me to travel with Carl and Lance.

Preparations became intensive, and while we were packing, Damaris said to me, "I wonder if you would mind if I kept Jeanne here. She seems to manage Sabrina better than anyone."

I was disappointed, because I had grown so fond of Jeanne, and her bright Anglo-French conversation was always amusing to listen to. However, I did know how useful she was to Damaris and I was so excited at the prospect of my journey that I readily said of course she must stay.

It was a warm day—the last of September—when we set out; we could not have left much later. Damaris had said a tearful farewell to me, and Jeremy stood beside her, a little reproachful because I so obviously wanted to meet my father's family. Jeanne was both tearful and voluble. She was torn between her desire to be with the new little baby and to come with me whom she regarded as her very own.

I was really rather glad to get away and felt ashamed of myself for this. I will get back before Christmas if that's possible, I thought, for I knew they would hate to celebrate Christmas at Eversleigh without me.

I rode between Carl and Lance Clavering, and we were all very merry once we were on the high road and had left the sadness of parting behind us.

It was a beautiful morning. The warmth of summer was still with us although the leaves of the oaks had turned to a deep bronze and in the hedgerows the field maples were showing their orange and red banners. The tang of the sea was in the faint mist which enveloped everything and gave a touch of misty blueness to the woods.

With us were two serving men and two more to look after the packhorses. They rode behind us, keeping a watch on the roads.

Lance said, "How I love setting out on a journey. It's an adventure in itself. Do you think so, Clarissa? The sun will break through at any moment. But I like the mist. Do you? There is an air of mystery about a mist ... mystery and adventure. What say you, Clarissa?"

His questions were rhetorical. He never waited for answers. "It's a morning for singing," he went on. "What say you?" Then he broke into song.

> *There came seven Gypsies on a day*
> *Oh, but they sang bonny O*
> *And they sang so sweet and they sang so clear*
> *Down came the Earl's lady O*
>
> *They gave to her the nutmeg*
> *They gave to her the ginger*
> *But she gave to them a far better thing*
> *The seven gold rings off her fingers.*

"You'll awaken the countryside," said Carl.

"They should be about at this hour," retorted Lance. "It's such a pathetic story. Do you know the rest of it, Clarissa?"

"Yes," I replied. "The Earl's lady went off with the Gypsies."

"So you do know the story." He went on singing:

> *Last night I lay on a good featherbed*
> *And my own wedded lord beside me*
> *And tonight I'll lie in the ash corner*
> *With the Gypsies all around me.*

"The castle lost for the love of the Gypsies. What do you think of the Earl's lady? Was she a wise woman or a foolish one?"

"Foolish," I replied promptly. "She would soon get tired of the ash corner and the Gypsies all around her. She'll be wanting her high-heeled Spanish shoes before long, you can be sure."

"What a practical girl you are! I thought you would have more romantic ideas. Most girls have."

"I am not most girls. I am myself."

"Ah, we have an individualist here."

"I think the lady was not only foolish but unkind." I sang the last verse of the song.

> *The Earl of Casham is lying sick*
> *Not one hair I'm sorry*
> *I'd rather have a kiss from his fair lady's lips*
> *Than all his gold and money.*

"And you find such sentiments foolish?" asked Lance.

"Extremely so."

So we chattered rather frivolously until we stopped at an inn for refreshment and to rest the horses. But after a short stay there we were on our way again. We passed through villages and towns and I noticed that Carl was watchful, as though he were looking out for something. I knew, of course, that they were going to York for some secret purpose and I was glad, for to travel in their company—and particularly that of Lance—was exhilarating.

Through the golden afternoon we rode on, and at dusk came to an inn which they had previously decided should be the one where we spent the night.

Rooms were prepared for us, and we had a grand meal of fish with a delicious sauce, followed by roast mutton and a kind of syllabub which was a specialty of the innkeeper's wife. I was given cider and the men sat back sipping their port. While we were at the table a man came into the dining room. I don't know why I noticed him. He was dressed in a dark-brown frieze coat with black buttons, brown shoes and black stockings. On his formally curled peruke was a three-cornered hat, which he took off when he came into the inn parlor.

He sat close by, and I had the impression that he was interested in us. It might have been that Lance Clavering's elegance would arouse interest wherever he went. Uncle Carl certainly looked less impressive without his uniform. As for myself, I was only a very young girl, and I had a feeling that it was the men who were arousing the stranger's interest. He sat quietly in a corner and after a while I forgot him.

I was tired out with the day's riding. The fresh air had made me sleepy, and as soon as I was shown to my room I went to bed and slept deeply. I was amazed that morning came so swiftly when I was aroused by the stirring of the inn folk. I got up and looked out of my window. I saw Lance down there. He looked up and saw me.

"Did you sleep well, beauteous maid?" he asked.

"The sleep of exhaustion," I told him.

"What tired you so? Not my company, I hope."

"No, that was enlivening. I went to sleep thinking about the Earl's lady."

"That foolish one! There's no need to hurry this morning. We shall be late leaving. One of the horses has cast a shoe. They'll be taking her along to the smith."

"Oh . . . when did this happen?"

"I've just discovered it. We shall be leaving at eleven. That will give us a chance to go to the fair."

"The fair? What fair?"

"With your entertainment in mind, I have been acquainting myself with the lie of the land. It seems that in the village of Langthorn . . . or is it Longhorn? I am not sure . . . in any case, the fair comes to the village twice a year, and it so happens that this day is one of its biannual visits. Fortuitous, you may say, and so it is. The powers that be are determined that this shall be an interesting journey for all concerned."

"What does my great-uncle say?"

"He is resigned. He has some business to do here in any case. So he said to me, 'Will you look after my little niece for an hour or so, Clavering?' I replied, 'Indeed I will, sir. Nothing would give me greater pleasure, sir. If you have no objection, your little niece and I will visit the fair.' He gave his willing consent to this excursion."

"Are you always so exuberant and talkative?"

"Only when I have an appreciative audience."

"You find me appreciative?"

"I find you everything I would wish you to be at the precise moment I would wish it. Now that, my dear Clarissa, is the definition of an attractive woman."

"I suspect that you do not mean all the flattering things you say."

"A statement of fact is not flattery, is it? One eulogizes because the spirit moves one to do so. One speaks as one finds, and if there is a flow of words . . . well, that is useful, but it is not flattery. To you I speak the truth, and if it seems overfulsome, that is because modesty is yet another of your excellent virtues."

"Have you ever been at a loss for words?"

"There have been times. At the gaming table, perhaps, when I have lost more than I could afford."

"That must be alarming."

"Well, it is part of the gamble. If one man won every time, there would be no excitement, would there? But I must not talk to you of gambling. Your family would heartily disapprove of that. Well, what say you to a visit to the fair?"

"I should love it."

"Then break your fast early and we'll set off. I promise you an exciting morning."

"I will be as quick as I can."

I turned from the window, pulled the bell rope and asked for hot water. I washed and went down. While I was eating hot, crisp bacon on crusty bread and drinking a mug of ale the man in the frieze coat came in. He was dressed for departure. He talked to the landlord about his horse. He was obviously rather anxious to be on his way.

. When I left the dining room Lance was waiting for me, and he told me we had a couple of hours before we need be back at the inn. As we walked into the village we heard sounds of merriment. The fair was set up in a field where there were brightly colored booths and such crowds that I guessed many people had come in from the neighboring countryside.

Lance took my arm. "Keep close to me," he said. "At fairs like this robbers abound. Keep your hands on your purse, and if anyone attempts to snatch it, shout and I'll prevent the robbery. Above all, keep close and don't stray from your protector."

"Who are you . . . Sir Lancelot?"

"I have a confession to make to you. That is my real name. As soon as I became aware of its implications—that was when I was seven years old, for I was a very intelligent child, as you have gathered, and the quality stayed with me in afterlife—I changed it. Lancelot! Imagine. Lance is so much more suitable. There is something rather aggressive about a lance. A weapon of war."

"Lancelot was aggressive at times, I believe. And then there was all that trouble over Guinevere."

"All the same, I should hate to go through life with the label of knighthood attached to me."

I laughed.

"You are amused?" he asked.

"We seem to get into discussions about matters which are of no real importance."

"My name is of the utmost importance to me . . . and I hope it will be to you. As for those Spanish leather shoes you were so anxious about, I think I learned something about you through your attitude to the Earl's lady—and that is what interests me, my dear Clarissa."

"I fancy you might be a little like Sir Lancelot after all," I said. "What is that smell?"

"An ox . . . roasting. A necessary feature of such occasions. They'll be selling it at so much a slice."

"I don't think I should want any of it."

"But you'll have a fairing, won't you? For I shall insist on that."

"I have an idea that you will not have to be too insistent."

I was fascinated by the fair. I had never seen anything like it. I felt I was stepping out into adventure. But perhaps this had something to do with the company of Lance Clavering. Perhaps it was because he did not treat me like a child.

The autumn sun was faintly warming and it gave a glow to goods displayed on the stalls. There was one section for the cattle. Horses were for sale too, but it was the stalls that fascinated me. Together Lance and I inspected the saddles, the boots, other clothing, pots, brushes, ornaments, potatoes in their jackets roasting in a brazier; there were chestnuts too. Lance bought a bag of these and we munched contentedly.

This was a special fair, Lance told me. There were side-shows with waxworks, dwarfs and conjurers. There was one extremely fat woman and a very thin one, and these caused great amusement because they were not very respectful toward their new monarch.

We went into one tent and watched a puppet show; we applauded wildly with the rest of the company, and I noticed that Lance's clothes attracted some attention. But the people were used to gentry looking in at the fair, so his presence was not as unusual as it might have been.

He took me to the fairing stall and asked me to choose what I liked. There were sweetmeats tied up with ribbons making lover's knots—most of them heart-shaped or in the form of some animals. There was a dog that looked rather like Damon. I hesitated over that, and then I saw a sugar mouse; it had bright pink eyes and a long tail, and about its neck was a piece of blue ribbon. I was reminded immediately of the sugar mouse I had had all those years ago when Hessenfield had held up the coach and I had given him the tail of my mouse because, although I had not known he was my father, I had loved him.

Lance saw that I was looking at the mouse, so he took it and with it a heart in pink marzipan decorated with lover's knots. He insisted on buying that as well, so we came away from the stall with the mouse and the heart.

He wanted to hear why I liked the mouse and I told him.

"Ah, yes," he said, "Hessenfield." And for the first time since I had known him he looked a little serious.

We went on through the fair. I wanted to stop time's passing. It was a magic morning and I was so happy to be there. I felt excited because I felt that anything could happen.

But as though fate were reminding me that it is not the way of life to give happiness all the time, I saw the hiring stall. I wished I had not passed that way as I looked at those sad people offering themselves for hire. They were people who had failed to find work in any other way. There was an old man who had desperation in his eyes and there was a girl of about my age. I felt it must be the ultimate humiliation to have to offer oneself in this way. There were others there too, some carrying the tools of their trade to tell prospective employers what they could do. I had never seen such expressions of mingled hope and desperation. Lance noticed my reaction, and taking my arm, gently turned me away from the hiring stall.

I walked very quietly, not seeing the stalls of pots and pans, the geese which had been cooked and were browning over a fire; I did not hear the quack doctors shouting of the benefits and miracles performed by their pills for lucky purchasers. I could only think of the desperate expression in the eyes of the old man and the girl who could have been myself.

"You have a tender heart, little Clarissa," said Lance, "and you have a great gift for putting yourself in the place of others. It is rare. Keep it. It will make life richer and fuller for you."

So there was, after all, a serious side to his nature, I reasoned, to talk like that and to mean what he said.

We came to the boxing booth.

"We'll go in here," said Lance, and I saw then that his seriousness had vanished. An excitement seemed to grip him.

We were inside a large tent. In this a ring had been set up and two men fighting each other. There were forms on which we sat.

It was warm in the tent. I could see the sweat glistening on the bodies of the fighters, who were bare to the waist. I found it rather repulsive and would have liked to leave, but when I turned to Lance I saw the rapt expression on his face as he watched the men pummeling each other.

After what seemed a long time to me one was knocked down. The cheers shook the tent, and a man came forward and held up the victor's hand. He smiled at the crowd although there was blood on his forehead.

Now someone was calling out, "Place your bets!" and Lance rose and joined the people around a man who was seated at a table. Money was exchanged.

Then two men came out and began to fight. I found it all rather nauseating, but I could not take my eyes from Lance, who was clearly engrossed in what was taking place and seemed to have forgotten I was there. When the fight was over he shrugged his shoulders, and when I suggested we leave he reluctantly rose and we did so.

"You don't care much for the sport of kings," he said.

"I thought that was horse racing."

"It depends on the king ... which he prefers, you see. I have not heard our noble George's likes in the matter."

"What were you doing at the table? We had already paid to go in."

"I was placing my bet."

"Bet? What bet?"

"On the winner. It was a little gamble."

"So you gambled on which one of those men would win?"

"Yes ... and on the wrong one."

"So you lost some money."

"Alas, I did."

"Oh, dear, I hope not too much."

"Five pounds."

I was aghast. It seemed a great deal of money to me. "Five pounds. That is terrible."

"Sweet Clarissa, to be so concerned. But think what would have happened if my man had won."

"You would have got a lot of money then, I suppose."

"Fifty, perhaps—fifty for five. Think of it. Wouldn't that have been wonderful?"

"But you lost."

"Ah, but I might have won."

I was silent. Then I said, "It was a great risk. And you lost."

"That's what makes it exciting. If you knew you were going to win all the time, where would be the thrill?"

"It would be more thrilling surely to win all the time."

"You haven't the gambler's spirit, I can see."

I did not answer. A faint cloud had settled over the outing. I had been so gloriously happy. Then I had seen the hiring stall and now Lance had lost five pounds. These two events shadowed my morning.

It was time, in any case, to return to the inn. I was surprised to see that the man in the brown frieze coat was still there, for previously he had been making such a fuss about his horse's being ready in time.

Within a short while we were on the road again.

Intrigue

I left Great-uncle Carl and Lance Clavering in York, and only then did I realize how much I had enjoyed Lance's company. His lively conversation had been so invigorating, and what I had liked most was to be treated like a grown-up person.

I had only the grooms now for the remainder of the journey. As the weather continued good, starting at dawn and riding till sunset, we had only two nightly stops at inns which had been recommended.

We rode over moors and along the sea. It thrilled and inspired me. This wild northern country was the home of my ancestors.

At length we came to Hessenfield Castle. It was not far from the coast—about a mile, I should say—and was a fine yellow-stone edifice forming a quadrangle enclosing a court, and finished at the four angles with tall square towers. At the corners of these towers were projecting octagonal turrets, machicolated and clearly intended for the convenience of archers, who could drive their arrows down on an invading army.

The projecting gateway, with its turret and battlemented gallery, was most impressive, and above were the carved armorial bearings of the noble Field family, whose title was that of Hessenfield. I looked at those mullioned windows and I felt a glow of pride because this was the home of my father's family.

As we rode through the gateway, grooms came running out to see who I was and I saw at once that I was going to be made very welcome.

"His lordship said as we were to be on the lookout these last two days," said one of them. "I'll take you to him without delay."

I dismounted and my horse was taken from me by another groom; two others came out to look after my guards and the saddle bags.

As I entered the castle I was immediately aware of its grandeur. I was accustomed to Eversleigh Court, which was a magnificent mansion; Enderby was a fine old house; but this was a castle. It owed its existence to the Normans; Eversleigh was Elizabethan and therefore comparatively modern. I was immediately struck by the thick stone walls and the spiral staircases with rope banisters in that part of the castle which was like a fortress. We emerged into the great hall—far bigger than the one at Eversleigh. On the stone walls hung weapons of another age; and when I looked up at the high vaulted roof I saw the minstrels' gallery and was reminded of Enderby.

"His lordship is in his sitting room," said the groom. "I will let him know you are here."

In a short while I was taken up a wide staircase, through a gallery hung with portraits. I took a quick look. All the men and women seemed very much alike. My father, I guessed, must be among them, but there was no time to search for him. The servant was hurrying me on.

We went through the gallery into a long corridor. Here there were carpets on the floor, which gave a more modern touch to the place. Comfort prevailed over antiquity.

The servant knocked on a door and I was advancing into a room. It was not a large room, but there was an air of extreme comfort there. The heavy blue curtains at the mullioned windows matched the blue of the carpet; there was a fire burning on the large grate, and seated in a chair was a man with a rug over his knees. On the chair opposite him was a young woman.

The man spoke at once but did not rise.

"You are Clarissa," he said. "At last you have come. I thought you would never arrive."

I went toward him quickly and he took my hand. I realized then that he was an invalid.

"Forgive my not rising," he said. "The plain fact is that I can't. I have to live my life in this chair. Aimée, my dear, come and greet Clarissa."

The young woman had risen. She was only a few years older than I . . . perhaps eighteen, I guessed. She was beautifully dressed in a gown of deep green velvet, cut away in front to show a gray silk petticoat.

She took my hand and smiled at me. Her look was searching. I was sure she noticed how untidy my hair was and that my hands were red from the cold.

"You will be tired and want to rest," said my uncle. "You will want to wash perhaps and change and then eat. Something warm, eh? I was not sure what you would want to do first, but I was so anxious to see you as soon as you arrived. Now, say ... which is it to be? Would you like to wash first? In the kitchens they will be preparing something good to eat, and we can get to know each other over a meal."

"It is so good to see you ..." I began.

"Uncle," he said. "I'm your uncle Paul. Your father was my eldest brother. I knew of your existence but only just became aware of where you were. I wanted so much to see you. Now, say what you would wish to do first."

Because I was aware of the elegant appearance of the girl called Aimée I said I would like to wash and change. I could wait for food to be served for everyone. We had eaten cold bacon with bread and cheese at an inn shortly before we reached the castle.

"Then Aimée will take you to your room. You can explain to Clarissa who you are, Aimée. You two are going to have a great deal in common. When you are ready you and I will have a long talk too. But first things first. I know how you ladies feel after a long journey, and our climate up here is less benign than yours in the south."

I thought he was charming. He resembled my father slightly, but the first thing that always struck one about Hessenfield was his towering height. To see his brother, my uncle Paul, in a chair had been a great surprise to me.

Aimée flashed a smile at me. "I am so glad you have come," she said. "You can't imagine how we've been longing to see you. Come along. Let's get you comfortable and then we can talk."

She led me out of the room, and we seemed to go through a maze of corridors and up several staircases until we came to a room in one of the turrets. I went to the narrow window. I could see for miles over the moorland and, in the distance, the sea.

Aimée came and stood beside me. She smelt faintly of some perfume, rather musky and vaguely seductive. I glanced at her. She had dark—almost black—hair and beautiful long dark-brown eyes with black lashes. Her skin was pale, her lips faintly carmined. I did not know then that she augmented her beauty with certain aids. I found her rather fascinating in a slightly disturbing way and I was very curious to know who she was and whether she was related to me.

"Uncle Paul selected this room for you," she said. "He thought you would like the view." I noticed that she had a slightly French accent and intonation, which added to her exotic aura. "The wind screeches across the moors when it blows from the east. Ugh." She shivered. "It creeps into the castle," she went on, "and then it is so difficult to keep warm. It is very cold here in the north." I noticed how she stressed her *r*'s and was reminded of Jeanne.

"Tell me," I said, "are you my cousin . . . or are we related in some other way?"

She came a step nearer to me and regarded me with something like amusement.

"Not cousin," she said. "Closer . . . much closer. . . . Can you guess?"

"No," I said and began to wonder whether Uncle Paul had married a young wife.

Her next words so startled me that I thought I must be dreaming. "We are sisters," she said.

"Sisters! But . . . how. . . ."

She was smiling. "How do you call it? *Demi-soeur*. What I tell you is this. Your father . . . he was my father too."

"Hessenfield!"

"Ah, yes," she said with a great effort to pronounce the *H*. "Yes, Hessenfield."

"But how . . . ?"

"Very simple. In the usual way. You understand?"

I flushed and she went on. "Ah, I see you do. Our father was a very loving man. He loved my mother . . . very much. He loved me too . . . very much. He was a very loving man."

"You mean you are his illegitimate daughter?"

"It is an honor we both share. He was never married to your mother . . . nor to mine. Your mother was married already. Mine . . ." She lifted her shoulders in an entirely Gallic gesture. "Well, he was not a man to marry. But we came . . . you and I . . . all the same. We are *bâtardes*, eh? *Bâtardes* who share the same loving father."

"My sister," I murmured.

She put her hands on my shoulders, and drawing me to her,

71

kissed me on both cheeks. I was ashamed to admit to myself a certain revulsion. My mother had been known as Lady Hessenfield; she had lived with my father in his *hôtel*, and all the time there had been this girl, who must be some four or five years older than I. Perhaps that explained it. He had known her mother before he had known mine.

I was learning. The King had brought his German mistresses with him. Hessenfield had been like a king; he had had mistresses. My mother had been one of them; Aimée's mother another.

"Well," she went on, "how does it feel to find you have a sister?"

"It is so unexpected, of course. But it is exciting."

"You thought you were the only one, didn't you?" she said rather slyly.

"I was led to believe it."

"Not with a man like my lord."

"How long have you been here?"

"About a year. I could not come before the peace. It was not easy for us in Paris. And then I thought I should come here, for after all, it was my home. This was where my father meant to bring me when he had put King James on the throne. He always said so to my mother. He used to say, 'When this is completed we will go home to Hessenfield Castle.'"

"And you knew of me?"

"Oh, yes, we knew of you."

"And you knew that my Aunt Damaris had brought me to England?"

"No."

"Then how did my uncle . . . our uncle . . . know where to send for me?"

"He has ways of finding out. Perhaps we will tell you."

I said, "It is all such a surprise for me. I shall need time to get used to it."

"You will. I find it good . . . amusing. We shall have much to share."

"There is a lot I want to know. Did you just come here and tell my uncle who you were?"

"Are you thinking that I might not be saying the truth?" She looked angry suddenly. "I am as much his daughter as you are."

"No, no, you mistake me. I merely wondered how you came

here and what did our uncle think when he met you so suddenly."

"I had proof." She spoke vehemently, and then she smiled. "Ah, I could prove who I was. I had his signet ring—the ring worn by all the holders of the title. I brought it back to our uncle, who now wears it on the third finger of his right hand. Our father wore it on his little finger."

I nodded. I remembered that ring. It was gold, with a stone called bezoar. I could hear his voice then telling me this when I had shown interest in it.

"Our father was a big man. The ring just fitted his little finger. I brought his watch too—and there was the letter. These things I brought because they were given to my mother by Lord Hessenfield in case something should happen to him. He loved well his daughters did our father. He wanted us to be taken care of. That was what he always said. He wanted *me* taken care of as well as you."

A maid came in with cans of hot water and Aimée said she would leave me to wash. Then, if I would pull the bell rope it would tell them in the kitchen that I was ready to be taken to my uncle. We could then talk together until dinner was served.

I felt in a daze as I washed the grime of the journey from my hands and face. My saddle bags were brought up, and I was glad to get out of my riding clothes and into a red dress which I felt was rather becoming. I wanted to look my best so that I might not compare too unfavorably with Aimée.

When I was ready I rang the bell as I had been told to, and was conducted back to the room where my uncle was impatiently awaiting my coming.

"Ah," he said, "now you are ready."

I looked for Aimée, and he said, "I implied that you and I should best get to know each other alone at first. Were you surprised to find you had a half sister?"

"Yes, indeed I was."

"My brother was always a lusty man. All of the Hessenfields are . . . except those who are incapacitated." He spoke without bitterness. He had a very sweet expression and I began to warm toward him.

"John—your father, that is—was always an adventurer. He was the eldest of a family of brothers. We were all daring. As I said, it runs in the family. But he was always the leader. John led, we followed. Sometimes we shared his adventures.

73

He was a wonderful man in so many ways. It has always been as though he lives on. And so he does in a way in you two girls. Strange that he should have left *girls*. One would have imagined he would have had sons."

"Would you have preferred them?"

"Not now I have seen you both."

"How did you know where I was?"

He hesitated for a moment. "Oh . . . I was told. A friend of a friend—one of those coincidences."

For the first time he seemed to lose that open look, and I felt my question had embarrassed him. I decided not to probe just then but to try to discover who the friend was later.

"My brother sent messages from France. You know he was one of the leading Jacobites."

I nodded.

"If he were alive today . . ."

"You are going to say that he would bring the Chevalier of St. George to England."

"I am sure of it."

"And you share his views?"

He was evasive. "These could be dangerous times," was all he said. After a slight pause he went on. "Let me tell you what your father wrote to me about you. He said you were the most adorable child he had ever seen and he was proud of you. He loved you dearly, you know."

"Yes, I did know it. It is something one knows even at an early age. I still remember it."

"He loved your mother too. He regretted there could be no marriage. She was already married. He told me all about it. It was one of those adventures that came his way."

"And what about Aimée?"

"That must have been some time before. I don't know much about Aimée's mother, but he must have been fond of her to give her the watch and the ring—particularly the ring. I think he must have known your mother was dying. You see, this ring is a rather special one in our family. It has always been worn by the head of the house. It has special properties."

"Does it bring good luck?"

"It is not that. Here, take a look at it." He took the ring from his finger. I remembered it vaguely. I did not find it attractive. It was heavy gold, with a stone of a nondescript color. The setting was elaborate. "It meant a good deal to me to get this back," my uncle went on. "It is important in the family. When he knew that he was dying of the same fatal illness which took your mother too, he sent for Aimée's mother and gave her the ring and his watch to bring to me with the letter. I thought we had lost the ring forever and that because of his illness it would have been buried with him. When Aimée arrived with it she had brought back the Hessenfield heirloom. It convinced me that she was his daughter. I knew he would never have parted with the ring unless he was dying and could not give it to your mother. Of course, owing to the war, a long time elapsed before she was able to get here."

"When did you hear of his death?"

"A few months after it happened. Our friends could not get across immediately to tell me. We heard that your mother had died too. I wondered what had become of you. I asked for news but could get none. No one knew your whereabouts."

"Jeanne, one of the maids at the *hôtel*, looked after me. She kept me until my aunt Damaris—my mother's half-sister—came to look for me."

"Yes. I know that now. But I did not then. As soon as I discovered where you were I sent my nephew to invite you to come here. I wished you had come earlier."

"I should have done so if my aunt had not been expecting a baby."

"The good Aunt Damaris. Tell me more about her. Aimée says that her mother tried to find you and failed to do so. She said that after the death of your father and mother there was chaos in the house. Of course Aimée can only speak from hearsay. She only knows what her mother told her. It was all very mysterious to her before she had the opportunity of coming to England. It was what her mother had waited for. She wanted Aimée to present herself to her father's family— and to bring back the ring and the watch. Aimée tells me that her mother had recently married and set up home with her new husband just outside Paris. I can imagine that a grown-up daughter would be rather *de trop* in such a household. I was touched to see how delighted Aimée was by her welcome here, and when I suggested she stay as long as she liked . . . in fact, make her home here . . . she was overcome with joy."

"It is all so bewildering. I had no idea what was going on."

"How could you? What were you . . . five or six?"

"I just knew that I was there with my parents in that luxurious house, and then they were gone and I was in a damp, dark cellar, frightened, bewildered, wondering what it all meant."

"My poor, poor child! But you were brave, I don't doubt. You have a look of your father. What a waste of a life! I should have been the one. Here I am, condemned to a chair for the rest of my life. . . . That's self-pity. One should beware of that. It's taking your troubles out and nourishing them . . . pampering them . . . instead of shutting them away in a dark cupboard and forgetting them—which is the wise thing to do."

I said, "I'm sorry. Has it been long?"

"Fourteen years ago, when I was twenty-five. I was thrown from my horse when I was out hunting. I knew she couldn't take that hedge. It was too high. Others turned away and took a detour. But I had to do it. It was showing off . . . nothing more. I crashed. My mare was on top of me. She had to be shot. I sometimes think it was a pity they didn't shoot me. There's self-pity again."

"It's understandable," I replied.

"They never thought I should recover. I was engaged to be married to a beautiful girl. She looked after me in those first weeks. She said we would go through with the marriage . . . but old self-pity came along. I was impossible, I knew. I had a grievance against life. We had always been so active in our family; I couldn't endure it. And then there was the pain . . . the intermittent pain. The trouble was that I never knew when it was coming on. I had rages. In the end she saw how useless it would be. So did I. I couldn't condemn her to a life like that. She married someone else in time."

"I am so sorry. Now you seem so calm and gentle . . . so reconciled."

"That is what time does, Clarissa. Time is the great teacher, the great healer. I tell myself that it was tragic that John should die of a strange disease in Paris and that I, his successor, should be a cripple, spending his days in a chair. You might say it was the curse of the Fields, if you believe in such things."

"Is there supposed to be a curse?"

"No. We've been strong and vigorous through the ages, defending our lands and goods from marauding Scots when they made their forays over the border. It was just one of the misfortunes which beset most families at some time. I have been talking a great deal about myself. I want to hear about you."

I told him about life at Enderby and how we were close to the Dower House, the home of my grandmother Priscilla, and Eversleigh Court, where my great-grandparents lived.

"You have an uncle too, have you not? One who is in the army?"

"He's my great-uncle, actually. He's Carleton really, but we call him Carl always, to distinguish him from my great-grandfather."

"Yours is a long-lived family."

"My grandmother was very young when my mother was born and my mother was young when I was born."

"I see. It makes a small gap between generations. Do you see much of your uncle Carl?"

"No. Very little until lately. He came with me to York."

He nodded and was silent for a while, and then there was a knock on the door and Aimée came in. She had changed her velvet dress for one of brocade in a bluish shade. The bodice was low cut and her skin looked pearly. She wore garnets at her throat and in her ears. They suited her. I learned afterward that they had been a gift from Uncle Paul to his fiancée, who, when she had broken off the engagement, had returned all the presents he had given her. I thought he must be very fond of Aimée to have given her his fiancée's presents.

Before we dined, there were arrivals at the castle. The nephew who had visited us at Enderby came with his father. Matthew Field was very like what I remembered of my father—tall and commanding. He seemed very pleased to see me.

"You are as pretty as my son Ralph described you," he told me.

Ralph greeted me like an old friend. "It was good of you to come all this way," he said. "I trust the baby arrived in good condition."

"She did and she is flourishing. I had to stay until she was born. You did understand, I hope."

"But of course."

Dinner was leisurely and lavish. There were a great many dishes, some of which I did not know the name.

"We eat heartily up here," my uncle Paul explained. "More so than you southerners."

"It's due to the climate," said Ralph. "It can be bitterly cold up here, and we need hot soups, black puddings and hot roast beef in abundance to keep out the cold."

I felt exhausted after the food and unaccustomed wine, not to mention the journey and the revelations which had disclosed the fact that I had a half sister. I must have shown this, because Uncle Paul said, "What Clarissa needs most just now is a good night's rest. Aimée, take her to her room. She might get lost in the castle." He turned to me. "People do, you know. That's until they begin to know the place. It began life as a fortress, but so much has been added over the centuries. Sometimes I think it resembles a maze more than a dwelling."

Aimée rose obediently, and smiling at me, asked if I were ready. I said I was, for I felt a great desire to be alone and digest what I had heard. She took a candle from a chest and lighted me up the stairs.

As we ascended them she waved the candle about and turned to smile at me. "It is a little . . . what you say? . . . eerie by the light of the *chandelle*." Like Jeanne, she introduced a French word into her speech every now and then. It added a certain charm to the conversation.

"Yes," I said. "Our house is a little like that too."

She nodded. "But you are not afraid of shadows . . . not you."

"I try not to be."

"That is all we can do about anything . . . try."

When we came to my room she threw open the door and we entered. A fire was burning in the grate, which gave out a coziness. "I told them you must have a fire," she said. "It is so cold when the wind blows." Heavy curtains had been drawn across the window; the bed quilt was turned back and the four-poster bed looked very inviting.

"They have put in the warming pan . . . you will see."

"They are determined to make me comfortable."

"We want you to know . . . Uncle Paul and I . . . that you are with your family."

"You have certainly made me feel that."

"Now, is there anything else you want . . . for the night?"

"I don't think so, thank you."

"If you should want . . ." she waved her arms in an expansive gesture . . . "you will ring the bell. So." She indicated the bell rope. "Or if there is something I can do . . . I am not far away. We are both in the turret. I look out to the west . . . over the countryside . . . you look out to sea."

"Thank you. I'll remember."

"Good night, *ma soeur*. Sleep well."

She shut the door quietly and went out. I stood staring at it for a few seconds. It was a thick oak door with a latch and a bolt which could be drawn across. On sudden impulse I went to the door and bolted it.

Then I wondered at myself. Why had I done that? It was almost as though I were afraid. Suppose Aimée came back for something and heard me unbolt the door. It would seem very unfriendly. I drew back the bolt and undressed. The firelight threw flickering shadows round the room. It was warm, cozy . . . and yet . . . there was something alien here, something which was almost a warning, and I believed that, tired as I was, I should find it difficult to sleep in this room.

I drew back the curtains as though to let in the outside world. There was a half moon and it was a clear night. I could see the sea distinctly in the distance. There was a quietness in the air . . . no wind ruffled the grass of the moorlands. I could get a glimpse of the gate of the castle, majestic in moonlight.

I turned back to the comfort of the fire and got into bed.

I had been right. It was difficult to sleep. I knew there were all sorts of unusual noises in old houses. When darkness falls it is as though those who have lived out their lives within the walls and who cannot rest come out to live again. It was like that at Enderby, but I had grown accustomed to the creak of the wood there. I knew which stair seemed to protest every time one trod on it; I knew that the creaking went on until the early hours of the morning. It would be the same here, but they were to me as yet unfamiliar creaks.

I lay there for about half an hour, sleep eluding me. I dozed once and dreamed the door opened and Aimée came in. She was smiling at me, laughing at me, noting that I lacked her elegance. She was saying, "I am your sister . . . *ma soeur, ma petite soeur.*"

I awoke frightened, though there was nothing frightening in the dream. I expected to see her standing by the bed laughing at me. There was no one there. I rose from my bed and bolted the door. I knew that would help me to sleep.

I was so tired that I did fall asleep, and suddenly I was awakened by the sound of voices. They came from below. I sat up in bed, startled.

I thought I heard the sound of horses. I listened intently and went to the window. The moon shone serenely on the moors, and although I could see nothing below me, I was aware of the sounds of activity.

I went back to bed. The fire had died down and there was a chilliness in the room. My feet had grown cold. I tucked them into my nightgown, and I saw from my watch—which I had laid on the table beside the bed—that it was three o'clock. I tried to sleep, but it was impossible. I was wide awake now.

I lay still while my feet grew warmer and I went over every detail of my arrival at the castle, particularly my talks with Uncle Paul and Aimée. Such revelations as she had made were enough to create insomnia in anyone, I assured myself, and as I slept so well normally, I could easily cope with the very occasional bad night when it came along. Moreover, it was understandable, as it was the first night in a new bed. One had to grow accustomed to beds.

I was thinking how complicated life was and how the actions of the past created the future, and their effects could be felt through the generations.

Then suddenly I heard voices . . . low, sibilant voices. I got out of bed and went to the window. Men were coming out of the castle; they had come through the gatehouse. I saw my uncle Matthew and Ralph with them, and there were three other men. One of these three was vaguely familiar to me. He wore a brown frieze coat and black stockings; on his head was a three-cornered hat. I was trying to think where I had seen him before. The men were out of sight. I guessed they were going to the stables, where they would have left their horses. I was right. After a short while they emerged on horseback. The man in the brown frieze coat was with them.

I watched them ride away, standing at the window until they were out of sight. Then, cold and shivering a little, I went back to bed. I lay there for a long time wondering why I should feel there was something strange going on. Why shouldn't my uncle and cousin and their companions leave in the early hours of the morning? There was no reason why they should retire early because I did. But there were the three other visitors. They must have come very late. Well, why should they not do so?

I was imagining all sorts of strange happenings. Why? Because I had just discovered that I had a sister and had left the quiet world of my mother's family. I had escaped from the cocoon and perhaps was looking for adventure. I had come into the orbit of the bold Hessenfields. Already I was learning a little more about my exciting father and discovering that there was still much to learn.

Dawn now streaked the sky. I got out of bed again and unbolted the door. I did not want someone to bring up hot water and find that I had shut myself in. I did not want to betray my uneasiness.

I lay waiting for morning and suddenly the realization came to me.

The man I had seen below was the same one whom I had noticed in the inn.

How strange! He had seemed to take an interest in our party. And now he had turned up at the castle. What did it mean?

The comforting daylight was creeping into my room, dispelling the imaginings of the night.

How many men in England wore brown frieze coats, black stockings and three-cornered hats? The answer was: thousands. I was going to laugh at myself in the morning.

For a long time I was to remember those first days at Hessenfield Castle. There were the conversations with Aimée—light-hearted, frivolous chatter—which enthralled me because with them came an aura of the past and they brought memories which I had long forgotten. Then there were my sessions with my uncle Paul, my interest in the castle, and the strange atmosphere of tension, which I did not understand at the time. It was a suppressed excitement and uneasiness which seemed to affect them all except Aimée. I believed she was aware of it and that it both amused and exasperated her.

She had made herself mistress of the castle, and it was quite clear that my uncle Paul was fond of her. She made him laugh, and anyone who could do that would be a favorite of his.

He talked about her to me. "She has the true Gallic charm," he said. "That comes from her mother. I must say we have been more lively in the castle since she came. When the war was over and there was free traffic between the two countries, one summer's morning she presented herself at the castle, announcing who she was. She is a resourceful young woman. She gave me the ring, which she said your father had wished to be returned to me, and she brought his watch too, which he had presumably left to her mother, and there was a letter from my brother."

"When did he write it?" I asked, even though Aimée had told me this.

"It must have been before he died. He must have given it to Aimée's mother as a sort of guarantee that the child would be cared for. He died suddenly, but living was precarious for him. He never knew from one day to the next when he would run into an ambush or someone would assassinate him. There was a price on his head, you know."

"Could I see my father's letter? I have never seen anything he wrote."

"Certainly you may. It clearly states that his daughter shall have a share of his estate."

"Does he mention me?"

"Not in this letter. He had already written to me about you when your mother joined him in France. He said then that you should be his heiress."

He took some keys from his pocket and gave them to me. "Go and open that desk," he said. "You will see some papers there . . . just inside. Will you please bring them to me?"

I did as he asked and came back with the papers. He turned them over and brought out a letter which he handed to me. It had the address of the *hôtel* embossed on the top right-hand corner.

I read:

Dear Paul,

We had an unpleasant scare today. It made me realize that I could be a dead man at any time. I know that applies to us all, but to some more than others—and I am one of those to whom it could happen suddenly.

I have involved myself in certain responsibilities, and I want this daughter of mine to have a share in my fortune. Her mother will get the letter to you somehow. I will write in detail later, but just in case something should happen before I have an opportunity to do so, I want to make sure this girl is cared for along with my other liabilities.

I'll be setting it all out clearly later. This child is one of us, Paul, and I know I can trust you. I'll send this over when I can work out how the money should be arranged.

Your affectionate brother

John

"And he gave this letter to Aimée's mother?" I said.

"Yes. That was how it was done, I imagine."

"It is undated," I pointed out.

"Aimée said it was written a few days before his death. It seems as though he had a premonition of it . . . or perhaps he was then feeling ill."

"Then he must have been seeing Aimée's mother right up to the time of his death."

"My dear," said Uncle Paul, "you must not be shocked. He was like that . . . polygamous. There were always women . . . although your mother was the one he cared for in a very special way . . . and for you too . . . as her daughter. But he had clearly been fond of Aimée's mother, and he certainly was of Aimée. He was a philanderer, but there was a very sentimental side to his nature. He had a strong sense of honor and would never shirk his responsibilities!"

I looked at the letter in his handwriting. Bold and flowing, typical of the man.

"You can imagine how moved I was when Aimée arrived," went on Uncle Paul. "She told me that her mother had preserved that letter with the ring and watch and that she had planned to come to England herself as soon as she could do so. But when the opportunity came, Aimée was of an age to travel and her mother had married. It was only natural that she would not want to involve her new husband in a past love affair, so Aimée came alone. I trust you are pleased to have a sister. She is a charming girl, full of vitality. One would expect that from a daughter of my brother. You have the same quality, my dear. You must always keep it. I hope you two are going to be friends, as sisters should be."

I was getting very fond of my uncle.

Aimée and I rode a good deal and she undertook to show me the countryside. Uncle Paul insisted that we take a groom with us when we rode out. These were troublous times, he said. But Aimée usually contrived to arrange it so that we rode ahead of the groom and she tried to lose him. I refused to do this, as the groom would be reprimanded if he did not keep guard over us, but I did all I could to keep a distance between us so that we could indulge freely in one of those conversations which were so fascinating to me.

They took place partly in French, partly in English, and they taught me a great deal about life in Paris and quite a bit about the household in which I had lived in those early years.

She reawakened memories in me. I could almost smell the Paris streets. "Hot bread," she said. "It is one of the most delicious smells on earth. It filled the streets when the bakers came in from Gonesse with their baskets full of hot bread. Then there were the peasants with their farm products . . . chickens, eggs, fruit and flowers."

I remembered then the barbers, covered from head to foot with flour, with wigs and tongs in their hands . . . and the stalls of fish and apples in the marketplace.

"I would go into Les Halles with my basket on my arm," said Aimée. "Maman said I could drive a better bargain than she could herself. I was quick . . . I was . . . how you say . . . ?"

"Ruthless?" I suggested.

"Ruthless," she repeated. "I was the one to get the price less and come home with the *bon marché.*"

"I can well imagine it."

"So you think I am . . . *adroite*, little sister?"

"I not only think. I know!"

"Why do you say that?" she asked rather sharply.

"It is just something of which I have become aware."

She was ready to take offense over some matters. I think it was because she was quite at home in the English idiom. I had thought she would be pleased because I had noticed her cleverness.

"We were poor," she said defensively. "We had to watch every sou. When our father died it made a difference."

"It did to all of us," I reminded her. I knew something of poverty in the streets of Paris.

I told her about the cellar, and the horror of it all came flooding back as I talked.

"But you had the good Aunt Damaris to rescue you."

"You had your mother."

"But we lived through the hard times. Is it not comforting to live in a rich household when you have been so poor as to wonder where your next meal will come from? If you have been poor like that once . . . you never forget it."

"You are right," I answered.

"You appreciate. . . . You find it good. Money brings comfort. You would do a great deal to get it—and keep it."

"I should be terrified to go back and live as I did in the cellar."

"It has taught you what poverty is . . . and that is the good lesson. It will make you understand those others who have suffered it."

"Oh, yes, I agree. Tell me about my father. Did you often see him?"

"Yes. He came to us often."

"My mother did not know . . ."

"My dear sister, a man does not tell one mistress when he is visiting another."

"I am sure my mother had no idea."

"No. But we knew he was living with her. We could not help knowing. She was the *maîtresse en titre*. You see, Hessenfield was like a king. He could do these things as he willed."

I tried to remember my mother, and even though the pictures were hazy, I could not believe she would ever have knowingly accepted such a situation.

Aimée seemed to think it was something of a joke.

"I am four years older than you," she said. "There is much I can remember. He used to look a little . . . how you say it? . . . out of place . . . in our rooms in the Rue St. Jacques. We live there many years over the shop of a bookseller." She wrinkled her nose. "I can still smell the books. Some of them not very nice . . . not savory. He filled our little room when he was there. He looked so grand, he used to make us feel shabby . . . but he did not seem to notice. He was so happy to see us. He used to take me on his knee and say I was a little beauty. It was so *désolé* when he die. Those were the unhappy years. We were poor then. The bookseller was good to us, though. My mother worked in his shop and I helped. We could have sold the watch and the ring, but my mother said no. Never. She say, 'One day you go to England. When war is over . . .' Then she marry and I come to England. She did not want me when she married. She have the new family. Well, I found mine, did I not? Uncle Paul is good to me. If I was not his niece I would marry him. Then I have found my little sister."

She liked to shock me. She was constantly reminding me that I was a bastard; so was she, for that matter.

"Love children are the children of love," she said once. "That sounds romantic, does it not? I do not mind at all being a love child—as long as I am cared for by my family."

She did admit that when she had seen the lords and ladies riding in their carriages she had been overcome with envy.

Then there were the old dowagers in the sedan chairs in the mornings, usually going to Mass. She did not envy them so much, because they were old and it was a fearful thing to be old. But always she had wanted to be a lady in a carriage, patched, powdered, bewigged and perfumed, riding through the streets, splashing the Paris mud on passersby and attracting the attention of equally elegant young men in their carriages, pulling up, slyly making assignations, visiting the theater and being admired by the male audience and envied by the females. Life in Paris had been very much more exciting than it was at Hessenfield, but Paris had meant poverty and Hessenfield affluence.

I felt as though I had been at Hessenfield a long time, but it was only a week or so since I had arrived. My talks with both my uncle Paul and with Aimée had made me feel I was part of the place. Uncle Matthew and Ralph were frequent visitors, and there were other people, mostly men, who came to the castle. Sometimes they dined with us. When they did, I noticed there was a wariness about the conversation, and I could not help noticing that the tension I had observed when I arrived increased rather than diminished.

One day I went into my uncle's private sitting room. He was in the chair, the tartan rug over his knees, and I saw that some papers had slid to the floor. He had fallen asleep and dropped them. I hesitated. There were about six sheets, and some of them had fallen quite a little way from his chair. I went forward quietly and picked one up.

I looked at it in amazement. There was a picture on it of a very handsome man. "James the Third, King of Britain" was the heading. My eyes glanced down the page. It was an account of the virtues of the true King, and it stated that he would soon be returning to claim his kingdom. When he did, he must find his people ready to declare their allegiance to him.

I felt the color rush into my cheeks. This was treason to our crowned King George.

I looked up. Uncle Paul's eyes were on me.

"You seem absorbed by what you are reading, Clarissa," he said.

"I found these on the floor." I started to gather up the other sheets and I could not help seeing as I did so that they were the same as the one I had read.

"They slipped from my lap while I dozed," he said.

"They are . . . treasonable!" I whispered.

"They would be called so, it is true. Nevertheless they are being circulated in certain places."

I shivered. "If they were discovered . . ."

He said slowly, "There is strong support for James in Scotland. There are even certain members of Parliament . . . men in high places—who support him."

"Yes, so I have heard. My great-grandfather talked a lot about Bolingbroke and Ormonde . . . and men such as that."

"Give the sheets to me. I think they should be locked away in the desk, don't you? Will you put them there for me? Thank you."

He started to talk of other matters, but I knew there was something very dangerous afoot. Of course they would be Jacobites at Hessenfield. My father had been a leading one. That was why he had been in France . . . working to bring King James back to the throne. That James had now died, but there was this other James, his son, the Chevalier of St. George.

I wanted to talk to my uncle about this, but he quite clearly did not intend to discuss the matter with me. I wondered what my great-grandfather Carleton would say if he knew Hessenfield Castle was what he would call a "hotbed of traitors." He was intolerant, of course. He never admitted that there might be another side to a question than the one he took. I felt as my grandmother Priscilla did, that one side was not entirely right any more than the other was. I only wanted them all to be friendly together.

My uncle said suddenly, "When I first invited you to come here I planned all kinds of pleasures for you."

"Pleasures?" I asked.

"Yes. I wanted you to meet the people of the countryside. Perhaps a ball or two. It may be that you are overyoung for such. However, we should have made some attempt to show you that life is not as dull as you might think up here in the north."

"But I have not found it dull. I am having a very interesting time."

"It is fortunate that your sister is here. She provides the company. I am sure you would find it very dull otherwise. But it is not always so. My younger brothers are in Scotland at this time. Only Matthew is here."

"Something is happening," I burst out. "You are preparing

for something." I was thinking of the papers I had found on the floor.

He did not answer me. He merely said, "Perhaps later . . . if you stay with us . . . we shall be celebrating. Then we shall show you a little castle entertainment. But just now . . ."

"I understand. You cannot celebrate something which has not happened."

"We shall see. Now would you please go and find Harper and tell him I am ready for my beef tea."

Thoughtfully I went to the butler's pantry and there found Harper already warming up the beverage my uncle took at this time. I understood now what the tension in the house meant. They were preparing for a coup, which meant that they were planning to bring James back to England. It was only natural that Hessenfield Castle—the home of staunch supporters of the Chevalier—should be at the heart of the plot.

I thought of my great-grandfather, my great-uncle Carl and Lance Clavering. I did not believe the plotters could succeed, and I knew that there would be war.

I wanted to be alone to consider what this meant. As Priscilla had said, what did it matter which King was on the throne? But it mattered to fierce Protestants and perhaps fiercer Catholics. Wars, it seemed, were always about religion. Why was it that people who thought one thing was right wanted to force their views on others?

Uncle Paul was mild and gentle normally, but he had looked quite fierce when he had talked about the return of James.

I wondered what the family at Eversleigh would do if there was war and I was up in the north, which I presumed could be called Jacobite country, for the Scots would be more likely to support the Stuart line than the Hanoverian, although they were not of Catholic opinion by any means—except perhaps in the Highlands.

It was later in the afternoon when I went to my uncle's sitting room. I had made up my mind that I would ask him to tell me more of what was happening. I knew that there had been a company of Jacobites whose goal it had been to set James on the throne, though during the reign of Anne we had not heard a great deal about them—but perhaps I had not been sufficiently interested to notice. They had been mentioned from time to time, it was true, and there had always been a colony of them on the Continent, but I could see that now a new branch of the royal family had been brought to England, they might consider it was time to rise.

I came into the sitting room, but my uncle's chair was not there. I was just about to leave when I heard the sound of a movement in the anteroom which led from the sitting room. I went over to it, my footsteps silenced by the thick carpet. Then I heard someone—in a voice I had not heard before— mention me. I stood still, listening.

"But is it not strange that she should be here just at this time? I'll warrant she's acting as a spy. I suspected that from the moment I saw them on the road. She was with Eversleigh . . . General Eversleigh . . . though he was disguised as a plain citizen, and there was another of them with him . . . a fop . . . who perhaps is not such a fop . . . Clavering. They were with the girl . . . priming the girl. That's what she's here for. Who would suspect a girl of that age . . . little more than a child?"

"No. no." That was my uncle. "She came because I invited her."

"Why did you invite her . . . at such a time?"

"It was before this seemed possible. Her visit was delayed."

"Delayed! Of course it was delayed. I tell you they had wind of it. That's why she's here . . . at this moment. She'll be peeping and prying into everything. I tell you she's a danger. She's putting us all at risk."

I was too stunned to do anything, though I knew that at any moment the door would open and someone come out and find me here.

Yet I felt it was necessary for me to stay and listen. On the other hand, I wondered what they would do if they discovered me.

"You are making a great matter over nothing, Frenshaw," I heard my uncle say. "She is young . . . innocent . . . she knows nothing of these matters. She is concerned with riding and what color sash she will wear and visiting a family she has just discovered . . ."

"They have made a Hanoverian of her, Hessenfield. Don't you see that? She's here to spy. Why, I wouldn't be surprised if . . ."

I turned but I was too late. The door between the two rooms was suddenly opened. I swung round. The man in the brown frieze coat and black stockings was looking at me, and his expression in those first seconds of confrontation was frightening. There was triumph and malevolence. He was proved right and at the same time he was face to face with someone whom he believed to be a spy from the enemy's camp.

"I came to see my uncle," I said as firmly as I could. "I was surprised not to find him here."

"He is with friends," said the man, advancing toward me.

My heart was pounding so fiercely that I thought he must have noticed its beating against my bodice. I put my hands behind my back for fear he should see them trembling.

"Then I must not disturb him now," I said.

"Have you been waiting long?" The eyes, I noticed, were gray and penetrating. I felt that he was trying to look right into my mind and was convincing himself that he found there what he suspected.

"No . . . I had just come in."

"You must have heard us talking and known that he had visitors."

"I did not realize it until a moment ago."

He hesitated, and for a moment I thought he was going to seize me and make me his prisoner. He was a fanatic if ever I saw one.

My uncle called out, "Who's there?"

"It's your niece," said the man.

"Tell her I'll see her in about an hour."

The man looked at me. I nodded and escaped. I ran to my room. I was trembling. It was not pleasant to be caught eavesdropping, but to hear something which could be dangerous was quite terrifying.

I had no doubt now that I had walked into intrigue. I had chosen this time to come when something important was about to happen. I knew now what it was and that they were planning to bring James back to England and crown him King. But George of Hanover would not stand by and let that happen. There would be war, and at Eversleigh they would be staunchly for George, while here, in my father's family, they were the leaders of the plot to bring James back.

Aimée came to my room. I was lying on the bed, for I felt very shaken after that encounter.

"Are you not well?" she asked in astonishment.

"A headache," I replied. I did not wish to talk to her about what I had heard and what I knew was happening. Not yet, at any rate—not until I had sorted out my thoughts.

"I was just going out for a ride and hoping you would come with me."

"I won't today, thanks, Aimée."

"Ça va. Au revoir. I will see you later on."

I was relieved that she did not want to stay and talk.

It must have been about an hour later when I heard the sounds of departure below. I went to my window and saw a party of men riding away.

Then my uncle sent for me.

When I went to his room he was sitting in his chair in the usual place.

"Clarissa," he said as I entered, and he held out his hand to me. I went to him and took it and knelt down beside his chair. "My dear child," he went on, "this is so difficult for me. I have so enjoyed your being here . . . but the times are dangerous."

"I know," I replied. "I have gathered that there is a plot to bring James back to the throne."

"It has always been our desire to do that. All these years we have promised ourselves that we would. Your father, as you know, was devoted to the cause. You could say he gave his life for it. Had he not been in Paris on the King's business he would not have died as he did. Yes, we have never forgotten, and this time we are going to do it. It is unfortunate that you should be here now. It would have been far better if you had come when I asked you. Then this was not imminent. Now . . . it is."

"Uncle Paul," I said, "when I was in your room and you were in the anteroom I could not help overhearing those men . . . Frenshaw, was it . . . talking about me. He thought I was here to spy. You don't think that, Uncle?"

"Of course I don't."

"I knew nothing of all this before I came. It is true that I did come as far as York with my great-uncle Carl and Sir Lance Clavering, but that was only because they were coming this way and my aunt Damaris wanted me to have their protection on the roads. You do believe that."

"Yes, I do. I believe you so entirely that I am going to trust you. A Jacobite rising is imminent. There are many Scotsmen who are with us—that is why it will start in Scotland. Lord Kenmure has already proclaimed James King at Moffat. Lord Mar is rallying an army. The Lords Nithisdale, Wintoun and Carnwarth are coming to his aid. They are already preparing to cross the border and James is on his way to England."

"Uncle," I cried, "there will be war, civil war."

"Now, listen to me. You must go back to Eversleigh. My friends suspect you of spying. If we found ourselves in difficulties they would be ruthless. I want you to prepare to leave at dawn tomorrow. I will send for your grooms and prepare them. Get your things together, but don't let anyone know. In the morning I will tell them that you have been called away."

"Shall I not say goodbye to Aimée?"

He hesitated. Then he said, "I think we can trust her, but wait until last thing tonight."

I took his hand and kissed it. "I shall be so sorry to leave you," I said. "We have not had enough time together. There is so much I want to talk about."

"There will be other times. When all this is over, the country will settle to peace, and once the true King is here the German can go back to Hanover. I hear he prefers it to England in any case."

"Do you think it will work out like that?"

"I know it will. And think, Clarissa, when it does, it will be success for all we have been working for. Your father lived and died for this cause. You should be one of us for his sake, you know."

I thought of Eversleigh then and that warm, protecting love I had had from my maternal relations, and I felt a sudden anger that there should be all this trouble and people should die just for the sake of putting one man on the throne against another. I was in complete sympathy now with my grandmother Priscilla, who was always more fierce than any of the others in her condemnation of war.

"You will come again in happier times," went on my uncle. "Dear child, it seems so churlish of me to send you away, but I know these men I work with. I am not able to keep them in order as your father could. You understand?"

I kissed him tenderly and told him how much I had enjoyed meeting him and that I would come back as soon as I could.

He was frowning. "You will have to be careful," he said. "We don't know what the state of the country will be later, but for the next few days it should be safe for you. Get south as quickly as you can. The grooms are good fellows, and I have impressed on them the importance of taking the utmost care. I shall pay them well, and I have promised—on behalf of your family at Eversleigh—that they will be amply rewarded when they deliver you safely to them. Will you see that my promise is honored?"

"I will, Uncle. I will."

"Then be prepared to leave at the first signs of dawn in the morning." He hesitated, then he went on. "Before you go, there is something I want to give you. Wheel me into the anteroom."

I did so and took him to a bureau there which he indicated. He unlocked it and took out a case. He sat for a while thoughtfully holding it in his hands.

"This is a ring," he said. "It has been in our family's possession since the days of Elizabeth. In fact, it is very valuable because she gave it to one of our ancestors . . . one of her attendants of whom she was very fond. You see . . ." He had taken the ring from the case, and I saw that it was similar to the one he wore on his finger. "It is not as beautiful as diamonds, sapphires or emeralds, but because of its antiquity and what it stands for it is more valuable than those stones. Try it on."

I put it on the third finger of my right hand. It was much too big.

"You have some growing up to do," he said with a smile. "Surely there is one finger it fits."

There was. It was my forefinger.

"There," he said. "It is yours, and you will give it to your eldest daughter. The eldest daughters in the family always have it."

I looked at him sharply and said, "But Aimée—"

He was frowning again. "Yes, I suppose she should have it, but I hesitated. Your father wanted to marry your mother, and he would have done so if she had not been already married. He felt about her as though she were his legitimate wife and you his legitimate daughter. He could not have felt the same about Aimée and her mother, for he did not mention her to me . . . except in that last letter. I think there may have been many women in his life who meant as much to him as she did. But with your mother it was different. That is why I am giving the ring to you. I am obeying some instinct. Preserve it. It is worth a small fortune. Look at the setting. It was designed by Elizabeth's favorite jeweler and is recognized as such by experts. The Queen herself once wore it."

"I have never seen this stone before."

"No. It is fairly rare nowadays, but at one time it was worn a great deal by monarchs. They wore these rings because they were in constant danger of being poisoned. These stones are said to absorb arsenic from any liquid, and they were generally worn by people who feared someone might attempt to make an end of them."

"It is all very interesting, but I don't think anyone is likely to put arsenic in my goblet."

He smiled. "The ring is a sort of talisman . . . as things become when handed down through families."

"It is a very unusual stone," I said.

"Yes. It is formed in the digestive organs of the Persian mountain goat."

I gave a little exclamation of disgust.

"It is all right," he said with a laugh. "It is purified, but that is what it is. It is formed by digested hair, and it is this which makes it a good antidote to poison. In the Persian language, 'bezoar' means 'against poison.' And that is the name of the stone."

"How very interesting." I held out my hand and surveyed the ring. My uncle took my hand and held it tightly for a moment or two. "Now," he said, "you look as though you truly belong to Hessenfield."

I thanked him warmly, and as I knelt before him he took my face in his hands and kissed me.

"Good luck, little Clarissa," he said. "Come back to us soon."

When we were retiring that night I told Aimée that I wanted to speak to her. She said, "Come to my room," so I went.

She lay on her bed, her lovely dark hair hanging loose about her face, her eyes alert with interest. I sat by the bed on a chair, looking at her, thinking how attractive she was without being really beautiful.

"I have come to say goodbye," I told her. "I am leaving early tomorrow morning."

She stared at me incredulously.

"Uncle Paul thinks it best," I went on. "There's trouble coming."

"Oh, those wretches! Jacobites and Hanoverians, I suppose."

"Yes."

"Uncle must be *triste* because you are not a good little Jacobite."

"Uncle is too wise for that. He wouldn't try to persuade anyone to be what they didn't want to."

"And you *are* against these Jacobites."

94

I shrugged my shoulders. "We have a King. We have crowned a King. There will only be trouble if they try to force another on the people."

"They seem to think here in Hessenfield that it would be a good thing for the people to have James back."

"It is never wise to decide what is good for others and to try to force it on them because it would be good for *us*. The people, in any case, will decide what they want."

"You are a little statesman, I see."

"If you mean I have some plain common sense, I would agree with you."

"But what is all this—about your leaving us?"

"Our uncle thinks it better if I leave now, before the trouble breaks out in earnest. He thinks I should get back to my home in Eversleigh."

She nodded slowly. "They are on the opposing side, eh?" she asked. "Then is it goodbye for us?"

"Only for the time being. I shall see you again, Aimée. You must visit us at Eversleigh. I know my aunt Damaris would be pleased to see you . . ."

I hesitated. Would she? Would Jeremy? Would Priscilla and Arabella? They would not like to think that Hessenfield had kept a mistress when he had been all but married to their darling Carlotta. But Aimée was my sister. They had a strong family feeling and they would remember that.

She noticed my hesitation and smiled secretly. Sometimes I thought Aimée read my innermost thoughts. Aimée was clever. She was subtle, but perhaps I was a little more astute than she gave me credit for. She expressed great sadness because I was going away but I thought I detected a hint of elation. I wondered if she were a little jealous of my friendship with our uncle Paul and perhaps was rather glad that I was leaving the field to her.

I said goodbye with assurances that we should meet again as soon as was convenient; then I went to my room and made my final preparations to leave. When everything was ready for the early departure I went to bed, but I lay sleepless, fearful that I should not awaken in time, though my uncle had said that I should be called half an hour before dawn, when cold bacon and bread with ale would be sent to my room. Food for the first part of the journey had been put into saddlebags so that we need not stop at an inn until we were well away from the neighborhood.

All went according to plan, and when the first streak of

dawn was in the sky I said goodbye to my newfound uncle. I was touched because Aimée had come down to see the last of me.

So in the very early hours of the morning I rode away from Hessenfield and with my grooms began the journey south.

The Captive

As I turned my horse southward I could not help feeling a glow of pleasure at the prospect of seeing my family again. They would be aware of what was going on in the north and worrying about me, I was sure.

The countryside was beautiful on that morning. There were little clumps of gorse in flower on the moors. The mist hung heavily over them, and here and there trees lifted their denuded branches to the sky. We left the open country behind us and came into lanes, past woodlands, and I thought how beautiful the trees were with their bare branches making a lacy pattern against the sky. The winter was more advanced up there than it was in the south, but we should be lucky if we reached Eversleigh before the snowstorms came.

We stopped for a meal in the shelter of a hedge and did full justice to the good things which had been provided for us at Hessenfield. There was new bread and capon, with ale to wash it down with. The four grooms said it was right good fare indeed and the best thing about the northerners was that they knew how to eat.

They were Jim, Jack, Fred and Harry, and they had enjoyed their stay at Hessenfield mainly, I gathered, because of the excess of victuals. Not that they were inadequately fed at Eversleigh, but at Hessenfield there was what I heard one of them describe as "a mountain of vittels."

They were all delighted, however, to be going home, and they looked upon this jaunt as an adventure.

After eating, we continued our journey, and just before dusk were at the inn which Uncle Paul had told us to make for. The first stage of the journey had been completed with success, and we were all tired and hungry and ready for the excellent meal our host was ready to serve in the inn parlor— hot soup, roast beef and veal-and-ham pie, with cheese and fruit to follow. Fortunately there was room for us all, and we decided to retire early that night and continue our journey at dawn.

After that most satisfying meal I went to my bedroom, which overlooked the inn yard, and it was a great relief to take off my clothes and get into bed; having slept scarcely at all the previous night, I was soon fast asleep.

I was awakened by the clatter of horses' hoofs below. More arrivals, I guessed, and I listened a while to the voices of the grooms and the host. There was some sort of argument going on, and I imagined the trouble was of that nature which was not unusual on journeys like this. Someone had arrived too late to get a room. I and my party had taken up a fair amount of space, I knew. Well, it was only two rooms—the four grooms were in one, I was in another. However, the altercation seemed to go on so long that I slipped out of bed and looked out the window.

I half wished that I hadn't. One of the horsemen down there was Frenshaw, whom I still thought of as the man in the brown frieze coat. What was he doing at the inn? I had a horrible fear that he was looking for me.

I waited at the window, keeping well in shadow. The host was wringing his hands. His inn was full. It was most unusual. The Rising Sun was not a big inn, my lord must understand. He could accommodate three of the party, but unless they all wished to sleep in one room, some of them must go elsewhere. The Stag and Huntsmen was only two miles up the road. There were a lot of travelers about ... which was strange at this time of the year.

They seemed to come to terms. Frenshaw and one other would stay. The rest would go on to the Stag and Huntsmen.

I did not go back to bed. We must be off very early in the morning. *Before* dawn perhaps. I guessed that Frenshaw would be on the lookout for us, and it was very possible that he was here looking for me.

I hastily dressed and went along to the room where the grooms were sleeping. I had made up my mind that we should leave without delay—steal away when the inn was quiet and settled for the night.

I tapped on their door. It took a little time to wake them, for they were all fast asleep. When I told them we were to leave at once they all looked dismayed.

"The horses need a night's rest, mistress," said Jim.

"I know, and so do we, but we must get away from this inn. We left in a hurry because my uncle feared for us. I know now that we have been traced here, and we must go at once and quietly. I settled with the landlord last night, so we can get away quickly. But we must be quiet."

It took me a little while to impress on them the urgency of the situation, but at last I managed to do so. They had heard the rumors that there was trouble in the north, for they had talked with other stablemen at Hessenfield. At length they roused themselves and said they would be in the stables preparing the horses without delay.

I went back to my room, collected my things and was ready to leave.

It was a very starry night and about two in the morning when we rode out of the inn yard, and I was very relieved when the Rising Sun was several miles behind us. We had passed the Stag and Huntsmen and I had looked anxiously at the inn as we passed, wondering how many of Frenshaw's men were there.

With the coming of the dawn my spirits rose and I found I was enjoying the adventure. We should make our way to York and in doing so would pass the little village of Langthorne. Our jaunt at the fair there seemed a long way in the past. I had almost forgotten Lance Clavering, because, I supposed, so many impressions had been imposed over that one, but it would be exciting if, when we arrived in York, he was still there.

It was midday. I had meant to get food from the inn, but there had been no time for that. There was a little of the capon and bread left and also some ale, but it had lost its freshness and the meal was not as good as it had been on the previous day.

We had come to a wood. We were very tired and the horses were in need of a rest. There was a stream nearby and Harry took them down to it. We stretched out under the trees and before long were fast asleep.

I awoke with a start. I was cramped and cold. The sun would be gone in another hour, I reckoned. It was a pale wintry sun, but at least it was there, and I was annoyed that we had slept so long. We should have found ourselves an inn for the night by now.

The four grooms were fast asleep and the horses were tethered to trees. I felt the need to stretch my legs before awakening the men, so I walked down to the stream. My mouth felt parched and dry, and perhaps the water would be fresh and clear.

It was not far, I knew, because Harry had taken the horses there. I knew the direction. There it was—clear, pure water.

I looked back. The grooms and horses were hidden by the trees. I must not be long, for they would be alarmed if they woke up and found me gone. Moreover we must be on our way if we were to find an inn before nightfall.

I was about to kneel by the stream when I heard a movement behind me. I turned. I was suddenly caught in a pair of strong arms. I gave a little scream and a hand was immediately clapped over my mouth. Something like a hood was slipped over my face so that I could not shout.

"Good work," said someone. "Now to the horses."

I tried to struggle free, but it was useless. My strength was puny beside that of the one who held me, and I was carried off under someone's arm as though I were a bundle of hay. I was aware that I was slung across a horse, and then we were galloping away.

I was bewildered and very frightened. I was not sure who had captured me, but I feared it had something to do with Frenshaw. They had followed me to the Rising Sun and in the morning must have discovered that we had left. This was the road to the south, and they knew I was going that way, so it had not been very difficult to find me.

I did not know what I could do. To attempt to wrest myself from the arms of my captor would be folly while we were galloping at this speed. There was only one thing I could do and that was wait and see what they wanted of me.

After what seemed like hours we began to slow down and I gathered that we had arrived at our destination. We clattered into a courtyard.

"Bravo!" said a voice which I recognized as Frenshaw's.

I was lifted from the horse and the hood was taken off. I could see nothing for a few moments, then I was aware of a house. Two flaming torches were on either side of the door and a man was standing there. It was Frenshaw.

"Bring her in," he said. My arm was seized and I was propelled into the house after him. We were in a hall, not large by Enderby standards but paneled, with heavy beams across the roof, and a fire blazing in a large fireplace.

I was dizzy and my legs felt stiff. I swayed a little.

"Give her a stool," said Frenshaw.

They did so and I sat down.

"Now," he said, "I want you to tell us without delay what

you have discovered at Hessenfield and to whom you have sent your discoveries."

I was numb with the shock of having been kidnapped and brought here in this fashion. I had been afraid of this man from the moment I had seen him at the castle, but even before that he had filled me with some eerie premonition that I should come to no good in his hands.

I stammered, "You are mistaken. I know nothing. I have not sent anything to anyone. I am ignorant of these matters. They have nothing to do with me. I am not interested . . ."

"Your uncle was misguided to send you away," said Frenshaw. "He will have to answer for that. I myself discovered you listening at the door. Quite clearly you were sent to spy on us. General Eversleigh primed you on what you must do. He thought it ingenious to send a young girl into the enemy's camp. It was a God-sent opportunity for him that Hessenfield happened to be related to you."

"You are quite wrong. There was no question of my finding out anything. This attempt to put another King on the throne only came about after I arrived at the castle."

"Don't think to fool us with infantile babblings. You know and we know that we have been trying for years to bring the rightful King back to the throne."

"I didn't think of it."

"Oh, come, come . . . and you in a hotbed of Hanoverian supporters! We all know that General Eversleigh is one of George's greatest commanders. Tell us what you have discovered. We know that you sent your findings to the General in York."

"I did nothing of the sort. I have had no communication with him since I left him in York."

"Do you think we are going to believe that?"

"I have no idea."

One of the guards slapped me hard on the side of my face. I cried out and Frenshaw said, "There is no need for that . . . yet."

"She was insolent to you, sir."

"She will tell us in time."

"How much time is there?" asked one of the men whom I had just noticed.

I was so tired and it was only my terrible apprehension which was keeping me awake. I had had no sleep the previous night and all I had was the hour I had snatched in the woods just before my capture. I was hungry, but what I wanted most was sleep.

"We will get what we want from her," said Frenshaw. "She seems dazed just now."

"She could have had no sleep last night, leaving the Rising Sun in the dead of the night. Look, she's exhausted."

I realized that the best thing I could do was to pretend to fall asleep. That would give me a little time to think of what I could do and to discover if there was some means of escape.

As Frenshaw rose and came over to the stool on which I was sitting, I closed my eyes and let my head fall to one side. He leaned over me and shook me. I opened my eyes sleepily.

"Where . . . am I?" I said, and shut my eyes again.

"You're right," he said. "Shut her up for the night. We'll deal with her in the morning. There's time."

I was shaken and made to stand up. I did so, yawning.

I was half-dragged across the hall to a staircase. I tried, under the guise of sleepiness, to note where I was going. As we left the hall the two men who were escorting me took candles from a shelf by the staircase and lighted up the stairs. We came to a landing on which there were several doors. I was prodded toward another staircase, which we mounted and which led to a long gallery. We walked through this to a wooden door, beyond which was a passage with more rooms. Then we ascended a pair of steps to a kind of attic. It was large, and the roof, which had two windows in it, sloped steeply. I noticed a bed, a stool and a table. I was pushed inside and left alone. I heard the key turn in the lock.

I stood in the center of the room, my heart beating wildly. I was wide awake in spite of my exhaustion. How was I going to get out of here? The windows were in the roof; I should have to stand on the stool to see out of them and then all I would see would be the sky. There was a curtain at one end of the room. I went to it, drawing it back, disclosed a hip bath and a small table. I turned away, and going back to the bed, sat on it.

How could I possibly escape? If I told them all I knew they would not be satisfied, because I knew nothing that was of importance. It was common knowledge that the Jacobites had always been a threat. They had been for years. What could I tell them more than that?

And they would not believe me.

I lay down on the bed, and in spite of my bewilderment and fear, in spite of my growing apprehension, I fell fast asleep.

When I awoke the attic was filled with light, which came through the windows in the roof. I was stiff with cold. At first I could not remember where I was, and then the horrible realization dawned on me.

I got off the bed and went to the door. I shook it, which was a foolish thing to do, for it was a heavy oak and I had heard the key turn in the lock. I wondered what my captors intended to do with me, and horrible thoughts came into my mind. I thought of what I had heard of prisoners tortured in the Tower of London. I visualized the thumbscrews, the rack, the scavenger's daughter—that fearful iron case shaped like a woman, with nails lining it, into which victims were forced and, as their tormentors cruelly joked, were "embraced" until the nails entered their flesh.

They would not have one of those, I reassured myself. But there were other cruelties they could inflict without such complicated instruments.

I was growing more and more frightened as the minutes passed. I had longed for adventure. Now I longed for nothing so much as to be back in my cozy cocoon.

I started, for I thought I heard footsteps.

I looked at my watch, which was still hanging on the chain round my neck. I was surprised to see that it was nine o'clock.

Yes, the footsteps were coming to my door; a key was turning in the lock, and the door wheezed open. I realized later that the attic was rarely used.

I expected to see the villainous Frenshaw but instead a young boy stood there. I was astonished because he seemed to be about my own age, and that comforted me. Moreover, having expected Frenshaw or one of his men, this boy looked beautiful by comparison. He was wigless and his waving hair was cut to a fringe, so that it made a shiny bell about his face. His skin was clear and pale, his eyes deep blue. I thought I was dreaming or perhaps that they had killed me and I had gone to heaven. This boy's face had that purity of expression that might have belonged to an angel.

He looked at me steadily and said, "Are you ready to tell us what you passed to the enemy?"

So he was one of them after all. It was strange that he should be so young and look so innocent of evil.

"I told them I knew nothing," I said shortly. "I have nothing to tell. You had better let me go from here. When my family hears how I have been treated. . . ."

He held up a hand. "I shall not let you go from here until you have told us all you know."

I cried out in desperate exasperation, "How can I tell when there is nothing to tell! If you keep me here until I die of cold and starvation, I can tell you nothing ... because I know nothing."

"Are you hungry?" he asked.

"I have not eaten for a long time."

"Wait," he said.

He went out, shutting and locking the door after him.

I felt a certain lifting of my spirits. He looked so young and as if he might listen and take heed of what I said. I might be able to convince him that I was speaking the truth. But what about the others?

It was a tense ten minutes before he returned. I heard his footsteps coming along the gallery and mounting the three or four steps to the attic. He opened the door and came in bearing a tray on which was a bowl of oatmeal.

"There," he said. "Eat that."

I took the tray. I was ravenously hungry and food had never tasted so good.

When I had eaten it all he said, "Do you feel better ... more inclined to talk?"

"I feel better," I replied, "and inclined to talk, but I cannot tell you what you want me to simply because I do not know it."

"You are a good spy," he said, almost admiringly, "but you will weaken in the end."

"How long will you keep me here?"

He lifted his shoulders. "It depends on so much."

I was sitting on the bed; he took the chair and studied me intently. "When were you born?" he asked.

"February, 1702."

"I was born in November, 1701, so I am quite a bit older than you are."

"I make it three months."

"Three months can be a long time. I am your jailer now, until the men come back."

"Come back ... from where?"

My heart had begun to beat faster. Everything seemed brighter since this handsome youth had come into the attic.

"Did you hear the commotion in the night?"

"No."

"No, I suppose you wouldn't, up here. They have all left in a hurry. It will soon be over now. The loyal Highlanders are marching into England. The call came for all here to join the triumphant army of Highlanders. They are marching toward Preston."

"Do you mean to say they have invaded England? Is there a war, then?"

"It will all be over soon. The English are falling back before the brave Highlanders. James will soon be here to claim his throne."

"You are a staunch Jacobite."

"Of course. And you have been brought up in error. I know about you. They told me some of it and I gathered the rest. They didn't know what to do with you. Some of them wanted to kill you."

"Kill *me!* They must be mad."

"They said my uncle was mad to let you live."

"Who is your uncle?"

"Sir Thomas Frenshaw."

"Oh! So you are *his* nephew."

He nodded. "I live with him here. He brought me up. Of course I see very little of him. He is a brave, good man."

"He has scarcely been good to me. As for his bravery—to bully an innocent girl does not show much evidence of that quality."

"You have a sharp tongue."

"Sharp tongues are often good weapons. Not quite as effective as swords, but they have their uses."

"You are a most unusual girl. You seem much older than you say you are."

"That may seem so to you because you are young for your age."

"I am not. I can outride many of the grooms, and my fencing master says I could fight a duel with success tomorrow."

"Great achievements," I mocked. "You can also act as jailer to a girl who is not even in a position to attack you . . . except with her sharp tongue."

He laughed. "You are different from anyone I have ever known before," he said.

"Of course I am. I'm a spy."

"You admit it, then," he said quickly.

"You are very young," I said loftily. "You don't even know when that tongue of mine is mocking you."

"Remember, you are my prisoner. Until the men come back I have sole charge of you."

"Then beware . . . I might escape."

"You can't. There are servants here. They all know that you have to be kept prisoner. My uncle and his friends will soon be back."

"Then if they are victorious and poor George is sent packing to Hanover and James the Saint is crowned, then *my* little sins won't amount to much."

He considered this. "It's true," he said. "That might be your salvation. So you hope for James to be triumphant?"

"Nay!" I cried. "George forever."

"That's treason."

"On the other hand, you are the one who is guilty of treason."

"You *are* a spy."

I laughed at him derisively. Odd as it seemed, I was beginning to enjoy this. I was a captive, it was true, but my jailer was only a boy and I believed I could outwit him.

He was angry with me. He picked up the tray and went out, carefully locking the door behind him. I had been foolish. I should have played along with him. I should have found out more about the arrangements of the house. I might now be planning a way of escape.

I sat on the bed. In a few moments I heard the footsteps again. He had returned and he had a scared little maid with him.

"This is Janet," he said. "She will take you where you can wash and see to your toilette. I shall be on the alert, so do not attempt to escape."

I was grateful. I followed Janet out of the attic and down the stairs. There was a small place where I could wash and make myself generally comfortable. I saw cans of hot water standing there with an ewer and basin. She went out, shutting the door behind her, after she had indicated that she would be waiting for me.

In due course I emerged and was conducted to where my young jailer was waiting for me. We went back to our attic, and I sensed that he was still annoyed with me, as he said nothing. However, I thanked him. "It was very thoughtful of you," I said. "Not the sort of treatment a spy would expect."

"We are not savages," he said, and went out, locking the door after him.

I felt better now. In fact, I was aware of a certain elation creeping over me. I was a prisoner in this house; my captors had hurried away to join in the victory they were expecting

106

and my jailer was a boy more or less my own age. It did not seem such a desperate situation as it had when they had first brought me here.

It was midday when he came again. This time he brought me hot soup and a chicken leg. It tasted like ambrosia.

"You enjoy your food," he said.

"Have you ever heard that hunger seasons all dishes?"

"Not an original remark, I believe," he said.

"That does not detract from its truth. However, thank you for my excellent meal."

He smiled and repeated that they were not savages.

"Is that so?" I said. "Thank you for the information. I might not have known . . . had I not been told."

"You are very foolish," he told me. "You should be trying to ingratiate yourself with me."

He was right, of course. My mocking manner was making things worse for me.

"I see," I said. "Good, kind sir, I thank you for the benefits you have bestowed on me. To feed one in my position is gracious of you. I bow before your magnanimity."

"That," he said severely, "is worse than ever."

I began to laugh, and to my amazement he was laughing with me.

I thought, He is enjoying this too. Of course he is. He has a position of responsibility, but I think he rather likes me.

From that moment our relationship began to change. At moments I thought we were like two children playing a game in which I was taking the part of the kidnapped girl, he her guard.

He sat in the chair and looked at me.

"Tell me about yourself," he said.

I began to tell him how I had visited my uncle Hessenfield and had come north from my home in the south, but he interrupted: "Not that. I know all that. I have heard them talk about how you came to York with your uncle, General Eversleigh, and on to Hessenfield. They thought it was a good opportunity for you to do a little spying for them and . . ."

"You are wrong about the spying, but the rest is right."

I told my story. It seemed very romantic. My beautiful mother . . . my incomparable father, the great Hessenfield.

" 'The great Hessenfield,' " he repeated, his eyes shining. "He has always been a hero to us. I was always taught that I must grow up like him."

"He was wonderful. I used to ride on his shoulders."

"*You* rode on great Hessenfield's shoulders?"

"I was his daughter."

"And you could bring yourself to spy for the other side!"

"I keep telling you I did not spy."

"You really came up here to work for us."

"I did not. I did not. I want none of your wars. I want old George to stay where he is and for everyone to stop shouting about it."

"Can this be Hessenfield's daughter?"

"The very same."

I told him how my parents had died and I had been taken by a faithful maid and how Aunt Damaris had come to Paris to find me.

"Yes," he said, surveying me with admiration. "I can imagine all that happening to you."

Then he told me about himself. It seemed very mild compared with my adventures. His father had died at the Battle of Blenheim when he was about five years old.

"Not for the Jacobites?" I asked.

"No. My father was not one. But I was sent to my uncle soon after, when my mother died, and I learned all about the cause, so I became a Jacobite—and you can mock all you like, but I tell you King James is coming back to rule over us."

"You should never be too sure of what is going to happen. You may be wrong, you know."

"Soon my uncle will be coming back from Preston with good news."

"And then what will happen to me?"

"So much will depend on what it is necessary to do."

I shivered. "At least they are not here yet," I said.

We talked of other things, including horses and dogs. I told him about Damon and he said he had a mastiff. He would show me—Then he stopped. "But you are a prisoner," he said.

"You could let me free—just to see the dogs."

"What if you ran away?"

"You could catch me and bring me back."

"You are mocking again."

"I'm sorry. I didn't mean to."

And so the day passed, not unpleasantly, and when it was dark he came up with a fur rug and two candles for me.

Even now it is difficult for me to know what exactly happened to me during those days I spent in the attic. They seemed, even looking back, to have been touched with a mystic light. He came to me every morning with my oatmeal, and he would stay during the morning, then go away and return with my midday meal. Before the second day was over we no longer pretended to be antagonistic toward one another. I did not disguise the fact that I greeted him with joy any more than he could pretend he did not want to be with me.

He was called Richard Frenshaw, and, he told me, those who were intimate with him called him Dickon. I called him Dickon. I thought it suited him. Clarissa suited me, he told me. We used to look at each other in silence sometimes. I thought he was the most beautiful human being I had ever seen—with a different sort of beauty from that of my parents. I suppose it was what is called falling in love, but neither of us realized it at first, perhaps because it had never happened to either of us before.

We argued incessantly. He put the case for the Jacobites with fervor. I laughed at him and shocked him by telling him I simply did not care which King was on the throne. I only wanted people around me to live happily, without fighting or getting angry because others had different views.

I would have found it easy, I think, to have persuaded him to let me escape. I could have asked to see the horses and mounted one and ridden away; I could have got the key of the attic from him. But I would not. I could not let him betray his uncle's trust. There was something essentially honorable about Dickon.

He brought his mastiff to show me. The dog was called Chevalier after the would-be King. He took a fancy to me, and this was an added bond between us. The little maid who had brought up the water for me on the first day knew how it was with Dickon and me. She was a romantic at heart and, I believe, thought it charming to see the love springing up between us. I began to get special delicacies brought up from the kitchens—and I wanted this episode to go on and on. It seemed more than three days I spent in the attic. It was like a dream. Dickon felt it too—so he told me afterward.

We were avid to know everything about each other. The smallest detail seemed of the utmost importance. This was the strangest and most beautiful thing that had ever happened to me.

It was on the fourth day that he came to me, and I knew that something was wrong from the moment he stepped into the attic. He was paler than usual and his hair was ruffled. He had a habit, I knew, of running his hand through it when he was disturbed.

I went swiftly to him and put my hands on his shoulders. It was the first time I had ever touched him. His reaction was immediate. He put his arms about me and held me close to him. He did not speak for a few moments and I did not ask him to. I was savoring the wonder of being close to him.

At length he broke away from me, and then I saw how frightened he was. He said, "You must get away from here. They are coming back. They are only a few miles away. One of the men reached here in advance with the news. There has been a disaster at Preston. Most of the Highlanders have surrendered; the rest are in retreat. My uncle will be back soon . . . and I fear he will kill you."

This was bringing me back to reality. I should have known that my idyll could not last. Dickon had changed. He was remembering too.

He looked at me very seriously. "You must not stay here," he said. "You must get away."

"We shall have to say goodbye," I murmured.

He turned his head aside and nodded. A terrible desolation came over me. "I should never see you again," I said.

"No—no—That must not be." Then he held me against him and kissed me. He said, "Clarissa!" and went on saying my name over and over again.

Suddenly he was alert. "There is no time to lose," he said. "You must get out of here."

"You . . . will let me go?"

He nodded.

"Your uncle . . ."

"If they find you here they might kill you."

"But they will know you have let me escape."

"I will make some excuse . . ." he muttered. "Come . . . now. They could be here at any moment. You will have to be careful. Follow me . . . quietly."

He shut the door behind us, carefully locking it. I followed him down the steps and through the gallery. He went ahead, beckoning to me when the way was clear. We reached the hall safely and went out to the stables. Quickly he saddled a horse.

"Here," he said, "you will have need of this. Get to York. There send a message to your family. Perhaps your uncle is still there. There is a coach that goes to London from York. It starts from the Black Swan, in Coney Street, every Monday, Wednesday and Friday. It takes four days, providing there are no mishaps. Perhaps you could take that. I don't think they will follow you south. They will have to go to Scotland and join the men there."

"Oh, Dickon," I said. "You have done this for me. I shall never forget. . . ."

I was not generally given to tears but they were in my eyes then. I saw, too, that he was also trying to suppress his emotion.

"It will be dangerous on the roads," he said. "A girl alone. . . ."

Then he began to saddle another of the horses.

I said, "Dickon . . . what?"

"I am coming with you. How can I let you go alone?"

We came out into the frosty morning air.

"Oh, Dickon," I said, "you must not. Think what you are doing. . . ."

"There is no time for talking," he said. "Ride . . . gallop . . . We must get away from here as fast as we can."

I knew I was in danger. I believed that they would be capable of killing me if they returned and found me there. There was indeed no time for delay. They were in retreat and would want to set out for Scotland immediately. They would not want to waste time with me, and on the other hand, they would not want to let me go free. Yes, I was in acute danger. But I knew I had never been so happy in my life.

Our horses' hooves rang out on the frosty road and it was exhilarating riding along beside Dickon. The countryside seemed more beautiful even than in the spring. The black lacy pattern of branches against the sky, the gray tassles of the hazel which shivered in the breeze, the jasmine round a cottage door which was beginning to show shoots of yellow— they all enchanted me. I heard the song of the skylark which was soaring over the fields, followed by the wild cry of the mistle thrush. It was strange that I should notice such details at such a time. It was perhaps because Damaris had made me aware of the wonders of nature.

In any case I was happy. I refused to look beyond the moment. Dickon and I had escaped together, and he had rescued me—at what cost to himself I could only guess.

In the early afternoon he called a halt. "We must refresh not only ourselves but the horses," he said. We went into an inn, which I saw was called the Red Cow, according to the sign which creaked over the door.

"We are brother and sister," he told me, "if any should ask your business. We live at Thorley Manor. No one will ever question that, for, as far as I know, there is no Thorley Manor. We are visiting our uncle in York. Our grooms with the saddlebags are going on ahead. Our name is Thorley, and you are Clara. I am Jack."

I nodded. The adventure was growing more and more exciting with every passing moment.

With an air of authority, Dickon ordered that our horses should be fed and watered. Then we went into the inn. I am sure I had never known such a happy hour as I spent in that inn parlor. The fire in the great fireplace was warm and comforting, and the innkeeper's wife brought us bowls of pease soup and hot barley bread with bacon and cheese; there were two large tankards of ale to go with it, and never had food tasted so good, even in my needy days in Paris. Paradise was an inn parlor in the Red Cow on the road to York, and I never wanted to leave it.

I regarded Dickon with eyes from which adoration must have shone out. We were both of us so happy to be together and we did not want to look ahead to what this impulsive action might bring. To him it could mean disaster. He had betrayed his uncle, who was his guardian; he had betrayed the Jacobite cause, and he had done it for me.

In the parlor there was a grandfather clock noisily ticking away the minutes. It was a constant reminder of the passing of time. I wished I could stop it.

I said, "I should like to stay here like this for the rest of my life."

"So should I," said Dickon.

We were silent contemplating such bliss.

"We shall have to go soon," Dickon went on at length. "We really should not have stayed so long."

"Do you think they'll come for us?"

He shook his head. "No. They will have to go north . . . to the army there. The invasion of England will come later."

"And you, Dickon?"

"I shall have to be there with them."

"Let's stay here for a while."

He shook his head but he made no attempt to get up. I gazed at the flames in the grate making fairy-tale pictures of castles and riders—all beautiful, enchanted, like this inn parlor.

I suddenly noticed that the sky had darkened and that a few light snowflakes were floating down past the window. I said nothing, for I knew if I did, Dickon would say we must leave at once.

The innkeeper's wife came in. She was plump, redfaced and smiling and wore a white mobcap on her untidy hair.

"Wind's getting up," she said. "Coming from the north. 'The north wind do blow, and we shall have snow,' so they say. You two got far to go?"

"To York," said Dickon.

"Why, bless my soul! You'll never make that before dark. Why, you'd be caught in the snow if you tried to get there today."

Dickon went to the window. The snow was now falling fast. He turned to me in dismay.

I said, "Perhaps we could stay here for the night. Could we pay?"

Dickon nodded.

"Why, bless you," said the host's wife, "I reckon your father would see to that. Live about here, do you?"

"Thorley Hall," Dickon told her boldly.

"Can't say I've heard of it. Have you come far?"

"Some twenty miles."

"That accounts for it. Now, Master Thorley, if you can pay me on the spot I'll find room for you. No question of that."

"My sister and I will consider what is best to be done," he said.

"Well, you'd better consider fast, young gentleman, for I hear horses coming into the yard. There'll be others looking for a night's lodging on a night like this is going to be."

When she had gone we looked fearfully at each other. Who were the new arrivals? What if, discovering our disappearance, Sir Thomas Frenshaw had sent someone after us to bring us back—or perhaps come himself?

I stretched out my hand and Dickon took it and held it comfortingly.

"You should not have come with me," I said. "You could have let me escape and told them it was no fault of yours."

"No, no," he replied. "I had to come with you. How would you have fared alone?"

We stood still, looking at each other, and in that moment of danger we knew without doubt that we loved and that life would be empty without the other.

Our fears were momentarily lulled, for the arrivals were a party of travelers who, in view of the sudden change in the weather, had decided they could not continue with their journey but would spend the night in the Red Cow.

They came into the parlor noisily and boisterously, invading our privacy and dispersing as they did so that wonderful intimacy I had shared with Dickon. We sat side by side on a settee in a corner of the room while the three men and three women occupied the table and were served with hot pease soup.

The women looked at us with curiosity and gave us friendly smiles. We were ready when they began to ask questions and we told them that we were a brother and sister who were going to York and that our grooms with the saddlebags were following us.

"Two young 'uns like you on the road," cried the eldest of the women. "My patience! I wouldn't like one of mine to be traveling like that."

"My brother has a strong arm," I said.

"And proud of him you are, I can see. Well, we're going to York. Best ride along with us, eh, Harry?" She appealed to one of the men.

The man addressed as Harry surveyed us genially and nodded. "Safety in numbers," he said with a wink.

The innkeeper's wife came bustling in. "Eee," she said. "Be wanting to stay the night, then?"

"Reckon there's no help for it, missus."

"Inn's full," she answered. She looked at us all and scratched her head, pushing the mobcap back to do so and then carefully replacing it. "What I'll have to do is give you pallets in the gallery. We call it Makeshift Gallery." She tittered. "Nights like this you often gets more than you've beds for."

The woman who had spoken to us said that reckon they'd be glad to have a roof over their heads on a night like this was going to be.

The innkeeper's wife looked at us. "These two young 'uns will be in the gallery too. It's all we can offer."

My heart sank. I could see that these hearty, well-meaning travelers had broken into our magic. We were members of a party now, no longer alone.

"It could have been worse," Dickon whispered to me. "It could have been my uncle to take us back to . . . who knows what."

All during the late afternoon the snow fell so that there was a blanket of it on the roads and the windowsills were covered. Our companions did not mind in the least. It was an amusing adventure to them. The woman came over to us and asked questions. What about our poor mother? She would be worried about us, wouldn't she? But she would be thinking we were with the grooms. Had we been a bit wicked? Had we lost them a-purpose?

I thought it was best that they should think we had, and tried to look arch and coy.

"Wicked . . . wicked . . ." said the youngest of the women, shaking her finger at us. And we came from Thorley Hall, did we? Gentry, eh? Well, she could see that. It didn't need no sign, like, to tell her. We'd got gentry written all over us . . . the both of us. Never mind, they would look after us. Mercy had it that they, too, were on the road to York. We should go along with them. There were some rough characters on the road. They'd think nothing of slitting your throat for the price of a goblet of ale. Never mind. Luck was with us. We'd fallen in with the Macksons and the Freelys, who were in the business of wool. Partners they were, and traveling to York with their families, all for the purpose of selling wool.

They were kindly, they meant well, and we could not help liking them.

They sang. Their raucous voices filled the inn parlor, and the innkeeper and his wife came in from time to time to supply their needs. There would be sucking pig for supper that night, we were told almost conspiratorially, and there were cries of approval, and one of the men shouted, "And plenty of stuffing, missus."

"Eee, I'll see to that," answered the innkeeper's wife.

The snow continued to fall; the candles guttered and the company sang. The youngest of the men had a good voice.

You gentlemen of England [he rendered]
Who live at home at ease
Full little do you think upon
The danger of the seas. . . .
And they all joined in at the end of each verse:
When the stormy winds do blow . . . o . . . o . . . o . . . o
When the stormy winds do blow.

And one of the women sang "The frog he would a-wooing ride."

I knew that whenever after I heard that song I should be back in that inn parlor, with the fire blazing and the snow falling fast outside.

The sucking pig arrived in due course, and we were all one

merry party with the other travelers who were staying at the Red Cow. The men talked about the troubles.

"They say the Pretender's on his way . . . may even have landed by now."

"He should stay where he is. Don't he know when he's not wanted?"

I caught Dickon's hand and pressed it warningly, for I was afraid he might betray himself. The company would not be very pleased to have a Jacobite among them.

"They came down as far as Preston," said one of the travelers. "We was ready for him. Routed they was . . . the Highlanders of Scotland. What are they up to coming into our country? Up to no good, that's what."

"We soon sent 'em packing."

"You don't think there'll be war?" asked one of the women. "We don't want none of that. I remember hearing my grand-dad tell me what it was like when there was war in the country."

"There's been war only a little while back," said one of them.

"Oh, that wasn't here. Don't call that a war. I mean war . . . when they're fighting here . . . on English soil . . . Englishman against Englishman, so your friend today is your enemy tomorrow . . . and who's to know what's what. That's what I mean. We don't want none of that."

"There's not going to be none of that. The Jacks is beat before they start. Come on, Bess, give us a song."

So they sang, and Dickon and I sat listening and at last we all retired to the gallery and lay down on our pallets. Dickon and I were very close to each other. We held hands but did not speak for fear of waking the others. There was no need for words. I lay there thinking of the enormity of what he had done for me. He had set aside his loyalty to his uncle, his entire belief in the righteousness of his cause; and he had done this for love of me. I did not know how I could ever repay him.

I lay sleepless, and I know he did too. During the night the rain started to fall, and in the morning it had washed the snow away.

We were up early and ready to leave. We set off in the company of our fellow travelers, and just as dusk was beginning to descend we saw the towers of the minster and the ancient walls of the city.

"Your friends are here?" said the wool merchant to Dickon.

"Yes," he answered. "I thank you for allowing us to ride with you."

"Eee, nothing to that, lad. 'Twas only decent. Two young 'uns like you shouldn't take journeys alone. Where be going?"

"To the mayor's house," said Dickon. I caught my breath. I had told him that when we were in York my uncle, Lance Clavering and I had stayed at the mayor's house.

The party was impressed.

"Didn't I tell you they was gentry?" whispered the oldest of the women.

We came through Goodramgate up to the Shambles and there we said goodbye to our companions. I had come along this road before so I knew the way to the mayor's house. There it stood, an imposing residence, apart from the small houses of the narrow streets.

As we approached, my heart leaped, for Lance Clavering was walking out of the house. He stopped in amazement and stared.

"Clarissa!" he cried. I had forgotton how handsome he was. He looked quite magnificent in his embroidered coat, the cuffs of which were decorated with mauves and blues of the most delicate shading. His cravat was a mass of frills, and his pale-blue stockings were rolled above the knee, which I learned was the latest fashion. On his high-heeled shining black shoes buckles glittered. He swept off his three-cornered hat and bowed low.

"Oh . . . Lance!" I exclaimed.

He took my hand and kissed it.

"Why . . . ? What does this mean?" He looked at Dickon, who was gazing at him in a kind of wonder, as though he could not believe this scintillating apparition was real.

"This is er. . . ." I hesitated, for fear had seized me. There was danger in the air and I must be careful not to betray Dickon. "Jack Thorley," I added. "He brought me here."

"Good day to you, Jack Thorley."

"This is Sir Lance Clavering," I said. "A friend of my family."

There was no need to explain. I had already told Dickon how my uncle Carl and Lance Clavering had brought me to York. In fact, it was for this reason that I had been held captive.

"You had better come into the house," said Lance. "Then you can tell us all about it. We thought you were at Hessenfield. And we were anxious about it too, I can tell you . . . the way

117

things have gone. Let's take your horses to the stables." He walked beside me. "I'm surprised that your uncle let you leave Hessenfield."

"There is a great deal to tell you, Lance. Is my uncle Carl here?"

"He will be back this night. There is a grand deal to occupy him. Things have been happening since you left."

"I know."

Dickon had said nothing all this time. I guessed he was not sure what he ought to do now, having delivered me into the safekeeping of Lance Clavering and wondering whether it would be wise for him to leave immediately.

"Did you come alone?" asked Lance. "Just you two?"

"Well—we traveled with some other people," I said evasively.

"You had a good journey, I trust." Lance's glance took in Dickon.

"Yes, thanks," said Dickon. "No trouble at all."

"Well, you must be weary. We'll see that you get some food and a bed for the night. I suppose you'll want to get back to Hessenfield as soon as possible."

"I must do that," answered Dickon.

"You won't run into trouble. We've sent off those accursed Highlanders. The impertinence! Do you know, they got as far as Preston. They're well and safely back across the border now—those that got away."

I watched Dickon wince.

"Hopeless!" went on Lance. "What they thought they were doing, I can't imagine. What happened, Clarissa? Did you long to come home?"

"It seemed time that I did."

Lance laughed out loud. "She's a determined young lady," he said to Dickon. "I expect you found that out at Hessenfield."

Dickon nodded.

When we came into the house, Laura Garston, the mayor's wife, after she had expressed her amazement at seeing me, greeted me warmly.

"These two young people are exhausted," said Lance. "Clarissa is going to tell us all about it later on. In the meantime they would like to wash and eat and rest, I do not doubt. This is Jack Thorley, one of Hessenfield's young men."

Dickon had a nobility of manner which was immediately discernible to Lance. He had at first thought him to be a groom, but in a few seconds, man of the world that he was, he was treating Dickon as an equal. I liked him for it, and in

118

spite of the fact that I was worried about Dickon I felt a glow of pleasure to be in his exhilarating company again.

In the house rooms were prepared for us and we washed away the grime of the journey.

As soon as we had done this we had a meal, during which Dickon and I had a chance to exchange a few words together.

"I cannot stay here," he said. "I shall have to go."

"Shall we see each other again?"

"We shall. We *must*. I will think of something."

"They will send me home. We shall be miles apart."

"I tell you I will find a way. If I stay here . . . if they know who I am . . ."

"Yes, yes. You are in as much danger here as I was in Hessenfield. These stupid . . . stupid men! I get so angry with them."

"This is no time for anger. I must leave here at once."

"Yes, you must go. I see that. When my uncle comes back . . . when they start asking questions . . ."

"They will not be so friendly toward me then. Oh, Clarissa, why did you have to be with *them*? You belong with us."

"I belong to myself and I am aloof from these foolish quarrels. I don't care whether you are for George or James. You know that."

"I love you," said Dickon.

"I love you," I replied.

We smiled at each other. "Those days in the attic. . . . I shall never forget them," he said.

"Nor shall I. I wish I were back there. I wish I were still on the road. I wish I were in Makeshift Gallery."

"Oh. Clarissa, Clarissa . . ." That way of repeating my name never failed to move me. "I will come back for you. No matter what happens, I swear I will come."

"Yes, I know. And you must go now, Dickon. You are facing dangerous risk, and the longer you stay the more dangerous it becomes for you. I shall be thinking of you . . . on the road . . . back there . . . Shall you go to Scotland? Oh, Dickon, don't. Leave them to fight their silly wars if they must, but not you . . . not you. . . . Let us think of a way we can be together."

"When it is over. When the rightful King is on the throne . . . I will come for you. I will ask you for your hand in marriage. I will take you away with me and we shall live happily ever after."

We sat silently holding hands. Then he rose and said, "Now

I shall go to our hostess. I shall tell her I must leave first thing in the morning. It is better so. When I am gone you can tell them the truth, who I am ... everything. It will be easier that way."

I nodded miserably.

So that sad night passed. We were taken to our separate rooms. He had to share with one of the higher servants because that was all that was available. I had a small room of my own. I lay awake thinking of him, and I knew he was thinking of me.

At dawn I went down to the stables.

We clung together for a few moments. His last words before he rode away were, "I'll come back. Remember it. I shall come back for you, Clarissa."

I stood watching him ride away in the early morning light.

There was a great deal of explaining to do, and when Uncle Carl and Lance heard my story they were horrified.

"How could Lord Hessenfield send you away like that!" cried Uncle Carl.

"How could he keep her there?" asked Lance. "He did the right thing. Gad, what could have happened to her in the hands of Frenshaw!"

"They thought I was spying," I explained.

"A pretty kettle of fish," said Uncle Carl. "Now the problem is, what are we going to do with you? You know what's happening, don't you? The country's in a state of tension. The fact that those Highlanders got as far as Preston has shaken us all up a bit. Who would have believed that possible? The north is a hotbed of treachery."

"They say the same of the south."

"Ah," cried Lance, "have they made a little Jacobite of you?"

"Indeed they have not! I think the whole matter is stupid. Who cares ... ?"

Lance took my hand and kissed it. "Your feminine reasoning doubtless displays wisdom," he said, "but men will never see it. They will continue to wage war, and that is a fact we must face. Besides, Clarissa, James is no good. The people would not unite under him. He's a bigot. He would bring Catholicism to the country, and since Bloody Mary's Smithfield fires and some of our sailors have had experience of the Inquisition in Spain, that is something Englishmen will not endure. George may not be all we desire, but he is peaceable and he doesn't interfere with the people too much. Trade will prosper under him, you'll see. That's what we want—a nice 'German boor,' not a fiercely romantic, bigoted Chevalier."

"The immediate question is, what are we to do about Clarissa?" interrupted Uncle Carl.

"I believe there is a coach which leaves Mondays, Wednesdays and Fridays. It goes from York to London."

"You are well informed," replied my uncle, "but I should not allow you to travel alone on such a coach."

"Why not? People do."

"Not ladies of our family. Lance. . . ."

Lance smiled at him almost as though he knew beforehand what my uncle was going to suggest.

"You will be going to London in a few days' time."

"That's so," said Lance.

"If you could take Clarissa with you . . . Perhaps we could arrange for someone to come to London and take her back from there to Enderby. I am sure Jeremy or Leigh would be able to."

Lance said, "It shall be my great pleasure to conduct the lady Clarissa not only to London but to Enderby itself."

I smiled faintly. My thoughts were with Dickon.

All through the days which followed I thought of Dickon, but the best possible companion I could have had was Lance Clavering. His lively conversation and his observations on life and the passing scene diverted my thoughts from the recent parting as I was sure nothing else could have done.

Moreover, I think he understood what had happened. He was gentle with me, a little wistful, I thought; but all the time he was ebullient, and his merry wit did bring a certain comfort to me.

We were fortunate in the weather, which grew more clement as we journeyed south. The skies were even blue and there was little wind. When we left in the early morning there was rime on the tree branches and on the road, but by midmorning, when the sun had come up, it disappeared, and although there was a sharp bite in the air, it was good for getting along.

Lance sang, laughed and talked a good deal, determined to comfort me, and after a few hours in his company I really did begin to feel better. There was a bright optimism about his attitude to life, and it was easy to catch this and believe that one day this stupid trouble would be settled and Dickon could come to visit us. I was sure Damaris and Jeremy would like him; and they would make him welcome when they realized I loved him.

This was the effect Lance had on me. Life was to be enjoyed, and there was always something to laugh about.

I even found myself joining in his singing as we rode along because he urged me to do so—and I was grateful to him.

We traveled with two grooms, so we were a party of four. A highwayman would think twice about attacking three strong men.

At dusk on the first day we reached an inn which was known to Lance and where, he said, we should be assured of good service.

He was right. The landlord greeted us effusively and provided two of the best rooms for us; the grooms were accommodated in another room. It all seemed very satisfactory. When we had washed the stains of the journey from our faces and hands we went down to the inn parlor for our meal. It was delicious, as Lance said it would be. Thick slices of succulent beef were served with dumplings, and there was also pigeon pie, with sweetmeats to follow. Wine was especially brought from the cellar to satisfy Lance's refined palate, and if I had not been wondering what had happened to Dickon I could have been very content in Lance's company.

We talked all the time about his adventures in the army, deliberately not mentioning the present troubles, because he sensed that would only increase my anxieties. I did really appreciate his kindness during that journey.

The innkeeper's wife came in while we were finishing the meal to ask if Lance would like some port wine. He said he would, and she told us that she was expecting the coach to arrive at any minute, because this was the day for it.

"They'll be a hungry lot, they will," she went on, "but we're ready for them. These coaches have been good for business. They're regular, like . . . more or less. I've got enough beef for the coachload of them . . . and all hot and ready to serve the minute they arrive."

The port was brought, and as Lance was sipping it the coach lumbered into the inn and the weary passengers spilled out of it—cold, hungry, their faces pinched and pale.

"Come along in," said the host. "There's a fire to warm you and you'll be fed in next to no time."

The host's wife came running into the parlor. "They've come," she announced. "I doubt the likes of you will want to be in the same room with 'em. I'll keep them out, though, till you've finished your port, my lord."

I liked the way Lance stood up. "No," he said, "let them come in. I can take the port to my bedroom. Poor things, it's no joy traveling in those coaches. Boneshakers, I've heard them called. Come on, Clarissa, let's leave them to their food."

"Well, thank'ee, sir," said the woman. "That's real kind and thoughtful of you."

I smiled at Lance, thinking that for all his finery and dandified ways he was a true gentleman.

As we walked out of the inn parlor there were more sounds of arrival from without, and before we could ascend the stairs to our room three men came hurrying in. They were fashionably dressed, and one of them, smelling the food which was about to be taken into the dining room for the stage-coach passengers, cried, "Gad! The smell is appetizing. What is it, woman?"

The innkeeper's wife, with that unfailing instinct for recognizing the gentry, bobbed a curtsy and said, " 'Tis the food we be about to serve to the stage which are just come in, my lord."

"Then serve us with some of this goodly smelling fare before you deal with the stage."

The landlord came out rubbing his hands obsequiously but showing that he was uneasy.

"My good lords," he said, "we have only enough for the coach. 'Tis bespoke, you see. The coach is regular and we have a duty to be ready for it. There be the end of the hot food we have. But I have some fine cheese and fresh-baked barley bread, with good wine—"

"Fine cheese! My good man, we want the hot meal. Let the coach crowd share out what is left of the hot food when we have had our fill. Or let them take the fine cheese. I doubt not that it will satisfy them. Serve the hot dishes to us—and without delay. We have ridden far and are hungry."

One of the women from the coach had heard what was going on. She was a large red-faced woman with a determined jaw; she was clearly one who was accustomed to having her own way.

"Oh, no, you don't," she cried. "That food is for us. It's bespoke for the coach. So don't try none of your fancy tricks, my lord High-and-Mighty, for me and my party are not having that."

The leader of the new arrivals held the eyeglass which had been dangling from his elegant jacket and surveyed the woman with astonishment.

"Landlord," he said, "this creature offends me. Have her removed."

The woman put her hands on her hips and regarded him steadily. "Watch yourself, me little cock sparrer," she shouted, "or it won't be me what gets put out."

"The creature would be insolent."

He took a few steps forward, and she came to meet him. He put up a hand as though to brush her aside, but it was a blow which sent her reeling against the stairs.

Lance stepped forward then.

"This is no way to treat a lady, sir," he said.

The man stared at him and seemed to be taken aback by coming face to face with one who, on the surface, appeared to be of his own kind.

"A lady, did you say, sir?" said the man with a sneer.

"I did indeed. I have listened to this dispute. The hot food has been prepared for the coach, which was due at this time. Unexpected guests cannot expect to take that which has been made ready for others."

"Can they not, sir? And may I ask if you are prepared to dine off bread and cheese?"

"I am not, having just dined off the most excellent beef. But I came in time. I took nothing that was not my due."

"You are interfering in what does not concern you."

"On the contrary, I am deeply concerned and I will not stand by and see these good people deprived of what is theirs by right."

"*You* will not, eh?"

Lance drew his sword and stood there smiling. I was terrified for him. There were three of them against one. But I was proud of him all the same.

"Damme," said one of the men, "if it is not Clavering."

"Ah," retorted Lance, "so it is you, Timperly. I am surprised to see you in such company."

"Come, Clavering, what is it to you? These are a mob of coach people."

"They deserve their rights whether they travel by stage or private carriage. I say they shall have their dinner, and you would eat very well I am sure—for the Plump Partridge is an excellent inn—on hot bread and fine cheese. The port is good too. You'll enjoy it, Timperly."

"Look here, Clavering," said the first man, "what is it to you? Why bother yourself with this?"

"No matter," replied Lance. "Just let it stand that I do. I'll challenge any one of you to single combat. Let's fight it out."

"Taken," said the first man.

"Careful," added Timperly. "You know Clavering's reputation with a sword."

"Afraid?" asked Lance. "Come on. Which one of you? We'll fight it out for hot beef with dumplings against bread and cheese."

"I'll take you on," was the answer. It was the first man, who had drawn his sword.

"Gentlemen," cried Lance, "we can't let this take place without a gamble. What'll you offer? Twenty pounds between you for me if I win. And if I don't—But, dammee! I'm so certain of victory that I'll make it twenty apiece if he pricks me first."

"And the matter is settled at the first prick?" said Timperly, brightening considerably.

"So be it," said Lance.

"When do we start?"

"Here and now."

The host and hostess were standing by in dismay and several of the coach passengers looked on in amazement. They whispered together about the cause of the fight, and they were eying Lance with something like adoration. I felt proud of him and at the same time afraid, but I knew in my heart that he was going to win. I could not imagine anything else, and as their swords clashed I was caught up in the excitement. I was praying for Lance's success.

"Lance . . . go on. Win, Lance," I whispered. The coach passengers were vociferous. They shouted and called, while the host stood by clasping and unclasping his hands.

In a few tense moments it was over. Lance had won. He had pricked his opponent and blood was spurting onto the man's elegant cuff. Lance gave a cry of triumph as he held up his sword and stood there for a second or so looking like a medieval knight who had fought the good fight and overcome evil.

"Twenty pounds for me and hot dinners for the coach," he cried. "A most satisfactory encounter."

The three men were rueful but accepted their fate. The money changed hands and they went into the inn parlor while the stage-coach people trooped into the dining room chattering about the adventures they met with traveling by coach.

Lance laid his hand on my arm and said, "It is time we retired. We have to be up early in the morning."

He slipped his arm lightly through mine and we ascended the stairs. When we reached my room he said, "What do you think of our little fracas?"

"I was proud of you," I said.

"Oh, bless you for that."

"But I was sorry about the money. That spoilt it somehow."

"That made it worthwhile for me as well as for the coach passengers."

"It was a pity. Up to that time it seemed such a noble thing to defend the coach people. Then it seemed as though you had done it for a gamble."

"I never miss an opportunity to gamble."

"I know. But it would have been so much better without."

He took my chin in his hands and looked into my face. "The trouble with you, Clarissa, is that you always look for perfection," he said. "Don't. You're never going to find it, you know."

"Why not?"

"Because it doesn't exist in this world."

I thought of Dickon then. Hadn't that been perfection? Yes, until we had to part. Perhaps Lance was right. There was no perfection in life. One had to be prepared for that. Not look for it. Not hope for it. Just accept what there was to take.

Lance smiled at me thoughtfully. Then he bent forward and kissed me lightly.

"Sleep well, my dear," he said. "And rise early. We must be on our way at dawn."

The Verdict

We were riding off when the first streaks of light were in the sky. It was not really so early, for the days were short at this time of year. Lance said that at least we should be home in time for Christmas, and he was sure my family would be pleased at that.

We did not see any more of Timperly and his friends. Some of the coach people had been there when we left, and one of them said to me of Lance, "You have a very fine gentleman there."

I glowed with pride and agreed with her.

Then we were off. Lance seemed to have forgotten the incident. Perhaps such were commonplace in the exciting life which he led. He sang as we went and again and again urged me to join in. I did, and I could not help feeling my spirits rising. Such was the effect his company had on me.

In due course we came to the Hoop and Grapes, which was another inn where Lance knew we should be well looked after. I commented on the fact that he was knowledgeable on the subject of inns.

"Seasoned traveler," he replied.

We went in and had an excellent meal and once more became involved with the company—this time in a friendly fashion.

Two men were traveling with their wives, and it was obvious from everything about them that they were of the gentry. We chatted amicably with them and discovered that they were on their way to their home in London. They knew Lance by repute and were clearly pleased to be in his company.

We had dined together and during the conversation it transpired that Lance and the gentlemen had several mutual acquaintances.

"I remember old Cherrington," said one of them. "Lost

twenty thousand one night at that place—what was it called? the Cocoanut Tree?"

"Fortunes were won and lost there," said Lance, his eyes sparkling. "At one time it was the most frequented gambling den in London."

"I say," said one of the men, "what about a little flutter now?"

"Nothing would suit me better," cried Lance.

My heart sank. I had hoped that we might sit and talk, for I found great comfort in his company. But I could see the gambling fever was on him and how excited he was at the prospect of indulging in it.

As soon as the meal was over they were impatient to begin. He turned to me and said that he thought I needed an early night, as we must be off at the crack of dawn if we were to reach London the next day.

I felt I was dismissed, and holding my head rather high to feign indifference, I said good night to the company and left them.

Although I was thinking of Dickon and wondering what had become of him, I felt hurt that Lance should prefer the company of these strangers to mine. Why must he always seize every opportunity to risk his money? Moreover, he had left me alone. He had explained to our fellow travelers that I was the niece of General Eversleigh and that he had been commissioned to take me to London—which, he hastened to add, was one of the most pleasurable duties which had ever been assigned to him.

I was unmoved by such blandishments and angry that he should have dismissed me so cursorily, merely so that he could enjoy a gambling game with his new-found friends.

I undressed and went to bed but could not sleep. I kept going over the days I had spent with Dickon, remembering everything he had said and the wonder of discovering the love between us. I likened it to the rising of the sun. First a few streaks of light in the sky and then the sudden emergence and the bursting forth in glory to touch all life with some mystical magic.

The more angry I grew with Lance the more poetic I became about my relationship with Dickon. But I was surprised that even in the midst of my anxieties I should still feel such deep resentment toward Lance.

"He is an inveterate gambler," I told myself. "It is a great flaw in his character. Oh, he was noble enough when he stood

128

up for the coach people, but I think he did it because it was a gamble to him."

The night was passing and I had not heard him come upstairs. I went to my door and looked out. All was quiet. I tiptoed along the corridor to his room and opened the door very cautiously. He had not come up, for the room was empty and his bed undisturbed. So he was still down there gambling with those people. My watch told me it was two o'clock. I returned to my bed and lay there wondering how much he was losing . . . or winning.

It was past three o'clock when I heard him come upstairs, quietly tiptoeing. I leaped out of bed, and, opening my door, confronted him.

"Clarissa!" he cried,

"Do you realize what time it is?"

He laughed. "Past three?"

"All this time you have been down there . . . gambling."

He came toward me. "Couldn't you sleep?" he asked.

"How could I? I was worried."

"About me?"

"I was thinking of Dickon."

"Ah, yes. Well, it was foolish of you. You should have been fast asleep. So you realize that in a few hours we have to be on our way?"

"Did *you* realize that?"

"I can do with very little sleep."

"Did you . . . win?"

He looked at me ruefully and shook his head. "It was good play, though."

"So you lost!"

"The hazard of the game, you know."

"How—how much?"

"Not a great deal."

"How much?" I repeated.

He laughed. "You look so severe. Well, fifty pounds."

"Fifty pounds!"

"It was a long session."

"I think it is foolish. Good night."

"Clarissa." He took a step toward me and laid his hands on my shoulders. "Thanks for your concern," he said. Then he drew me toward him and kissed me.

I drew back in some confusion.

"Good night," he said quietly. "Go to sleep now. Remember, we leave early."

129

Then he went to his room and I went back to mine. He had disturbed me. He had really startled me when he kissed me. I had been very much aware of my scanty apparel, and perhaps my feelings were somehow involved with what I felt for Dickon.

I told myself I was annoyed with Lance and that it was not very gallant of him to have sent me off to bed as though I were a child.

I sank back into my bed. I was cold and still found it hard to sleep, but finally I did so, and almost immediately, it seemed, I was awakened by a knocking on my door informing me that it was time to get up.

We left early, as planned. Lance seemed none the worse for what must have been a very short night for him. He was as merry as ever and prepared to entertain me with stories of his adventures as we rode along.

I could not stop myself referring to the previous night and again expressing my disapproval of his losing so much money.

"You won twenty the night before," I pointed out, "and then lost it . . . and more besides."

"That's how it is with the gambler," he said. "He is spurred on by his winnings, only to lose much more with them."

"Then surely it is a foolish habit."

"Indeed you are right. But as you go through life you will discover that so many things which are foolish are also irresistible. That's the tragedy of it."

"I should have thought a little strength of mind."

"You are absolutely right . . . only it is not a little that is needed in this case but a great deal."

"I was so pleased that you won twenty and in such a noble way."

"It is no use brooding on these matters, dear Clarissa. That which was won at the Plump Partridge has now found its way into another's pocket, and the coach people have long forgotten their good dinner."

"I think they will remember you for a long time. They will talk of it to their children in the years to come."

"It will be like a candle in a dark world. Candles gutter, Clarissa, and soon go out. What a dismal conversation! Soon we shall be in London. There we shall spend one night at my residence and the next day set out for Enderby. Your adventure is nearly over. Thank you for letting me share in it."

"It is I who should be thanking you."

"It has been a wonderful journey. A duel of sorts in the Plump Partridge, losing fifty pounds last night, a lecture on the evil of my ways—and best of all, my dear sweet Clarissa, your company."

I was mollified. He had great charm of manner, and perhaps I liked him better because of his obvious imperfections.

So we rode on, and I was moved when I saw the great stone walls of the mighty tower of London and the river running like a ribbon between the fields and houses. It was growing dusk as we came through the city to Albemarle Street, where Lance had his London residence. As soon as we arrived there was a bustle of excitement. There seemed to be innumerable servants. He explained that a room was to be prepared for the niece of General Eversleigh, whom he was taking next day to her family in the country. In the meantime our main desire was for food, and we were very tired after having ridden so far.

It was a beautiful house—by no means old. It had been designed, I learned later, by Christopher Wren soon after the great fire of London, when the famous architect was rebuilding so much of the town. It was not large, by Eversleigh standards, but it had an elegance which bigger houses lacked. The paneling was beautiful, the curved staircase of exquisite design and everything as I would have expected, knowing Lance, was far from flamboyant, but at the same time impressed even those, like myself, that it was in the best possible taste.

The household was impeccably run. That was obvious by the speed in which our rooms were made ready and the meal served.

We sat in a room with windows which reached almost from floor to ceiling that they might let in the maximum of light. There was a silver candelabrum on the table and in the mellow lighting I found the surroundings extremely gracious.

"I think your house is beautiful," I told Lance.

"Thank you, Clarissa. I am rather fond of it myself. I spend a great deal of time here—rather than in the country. I am, as you may have observed, what is generally known as 'a man-about-town.'"

"Well, naturally," I replied. "The gaming houses are here."

"Oh, you can manage very well in the country. There are all sorts of ways of losing your money there, I assure you."

"And saving it would not provide the same excitement, I suppose."

"How could it?"

"It would to me," I said. "I should enjoy watching it accumulate."

"Dear, saintly Clarissa! A lesson to us all ... and in particular to foolish gamblers. Try some of this soup. It is my cook's very special pride. I believe there is always a cauldron of it bubbling in the kitchen."

"You are very well cared for here."

"I see to it. It is one of the passions of my life to be well cared for ... second to gambling, of course."

"I am learning a great deal about you."

"Oh, dear, that sounds ominous. I am learning a little about you too."

"I often think it is a mistake to know too much about people."

"That could be a very profound statement," he said.

So we bantered.

I spent the night in a delightful room. There was a fire in the grate, and no sooner had I sunk into my featherbed than I was sound asleep.

I was awakened by a serving girl who brought me hot water. It was still dark, but she told me that Sir Lance had said we were to be ready to leave as soon as it was light.

Oddly enough, I felt a certain regret that the adventure was nearly over. I was still dazed by all that had happened. I was just beginning to realize how much I had enjoyed my days with Lance.

We left the comfort of the house in Albemarle Street and took the road to the southeast. There were two stops on the road and the last was at the historic town of Canterbury. We were then a day's riding from Eversleigh.

In all the places we passed through, if we engaged in conversation with anyone, the talk always turned to the attempted rising of the Chevalier of St. George—or the Pretender, as he was more frequently called.

There was fear of war in the air, and I was uneasy, thinking that if it really came, Dickon would be on one side, my family on the other.

Lance was a little subdued, I thought, as we rode out of Canterbury.

I asked if he was thinking of the martyr who had been slain in the cathedral. Was it the fate of St. Thomas which occupied his mind and made him melancholy?

"No," he cried. "I must confess I had hardly given him a

thought. Surely you know there could be only one cause for my melancholy. It is because soon I must part from you."

I was so happy to hear him say that that I laughed with pleasure; then I remembered Dickon and was ashamed that I could do so.

"You have a habit of saying what people want to hear," I said.

"Not a bad habit, you will agree."

"If you mean it . . ."

"That," he said, "is an added bonus. I assure you I mean what I say when I tell you I have rarely enjoyed anything more than our little jaunt together. Thank you, dearest Clarissa, for giving me such a happy time."

"Nonsense. You know it is I who should be thanking you," I replied. "I am afraid I have been a melancholy companion."

"Indeed you have not. In spite of all that happened, you have made me feel you have enjoyed our journey."

"I have been as happy as it was possible for me to be considering how worried I have been."

We rode on in silence. I think we were both a little moved.

That day we reached Enderby. Damaris rushed out in amazement when she realized who it was. She hugged me tightly and then I was seized by Jeremy.

"Oh, Clarissa . . . we've been so worried . . . so anxious . . ."

Damon jumped round, and I was glad he took an immediate fancy to Lance.

I must see Sabrina, who had grown since I left; messages were sent over to the Court and to the Dower House. They would all be coming over to Enderby. This was a great occasion.

Lance stayed the night and received the thanks of every member of the family for bringing me home safely. They listened spellbound to my story, which I told them in detail, for I saw no reason to withhold anything except, of course, my love for Dickon and his for me.

"Thank God for this Dickon," said Damaris. "Oh, my darling, you were in great danger."

"Damned Jacobites," growled Great-grandfather Carleton. "I'd string up the lot of them. As for that Pretender . . . hanging's too good for him."

So I was back in the bosom of my family, and it seemed strange to be sleeping in my own bed again.

* * *

Christmas came. Damaris kept telling me how delighted she was that I was home in time for the celebrations. Besides, this was no time to be traveling about the country. There could be civil war—and what a disaster that would be, and all because some people wanted to put this Pretender on the throne.

She was sure the loyal army, with men like Uncle Carl commanding it, would soon put a stop to all that nonsense— but there might be trouble first.

Jeanne was delighted that I was safely back. She wept and crooned over me.

"Oh, Mademoiselle Clarissa, you are the one things happen to," she cried. "It is the way with some. Oh, how 'appy I am that you are with us again. 'Christmas,' I said, 'what is Christmas without the little Clarissa?' I have *la petite* Sabrina . . . yes. I have the little one. But for you there is something special . . ." —she touched her heart. "Something in here . . ."

"Jeanne," I said solemnly, "I shall always love you."

Then we wept together.

I could not join wholeheartedly in the festivities. All the time I was wondering where Dickon was and whether I should hear from him. We did hear scraps of news about the Pretender. He had left Bar-le-Duc, where he had been living— for he was no longer welcome at the French court—and disguising himself as a servant, had traveled to St. Malo where he had tried to take ship to Scotland. This he failed to do, and made his way to Dunkirk. It was at that time the middle of December, but, accompanied by a few attendants, he managed to find a ship to take him to Scotland, and landed at Peterhead three days before Christmas.

This news filled me with dismay, for I felt certain there would be bitter fighting, and if there was, Dickon might well be in the thick of it.

The days passed and there was no news. The family had been amazed to hear that I had a half sister. It was something they did not want to discuss openly, though, because they deplored the fact that my parents had not been married, and they found it rather shameful that Hessenfield should have had another illegitimate daughter.

I thought a great deal about those days in Paris when Aimée must have been living not so very far from me, and chatting with Jeanne was the best way of recalling them. Naturally she remembered so much more of our life there than I could. I asked her a great many questions, and I began to feel that I was back there living it all again.

I made her tell me about the life at the *hôtel*. "Did you ever hear of Aimée and her mother?"

"Never," declared Jeanne. "But never ... never. My Lord was always with your mother when he was in Paris. He did go away now and then ... it was all rather secret. He went to and from Paris to the Court of Saint-Germain. But never did I hear that there was another woman."

"Are you sure, Jeanne?"

Jeanne nodded emphatically. She closed her eyes and lifted her head to the ceiling.

"I remember it well," she said. "I remember Yvonne, Sophie, Armand ... he was the coachman. And there was Germaine; she was above herself ... what you might say, too big for her boots. Germaine, she thought she should not be there ... she should be a lady in her carriage, not a servant in such a house. Then there was Clos ... who cleaned the boots and grates and whatever he was told to do. A happy boy he was ... always a smile. Then there was Claudine, another such as Germaine ... only not quite so haughty. Oh, I remember them well. There was one day when my Lord and Lady Hessenfield were away at Saint-Germain, and Germaine dressed up in my lady's clothes. We laughed and laughed. She did it all so well. Only trouble was, she didn't want to take those things off ... she didn't want to go back to work."

"And was I there at the time?"

"You might have been with my lord and lady—or you might have been in the nursery."

"I don't remember any of them except you, Jeanne."

"Mon Dieu! You were only a baby. I'd take you out sometimes, perhaps to the druggist to get something for my lady ... something sweet-smelling to scent herself with ... or to the glovemaker's to collect gloves. Little errands like that. I'd orders never to venture with you into the forbidden places ... never to the Pont-au-Bled or the Rue du Poirer. I remember one morning a man in a carriage drove by ... some young lover chasing his mistress' carriage—and you were spattered with mud. I had to get one of the brushers-down at the street corner to deal with you. I couldn't take you back like that, and I'd have to get that mud off you the minute it went on or it would eat into your clothes."

"When you talk, Jeanne, it brings it back to my mind."

"Well, there's much that's best forgot. We came through it

all, didn't we? I often wonder what became of Germaine. She had a lover, and she was proud of him. He lived somewhere on the Left Bank. I remember once she stayed out the night with him. Clos let her in in the early morning. Monsieur Bonton did not know. Do you remember Monsieur Bonton? He led us all, you might say. He was reckoned to be one of the best chefs in Paris, and it was said that the King himself would have liked him for his kitchens. But that was just talk, maybe. But we all feared him. He had the power over us. One word from him and we could be sent off . . ."

"Jeanne, it seems so strange to me that there should have been this woman . . . Aimée's mother."

"He would have been finished with her by that time."

"No, I don't think so. She had a letter from him which said he wanted Aimée taken care of. He must have been seeing her."

"Who can say with men! The best of them has his secrets and often that secret is a woman. It is just men, *ma petite*. We must never be surprised by what they do."

I supposed she was right, but I found it difficult to accept.

With the coming of the new year there was a great deal of talk about the Pretender. He was to be crowned at Scone, and the Jacobites were persuading their women to give up their jewels to make a crown for him.

There were rumors—that was all. On the pamphlets which had been circulated James had been represented as godlike— tall, handsome, noble and full of vigor, determined to win what was rightfully his. It seemed that the reality was quite different. James had no charm of manner; he did not know how to attract the ordinary man; he had no conversation; moreover, he was melancholy and seemed more ready to accept failure than inspire victory.

The truth was that he lacked the gift necessary for leading men. The Earl of Mar, who was the real spirit behind the rising, sought in vain to imbue him with the qualities essential for the success of the enterprise. It was hopeless, and even Mar had to realize that he was involved in a lost cause. The only people who were ready to support James were the Highlanders, and it was soon apparent that the wise course of action was to retire while it was possible to do so and await the opportunity to rise again.

The loyal troops of King George were on the march, and the only thing left for James to do was to go back to France. At Montrose he and the Earl of Mar embarked on a vessel and sailed toward Norway, hugging the coast until they came to Gravelines, where they landed. That was the tenth of February. The enterprise was over.

"Thank God," said Priscilla. "Let us hope they will never consider such a foolhardy expedition again."

"Well, it is all over now," echoed Damaris.

Alas, it was not over. There had been many captives, and it was not to be expected that they would be dealt with lightly. Lessons had to be taught and learned.

Prisoners had been taken, and many of them were being brought to London to be sentenced. I was overcome with anxiety.

Uncle Carl came home. He would stay a while, he said, now that the little trouble in the north was over.

"Your friend Frenshaw is one of the prisoners," he told me. "He won't escape execution. Hessenfield is in trouble too. By gad, Clarissa, you were in the very heart of it up there."

"Thank God she got away," said Damaris.

I longed to know what had happened to Dickon. I must find out. I was anxious about my uncle Hessenfield. I had grown fond of him.

Lance arrived. He said he had come to see me. He spent a long time talking to Uncle Carl, but it was Lance himself who broke the news to me.

He asked me to walk in the gardens with him. It was warmish for February and he remarked that there was a sniff of spring in the air.

I soon discovered why he had come. "Clarissa," he said, "this is going to be sad for you, but I think you should know."

I whispered, "It's Dickon . . . isn't it?"

"He's here . . . in London."

I caught my breath. "Can I . . . ?"

He shook his head. "He's one of the prisoners. He was taken with his uncle. There's no hope for them. They'll all be condemned as traitors."

"But he is only young and . . ."

"He was old enough to fight against the King's troops."

I caught his arm and looked up at him pleadingly. "Something can be done . . . something *must* be done. Remember, he saved my life."

"I do remember that. If I could do anything, I would. But they are doomed, all of them. People cannot commit treason against the King and be allowed to escape punishment."

"Dickon is different."

"I know Dickon is different for you, Clarissa. But not to His Majesty's judges. I wondered whether to tell you that this is about to happen . . . or to have said nothing."

"No, no. I want to know what happens to him. Lance, could you take me to him?"

"That is quite impossible."

"Could you not *do* something?"

Lance bit his lip as though considering, and my hopes rose.

"Lance," I cried, "you could do something. I know you could. You can do it—if anyone could."

"You have too high an opinion of my powers. There is nothing I can do. Your uncle Carl is in a high position in the army . . ."

"I will ask him," I cried. "And he is here now."

"Don't let him think . . ."

"What do you mean?"

"It would be a good idea if you gave the impression that you wanted to save this young man's life because he probably saved yours. If there was anything that your uncle Carl would call 'romantic nonsense' he would be less inclined to save Dickon. The last thing Carl or any of your family would want is an alliance with a disgraced Jacobite family. Perhaps it would be better if I spoke to him."

"No, no. I want to be there."

"Very well," said Lance, "but be careful."

Uncle Carl listened thoughtfully.

"You see, Uncle," I said, keeping a curb on my emotions, "he saved my life. I feel for that reason we ought to do something for him."

"It's true, of course," Lance added his voice to mine. "Is there anything you could do?"

"I should not think so for one moment," replied my uncle.

"But," persisted Lance, "it is worth a try."

"I should have to go to London."

"I'll come with you," said Lance.

I loved Lance in that moment. He had made my cause his. He understood how I felt and he was on my side. I felt optimistic because of his support.

"We could leave tomorrow. They're getting a fair trial."

"A word from you might make a difference. After all, there is his youth."

"I doubt that will be considered," said Uncle Carl. "Anyone who is old enough to fight is old enough to pay the penalty for treason to the King."

"Well, we can try," said Lance.

I could see that Uncle Carl thought it was a lost cause, and although Dickon had saved me he was not eager to make the journey to London for his sake. But Lance persuaded him. There was something good and kind about Lance. I had seen it when he spoke up for the coach people who were about to be denied their dinner. He could put himself in other people's places and see from their points of view. It was a rare gift, and most people who had it were too selfish to do anything about it.

The next morning Lance and Uncle Carl left for London. I wished that I could have gone with them, but Lance said they would be quicker without me, and they must get there before the trial started.

I want to forget the days that followed. They were some of the most wretched I had known up to that time.

I was desperately afraid, for I had gathered from Lance's attitude that there was very little hope. I waited every day for news. I could not eat; I could not sleep; and Damaris was worried about me.

"My dear Clarissa," she said, "you must not fret so. It's true he saved you, but he must have gone back to fight with them."

"He believed it was right," I cried. "Don't you know what it means to believe in something!"

There was no comfort anywhere, and for a whole week I fretted.

"You'll be ill if you go on like this," said Damaris.

At last Lance came alone for Uncle Carl was kept hard at work in London. I knew as soon as I saw Lance's face that all was not well.

"Lance . . . Lance . . ." I cried, flinging myself into his arms. He held me tightly for some seconds. Then I wrenched myself free and looked full at him.

"Tell me," I begged. "Tell me the truth."

"He is not to be executed. We managed to avert that."

"Oh, Lance . . . Lance . . . thank you . . . thank you."

"But . . ." He hesitated, and I felt I was going mad with the suspense.

"He is being transported to Virginia."

"Transported!"

Lance nodded. "He'll be on his way now . . . to the colony there. Quite a number of them have gone. It was his youth

... and the fact that Carl did what he could ... that saved his life."

"But he has gone away ... to Virginia. That's miles and miles ... over the sea."

"It's a long way," agreed Lance.

"And when ... ?"

"For fourteen years."

"Fourteen years. I shall be an old woman then. . . ."

"Oh, no ... no ..." soothed Lance.

"I fear I shall never see him again," I said quietly.

Lance looked at me sadly.

"But we saved his life," he said.

The Wedding

It was a hot June day. The following morning I was to be married. I was trying to look into the future and kept telling myself: It will be all right. It's the best thing that could happen. Everyone is pleased. Everyone is sure I am going to be happy. They must be right.

It was more than three years since Dickon had been sent to Virginia, but sometimes it seemed as though he were still with me. I had been dreaming of him in those weeks before my marriage. I could see him clearly, remember every detail of his face as he had stood there when he said goodbye; I fancied his eyes were full of reproach.

We were only children, I told myself, and we had met in such strange circumstances. It was only natural that we should feel as we did. We did not really know each other—not as I knew Lance.

Over the last three years Lance had been a constant visitor to Eversleigh, and when I became aware that he came to see me, I will not pretend that I was not flattered. I looked forward to his visits. I began to realize that they were the highlights of the weeks. He brought little gifts from London or any part of the country he happened to have visited. We laughed a great deal together; we rode; we walked; and the family looked on with growing approval. And at last it came—the proposal of marriage.

I refused him. How could I marry anyone while I was waiting for Dickon? He will come home for me, I used to tell myself, and when he does I must be ready for him.

The family was disappointed. They had made up their minds that Lance would be the ideal match for me. He was older than I, but as Damaris said, I needed an older man. He was comfortably off financially, of an extremely pleasant humor; he was excellent company and approved of by Uncle Carl and therefore a very welcome visitor to Eversleigh.

Damaris tried to persuade me to reconsider his proposal. Arabella said it would be a good thing if we married; Uncle Carl said it would be an ideal match; and even Great-grandfather Carleton said he could see nothing wrong with the young man.

Lance seemed to take my refusal more calmly than anyone. He continued to call and made it clear that he enjoyed my company still. That suited me, for I knew now how much I should hate it if he removed his friendship and his visits ceased.

He understood about Dickon, he said. That almost uncanny understanding of other people's minds was one of the most attractive aspects of his character. He was patient, gentle and tender and gave me the impression that, while he would not worry me with his importunings, he was sure it would all come right in the end.

There came a day when I paid a visit to London with Damaris and Jeremy. It had been planned suddenly, as Jeremy had to go to town and Damaris had thought it would be a good idea if we accompanied him. We arrived in the late afternoon and went immediately to the family's town house, where we were to stay for the few days we should be there.

The next morning I was up early and suddenly decided that it would be amusing to pay an early call on Lance. I was sure he would be delighted to see me and that we were to stay for a little while.

I took a sedan to the house in Albemarle Street. It was only about ten o'clock. I had always enjoyed the streets of London and was thrilled to be carried through them in my chair. Everything was so colorful. I delighted in the sedans, such as the one in which I was traveling, carrying, even at this hour, elegantly clad ladies and gentlemen. One could see the latest fashions, which these bewigged and painted ladies and gentlemen liked to display. I was quizzed by one or two gentlemen passing in their chairs and I shrank back farther into my seat, feeling very much the country girl. In contrast to these brilliant people were the beggars and street tradesmen. These fascinated me, and I was conscious of the tremendous noise everywhere. The newsmen were blowing in their tin trumpets to announce they had the *Gazette* or whatever journal they were selling; the bellows menders and the knife grinders squatted on the cobbles working at their tasks and calling out all the time; while the Colly Molly Puff man who sold his pies stood side by side with a milkmaid.

I was smiling, thinking of Lance's pleasure when he saw me, and when I reached his door I told the chairman to wait just in case Lance should not be at home and I needed him to take me back at once.

I knocked at the door and Lance's very excellent footman opened it.

"Hello, Thomas," I said. "This is a surprise visit."

He stared at me as though he could not believe his eyes. It was the first time I had seen him nonplussed. He knew me well, of course, for I, with my family, has often visited the house in Albemarle Street.

"Is Sir Lance at home?" I asked.

He floundered a little, which was odd, because he was usually so precise. "Oh, yes, Mistress Clarissa, but. . . ."

I had stepped inside. "Oh, I am glad he's at home. I should have been so disappointed if he had not been. I'll go and find him. I want this to be a surprise."

Thomas put out a hand as though to restrain me, but I had gone past him, laughing to myself at the prospect of seeing Lance's face when he saw me.

I opened the door of the dining room expecting to see him at breakfast, but he was not there.

"Mistress . . . you can't." Thomas was close behind me.

I took no heed. I bounded up the stairs, taking them two at a time. He must be still abed. I would tease him about his laziness. It was wrong of me to go to his bedroom. Damaris would not have approved, but there was a special relationship between us. I was being unconventional, but Lance himself had often said that conventions were for the unimaginative, and individualists disregarded them when it was expedient to do so.

I was doing that now.

I came to his bedroom door. Thomas was puffing after me. I knocked at the door.

"Come in," said a woman's voice.

I opened the door. She was seated at the dressing table in her nightgown combing her long dark hair.

"Put the tray down there," she said, without turning her head.

I was astounded. What was this woman doing in Lance's bedroom?

Then Lance himself appeared. I stared at him in amazement. He was wearing light-colored breeches and was shirtless, so that he was naked from the waist.

143

"I'm ready for breakfast, darling, are you?" he said. Then he stopped short, for he had seen me.

My face was scarlet. I turned and ran out of the room, almost falling over Thomas, who was beside himself with dismay. I started down the stairs. I heard Lance call after me, "Clarissa, Clarissa, come back."

I took no notice. I ran out of the house to the chair, which was mercifully waiting for me.

I did not see the colorful streets now; I did not hear the raucous cries of the street sellers. I could only see Lance with a woman in his bedroom. Lance . . . who had asked me to marry him.

I never want to see him again, I told myself fiercely. I was very upset and most unhappy.

Lance, of course, did not let the matter rest there. He came to see me later in the day. I pleaded a headache and refused to leave my room. But he kept calling until I did see him.

"I want to explain," he said.

"It was self-explanatory," I retorted.

"I daresay it was," he agreed ruefully.

"That woman . . . who is she?"

"A very dear friend of mine."

"Oh . . . you are shameful."

"You, my dear Clarissa, are very young. Yes, your inference is correct. Elvira Vernon is my mistress and has been for some time."

"Your mistress! But you have asked me to marry you."

"And you refused me. Do you deny me consolation?"

"I don't understand you."

"There is a great deal you have to learn of the world, Clarissa."

"I have already learned so much about you! What if people knew. . . ."

"My dear, a great many of them know. There is nothing terrible or unusual about this situation. It is a very amicable arrangement. Elvira and I suit each other very well."

"Then why don't you marry *her?*"

"It isn't that sort of relationship."

"It seemed that that was what it was . . . exactly. Oh, how wise I was to refuse you. Suppose . . ."

"Suppose you had agreed to marry me? Then I should have brought to a close my relationship with Elvira and begun my life as a respectable married man."

"You are so . . . glib."

"Listen, Clarissa, I am fond of Elvira in a certain way, but I don't want to marry her any more than she wants to marry me. We just like each other. We console each other. I love you. I want to marry you. You must believe that."

"I do not, and I have no wish to see you anymore. I think it is . . . horrible. I suppose you have had lots of mistresses."

"A few," he admitted.

"Then go back to them and leave me alone. What a lucky escape I have had!"

"So you did consider me, then?"

"I have told you I love someone else and I am waiting for him. But it is no concern of yours, because I shall never see you again."

He regarded me with a smile, half tender, half mocking. One of the things which exasperated me was his inability to be serious about any subject—and in a way it fascinated me. It gave him an added stature, as though he was completely competent to deal with any situation.

After he had gone I realized how angry I was, how hurt, how humiliated. Why should I be? I asked myself. What he does is no concern of mine. Let him have a houseful of mistresses if he wants them.

He continued to visit the family. When he saw me he behaved as though nothing had happened. I kept wondering about him and visualizing Elvira Vernon in his bedroom. I was not entirely sure what lovemaking entailed, and I began to develop a great curiosity about this. Occasionally I saw Elvira Vernon. She was poised and sophisticated. Quite old, I thought a little maliciously.

I became jealous if Lance did not pay enough attention to me. I could not understand myself. I was thinking more often of him than I did of Dickon. He seemed half-amused by what had happened and not in the least ashamed.

Once he said to me, "I'm not a saint. I'm not even a monk. Elvira and I are good for each other . . . at the moment."

"I suppose," I retorted, "one could say that mistresses are as much a part of your life as gambling."

"I suppose one could," he replied. "What a dissolute character that makes of me. But lovable withal, eh, Clarissa?"

Then he put his arms round me and held me tightly, and suddenly he kissed me.

I drew away breathless, assuming an anger which I did not feel. The fact was that I was tingling with excitement.

After that I began to realize that life was rather dull when

145

he was not around. I thought a great deal about us. Lance, with his mistresses and his gambling, would be far from the perfect husband. And what sort of wife would I be to him—in love with someone else who was lost to me?

I talked a great deal about Dickon to Lance, stressing his innocence, his gallantry, his purity.

"And sent overseas for years and years," said Lance. "Few ever return. Are you going to spend your life in single blessedness waiting for something which may never happen? People change with the years. Your Dickon, even if he came back, would not be this pure and gallant boy who went away. And what are those years going to do to you, my sweet Clarissa? Take what is offered you now. Think what we can do for each other. You can lure me from my vices; I can make you forget an impossible dream."

I thought a great deal about what he had said. Our relationship was changing. He would embrace me when we met, kiss me in a strangely stirring manner. Sometimes I thought he was laughing at me because I was so innocent of life that I thought it was so dreadful for a man to have a mistress.

"If," I said, "I should agree to marry you, you would have to say goodbye to your mistress of the moment."

"Done," he said.

"You would have to be a faithful husband."

"I promise."

Then he picked me up and held me tightly, and when Damaris came into the room he said, "It's happened at last. Clarissa has promised to marry me."

I told myself I must stop thinking of Dickon. That encounter with him was one little incident in my life. Lance was here, my future husband, kind, worldly, tender, taking life as it came along, enjoying it, never allowing it to oppress him. That was how I wanted to live. He was a gambler. He gambled with life. He took chances, and if he lost he shrugged his shoulders and was sure he would win next time.

He had been an only child. His father had died when he was a boy and his mother had lived only a few years longer. He had inherited estates on the border of Kent and Sussex, and if he was not exactly wealthy, he would have been if he had not lived so extravagantly and not lost so much at the gaming tables. My family, of course, was naturally interested in his financial position. I know now that my grandmother Priscilla had an obsession about my being married for my money, for I was a considerable heiress.

My mother had been left a fortune, and as I was her nearest of kin, that came to me. It had been looked after by Leigh, who had a head for such matters, and had accumulated during my mother's absence in France and my coming of age. The money was to be mine on my eighteenth birthday or when I married.

There was also my inheritance from my father, which Lord Hessenfield, who had charge of these affairs, had decided should be divided equally between myself and Aimée. He had made the provision that the money should not pass to either of us until my eighteenth birthday—which was strange, because Aimée was a few years older than I. I wondered why he had arranged this, for he had accepted Aimée, and yet she must wait for her share. If either of us died, her share was to go to the other living sister.

However, I did not think very much about the money. My family was sure it had not influenced Lance's desire to marry me. He was sufficiently comfortably off without it.

Now here I was, not only on the threshold of marriage but about to become a rich woman in her own right. Sometimes I felt very happy. Then I would think of Dickon.

The day had begun. I lay in bed listening to the sounds of the house beginning to stir. In the cupboard was my wedding dress. Lance was staying at Eversleigh Court and Uncle Carl was there too. Jeremy was going to give me away, and Priscilla had wanted the traditional wedding as she remembered it in the past.

While I was brooding on all this my door was pushed open and a small figure came into the room. This was Sabrina, nearly four years old now, a high-spirited and enchanting little girl. She climbed onto my bed and snuggled down beside me.

"It's the wedding," she whispered.

I held her tightly. I had always been very fond of Sabrina. She was exceptionally pretty; they said she had a look of my mother, Carlotta, who had been one of the beauties of the family. Moreover, she was well aware of her charm and made good use of it to get her own way. She was always darting about the house. She would be in the kitchen one minute, standing on a chair watching them make pies and cakes, sticking a greedy finger into sweet mixtures when no one was looking, dashing out to the stables and coaxing one of the grooms to take her round the paddock on her newly acquired pony the next, playing with the gardeners' wheelbarrows, hiding in the minstrels' gallery, jumping out at Gwen, the parlormaid, who believed in ghosts, finding an irresistible desire to do everything she was told not to do—that was Sabrina.

But she had the greatest charm, and she had quickly discovered that one of her enchanting smiles coupled with an air of penitence could extract her from most trouble.

Now she was chattering about weddings. It was mine, wasn't it? When was she going to have a wedding? She was going to wear a pink silk dress. Nanny Curlew was still sewing it. She was going to have flowers in her hair . . . and she was going to stand beside me. So it was really *her* wedding too.

She put her arms round my neck and her face was close to mine.

"You're going away from here," she said.

"Well, I shall be back often."

"It's not your home anymore. You're going to Uncle Lance's home."

"Well, he'll be my husband."

Her face puckered a little. "Stay here," she whispered. She tightened her arms about my neck and added pleadingly, "Stay here with Sabrina."

"Wives always live with their husbands, you know."

"Let Lance come here."

"We'll be here often. You'll see."

She shook her head. It wasn't the same. "I don't want you to get married."

"Everyone else does."

"Sabrina doesn't." She looked at me calculatingly, as though that was the best of all reasons for calling off the affair.

"When you are older you can come and stay with us," I said.

"Tomorrow?" she asked brightly.

"That's a little soon."

"I'll be older."

"Only one day. It'll have to be more than that."

"Two days? Three days?"

"Months, perhaps. Go and open the cupboard door and you'll see my dress."

She leaped out of bed. "Ooo," she said, stroking a fold of satin.

"Don't put your fingers on it," I warned.

She turned to look at me. "Why?" she asked. Sabrina always wanted an explanation of everything.

"They might be dirty."

She looked at them and then at me; she smiled slowly and deliberately touched the dress. That was typical of Sabrina. "Don't touch" meant "I must touch at all costs."

"Not dirty," she said reassuringly. Then she pounced on my shoes, which were of white satin with silver buckles and silver heels. She picked one up and smiled at me, stroking the satin and looking at me with a mischievous twinkle in her eyes, presuming, I supposed, that if the dress must not be touched, nor must the slippers.

There was a knock on the door. It was Nanny Curlew.

"I knew I'd find you here, miss," she said. "Begging your pardon, Miss Clarissa. The child is into everything."

"It's a very special morning, Nanny," I said. "She has caught the general excitement."

"It's my wedding, really," announced Sabrina.

"Come along," said Nanny Curlew firmly. "Miss Clarissa has other things to think about than you, my lady."

Sabrina looked puzzled. "What things?" she asked, as though it were inconceivable that there could be any subject more absorbing than that of herself.

But Nanny Curlew had her firmly by the hand, and with an apologetic smile at me, dragged the child away. Sabrina gave me one of her enchanting smiles as she disappeared.

My next visitor was Jeanne. She came in bristling with importance.

"Ah, is it awake, then? To do . . . there is so much. I have sent for a tray for you. That is best."

"I couldn't eat anything, Jeanne."

"That is not the way to talk, milady. You must eat. Do you want to faint at the feet of this new 'usband?" Jeanne had never completely conquered her *h*'s and could manage them only in calm moments. "Oh, this is the great day," she went on. "I am so 'appy. Sir Lance, he is a good man. He is the charming man." She closed her eyes and blew an imaginary kiss to Lance. "I say to myself, I say, 'This is the one for my little *bébé*. This is the 'usband for Clarissa.' So beautiful . . . the brocade waistcoat . . . 'e dresses like a Frenchman."

"There could be no greater praise than that, Jeanne. But I wonder whether Lance would appreciate it."

"Now come . . . the bath . . . then the food . . . and then the 'air. I shall make you so beautiful thees day."

"As beautiful as Lance?" I asked.

"I say this: no one shall be as beautiful as my lady. This is 'er day. She will be the most beautiful of all brides . . ."

"Made so by the deft hands of Jeanne."

"So . . . so . . ." she murmured.

Jeanne and I had grown very close to each other over the years. She was very fond of Sabrina. "There is a big charm in that one," was her comment. "But naughtiness too. She will have to be watched. You were not like that as a little one. No."

"I lacked the charm."

"That is a no sense." Jeanne had an amusing way of adapting words to suit herself, and I sometimes found myself using them. "You have the charm," she went on. "But you were a good little girl . . . more caring for others . . . per'aps. You were more like the ladies Priscilla and Arabella. Not like your mother and father . . . they cared first for themselves. So with the little Sabrina."

"She is only a child."

"I know much of children. What is in them at three is in them at thirty."

"My dear, wise Jeanne. . . ."

"So wise that I will get you up this minute. We have good time, but let us not waste it."

I put myself in her hands. I was content to sit at the mirror while she waited on me, brushing my hair and coiling it round my head so that it would show to the best advantage.

I watched her in the mirror, intent and proud of me. Dear Jeanne!

"I have so much to thank you for," I said with emotion. "What can I do to show you that I appreciate all you have done for me?"

She touched my shoulder lightly. "It is not to be measured out," she said. "You have change my life. You let me come here . . . be your lady's maid. That is what I ask. But we do not count what we do."

"Yes, Jeanne, of course."

"I am to be with you. It is what I want. We shall leave this house. You go to your husband and I go with you. I am glad of that. I would not wish to stay here . . . without you. And you let me come with you and Sir Lance, 'e say yes. 'I hear you are coming with us, Jeanne,' he say. 'That is good . . . very good.' That is what he say. And he smile his beautiful smile. He is a beautiful *gentilhomme*."

"I am glad you approve of him, Jeanne."

, "He is what I would choose for you. Stop thinking of this . . . Dickon. He is a boy. He is far away. He would not have been the one for you."

"How can you know?"

"Something tell me. He is away fourteen years . . . that one . . . that boy. Fourteen years! *Mon Dieu!* He will have a wife out there in that foreign place. No, Sir Lance . . . he is the one for you."

"He certainly has a champion in you."

She nodded, smiling.

"How will you like leaving Enderby?" I asked.

She was silent for a few moments, holding the brush over my head and staring down at it. Then she said rather vehemently, "I am 'appy. I go with you and that is good. Enderby is not a good house."

"Not a good house! What do you mean?"

"Shadows . . . whispers . . . noises in the night. There's spirits about it . . . long-dead ones that can't rest."

"Really, Jeanne, surely you don't believe that. Where is your practical French realism?"

"It is a 'ouse where 'appiness do not stay . . . long. A little time maybe, but it flits away. I am glad we leave. I could not have borne not to go with you. So . . . now I am 'appy. It is what I always want . . . to be lady's maid. I remember your mother . . . so . . . so beautiful, and Claudine was her lady's maid. She was very important, Claudine. Not like the rest of us. I always wanted to be lady's maid . . . to comb the 'air, to touch up the cheeks, to make little black beauty spots . . . that was my dream. Germaine was jealous of Claudine. Germaine always wanted to be lady's maid. And now I am one and I go with you and your beautiful 'usband. We shall go to London . . . Ah, that is a great place to be."

"And in the country sometimes."

"That will be good too."

"And we shall come back here to Enderby for visits."

"For visits. That is not the same as living here."

"You talk as though we're escaping from some evil spell."

"Per'aps," said Jeanne shrugging her shoulders.

She looked down at my hands. "You are not going to wear that ring at your wedding?"

I twisted round and round the ring, which now fitted my middle finger. My hands had grown since Lord Hessenfield had given it to me.

"It's my bezoar ring," I said. "A very special ring."

"It will not match your dress."

"Never mind. I shall wear it all the same. Don't look at it like that, Jeanne. It's a very precious ring. Queen Elizabeth gave it to one of my ancestors and it has special properties. It's an antidote against poison."

"What do you mean?"

"I mean that if someone gave me a drink with arsenic in it—or perhaps some other poison—this ring would absorb the poison. It acts as a sort of sponge."

Jeanne made a noise of disgust. "A likely story," she said, but she took my hand and studied the ring. "Queen Elizabeth, did you say? Was it one of hers, then?"

"Yes, and that makes it very valuable. It has her initial engraved inside."

"Well, in that case you can wear it."

"Thank you, Jeanne."

I was almost ready now. Very soon I would go to the church and be married to Lance. I was both excited and apprehensive. I wished that I could forget going into Lance's bedroom and seeing Elvira sitting at the mirror. They had seemed so unconcerned, so natural. There was so much I had to learn. I could not resist slipping away from Jeanne and taking a look at the bridal chamber which that night I should occupy with Lance. It would be that room which had once been in red velvet and which Damaris had changed when she came to Enderby. Now it was white-and-gold damask and had been decorated for the wedding with blue and green ribbons. Two serving girls were tieing sprigs of rosemary to the posts.

They were giggling together and were suddenly silent as they saw me.

"It looks very pretty," I said, trying to speak without emotion. Somehow I had never really liked this room. Perhaps it was because, as a child, when Damaris and I had been very close to each other, I had sensed her dislike of it. She hardly ever came to it, but it was, of course, the most elaborate and biggest of the bedchambers, and it was natural that it should be turned into the bridal suite for this occasion.

"It's a great day, Miss Clarissa," said one of the maids.

I agreed that it was.

When I went back to my room Jeanne was searching everywhere for one of my shoes.

"I've looked 'igh and low," she declared. "I am certain they

152

were both here. Where can it have got to? You can't be married in one shoe!"

I joined in the search without success, and Damaris came in while we were still hunting.

"You look beautiful, darling," she said. "Oh, Clarissa, I am so happy for you."

Dear Damaris. I knew she was thinking of the day she had found me in the cellar. She embraced me and then Jeanne.

"Oh, madame," said Jeanne, "no tears today, please. It spoil the eyes."

We laughed. Jeanne had prevented an emotional scene.

"And," she went on, "where is this shoe? We do not know where it 'ave gone."

"Well, it must be found," I said. "Sabrina came into my bedroom this morning. She looked at the gown. The shoes were there then."

"Ah," cried Jeanne. "I have the idea. One moment, please."

She went away, and soon came back holding Sabrina by the hand and the shoe was in the other.

"This wicked one had 'id it," announced Jeanne.

"Oh, Sabrina!" said Damaris.

"It was so she wouldn't be able to get married," explained Sabrina.

"You have cause great trouble and you should be spank," said Jeanne.

Sabrina's face crinkled in dismay. "I only did it so that Clarissa wouldn't go away and leave me," she explained.

Damaris knelt down and put her arms around the child. "Darling," she said, "Clarissa is going to be very happy. You want that, don't you?"

Sabrina nodded. "But me too," she said.

Damaris was touched, but I was not sure whether the spirit of mischief in Sabrina had been responsible for her act as much as her desire to prevent my marrying. However, the shoe was found and my toilet was complete now and I was ready for marriage.

Lance was waiting in the church with the family from Eversleigh Court. Great-grandfather Carleton looked on with a certain pride, although he tried to hide it. Leigh was there with Benjie and Anita. I guessed they would all be thinking of Harriet, as we must at a time like this. Arabella and Priscilla were alternating between their delight and that emotion which women feel at weddings.

So we were married, and as I came out of the church with

Lance I tried to suppress my uneasy feelings and assure myself that I had done right in accepting him. It would have been foolish to go on dreaming of a boy who had been transported to the colony of Virginia and whom I could not see until we were so much older. So much happened over the years, and it was hardly likely that, even if we did meet again in the far distant future, we should still be the same people who had met so romantically and parted so tragically.

At Enderby the celebrations were taking place. Everyone who had gone to church had carried a sprig of rosemary, in accordance with the old custom, and when we were all seated at the table a great punch bowl was passed round so that everyone could drink the health of the bride and groom. As the bowl came to them each of the guests dipped into it the rosemary they had carried to church, and so they wished us married joy.

Lance held my hand firmly and I was reassured. I had done what was right. In my heart I whispered wistfully, "Goodbye, Dickon. Goodbye forever."

Healths continued to be drunk, people made speeches, and there was a great deal of chatter and laughter. Then we went to the hall, which was decorated as a ballroom, and in the minstrels' gallery the musicians played for our dancing.

There were no ghosts there that night.

At midnight Lance and I retired to the bedroom with its brocade-covered bed and sprigs of rosemary, and the moments I had been dreading were at hand. I was terribly apprehensive; I was both ignorant and innocent. I had vague ideas of the relationship between men and women. I had come across servants in embarrassing situations. I had heard giggles, seen certain fumblings in dark corners; I had once come across a couple in the woods merged into each other under a tree, moving and moaning. I knew one of the kitchen maids had been, as the cook said, "anyone's for the taking," and finally she had had a baby. I will not pretend that I had not thought about an idyllic relationship with Dickon and when we had lain side by side in Makeshift Gallery we had both deplored the fact that we were not alone. I think we both knew that if we had been, our emotions would have swept us into physical union, which would have been irresistible to us both. I thought now that if we had been, we should have been bound irrevocably together and I should not be in this bridal suite with Lance at this time.

But it had not been so, and there I was, seated at the mirror brushing my hair, brushing on and on because I was afraid to stop. Lance had removed his coat. He was standing there bare to the waist, and I could not help seeing in my mind's eye that other scene—Lance as he looked now, but another woman at the mirror. She had been relaxed and smiling, luxuriously dreamy, like a satisfied cat. How different I was—ignorant and inadequate.

Lance came and stood over me, smiling at me in the mirror. He slipped the robe over my shoulders until it fell to my waist. Then he kissed me . . . my lips, my neck and my breasts.

I turned to him suddenly and clung to him.

"Don't be afraid, Clarissa," he said. "It's not like you to be afraid. Besides, there's nothing to fear."

He pulled me to my feet and my robe fell to the floor. I felt unprotected without my clothes. But Lance was laughing softly as he picked me up and carried me to the bed.

So my wedding night had begun. It bewildered me. I felt I had stepped into a new world where Lance was my guide and teacher. He was gentle and sympathetic. He understood my ignorance, and something told me that he knew I was thinking of that occasion when I had seen Elvira in his bedroom. He was determined to make me share his pleasure in our relationship, but at the same time he respected my virginity and understood that I must come to understanding gradually.

Finally he slept. But I did not. I lay awake thinking of all the young brides who had come to this room . . . all dead and gone now . . . but it seemed as though their spirits lingered on. I seemed to hear voices in the rustle of the curtains and the faint moaning of the wind in the trees. Then I thought, Oh, Dickon, it should have been you. It would have sealed our love forever.

The curtains had been drawn back and there was a full moon. It shone into the room through the mullioned windows, making shifting patterns on the wall from the swaying branches of the trees outside. Lance lay on his back. I could see his face clearly in the moonlight—the well-chiseled features and fine bones, the Roman nose, the high forehead and the hair which grew back thick and wavy. As I watched him the moonlight touched his face and in the shifting pattern his face seemed to change. I could believe he was an old man now . . . the shadows did that to him. I thought, He may look like that in thirty years' time. It made him seem vulnerable, and suddenly I felt how very dear he was to me.

The moonlight shifted—he was young and handsome again.

I must love him, I told myself. I must cease to think of Dickon. Even if he comes back, we shall be two different people. Lance is my husband. I must remember that . . . always.

So I continued to lie sleepless in the big four-poster bed, my husband beside me.

So I became Lady Clavering, and the days that followed were full of new experiences. Lance was always the tender lover, at ease in every situation, and his exquisite manners were in evidence in the bedchamber as everywhere else. He was sweeping my fears aside; he tutored me in the arts of love, as he had in those of living when we were on the road from York together. I could see that life with him would always be lived graciously. Our intimacy had brought us very close. I do love him, I assured myself. I was certainly proud of him; he was charming, easygoing and distinguished in company.

Jeanne's delight increased with every day. Unmarried herself, yet she was knowledgeable in the ways of men and women. He was the beautiful man; as far as she was concerned, we were worthy of each other.

Everyone around us was content.

My grandmother Priscilla was, I think, particularly so. She said I must read the family journals and contribute to them myself.

"You will see how it was with your mother," she said. "She was a stormy girl from the beginning. She was far too beautiful. Your character is quite different from hers. You had a harsh beginning, my child—I think it developed you in a certain way. But you have been happy since Damaris brought you home."

"Damaris did so much for me. I shall never forget it."

"You did a great deal for her, my dear," said my grandmother.

On the day Lance and I were to leave for London I received a letter from Aimée. Over the last three years I had had about two or three letters. They had come at Christmastime.

I did know that there had been a close watch on Hessenfield Castle after the flight of the Pretender when the Jacobites were being rounded up and brought to trial. Lord Hessenfield had been questioned and suspected. His fate had been undecided for some time, and then, no doubt because of his disability, he had been left in peace.

My dear sister, [wrote Aimée]
Everything has changed at the Castle. Our dear uncle has passed away. You can guess what an upheaval there has been, and now we have a new lord. Alas, I am unwelcome here. He is the son of one of our uncles, a younger brother of dear Lord Hessenfield, whose brothers were all executed—so the title and estates have gone to the nephew.

The fact is I cannot stay here. I feel my life is in ruins. I cannot go back to France. My mother would not want me. She is settled in with her new family. She has stepchildren. No, I could not face that. I thank God—and our father—that I am not in need of money. But I feel bereft—alone—without family or friends. I often think of my little sister—the only relation I have here. Dear Clarissa, may I come and stay with you—just for a little while, until I know what I can do?

Jeanne came in while I was reading the letter.

"What is it, *chérie?*" she asked. "You look a little *distrait.*"

"I've had a letter from my sister."

Jeanne frowned. "So?" she murmured.

"She wants to come and stay with me for a while."

"But you are just married. You want to be alone with your 'usband."

"She is my half sister, Jeanne."

"Why now . . . she want to come?"

"A great deal has happened up there. My uncle has died and a nephew has the title and the castle now. There are changes, evidently, and they have made it clear that Aimée is not wanted there. There will be plenty of room in the London house and in the country. Of course she must come. I daresay she will marry if she comes to London. She wouldn't have many opportunities for meeting people up there. They were all intent on one thing—putting James on the throne."

Jeanne clicked her tongue. "Wasting time in silly plots when they might be marrying and having dear little babies!"

I laughed. "I shall tell Lance and see what he feels about it," I said.

I knew in advance what he would say. "Of course your sister must come."

So I wrote and told her she would be welcome to arrive at any time.

Lance and I traveled to London about a week after our wedding day. I was enchanted by London. In the first place, I loved Lance's town house, with its big windows which let in the maximum of light and its large, uncluttered rooms. After Enderby it seemed airy and welcoming—a happy house.

My delight in everything was a source of pleasure to Lance. He devoted himself to me entirely. He wanted to show me London, that city of contrasts, such a place as I had never dreamed existed, having only before savored brief visits. I was amazed at the wealth and splendor which I saw side by side with poverty and squalor. I wanted to give to every beggar I saw, and whenever a flower girl crossed my path I would buy her entire basketful. Flower sellers always brought back such poignant memories.

We went often to the theaters. There was one in Drury Lane and that one called the New Theatre, in Portugal Street; there was a theater and opera house in Haymarket. Lance was fond of the opera and was determined that I should also appreciate its delights. I found those days immensely exciting, full of new experiences as they were.

We would take our seats among those reserved for the quality, and I would often find the audience more entertaining than the play. After the first act, one of the theater employees would come round to take the money for the seats, which was a signal for many to sneak out—not, as they would imply, because they were disgusted with the play but because they did not want to pay for their seats. Lance said that many people made a habit of coming to first acts and then going to the coffeehouses, where they would discuss the play with a show of knowledge, and they called themselves patrons of the theater.

Up in the top gallery were the footmen who came with their masters and mistresses to the theater, where they had free seats, and oddly enough they were often the most vociferous among the audience, expressing their pleasure or, more often, their disgust.

"Although they have not paid for their seats," Lance pointed out, "they believe they have a right to disdain the play, which shows that the more people are given, the more they take as their natural right. I wonder they don't demand the price of the seat which they haven't paid for."

Lance was interested in people, but his attitude toward them was lighthearted and even cynical. He looked for something beyond the façade, and I was sure he was often right in his judgment. When I pitied some poor beggar in the streets he would suggest that the woebegone look was part of an act.

"I once knew a man," he told me, "who was a great figure in the night life of London. He'd wager a thousand pounds and think nothing of it. He lived in style in St. James'. I saw him one day disguised so that I scarcely recognized him. He was waylaying fine ladies as they came out of their houses and telling such a pitiful tale that there was scarcely one of them who didn't dip into her purse and give the plausible rogue some money. I had a game with him. I pretended not to recognize him and gave him five pounds on condition that when he was able to he should repay me threefold. 'May Gawd bless you, sir,' he said. He had a good line of talk, and although by night he spoke in a highly cultured fashion, the jargon of the streets came readily to his tongue. 'That I will right gladly, noble sir,' he said. 'I never forget them that hoffers a poor beggar what's in need.'" Lance laughed at the memory. "It was a fortnight later when I saw him in the Thatched House coffeehouse in St. James'. I said, 'Hello, you old rogue, you owe me fifteen pounds.' He was startled, but when I told him I had recognized him in the ragged beggarman, he was overcome with mirth. He paid out the fifteen pounds and made me swear to tell no one of his little subterfuge."

"I am sure his was an isolated case," I said.

"That may be. But how can you say how many men-about-town are hiding behind their rags and tatters? How many ladies of quality are telling their doleful tales to passersby? I always remember him when I see him. It teaches you something."

"It teaches me that he couldn't have been very successful at the gaming tables if he had to resort to such methods. Oh, yes, it teaches me that gambling is a foolish way to lose one's money."

"*Touché*," he said. "I wouldn't have told you this tale if I had known it would bring us round to this. As a matter of fact, he was fairly lucky at the tables. I think he did the begging out of a spirit of mischief."

After that, I must admit, I looked closely at the beggars and was less generous.

I had a dressmaker who came to the house and made a whole new wardrobe for me. The clothes I had worn at Enderby were scarcely suitable for London life. All the latest fashions, I discovered, came from France—a fact which delighted Jeanne. If it had been worn at Versailles, that was its accolade. My dressmaker would bring large dolls sent from her associate in Paris, and these dolls would be dressed in the latest fashions, all made in exact detail. There would be tight-fitting bodices with sleeves to the elbow, which ended in the most elaborate frills. Big collars and fichus were very much in vogue. Panniers were worn, and the widened skirts accentuated the narrowness of the waist. There was a new kind of gown called a *sacque*, and although the bodice was tight-fitting, there was a fullness at the back which I thought most becoming. The dresses were made of silks and satins, brocades and velvet. "The material is of the utmost importance," declared Alison, the dressmaker, with such seriousness that she might have been discussing the Treaty of Utrecht.

It was all very exciting and amusing. Then there were the cosmetics. I must be patched and powdered like every other lady of fashion. Jeanne quickly adapted herself to the art, as she had done with that of hairdressing.

"I am not having one of these fancy hairdressers doing your hair, milady," she announced firmly.

I was quite ready to leave myself in the capable hands of Jeanne and Alison.

I said to Lance, "I shall soon be as elegant as you are."

It must have been about a month after I had received that first letter from Aimée that I had another.

My dear sister, [she wrote]
A wonderful thing has happened to me. I am to be married. Just as I was thinking myself all alone and forlorn—it was a day after I wrote to you before—I met Joseph. He lives close by Hessenfield Castle in a fine old house. Is it not strange that we did not meet before? He was not one for the social life . . . until we met. We like each other . . . we meet again . . . and again, and then to my surprise he said, "Marry me!" Well, I am amazed, but after a while I say yes. He is a little older than I am . . . well, thirty years, to be truthful. But I do not notice. . . . I am so happy. Dear little sister, you must come and see us. You will one day, eh? I have a fine house and am mistress of it. It makes me feel happy to be wanted, for I was not at Hessenfield, and even dear Uncle Paul was never completely warm toward me. He was a most conventional man and I think he did not like the irregularity of our

160

births. But our father, being as he was, how could it have been otherwise?

I thank you for your warm invitation. It has made me so happy. One day we shall meet again . . .

I wrote back to say how delighted I was that she had found happiness with Joseph. I could see her as the mistress of some stately home with an elderly husband who adored her.

The summer days flew past, and I was too young and inexperienced not to believe that they would go on like that forever.

I could not have had a better companion than Lance. He was completely at home in London—far more so, I was to realize, than he could ever be in the country. He loved the coffeehouse talk, and we would go out, dressed more simply than usual so that we could mingle more easily. The Calf's Head, the Apollo, the October, the Mughouse—I was taken to them all. We would sit listening to the talk, which was clever and even witty, and Lance often joined in.

"The coffeehouse is one of the best things that has happened to London," he declared.

After the theater we would have supper in one of the restaurants which were springing up all over the town. We went to Pontac's or Locket's, which were two of the most exclusive, but sometimes we went to the less elegant ones— just for the adventure of it, Lance said. There were, for instance, the Salutation, in Newgate Street, and the Mitre, in Fleet Street.

The days and nights were filled with new experiences and I felt that marriage was a wonderful experience. I could now respond to Lance's passion, which delighted him. I was no longer the shrinking and reluctant maiden, and although I could not be said to be worldly, I was growing into a full-blooded woman.

Though the streets could be dangerous at night and pickpockets—and worse—lurked in the shadows, I always felt safe with Lance. His carriage, with its stalwart driver and footman, would always be waiting for us.

"They have, thank God, got rid of the Mohocks," Lance commented. "A scandalous club, that was . . . dedicated to making mischief. No one was safe from them. They'd run a sword through a sedan, and they once rolled women down Snowhill in hogsheads. It is a few years since they were disbanded, but memories of them linger on. Although the streets are still a danger, they are better for the removal of those men."

We were entertained a great deal. Lance had many friends in fashionable London. I visited gracious houses with him and we gave dinner parties. There was no anxiety for me, for arrangements were taken care of by an adequate staff; my own concern was that I should be a credit to Lance.

I was welcomed into society. I was known as a member of the Eversleigh family and Lance was a favorite everywhere. We did not go to court, though Lance supposed we should have to at some time.

"It's incredibly dull now," he said. "Those Germanic customs are not appreciated here. The King is dull and heavy, and there is no Queen . . . only those grasping mistresses, who, I believe, are making fortunes for themselves out of selling favors. George is criticized for putting his poor wife, Sophia Dorothea, away—they say she is more or less a prisoner—and all because he suspected her of being unfaithful with Königsmarck. And if she were, she was only following in the footsteps of her husband."

The London life absorbed me. I was a little disappointed when Lance said it would be necessary for us to go to his estates in the country for a little while.

Clavering Hall had been the house of the family for two hundred years, and I was back again in the kind of house I knew so well from Eversleigh and Enderby. After the airy comfort of the modern house in Albemarle Street I found the Hall a little oppressive. Like all such houses, it seemed to carry with it an aura of the past, as though those who had lived there before lingered on in spirit, endowing the place with their joys and sorrows—mostly sorrows.

Any house in which Lance lived could not be gloomy. There were elegant touches in curtains, carpets and such articles; but the court cupboards, the four-poster beds, and large refectory tables were relics of a bygone age.

The hall, of course, was the center of the house, with the east and west wings on either side, and there were two fine staircases, with handrails framed into the newels. The woodwork was exquisite, the doors intricately carved and the fireplaces, which were very fine indeed, were carved with scenes from the Bible. There were rich tapestries on the walls in beautifully blended colors. It was a gracious, lovely house and Lance was proud of it.

He had a large estate, which demanded a great deal of

attention, but he had several people who did the necessary work under a most efficient manager. That suited Lance, who, I discovered, did not care to do one thing for too long a time. He could be enthusiastic about the estate for a few days, and then, when some weeks had passed, it began to pall.

The house was frequently full of guests from the neighborhood; they came to dine and, I discovered, play games of chance.

I was dismayed one night after dinner when I, with the ladies, had left the table and we had chatted together, to rejoin the men and find them preparing to sit down and play with the cards.

I saw the excitement in Lance's eyes and I realized then that when the gambling fever was upon him he was like a different man. Before, I had always been aware of his tender attention at gatherings like this. He always looked after me, which was what I had wanted when I was first introduced to his friends. He would give me a detailed description of the people we were meeting—and always amusing—telling me their likes and dislikes, warning me of their foibles, making it easy for me to be a success in society. I had always been aware of that special care and had been grateful for it. Now I realized that he had forgotten me. I saw that gleam in his eyes which I was to see many times in the years ahead.

The play began. Those who did not join in were left to amuse themselves. Quite a number of the women did join, and I noticed that they appeared to play with the same feverish intensity as the men.

When all those who did not wish to play had left, I retired to my bedroom. Lance went on playing with those who had gone to the tables. I lay in bed waiting for him to come up. It was past three o'clock when he did.

He came to the bed and looked down at me.

"Still awake?" he asked. "You should be fast asleep by now."

"So should you," I said.

He bent over and kissed me. "A good night's play," he said. "I won two hundred pounds."

"You might have lost it," I said, aghast.

"What a dismal outlook! I win two hundred and you talk of losses. Never mind. I'll buy you a new dress when we get back to London."

"I have enough new dresses."

"Oh, come, a woman can always do with another. You sound a ittle piqued, sweetheart. Is it because I left you alone so long?"

I said, "I wish you didn't love gambling so much."

"Sweet of you," he said lightly, "to care so much for what I do."

"One day—" I began.

"Sufficient unto the day is the evil thereof," he quoted. "That's a good motto. It's one of mine. You should make it one of yours, Clarissa. There. I'm back now. I'll be with you in a moment."

I lay uneasy until he came. He slipped into bed beside me and took me into his arms.

"Let me kiss away the frowns," he said. "Remember, I'm the one you love ... full of imperfections ... but you love me all the same."

He made such ardent love to me that I forgot I had been left alone. In my heart I knew it was something I must accept, but just then I preferred to forget.

The Bubble

Christmas came and Lance and I went to Enderby. Jeanne came with us, of course, and it was wonderful to be in the heart of the family again.

Damaris was delighted to see us, and I was touched by the earnest way in which she studied me to assure herself, I knew, that my marriage was happy. Jeremy was with her when she greeted us, and although his welcome was more restrained than hers, I knew it was sincere. Sabrina ran headlong at me and embraced my knees.

"You've come home," she cried. "Clarissa has come home. Are you going to stay now? I want to show you my new pony. He's called Gypsy because Grandpapa Leigh bought him from the Gypsies. He can gallop miles and miles and never gets tired like other ponies. Come and see him."

"Not now, darling," said Damaris. "There's plenty of time."

"Oh, now . . . *please*."

"Let me wash and change first, Sabrina," I said.

The same Sabrina, whose own affairs were of such immediacy that she could not conceive that anything else could be of the same importance.

She ran up to our room with us. It was that one where we had slept on the first night of our marriage, the room which had such memories for Damaris—as, having read her story, I now understood. Dear Damaris. I was closer to her than ever, now that I knew how she had suffered and how she had at last come to happiness through Jeremy and myself. It made a special bond between us. I knew I should never forget what we had meant to each other, and although now I had moved out of her care and had a life of my own, the bond was still strong.

"Can I stay with you here, Clarissa?" asked Sabrina. "It's a nicer room than mine." She laid her cheek lovingly against the damask bed curtains and looked pleadingly at me.

Lance said, "You can't sleep with Clarissa now. I'm here."

"Why not?"

"Because it is my place."

"You can have my bed."

"So kind of you," said Lance, "but do you know, I prefer this."

She sidled up to him. "It's nice," she said. "Nanny Curlew comes to tuck you in."

"A delight I shall have to forgo," said Lance.

She frowned at him but with no real animosity. She liked him; the only thing she had against him was that he had taken me away.

He picked her up and she kicked a little in remonstration. He put her outside the door and shut it on her. I heard her laughing as she ran along the corridor.

"There is one who will want her own way in life," he said. "And get quite a lot of it, I should imagine."

"She is a dear creature."

"A little spoilt, I fancy, except by the worthy Nanny Curlew."

Then he held me tightly against him, and I knew that he was thinking of the first night we had shared this room.

It was a happy Christmas. There were the relatives to visit, and the celebrations took place mainly at Eversleigh Court in the traditional manner. There were the decorations with holly and ivy and the ceremony of bringing in the Yule log, carols, the midnight service on Christmas Eve, kissing under mistletoe. Eating mince pies in the shape of coffins, which were supposed to represent the manger at Bethlehem. Sabrina loved giving Christmas boxes on the day after Christmas, when everyone who had rendered a service to the household appeared to collect what he or she called "the box"—which was in fact a gift of money. Great-grandfather Carleton grumbled and said that he was the one who did the tradesmen a service by buying their goods, and why he should be expected to reward their servants he could not imagine. They should be giving him a Christmas box.

"Nonsense," said Great-grandmother Arabella. "You know you would never stop the Christmas boxes."

"Poor Great-grandpapa," put in Sabrina. "Nobody gives him a Christmas box."

Then she came up with a bright new penny and thrust it into his hand. And the old man, who was really very sentimental, said it was the best Christmas box he could ever have had, and he would carry it with him for the rest of his days and have it buried with him in his coffin.

This greatly intrigued Sabrina and spoilt her generous gesture, for she was clearly looking forward to seeing the penny placed in Great-grandfather's coffin.

"Don't grumble so, Carleton," said Arabella. "I declare, you'd be a thorough wet blanket if I let you."

Nothing changed at Eversleigh, it seemed. One Christmas was very like another; but of course there was really change taking place all the time. Sabrina was now five years old and Great-grandfather Carleton was more quickly out of breath when he went walking in the gardens; there was more white in Arabella's hair, and it was beginning to show in Priscilla's. I was a married woman of some months' standing. Yes, time was moving on.

When we went back to London, Lance was caught up in the enthusiasm which was sweeping through the city. He came in one day in a fever of excitement.

It was late afternoon, I remember, of a cold January day. There was a north wind blowing and it had started to snow. In the drawing room a great fire was burning and I was seated close to it when he burst into the room.

He threw off his heavy coat and came close to the fire. He lifted me up and held me against him, laughing up at me.

"We're going to be rich . . . richer than you've dreamed," he said. "Gad, this is the greatest chance that ever came to anyone."

Little shivers of alarm went through me. I was always apprehensive about Lance's gambling; he knew this and kept much of his activity in the field from me. He would occasionally report a fantastic win, but whenever he told me, I wondered what enormous losses had gone before.

"Put me down, Lance," I said. "And if this is another gamble . . ."

"It is the greatest gamble that ever was."

"Oh, no, Lance!" He had set me down and I drew away from him, looking steadily into his face.

"Oh, yes, Clarissa," he said, laughing, and his eyes were bright with anticipation. "Wait till you hear before you condemn," he went on. "No . . . it is not horses . . . It is not the tables. . . . It's a government venture, you might say."

"I am always suspicious of attempts to make money by gambling."

"This is different. Wait till you hear. I've gone into it

thoroughly. I know exactly what is happening. Let me explain and you will see how safe it is. The big trading company calling itself the South Sea Company has proposed to the House of Commons that they purchase the irredeemable annuities which had been granted in the reigns of William and Mary and Anne and amalgamate all the public funds together in one stock so as to become the only public creditor. Do you follow me?"

"No," I said.

"Never mind. You will. The Bank of England has entered into the bargaining and the two began to outbid each other. Now an offer has been accepted on the part of the South Sea Company to provide a sum of seven and a half million in order to buy up the annuities. The government annuitants are rushing to exchange their stock for that of the South Sea Company. Already two-thirds of them have done so. There will obviously be enormous dividends. It's a way of getting rich in the shortest possible time. We have to get into this quickly, Clarissa."

"Won't hundreds of people be saying that?"

"Of course they will. It's all so obvious. There will be a rush to get rich quickly. We mustn't be left out. Already the fifty-pound shares are worth one hundred."

"It seems imcomprehensible to me. How can they be worth so much?"

"It's the prospects, my dear. They are saying there will be a dividend of fifty percent. The thing is to buy cheaply and sell dear."

"Surely everyone will have that idea?"

"But the thing is to know the right moment to buy and the right to sell."

"And how can anyone be sure of that?"

He put his arms round me and hugged me tightly. "My dear, cautious Clarissa, you may trust your old Lancelot."

I was silent, disturbed as I always was by his gambling exploits.

"But suppose it shouldn't work out as you think?"

"My dear, don't you think I shall know the right time to sell?"

"I would rather not have anything to do with such ventures."

"What! And go on this way all our lives!"

"It's a very comfortable way."

"And see all those around us making fortunes!"

"If some are making them, you can be sure some are losing them."

"Leave it to me, my dearest."

"Lance . . . are you going to invest heavily in this South Seas Company?"

"Unless one does, there seems little point in it. And, Clarissa, I thought you would wish to share in it."

"I?"

"Why not? You're a woman of substance."

"I am not a gambler. I like things as they are. Besides, I couldn't touch my shares and things which Leigh manages for me."

"Perhaps not. But there is the money your father left you."

"Oh, no. I don't think I would touch that."

He shrugged his shoulders and laughed at me. But he said no more about the matter. He went out soon afterward and I did not see him for the rest of the day. We were dining alone that evening and during the meal he seemed abstracted.

I said, "I believe you are still dreaming of the fortune you are going to make out of this South Sea affair."

"It's going to stagger you, Clarissa."

"I do hope you have not invested a great deal."

"Enough to make me rich, very rich."

I shrugged my shoulders. "We have enough of everything. We can have what we want in reason. I cannot see why we want to clamor so desperately for more."

"You wait, Clarissa, you are going to be as thrilled as I am when you see the fortune which will be ours."

When we were in bed that night I sensed that he was restless. He could not sleep, nor could I.

Suddenly I felt his hand grasping mine.

"Are you awake, Clarissa?" he said.

"Yes. And I know you are. Oh, Lance, I don't like this thing. I have an uneasy feeling . . ."

"You think it's a gamble. It is not. It's a certainty."

"It doesn't make sense to me. Why should something one buys one day be suddenly worth a lot more the next? It hasn't changed its value, has it?"

"It is changed in value because so many people want it."

"They want it because they believe it will make them rich overnight."

"So it will."

"But surely they can't *all* become so rich."

"Oh, the shares will settle in time. That's what makes it

169

wise to buy now. But it is the dividends the money will bring in which make it such an excellent venture. Fifty percent. Just imagine that."

"I don't understand it and I don't believe it's true."

"You disbeliever!" He held me tightly and began to caress me. He told me how much he loved me and what a difference I had made to his life; how he had adored me from the time we had journeyed to York together; how jealous he had been of poor Dickon and how happy he was because he was going to spend the rest of his life with me.

Lance would always arouse a response in me. He was tender and gallant and fiercely passionate at the same time. I was happy, I told him. I wanted to please him for as long as we both should live.

I whispered an apology to Dickon as I invariably did at such moments. My encounter with him still stood out in my memory as something especially beautiful, but it was growing more and more like a dream as time passed, and it had more than a touch of unreality about it.

At length Lance whispered to me, "Clarissa, dearest, I couldn't leave you out of the excitement. You had to be in it. I wanted you to share . . ."

My heart started to beat more quickly. "What?" I asked.

"I have bought for you. You had to be in it. Everyone who can must be in it."

"What are you telling me?"

"That I have arranged for five thousand pounds of your Hessenfield inheritance to be put into the South Sea Company."

"You have what?" I drew away from him, but he held me firmly and began kissing my face and throat.

"I spoke to Grendall about it," he said. Grendall was the solicitor who managed the Hessenfield inheritance. "He wanted your approval, but as I am your husband he accepted mine. I had to do it for you, Clarissa."

"Five thousand pounds," I stammered. "Oh—Lance, how could you!"

"How could I not? Could I stand by and see everyone else making a fortune and my little Clarissa being left out!"

For a few moments I was speechless. It was half the money which my father had left me. I was furiously angry—first, because I hated this gambling, which offered him more excitement than I could. This must be so, because he could forget me when the fever was on him. And second, because he had dared act without consulting me.

He tried to soothe me, holding my quivering body against his, tenderly, passionately. I pulled away from him and sat up.

"How dared you!" I cried. "You cannot resist this urge to gamble. If you must risk money in future, confine yourself to what is yours to risk."

"Clarissa, my darling, you are really angry, aren't you? Wait until you see what this will bring you."

"I have no intention of frittering away my fortune, and you have no right to treat me as though you own me and all my possessions."

"I love you. I only wanted to do what was best for you."

I jumped out of bed. I wanted to escape from him. I did not want to be soothed and petted until my emotions were aroused and I was ready to forgive him and forget the matter. I felt it was important that he should understand how I felt. He must realize how deeply I resented his action.

He was leaning on his elbow, looking at me with that indulgence I knew so well, refusing to accept that I was serious in my condemnation of him, trying to shrug off this matter as though it were of no importance. It was very important to me.

"You must not think that you are going to placate me with a few soft words," I said.

"Come back to bed and talk reasonably. You'll catch cold standing there."

"I shall not come back to bed," I said. "I want to think what I shall do. I want to be alone."

I went toward the powder closet, which was roomy enough to hold a small couch.

"You're surely not going to sleep in there?" cried Lance.

"I told you I want to be alone."

"It's very cold on that couch and desperately uncomfortable."

I ignored him and went into the powder closet. I was trembling but not with cold.

Almost immediately he was there beside me. He put his arms about me. "If you insist on sleeping alone," he said, "there is only one course open to me . . . or two, rather. I must either offer you the bed and take the couch myself or use the rights of a husband and carry you back to bed. Which shall it be, Clarissa? Please choose the second alternative for I shall have a very uncomfortable night on that couch."

He began to laugh, and in spite of everything, I found

myself laughing also. It was typical of him to introduce a ridiculous note into a serious situation.

He had picked me up and carried me to the bed. I was momentarily reminded of that first night of our wedding when he had carried me thus. Then I had shivered with apprehension, now it was with resentful anger.

We lay in the bed together. He put his arm about me. I knew that he was trying to arouse desire in me; the act of love would make everything right between us. He always thought that was so. It was the same when he came home after a night of gambling. But I was not so easily to be won over this time.

"Don't try your blandishments, Lance," I said.

"All right," he answered. "I promise, no blandishments. But just tell me you are not angry with me anymore."

"But I am," I said. "I am very angry. I want to think about it."

I moved away from him to the edge of the bed.

"Good night," I said firmly.

He sighed. "Good night, my dearest," he said. "Tomorrow it will seem so different."

I did not answer. He respected my desire to be left alone and we lay on either sides of the bed.

I was trying to decide what I should do. That he had dared touch my money angered me. He would not be able to play such tricks with the fortune my mother had left, because he would have to deal with Leigh first, and I was sure Leigh would never allow it.

I knew that many husbands would have seized their wives' fortunes. Lance had always behaved as though my money was of no importance to him. He had never shown a great interest in it—so I had thought. Yet he had dared to go to Grendall's and use it to buy stock in my name in the South Sea Company.

I pretended to be asleep as I lay there planning what I would do. It was the first time I had been really angry with Lance. True, I had resented those occasions when he disappeared for hours at the gaming tables, deserting me, so I told myself in hurt pride, for the love of the game, but I had always forgotten that resentment when he had come back and charmed me, as he knew so well how to do. This was quite different.

I began to wonder whether he had married me for my money. He must have been fond of Elvira Vernon—but he had not intended to marry her. Why not? Presumably she did not have a fortune. This was not fair. He had explained to me about Elvira, and I was not now the simpleton I had been at the time of that discovery. I knew that men had love affairs before they settled down, and at least I had no cause to suspect Lance of infidelity . . . as yet.

Finally I dozed, and slept so late that he was gone from beside me when I awakened.

I had made up my mind. I was going to show him that I was an individual and had no intention of allowing anyone to manage my affairs—even the most charming of husbands.

I took a sedan to Grendall's in Cornhill, where I was shown into Mr. Grendall's office immediately.

He greeted me warmly and I told him the purpose of my visit. My husband had wrongfully assumed that I wanted to invest in the South Sea Company. This was not the case. I wished to cancel the order he had given.

Mr. Grendall looked dismayed. "But, Lady Clavering," he said, "the shares have already been bought. In these transactions it is always necessary to act with the maximum speed. They were bought two days ago."

Two days ago! So he had not told me immediately. I felt my anger rising.

"Then I wish them to be sold without delay," I said. "You look astonished. Is that impossible?"

"By no means. People are clamoring for these shares. But, Lady Clavering, the prospects are excellent."

"So I have heard, and there will be immense dividends. I am not interested. I want these shares sold at once."

"At whatever the market price?"

"At whatever the market price," I repeated.

"Your orders shall be carried out. I will let you know what price we obtained as soon as the transaction is through."

"Thank you, Mr. Grendall," I said. "And I should be glad in future if you will take orders for such transactions only from me in person. That is what Sir Lance and I both wish."

"I understand, Lady Clavering."

I was bowed out to my chair.

Lance was in when I returned. He was clearly waiting for me.

"Clarissa, I was worried about you. Where have you been?"

"I have been to Cornhill to see Mr. Grendall," I said.

"Ah." He was smiling at me.

"I have told him to sell the shares you bought with my money."

"To sell! But the market is rising."

"I have told him to sell and that all such transactions will in future come through me and me only."

I suppose any other man but Lance would have been furious with me. Not so Lance. He looked at me in astonishment for a moment and then laughed. There was no doubting the admiration in his eyes.

"Clarissa," he said, "my splendid Clarissa. I am forgiven, am I not?"

I could not resist him so I said I supposed he was.

"It was arrogant of me. It was wrong. It was foolish. But, believe me, I was only thinking of the pleasure I should have in confronting you with the fact that you had become a richer woman."

"I am quite content with what I have."

"The world's phenomenon," he said, "a contented woman!"

"Oh, Lance," I pleaded, "give up all this gambling. What is the purpose of it? We have enough. Why take risks in the hope of getting more?"

"It's not exactly money," he said seriously. "It's the fun of it . . . the excitement. I'll never get you to understand. However, my sweet Clarissa, you have taught me a lesson. I promise I will never be so foolish again. But I am forgiven my sins now. That's so, isn't it?"

"Of course, and I know you were trying to do what you thought was best for me."

We were lovers again.

It was the following day when Mr. Grendall sent a messenger to me. He had sold my shares in the South Sea Company. They had been bought at a hundred pounds and sold for a thousand. Thus my five thousand had become fifty thousand.

I had become a very rich woman overnight.

I shall never forget the months that followed. There was tension and excitement in the streets of London as the price of South Sea stock rose. Lance never said "I told you so" exactly, but he did point out how wealthy I might have been if I had not sold out.

He himself had put all the money he could raise into the company. Sometimes he was on the verge of selling, but he could never bring himself to do so. He always felt there would be another rise the following day.

Everyone was talking about the South Sea wonder. Sir Robert Walpole condemned the scheme from the start and warned the public about overinvesting. It turned out, however, that he himself had bought a number of shares, but, as I had, he had sold out at a big profit. The Prince of Wales had also invested and sold advantageously. There was euphoria throughout the country. Everyone who could scrape together a few pounds was clamoring for shares.

"Think how much you would have to pay for those shares which you bought at a hundred," Lance reminded me.

"I don't need to think, as I have no intention of buying more."

"You're throwing away a fortune."

"On the contrary, I have made one."

"But, my dear Clarissa, think how much richer you would have been if you had left the shares in."

"On paper," I reminded him. "I have really done very well."

"Thanks to what you thought of as my wickedness in the first place."

I agreed that this was so. "But," I said firmly, "my money remains where it is."

"Is that final?" asked Lance pleadingly. He had nothing left with which to gamble himself and was itching to get his hands on my money, I knew.

"Final," I replied with emphasis.

He would take me to the coffeehouses, which were full of people talking of the wonder of the South Sea Company; they discussed their plans for spending their newly acquired wealth. Even the sellers of spiced gingerbread and watercress talked of the wonders of the times to come when everybody would be rich.

All through the summer the fervor persisted, and always I refused to be drawn into it.

Then, as suddenly as dreams of prosperity had come, they began to disappear. It was a hot August, I remember. We should have been in the country, but Lance could not tear himself away from the excitement of London. Each day he studied the prices and calculated how rich his shares in the South Sea Company had made him.

He came into the drawing room where I was sitting reading and there was a look of intense excitement on his face.

I looked up and asked what had happened.

He threw himself into an armchair and said, "The stock is down to eight hundred and fifty."

"Eight hundred and fifty!" I repeated. I had taken little interest in the market and had deliberately refused to listen, but I did know that I had sold out at a thousand.

"I can't understand it," went on Lance. "It's all happened in a day. It's because of the spurious companies which have been springing up . . . trying to get in on the reputation of the South Sea Company. Some of them have been proved to be false and people are panicking. It'll pass."

But it did not pass. The next day the shares were down to eight hundred and twenty, and within the next two days to seven hundred.

The mood of the streets had changed. There were gloomy faces in the coffeehouses; the street merchants were looking anxious and the traders chattered in hushed voices.

"It'll pass," said Lance. "It's just a momentary panic. Then they'll shoot up higher than ever. People are beginning to sell. When the shares go up they'll have to pay higher to get them back."

By mid-September the shares had tumbled to one hundred and fifty. I marveled that what I had sold for a thousand would only bring in one hundred and fifty now. I shuddered to think how quickly fortunes could be made and lost.

Even Lance was uneasy now. On the last day of September the shares had dropped below a hundred. I remember that day so well. I had never seen him so downcast before.

I ran to him in consternation when he came in from the city.

"Why, Lance," I cried, "what has happened?"

He said, "Frank Welling has killed himself."

I knew Frank Welling. He was one of the first of Lance's friends I had met after my marriage—a wealthy man, with estates in the country and a magnificent town house in St. James' Street. I knew that he had been a gambling friend of Lance's and they often went to clubs together.

"He shot himself," said Lance. "He lost everything."

"How dreadful for his family."

"I'm afraid there will be others like him."

I was so passionately angry. Why could they not resist the desire to gamble! They knew the risk involved. How could they be so foolhardy!

I thought of Frank Welling's wife, and there were three children, I remembered. What tragedy had come to their lives which before had been so comfortable, and all because of an irresistible desire to grow rich quickly and take a gamble on it.

Frank Welling's case was one of many. Those excited people who had thronged the coffeehouses now assembled there to discuss the tragedy which had befallen them. Everyone was talking about what they called the South Sea Bubble.

Very few people had profited from that affair—only such people like Robert Walpole and the Prince of Wales, who had foreseen disaster, and those, like myself, who had no desire to gamble.

I was afraid for Lance, for I knew he must have lost heavily. He had. Fortunately the estate in the country was intact. I had been afraid that he might try to raise money on that. I believe he had been contemplating doing so when he realized how things were going. He still would have the town house, but everything else was reduced to a fraction of what it had been before.

For a few days he was very despondent indeed, but after that his spirits rose. I believed he was assuring himself that he would soon win back his losses. After a few days he was saying that it was all part of the gamble. He had lost this time but would win the next.

"Rather a big gamble and rather a lot to lose," I reminded him.

He conceded that. "You, dear Clarissa, the clever one."

"If it is clever to know how foolish it is to risk what you have in the hope of getting more, then I am indeed clever."

"So severe," he said, kissing the tip of my nose.

"Oh, Lance," I answered, "how I wish you did not feel this urge to gamble. I wish . . ."

"You wish I were different."

"Only in this respect."

He looked at me pensively and said, "It is a mistake to try to change people, Clarissa. I learned that long ago. So you have to accept me as I am . . . and, my dear Clarissa, please don't let my follies make any difference to that."

"I expect I have foibles."

"Adorable ones," he told me.

Then he held me to him and whispered, "One of us came very well out of this sorry business. My own clever Clarissa."

The Tragedy on the Ice

The effects of the South Sea Bubble went rumbling on through that year. There were many sad stories and countless suicides. A subdued air fell over the city. Cynical cartoons appeared. There was one, I remember, with Folly as the charioteer of Fortune which depicted a carriage drawn by foxes with the faces of agents for the company, and the devil was in the sky laughing and blowing soap bubbles.

Nobody talked now of getting rich quickly; instead, it was a matter of speedily reaching the reverse state.

When Lance reckoned up his losses, it was a very depressing time. He decided he would have to sell some of the land in the country merely to keep going. I might offer to help, but I did not want to do this. I think I must have had something of the reformer in me at that time, because I was determined he should learn his lesson. He must realize the folly of this incessant gambling.

We went down to the country after that. It was a relief to get away from London, but even in the country there were dismal stories of people who were facing ruin. It was impossible to escape from the disaster of the South Sea Bubble.

I think Lance was a little penitent. It was some time since he had been to the London gambling clubs, and when we arrived in the country, there were none of those gatherings the purpose of which was to play cards as quickly as possible. People were just not in the mood for it—nor now had most of them the means.

Lance had lost a fortune, but he had done so with a certain amount of cheerfulness and quickly began to think of what had happened as the luck of the game. "It could have gone the other way," he said. "Suppose I had sold just before the fall, as I might well have done. Think what I should have now."

"But you did not," I pointed out in exasperation.

"No. But I might easily have."

I knew that he had not learned one little lesson from what had happened.

At the end of October a letter arrived from Aimée. This was a real cry for help.

Dear sister,

I am writing to you in the hope that, because of the close bond between us, you will lend me a helping hand. I am in desperate straits. My husband has died. It was the shock of the Bubble. We had both invested heavily, with what result you can guess. We lost almost everything. I shall have to sell up and get what I can for what is left to me. Who would have believed this terrible thing could have happened? Everyone was so sure. It has been the most terrible shock. I know I am not the only one to find myself in such a position, but I shall have to decide what I can do. I could go back to France perhaps, and it may be that this is what I shall have to do. But I am not sure . . . particularly as . . . It is no use holding back the facts. I am pregnant, Clarissa. We were so looking forward to having a child. Poor Ralph. He thought it was so wonderful . . . and now he is dead. It was a heart attack when he heard that we had lost almost everything. I am desperate, because I was persuaded to risk what I had from our father in this miserable South Sea Company.

I don't know what I shall do. I may have to work, though I don't know how, with a baby to care for. But, dear sister, until I can straighten out my affairs, would you be so good—as you once offered—to let me come to you? I promise you I will help in the house. I will try not to be a trouble to you. But do understand I would not ask you if I were not desperate.

If you say yes, I will come to you, say, in three months' time. It will take me that time to settle up here and salvage what I can. If you do say yes, you will make me as happy as it is possible for me to be in these circumstances.

I think I shall be ready to travel in January, and the birth would still be three months ahead, so I should still be able to make the journey. I shall eagerly await your reply, but I shall begin making preparations now, because, knowing you, dear sister, I am sure you will not refuse me in my need.

Your loving sister,
Aimée

I showed the letter to Lance and he immediately said, "Poor girl. She must be anxious. Write and tell her at once that she must come to us. She'll be company for you."

So I dispatched a letter immediately and wondered what difference Aimée's coming would make to our household.

Once more we spent Christmas at Enderby. Damaris told me that she thought the great-grandparents were getting too old to preside over the festivities; and she and Priscilla both thought that Enderby would be a good place to have them.

We did all the traditional things, and the days flew past. We returned to London on the sixth of January. Aimée was due at the end of the month.

She was catching the coach from York and traveling to London, and we would meet her at the coaching inn and take her to Albemarle Street from there. We had planned that we would stay in London until the birth of the child.

I was excited at the prospect of having my sister to live with us. Looking back, I realized I knew very little about her, and what I had discovered at Hessenfield had been submerged beneath the importance of my later meeting with Dickon.

We were waiting at the inn when the coach arrived, a lumbering vehicle, leather-covered and studded with nails, windows covered by leather curtains, with a rounded roof and an outside seat over the boot.

The guard alighted first, hampered by the blunderbuss which he carried as a protection against any highwayman encountered on the road, and the horn, which he would blow on passing through a town or village. Then came the postilion, who had been riding on the foremost of the three horses. He was dressed in a green coat laced with gold and wore a cocked hat.

The passengers finally emerged, and among them was Aimée. She looked different from the others, and even a long and uncomfortable journey on rough and muddy roads could not destroy her innate elegance. She wore a woolen cloak, navy blue in color, over a dress of the same material, and she had on one of the latest fashions in cocked hats, which was blue and trimmed with touches of red. The garments were plain but in the best of taste. I could never understand whether it was the manner in which her clothes were cut or the way she wore them which gave them distinction. She had made them herself, I discovered later, for she had been apprenticed to a couturiere in Paris when she was a young girl.

She embraced me with great affection and gratitude. She treated Lance with reserved respect and thanked him warmly in that accent with its foreign touch, and I was delighted to see that they immediately liked each other.

Our coach was waiting to take us the short distance through London to Albemarle Street, and during the journey Aimée talked a little of the impossibility of her life in the north and her losses in the South Sea Company.

"Here you have a fellow sufferer," I said.

"You too, Clarissa?" she said in some alarm.

I shook my head. "Poor Lance," I replied. "As a matter of fact, I did rather well out of it, unwittingly."

I told her what had happened.

She leaned toward me and pressed my hand. "I am so glad for you. How ironical that this South Sea business should profit you, who are not in the least interested in taking a chance."

"It did, precisely because I was not interested."

"How perverse of fate! And there were we . . ." She glanced at Lance . . . "trying so hard to make the most of what we thought was a God-given opportunity . . . and we came to grief."

"The fate of most gamblers," I said.

"You see," said Lance, "I am an inveterate gambler. Clarissa deplores it."

"My husband was the same . . . with what dire results. But for the South Sea Bubble I should not be in these straits now."

"We'll forget the Bubble," I said. "We have plenty of room—haven't we, Lance?—and we are delighted to have you stay as long as you wish. I am thrilled about the baby. What do you want, a boy or a girl? We shall have to see about engaging a midwife. We thought it would be better to stay in London until after the birth."

Aimée turned to me with misty eyes. "You are making me feel very welcome," she said gratefully.

Aimée's coming wrought a subtle change in the household. I suppose the birth of a child is such an important event that it must dominate all else. We engaged a midwife who was recommended by a friend of Lance and eventually she came to stay in the house. Aimée and I—before she became too large—shopped to buy clothes for the baby. We visited mercers in Cheapside, Ludgate Hill and Gracechurch Street. We took great delight in ribbons and laces, and I was determined that my little nephew or niece should have the best of everything.

Jeanne was good with her needle, but we hired a seamstress to come to the house. Those three months before the birth were taken up with plans for the baby.

I had thought Jeanne and Aimée would get on well together, being of the same nationality, able to prattle away in French. What could be better? I spoke French tolerably well, and now that Aimée was with us I spoke it more frequently than I had with Jeanne. Oddly enough, there was hostility between them.

"Jeanne is inclined to be insolent," said Aimée.

"No . . . no . . . never," I replied. "She has been with me so long, and she came in rather exceptional circumstances. Jeanne was a good friend to me when I needed a friend. She could not be insolent . . . just aware that there is a rather special bond between us."

Jeanne said, "The baby will come, and it is good to have a dear little baby in the house. But she is not the mistress here. Oh, no—that is you, my Lady Clarissa, and no one is going to forget that if I can help it!"

"I am sure Aimée doesn't forget it."

"She is deep, that one," was Jeanne's comment.

But of course she was delighted with the prospect of the baby.

Aimée and I would talk of it for hours, and then little scraps of information came out about her past. I gathered her mother had been a dominating character and Aimée had had to obey her in all things. She described the book shop on the Left Bank, and how her mother had worked hard to give her a good education. She talked about the streets of Paris, of sitting by the river and watching the boats go down the Seine; she made me, as she had before, feel the atmosphere of those streets, see the crowds of gesticulating people, the traders, the ladies going by in their coaches, and the perpetual mud.

At last, with the coming of April, Aimée's pains started, and after a few anxious hours her child was born.

It was a son. I went in almost as soon as he was born to see that red, wrinkled little creature, and I was overjoyed to learn that he was sound in every way, with a pair of lungs which he liked to air.

Aimée herself made a quick recovery, and we had a lot of fun selecting names. Eventually she settled on Jean-Louis. Now we had two additional members of the household.

It is amazing how quickly people's lives become changed by a baby. The entire household was devoted to Jean-Louis. He only had to appear and he was the center of attention. When his first tooth came we were all excited, and I sent messengers over to Eversleigh to tell them of this astounding event.

We vied with each other for the privilege of holding him, and when he smiled at us we were in transports of delight. Even the male members of the household were not immune to the baby's charm. And Jeffers, the coachman, who had been with Lance's family for the last fifty years—since he was a stable boy of eight—and was as sour as vinegar, would try hard not to smile when he saw the baby, and could not prevent himself from doing so.

As soon as summer came we went to Clavering Hall, for we thought that it would be good for the baby to be in the country. There he received the same adoration as he had in London. He was rather a solemn little baby.

"That," said Jeanne, "comes of having an old father."

I noticed that she watched Aimée with a certain suspicion. I wondered whether she was a little jealous of my sister on account of me, for Jeanne was inclined to be possessive. Jeanne was the sort of person who wanted someone to look after. She had cared for her mother and old grandmother and now she had turned to me. She was a born organizer, inclined to dominate if given a chance, but her motives were of the very best. Lance always said, "Jeanne was born to serve." I suppose it was only natural that she should dislike Aimée, who had come into our household and, largely because of Jean-Louis, seemed to dominate it.

Jeanne repeated her assertion that Aimée behaved as though she were the mistress of the house.

"Oh, Jeanne," I said, "you see trouble where there is none."

"Do not be too sure." Then she leaned toward me and said, "She is French."

That made me laugh. "So are you," I said.

"Ah, that is why I know."

She touched her neck—a frequent habit of hers which I had wondered about until I discovered that beneath her bodice she wore a kind of locket on a gold chain. She had once shown this locket to me. On it was engraved a figure of John the Baptist. She called it her Jean-Baptiste; it had been put on her neck when she was a baby. She was never without it and regarded it as a sort of talisman against evil.

We had servants who were permanently at Clavering Hall and those who remained in London, but Jeanne, of course, was my personal maid and always with me. After the losses Lance had suffered in the South Sea Bubble he had thought he would have to get rid of some of his servants, and the fact really did worry him. He decided in the end to sell some land and horses rather than do so. It was typical of him. He loved his horses and hated to part with land which had been in his family's possession for generations, but he considered the welfare of his servants before his pride in his possessions. He was sad for a while, but as always with him, his depression did not last for more than a week.

We needed a nurse for Jean-Louis and I was determined to pay for her. I said to Lance, "Aimée is my sister, and it is good of you to make her welcome here. I insist on providing the nurse."

So it was settled, and Sabrina's nurse, Nanny Curlew, recommended a cousin of hers whom we were glad to employ. Thus Nanny Goswell came to us and immediately took over the care of the child with the utmost efficiency.

The summer came and we had no desire to return to London. When the baby was old enough we would take him to Eversleigh. I wrote frequently to Damaris to tell her of all that was happening, and I began to realize that my letters were full of Jean-Louis.

Damaris wrote back, "It is time you had a child of your own."

It was what I longed for; so did Lance, I knew.

Aimée and I rode together during that hot summer. She had learned to ride at Hessenfield and was not quite as proficient as I, who had been in and out of the saddle ever since my return to England.

Aimée had an air of contentment about her during that summer, which every now and then would slip into a certain . . . what I can only describe as watchfulness.

When we talked I began to understand her more.

She had suffered from being unwanted, I was sure. I imagined her birth had not greatly pleased either of her parents. Hessenfield's life would have been cluttered with women—some more important to him than others. I had no doubt that my mother—the incomparable Carlotta, whose beauty was a legend in the family—had been the most important woman in his life, one whom he had told his brother he would have married if she had been free. Aimée's mother could not have been so important to him, for I imagined he could easily have married *her* if he had wished to do so. But he had been fond of children, particularly his own, and he had clearly wanted to provide for Aimée.

Of course a man like Hessenfield could never visualize death. He was, after all, a young man. But at the end he must have had some premonition, and that was why he had written to his brother asking him to provide for Aimée and had given her mother the watch and the ring.

There must have been great insecurity in Aimée's life. I sensed that what she greatly desired was to be wanted, to have security for herself and her child.

She more or less admitted this when we lay in a field a mile or so from Clavering Hall. Our horses were tethered to a tree while we rested before returning to Clavering.

"I married Ralph Ransome," she said, "partly because I wanted a home and someone to care for me. I was never really in love with him. But he was kind to me. He was a widower and had a son and daughter who were married and lived in the Midlands. I had our father's money, so I was not destitute, but this seemed a wonderful opportunity. Ralph had a beautiful home and I became mistress of it. But I realized after our marriage that he was deeply in debt, and there were anxieties. Then, when this South Sea chance presented itself, Ralph risked almost everything he had to gain a fortune which would bring him out of his difficulties. We could have been happy . . ." She looked at me intently. "Not romantically so . . . as you and Lance must have been . . . but comfortably . . . adequate for a girl who has not had many advantages in life."

She picked a blade of grass and tore at it with her white, even teeth.

"Oh, you are the lucky one, *ma soeur,*" she went on. "You are rich. You have the handsome husband. You are one of the few who escaped before the Bubble burst."

"And you have Jean-Louis," I reminded her.

"That adorable one, yes, it is so. I have my baby. But you have him too . . . they all have him."

"Everyone loves him, but you are his mother, Aimée."

She touched my hand. "Yes, and thanks to you he has come comfortably into the world. But I cannot live here forever. I shall have to think what I am going to do. What does a woman in my position do when she is without the means to support herself and her child? Teach French, perhaps . . . to children who do not want to learn it? Be a superior servant in some noble household?"

"Nonsense," I said. "This is your home. You will stay here."

"I cannot live on your bounty forever."

"You will stay here because your home is with your family. Have you forgotten we are sisters?"

"Half sisters. No, I must make plans."

"Perhaps you will meet someone whom you can marry. We will entertain more. There are so many people here in the country whom Lance knows."

"The marriage market?" she said, with a glint in her eyes which I did not altogether understand. When I came to think of it, there was much I did not understand about Aimée.

"That's putting it crudely. But people do meet each other and fall in love."

She looked at me and smiled, and I thought, I will speak to Lance about it tonight. We must entertain more. I had the money to do this. I must try to find a husband for Aimée.

We stood up, stretched, and went to the horses. It was a silent ride back to the house.

I spoke to Lance about Aimée that night.

"The poor girl is unhappy about her position. It is worrying for her. She is proud and deeply conscious of depending on us. If we entertained here in the country we might find a husband for her."

"Then, my dear matchmaker, that is what we must do."

It was a few days later, when she was brushing my hair, that I told Jeanne we were planning to do more entertaining at the Hall.

"Will you like?" she asked.

"To tell the truth, Jeanne, it was I who suggested it."

"There will be card games, then. You want that?"

"No, of course I don't. But I think my sister should meet people."

"To find a 'usband for her?" asked Jeanne bluntly.

"I did not say that, Jeanne."

"No, but you do not always say what you mean."

"Well, if I did mean it, it would be a good idea, wouldn't it?"

"It would be very good. Madame Aimée is not the one you think her."

"Now, what do you mean by that?" I demanded somewhat

testily. I was irritated by Jeanne's frequent innuendoes concerning Aimée.

"You must watch 'er," whispered Jeanne. "I think she 'ave an eye for the men. And men are men . . . even the best of them."

I knew she was referring to Lance, for whom she had an inordinate admiration because of his handsome appearance, elegant style of dress and gracious manners.

"You talk arrant nonsense sometimes, Jeanne," I said.

She gave a rather vicious tug to a tangle, so that I cried out in protest.

"You will see," she said darkly.

It was not long before I was wishing that I had not suggested having these parties, for a round of gaiety began and almost always the gatherings ended at the card tables.

Lance, who had been considerably sobered by the recent disaster, became as fervently involved as before. Aimée, too, had a taste for the game. Lance said she played a very good hand at faro, and they played sometimes into the early hours of the morning. I would often retire before the games ended. No one seemed to mind; the only thing that mattered once the tables were set up was the play.

Lance had a run of luck and was sure he was going to retrieve all he had lost in time. This was the pattern of luck, he said. Up one day and down the next.

I became very uneasy again, but I did not want to become a nagging wife and I had long ago realized that nothing I could do would make Lance anything but a gambler.

I think I was almost as anxious about Aimée as I was about Lance. He at least could look after himself. I remonstrated with him about encouraging Aimée to play.

"Where can she find the money?" I asked. "You know her circumstances."

"Don't deny her the excitement, Clarissa," he answered. "Poor girl, she has had a hard time. She enjoys it so much, and she has a good card sense. She's a natural, and lucky too. Some people are, you know."

"But how can she afford . . ."

"Don't worry about that. I set her up, and if she wins she pays me back. If she loses, we forget it."

"Oh, Lance!"

He put his arms round me and kissed me, laughing as he did so. "Let the girl enjoy herself," he pleaded.

"It is not the right way."

"We can't all be like you, my darling."

I was silent, feeling that I was priggish, a spoilsport.

A few days later I heard a little altercation between Jeanne and Aimée. Before that the hostility between them had been silent, though pronounced.

I was on my way to Aimée's room when I heard their voices raised in anger. I hesitated and could not help hearing what they were saying. They spoke in French rapidly and angrily.

"Take care," Aimée was saying. "You are not in the Rue de la Morant now, you know."

"How did you know I was ever in the Rue de la Morant?"

"You know you were there with your mother and grandmother. You know only the lowest of the low live in such places."

"We lived there because we could afford no better. But how did you know?"

"I heard you say it."

"Never did you hear me mention it. Never. Never."

"Be quiet and don't speak so to your betters."

"You . . . you . . ." cried Jeanne in a fury. "Have a care. If ever you hurt my Lady Clarissa, I will kill you."

I did not wait for more. I turned and hurried away.

I did not like this growing hostility between Jeanne and Aimée any more than I liked the gambling which once more was becoming the main feature of our lives.

That summer and autumn passed uneasily, and it seemed that in a very short time Christmas was upon us. We were to go to Enderby as usual, and we set out from Albemarle Street on the morning of the twentieth of December, hoping to get as far as possible before darkness fell.

It was a somewhat hazardous journey, as the cold weather had set in early and it seemed that the winter might be a severe one.

It took us three days to reach Enderby, and Damaris was in a state of anxiety, visualizing the state of the roads. Aimée, of course, accompanied us, with Jean-Louis, and there was a great welcome for the baby, who was admired by them all except Sabrina. I was sure she thought he detracted from her own importance.

She was delighted to see me, however, and I was touched by her boisterous welcome.

"It's going to snow," she told me, "and freeze, and we shall

all go skating on the pond. I have a new pair of skates. I shan't get them until Christmas day though. My papa has bought them for me."

Now that Enderby was no longer my home I could see clearly what people meant when they said there was a certain foreboding about it. Whether this was due to long-ago tragedies which had happened in the house or whether it was just the way it was built, without enough light coming in and because the magnificent trees grew too close to it and darkened it even more, I did not know. But there was a kind of menace there which I noticed before the tragedy.

When we arrived great log fires were burning in all the rooms, and Damaris had had the place decorated as usual for Christmas, which dispersed most of the gloom . . . and yet it was there all the same.

I spent a great deal of time with Sabrina, who insisted on it. She had formed a deep attachment to me and looked upon me as her elder sister, which was natural, as Damaris had been a mother to me. She proudly showed me all her presents. There was pride of place for the skates, and next came the fur muff, which her mother had given her; and then there was my gift—a saddle for her pony, which I had heard she wanted. She gloated over them all and kept running to the window to see whether it was still snowing, and she asked Jeremy a hundred times a day whether the pond was hard enough yet to skate on.

She did not like Aimée, which I think was due to the fact that she was Jean-Louis' mother. She referred to him as "that silly baby."

"You were a baby once," I reminded her.

"I soon grew out of that," she answered scornfully.

"So will he."

"Well, he's a silly baby *now*."

Damaris was always trying to remonstrate with her. "You are too impatient, Sabrina," she said. "Remember, there are other people in the world besides you."

"I know that," retorted Sabrina.

"Well, they have to be considered."

"Everybody considers that baby more than . . ."

"Of course they do. He's only little. They consider other people too."

Sabrina muttered, "It's stopped snowing. Papa says it'll freeze up, and perhaps tomorrow. . . ."

She was off to consult Jeremy on the temperature.

"Sabrina worries me a little," Damaris confided in me. "She's so impulsive and self-centered."

"All children are."

"Sabrina more than most. It's strange that Jeremy and I should have such a daughter. She reminds me of your mother. I do hope she will be happy. I don't think your mother ever was . . . with all her gifts. Sometimes I tremble for Sabrina."

"You worry too much. Sabrina is all right. She is just a normal, healthy child, full of high spirits."

"You are fond of her, aren't you, Clarissa?"

"Of course. She is like my little sister."

"You have a new sister." She looked at me anxiously. "You get on well with Aimée, don't you?"

"Yes, of course."

Damaris looked sad. "I often think how much better it would have been if your mother had stayed with Benjie. He was, after all, her husband . . . and such a good man. Still, he is happy now. But if your mother had stayed with him, she might have been alive today."

"It is no use talking about ifs. It didn't work out that way and so things are as they are today."

"You'd always look after Sabrina, wouldn't you?"

"Of course I would. But she'll be here with you. You'll be the one to look after her."

"Yes, unless . . ." She smiled suddenly. "I have something to tell you, Clarissa. I am going to have another child."

"Oh . . . how happy you must be."

"Yes . . . yes, of course. We had Sabrina at last . . . and it is wonderful how full of life she is. Sometimes I wonder how Jeremy and I could have such a child. I look forward to another. Jeremy is so pleased. I should like a little boy this time."

"But you will be highly contented with whatever comes."

"Clarissa, it would be wonderful if you . . ."

"Yes, I know. I suppose I shall have a child one day."

"I do hope so. It is a great joy, but . . ."

I looked at her expectantly, and she went on, "I hope it all goes well. Sometimes . . ."

"Of course it will go well. You are in good health now."

"Yes, but there are times . . ."

I shrugged her gloom aside. Naturally she was a little uneasy at the prospect of another pregnancy. She had caught Jeremy's habit of looking on the dark side. I supposed it was because of what had happened to them.

190

By Twelfth Night the pond was frozen hard, and to Sabrina's delight, those of us who wished went skating. Jeremy was there with Lance and myself. The others watched from the bank. Sabrina shrieked with delight, and she looked a picture in her scarlet cloak and hat, clutching the fur muff in her hands and skating over the pond with her father beside her. The color in her cheeks matched that of her cloak, and her eyes sparkled. This was what she had been waiting for.

She was disappointed when darkness fell and we went back to the house.

"The pond will still be frozen tomorrow," prophesied her father, and Sabrina cried out, "How I wish it was tomorrow."

She was up with her skates the next morning, badgering us all to go skating.

On the third day, with the unpredictability of the English climate, it was a little warmer.

"If this goes on," said Jeremy, "the thaw will set in sooner than I expected."

Sabrina was very disconsolate. But her father said, "There'll be no skating until we are sure it is safe."

He went out in the morning and came back to tell us that there were cracks in the ice on the pond. "This is the end of our skating unless the weather turns icy again."

"But there is still ice on the pond," protested Sabrina.

"It'll be there for some days, but it is not safe for skating anymore."

"*I* think it is," said Sabrina with a touch of rebellion in her voice.

"You shall not go on the ice again until it is perfectly safe," said Jeremy.

Sabrina pouted, looking angry.

"Now, darling," said Damaris, "if your father says it is not safe, it isn't. So you must keep away from the pond until it freezes again."

Sabrina was silent . . . too silent. Perhaps we should have been prepared.

In the afternoon I thought I would take her round the field on her pony. She loved riding and was always delighted when I rode with her. One had to be watchful of her, for she was far too daring. Like most children, she did not know the meaning of fear, and it never occurred to her that anything could go wrong.

I could not find her. Nanny Goswell, who had accompanied us to Enderby to look after Jean-Louis, said that she had seen her running out of the house. I went to Damaris to ask if she had seen her, and when she heard that I could not find her, she grew perturbed. I said I would go through the house.

I wished I had stayed with Damaris.

I could not find Sabrina. I went up to the attics. Sabrina was rather fond of exploring them and up there I happened to look out of the small window and I saw Damaris running as fast as she could away from the house, and she had not stopped to put on a cloak. She will be frozen, I thought. And then, suddenly, a frightening thought came to me. Events clicked into place. I saw Sabrina's face, quiet for once, brooding, planning—and I guessed.

I did not stop for cloak or gloves. I ran out of the house as fast as I could and down to the pond.

It was clear what had happened. Sabrina had gone to skate in spite of being forbidden to do so. There was a gaping black hole in the whiteness and there was Sabrina's head in the red cap protruding from it. Damaris was lying full length on the ice supporting her.

I was panic-stricken, not knowing for a moment what to do. If I went out to try and help, my weight might break the ice. In fact, it might break at any moment, taking Damaris down with Sabrina.

I turned back to the house, shouting for Lance and Jeremy. Fortunately Jeremy was in the garden and heard me. Breathlessly I explained. Lance appeared.

Then we were all running as fast as we could to the pond.

It was a near disaster. I shall never forget those terrible tense moments. Jeremy was like a man possessed by despair. It was Lance, really, who calmly and practically saved their lives. I was proud of him. He acted almost nonchalantly, as though rescuing people from such situations was an everyday occurrence to him. Jeremy was handicapped by his lameness; but with amazing skill and firmness, Lance had Sabrina out of the water, and handed her to me while Jeremy helped Damaris to rise gingerly from the thinning ice.

Sabrina was white-faced and terribly cold; it was strange to see her still and silent. Smith, having heard what had happened, came running to the pond, and it was he who took the sodden little bundle from me and rushed toward the house. I saw Damaris then ... she was half fainting, and Lance had lifted her up and was carrying her.

We reached the house, where they were already getting

blankets and warming pans and wrapping hot bricks in flannel.

Someone ran to get the doctor.

I was with Nanny Curlew when she stripped Sabrina of her wet clothes and wrapped her in a warm towel to rub her dry. Then we put her into a blanket and bed already warmed. Her teeth chattered, which relieved me, for I had been terrified to see her so still and silent.

She opened her eyes and saw me.

"Clarissa . . ." she whispered.

I leaned forward and kissed her. "You're safe now, darling," I said. "In your own little bed."

"I was frightened," she said. "It cracked . . . and I was in. Oo, it was cold."

"Tell me about it later, dear." I stroked her face. "There. You're home now. You're safe."

"Stay with me," she murmured.

So I sat by her bed and she held my hand tightly.

"She'll be all right," said Nanny Curlew. "A chill, mayhap. But she'll be all right."

I sat looking at that beautiful little face, so different from usual—pale and quiet, with the lashes, looking darker than usual, lying fan-shaped on her white skin—and I rejoiced that Lance had saved her and thanked God that there had not been a tragic ending to this day's adventure.

But before the day was out I realized I had been over-optimistic.

Damaris was very ill.

The exposure had affected her so much that it was clear within a day or so that she was about to miscarry and that her life was in danger. She had been an invalid when she was in her teens and had suffered from rheumatic fever, which had left her unable to leave her couch. Then the miracle had happened. She had met Jeremy and made the almost super-human effort to rescue me. This had done something to Damaris; and although she had never been strong, she had been able to lead a normal life. Giving birth to Sabrina had been an ordeal for her although she had survived and wanted another child; but her health was not such as to allow her to expose herself with impunity to such an ordeal as that which she had undergone to save Sabrina.

And now . . . this miscarriage. It was a time of great suspense while we waited to hear news of her. I felt the house closing in on me . . . triumphant, almost . . . the house of

193

shadows, the house of menace, where evil was waiting to catch those who dared live in the place.

Strange . . . for it had been my home once and I had never noticed it then.

Sabrina recovered rapidly. After the first day she was sitting up in bed eating heartily. Nanny Curlew had decreed that she should stay in bed, and after what had happened—which was the result of her disobedience—she was for once submissive.

But the old Sabrina was ready to break out at any moment until Jeremy came to her. I was there, so I saw it happen, but it was only afterward that I understood that something very significant was happening to Sabrina.

Jeremy was fond of the child, but beyond anything in the world he loved Damaris. Damaris represented salvation to him. Having read their story, I now knew what she did for him. He had been morose and unhappy, resentful of life, shutting himself away, believing that nothing good could ever happen to him. Then she came along—a girl physically handicapped, as he was—to show him that there was something worthwhile for him in life after all. He had been with her when she came to rescue me in Paris, and I felt deeply about them, because I had played a part in their story. He had seen Damaris' courage during that adventure; he had realized her selflessness. She was his salvation; together they had built a new life.

Jeremy was still something of a misanthrope. He would never throw off that morbid streak in his nature. He expected disaster rather than good fortune, and luck to be bad rather than good. He was the absolute antithesis of Lance.

He was now in a state of deep despair. It was not only that he was disappointed in the loss of the child; his great anxiety was for Damaris. Her exposure on the ice would very likely bring back that affliction which had come to her in her youth. He was certain this would be so. Worse than that even—she was very ill, and knowing Jeremy, I realized that in his mind he had already buried her and had drifted back into the lonely, frustrated existence which had been his before Damaris came into his life.

His face was pale and his dark eyes glowed. I had never seen him look as he did now. Sabrina sat up in bed staring at him.

She had always been a little unsure of her father. Perhaps he was not quite so susceptible to her charm as most of us were; and she knew, of course, that a great deal of trouble had been caused by her naughtiness. She did not know then how much.

He stood at the end of the bed, looking at her almost distastefully and as though he wanted to put as great a distance as possible between her and himself.

Her lovely eyes were wide as she stared back at him and her lips were trembling. He said nothing for a moment, and Sabrina, who could never bear silences cried out, "Papa . . . I . . . I'm sorry . . ."

"Sorry!" he said, and he looked at her as though he hated her. "You are a wicked girl," he went on. "Do you know what you have done to your mother? She has lost the baby she wanted. And she is ill . . . very ill. You were told the pond was dangerous and that you were to keep away from it. You were forbidden to go on . . ."

"I didn't know . . ." began Sabrina.

"You knew you were doing wrong. You went out to skate when you were told not to, and your mother risked her life saving yours. It may be that you have killed her. . . ."

I cried out involuntarily, "Oh, no . . . no . . . *please* . . ."

But he did not look at me. He turned and went out of the room.

Sabrina was still staring before her. Then she turned to me and flung herself against me. Sobs shook her body; she cried and cried. I stroked her hair and tried to comfort her, but there was no comforting Sabrina. For the first time in her life she had come face to face with a situation from which her charm could not extricate her.

It was a very sad household. Anxieties over Damaris grew. She had lost the child, but that was not all. She was very ill indeed, and it was not only Jeremy's pessimism that pointed to the fact that she might not recover.

Priscilla and Arabella came over to Enderby every day, though there was nothing any of us could do. I was deeply concerned about Sabrina too, for she had changed drastically. She had lost her gaiety and had become silent, almost sullen. Nanny Curlew said, "She's as naughty as ever, though in a different way. She's more trouble than any child I ever had to handle. She teases dear little Jean-Louis. I think she's jealous of him."

I sat with Damaris often, for she seemed to derive comfort

from my presence. "She cares so much for you," Priscilla told me. "You mean a great deal to her."

I took Sabrina with me one day. She did not want to go, but I persuaded her.

Damaris smiled at her daughter and held out her hand. Sabrina shrank from it, but I whispered, "Go on, take it. Tell your mother how much you love her."

Sabrina took the hand and stared defiantly at her mother.

"Bless you, my darling," said Damaris, and I saw Sabrina's face soften. I think she was near to tears.

She needs gentleness now, I thought, as never before. Jeremy had wounded her deeply. It was wrong of him. She was only a child. She had acted thoughtlessly, mischievously— but that was all. I could see that Sabrina needed the love Damaris could give her, but Damaris was ill and I felt I must make Sabrina my special care.

It was time, of course, that we left Enderby. I knew that Lance had business on the country estate and could guess that he was longing to be in London. Aimée was restive too. Enderby was not a happy house to be in at this time.

I talked about it with Lance. He admitted that he wanted to go back, but I said I should not be happy leaving Enderby while the fate of Damaris was still uncertain. I was worried about Sabrina. Being Lance, he understood immediately.

"But we can't all stay here," he said. "There are too many of us. Besides, I think we are a bit of a drain on the household."

I thought fleetingly that he would find it dull here. We had intended to stay only for the Christmas festivities. Here there was no gambling. It might be frowned on at Eversleigh. Lance must find the quiet life of the country without such flutters very dull.

We arranged that Lance should go back to London and that Aimée, with Jean-Louis and Nanny Goswell, should accompany him, leaving me to stay a while until we knew for certain that Damaris would recover.

Jeanne shook her head over the decision. It was not good, she said, for husband and wife to live apart.

"Live apart!" I cried. "We are not living apart. It is only until my aunt Damaris has recovered."

"Meanwhile he go off . . . with Madame Aimée? I do not like."

"Oh, Jeanne, don't be so melodramatic."

"They gamble together. Such a beautiful man . . . and a woman like that." Jeanne narrowed her eyes. "She is . . ."

"Yes, I know. She is French, and so are you, so you *know*. That's it, is it not?"

"You may not laugh always," said Jeanne ominously.

Seen in the Looking Glass

Damaris did recover, but not completely so. She was very weak, but we were all overjoyed when she showed signs of improvement.

Jeremy was still cool with Sabrina, and I knew that there was something smouldering in the child.

I was able to talk with Damaris, which was a relief.

"Poor Sabrina," I said, "she feels this deeply. I know you will understand how this has affected her. She knows it was her fault . . . all the trouble, your illness, the worry everyone has had. Dear Aunt Damaris, I know you will understand."

She did of course, and she thanked me, with tears in her eyes, for what I had done for Sabrina. I said I had done nothing. She was the one who had done everything. Giving Sabrina life . . . and then saving it.

"She is my baby, of course—as you were once, Clarissa."

"I know. But I am able to take care of myself now. Sabrina isn't. You will know how to make her happy again."

I used to take Sabrina with me when I went to see her mother. At first she continued to regard Damaris with something like revulsion, which was due to the fact that she was responsible for her being in bed. But after a while Damaris' gentle nature and her love prevailed. The barrier was broken. Sabrina would sit on the bed and I would tell stories and play games, such as "I spy with my little eye," which meant that the others had to guess the object I was looking at, and the one who guessed took the turn of selecting the next; and very soon we had Sabrina rolling about the bed in fits of laughter. This mood did not always last, but it was good to see the old Sabrina coming out now and then; and I knew that Damaris understood perfectly.

I then decided that I could leave and that I ought to go back to my home. I explained to Damaris, who understood at once and made a great effort to appear better than she was.

"You must not leave Lance any longer," she said. She turned and took my hand. "Oh, Clarissa, you have brought such happiness into my life . . . always. I believe you understand Sabrina better than anyone. She loves you dearly."

"She is a delightful child . . . and very attractive."

"Yes, that is why I am afraid for her. Your mother was like that. She had that tremendous appeal. It turns up now and then in the family. I am not sure that it is an asset. Sometimes I think it is a liability. I worry about Sabrina, Clarissa."

"She will be able to take care of herself."

"She has been so strange lately."

"It is because she blames herself for what happened, and Jeremy blames her too."

"I have spoken to Jeremy about her. He worries so much about me."

"Dear Aunt Damaris, you must get well. You are Jeremy's life, and Sabrina needs you. You are so much . . . wanted."

She was emotional for a moment and then she said, "Clarissa, will you promise me something? You did once before, but I want to make sure."

"Of course I will. It's Sabrina, isn't it?"

She nodded. "Just suppose I didn't get well."

"Please don't think like that, even for a moment."

"I'm trying, Clarissa, but I want to be sure. Just suppose something should happen to me. Suppose I should die. Promise me *you* will look after Sabrina."

"Her place would be here. This is her home."

"Jeremy is a man who has suffered much. I cannot bear to think what he would do . . . if I were to die."

"I understand," I said.

"Promise me then that you will look after Sabrina. She loves you dearly . . . in fact, I think she loves you better than anyone else. Look after her . . . for me, Clarissa."

I took her hand and kissed it. I was afraid if I looked at her I should weep.

"I promise," I said.

A few days later, after listening to loud protests and reproaches from Sabrina, I left for London.

Back in London, life slipped back into the old pattern. We entertained a good deal now. Lance was elated. He had had a run of luck at the tables and with the horses. He was a devoted husband and a passionate lover and made me feel in a hundred ways how delighted he was to have me back. I felt happy. Damaris was improving; she would comfort Sabrina, and without me there the two of them would grow closer. And this was where I belonged—with my husband.

Aimée was settling into the household as though it were indeed her home. I was glad, though I knew that Jeanne remained suspicious. Aimée told me about the hospitality she—with Lance—had received during my absence and that now and then she had acted as hostess for Lance. They had had a most exciting time.

"Gambling?" I asked.

Lance burst out laughing.

"Now, don't scold, Clarissa," he said. "I had some very good nights. You didn't do too badly either, Aimée, did you?"

They laughed together. A tinge of suspicion came into my mind then. I dismissed it. It would never have come to me but for Jeanne's sly innuendoes.

Jean-Louis was now running all over the nursery and desperately trying to talk. Nanny Goswell said he was a bright child; he was certainly a handsome one.

"Little pickle," said Nanny Goswell fondly. "All he wants is for someone to show him he's not the only pebble on the beach."

I sighed. No one could long more for children in the nursery than I.

We spent the summer between the country and London, and a feature of our lives was, of course, the gambling sessions—through which, Lance assured me, he was fast recouping his losses in the South Sea Company.

I was not so sure of this, for I guessed I heard only of the winnings. The losses were probably just as great.

I often felt during those days how happy I could have been but for Lance's obsession with gambling. It was only when the fever was on him that he seemed unaware of me. It was like a demon that possessed him. He could never resist the desire. I had seen him wager on two raindrops falling down a windowpane . . . five . . . or even twenty pounds . . . all on the spur of the moment. I could not understand him. I should have thought the lesson of the South Sea fiasco would have changed him. It was not so.

I was more than a little anxious about his financial position, for I fancied he was in debt. Once I found a demand from his tailor for a long-overdue bill, and when I remonstrated with him he replied, "But, my darling, no man ever pays his tailor's bills for at least five years."

"Then they should. What if the poor man needs the money?"

"This man is far from poor. He served the court. He must be worth a fortune . . . in debts."

"That's not much use if he is never paid."

"In time . . . in time. . . ."

"Well, if you have been winning, surely this must be the time."

"Logic, my dear. Absolute logic. Leave it to me."

Casual, charming, unruffled, gallant, and a hopeless gambler. He was a man who would smile in the face of ruin. I was so different. Perhaps he should never have chosen to marry me.

As for Aimée, she was like him. I saw the excitement beginning to grip her. She could scarcely wait to get to the tables. I wondered if Lance was still financing her efforts. I often saw Jeanne watching her, shaking her head ominously.

"Aimée has the luck of the angels," said Lance. "I've seen few to rival her."

So I presumed Aimée, at least, was doing well.

Then I understood. It was quite by accident that I found out. After we had had a dinner party the guests settled down to the card tables and I invariably went to bed. Lance had tried, with no success, to persuade me to stay; but he had not been really pressing, and perhaps he thought one gambler in the family was enough.

It was early autumn, I remember. We had had a successful dinner and conversation flowed freely. I had sat at one end of the table and Lance at the other. He was a graceful, witty host, but these people were all players, all eager to get to the business for which they had come, and that was to win money from one another. I knew most of them very well, for Lance often went to their houses to play and they came to us often. Sometimes I accompanied him, but I dreaded the evenings, which were usually spent in rather dreary conversation with those members of the party who, like myself, did not gamble, waiting for the play to end which generally did not until the early hours of the morning. I often made excuses not to attend. Lance was tolerant enough to understand and sometimes aided me in avoiding them. All the same, nothing could prevent his going.

Aimée was often invited. She was popular with this set. "A regular little sport," I had heard them say of her. "Not afraid to take a risk." No, I thought, of course she was not if Lance was supplying her with the means to do so and she only paid back when she won.

But perhaps he no longer did this, since she was notoriously lucky. I did not care to ask either him or her.

On this night she was wearing a charming gown, which she had made herself. It had not cost a great deal. I had been with her when she had bought the material in Leadenhall Street. It was a light shade of red—at least the skirt was; the petticoat was cream-colored, and she herself had embroidered it in red silk the color of her dress. It looked enchanting flowing away from the tiny waist, cut down the front to show the embroidered petticoat.

I saw them all to the tables. There were three tables, and four people at each. Aimée was next to the rather aging baron who had sat beside her at dinner and seemed rather taken with her. At their table were another couple of middle age. Lance's friends were of all ages. The only thing they all had in common was a love of gambling.

Lance put his arm about me and kissed me lightly on the back of my neck.

"Slip away if you wish, my dear," he said.

I nodded. I intended to.

I waited a while and watched the play start, fascinated by the intent look on their faces ... Aimée's no less than the others. I felt a little uneasy about her. I thought, Lance has made a gambler of her. And I felt somewhat responsible.

In this room was a marble fireplace with a large mirror above it and on the mantelpiece a bowl of chrysanthemums. I myself had arranged them that morning. Someone must have brushed against them when passing, for one of them was almost falling out of the bowl. I started to adjust it while I listened to them calling their stakes. I shuddered. It was all so depressing to me, for many of them would come out of that room much poorer than they went in.

I was looking straight at Aimée in the glass. I could not believe that I saw correctly. Her hand moved inside the opening in her skirt to her petticoat. There had been no card in her hand when she put it in, and she was holding one when she drew it out. I saw her slip the card among those she was holding in her other hand.

I felt faintly sick. It was hot in the room. Or was that my imagination? I wanted to get out, but I stood there fixed to the spot, staring at Aimée in the looking glass.

She was smiling, and they were all congratulating her. She had won again.

I had to get away. I called good night to them and went to the bedroom. I sat down and stared at my reflection in the glass.

I must have been mistaken. Of course I had not been. I had seen it all so clearly. I kept going over it ... that vital moment when she had brought the card out from her petticoat, the smile on her face, her leaning forward and putting her elbow on the table, holding the cards fan-shaped before her.

She had great good luck. Of course she did. She made her luck by cheating at cards.

It was impossible! But it wasn't, of course. Cheating was the greatest sin among gamblers. What did they do about people who cheated? They were banished from clubs. No one would play with them. Duels had been fought between accusers and accused.

What could I do? One thing was certain. I could not allow Aimée to go on cheating in my house. Should I tell Lance? He would be horrified. That would be one of the things which could really move him. And where would she go if she were asked to leave? What would happen to Jean-Louis?

I was very upset and uncertain.

I undressed and went to bed. I lay sleepless, listening for the sounds of departure, for Lance's step on the stairs. I had not yet made up my mind what I should do.

I waited all next day, and in the afternoon when the house was quiet, I went alone to Aimée's room, for I knew she would be there. . . .

She gave me a warm smile when I entered.

I said quietly, "I have come to talk to you."

"That's nice," she said.

I shook my head. "You do very well at the card table," I said.

"Not so bad for a beginner."

"You must have won a considerable sum."

"Oh, a little. Enough to pay my debts to Lance and to give me a chance to recuperate my losses over the Bubble."

"Naturally your methods are successful."

She looked puzzled.

"I saw you cheating last night," I said.

All the color drained from her face. She stood up and stared at me, her eyes blazing.

"What are you talking about! You weren't there."

"I was . . . for a while. I saw you in the mirror."

"You were dreaming."

"No. I was wide awake. I saw distinctly. You had a winning card in the pocket of your petticoat. I saw you take it out after the cards were dealt."

"It is not true."

"I tell you I saw you do it."

"In the looking glass! That's quite impossible. What are you trying to say?"

"Only that I saw you cheat at cards."

"Nonsense."

"It is not nonsense and you know it. Lance would never allow it."

"Have you made this monstrous accusation against me to him?"

"Not yet."

"Not yet! You mean you are going to?"

I hesitated, and when I saw the hope spring up in her eyes I knew without a doubt that she was guilty.

"I am not sure what I shall do," I said. "Oh, Aimée, how could you do such a thing!"

"There is only your word against mine."

"Do you think Lance would believe you rather than his wife?"

"No . . . he'd believe you, and then . . ." She stared blankly ahead.

"Why did you do it?"

"I didn't. I didn't."

"Please don't lie to me. I saw you. I saw it all. I was terribly upset."

Her face crumpled suddenly and she began to cry. That touched me terribly. I always thought her rather hard and well able to take care of herself. To see her so abjectly miserable made me sorry for her.

"Aimée," I went on, "why . . . *why?*"

She took out a handkerchief and dabbed at her eyes. "I suppose I shall have to go now," she said. "You'll tell Lance, and he will send me away. He would never have anyone here who cheated at cards. I wasn't going to make a habit of it . . . only until I had things straight. You've no idea what it's like living on charity. I want to work ... to do something for myself and Jean-Louis. I want our independence. I want..."

"That wasn't the way to do it."

"I know. But I saw how it could be done ... and then I did it. I'm saving, Clarissa, saving for myself and Jean-Louis."

"It's taking money which doesn't belong to you."

"They are all rich. They can afford it."

"That's no reason why you should do it."

"I know it's wrong. I'm weak, I accept that. I deserve everything that's coming to me. You'd better tell Lance at once, and I'll start making plans ... though where I'll go I have no idea."

I watched her. There was no mistaking the despair in her face. I could see her gloating over her winnings, calling them her means to her independence. She turned her pleading eyes to me.

"It has been wonderful here. You have been so kind ... you and Lance. But I see I must go now. You're going to tell Lance, aren't you?"

"He will never allow you to play again," I said.

"I know. And he'll find some excuse to send me away."

"Aimée," I said slowly, "if I promise not to tell him, will you promise me never to cheat again?"

She had taken my hands and gripped them hard.

"Oh, I will, I will," she cried.

I came out of her room feeling emotionally exhausted. It seemed to me that I had emerged from the situation in the only way possible.

Aimée's luck at the tables had changed drastically.

"It is like that," said Lance. "You have a fantastic run of luck and then suddenly ... it's all over. It'll come back."

"I don't think it ever will," said Aimée sadly.

I was satisfied. She was no longer cheating.

I thought about her a great deal. I made excuses for her. She had come over from France on the chance of finding her father's people and a new life. Hers had been a precarious existence, and she had found great comfort in security. She had married for it—she had more or less said so—and then it had been lost with the bursting of the Bubble and the death of her husband.

She still attended the gambling sessions, though with less zeal than before. Sometimes she was flushed with success, at others despondent. I told her it was a mistake to join in, but I could see that she had caught some of that fever which obsessed Lance.

It was too late now for her to draw away.

Sabrina

The months passed quickly. I visited Enderby in the autumn. It was a sad visit, for as soon as I saw Damaris I realized that her health had deteriorated still further. She rarely left her bed now, and when she did she had to be carried downstairs to lie on the sofa in the drawing room. Jeremy insisted on carrying her himself, and tragedy was already beginning to look out of his eyes. His tenderness and devotion to Damaris was deeply moving to watch, but it was clear to me that he was still blaming Sabrina.

She clung to me when I arrived . . . a new Sabrina, who had lost that insouciant gaiety which had been so much a part of her nature. She brooded; she was disobedient.

"She's a handful," said Nanny Curlew, who was the only one who could manage her. I was shocked, for I understood that the tragedy on the ice was by no means over.

She was delighted to see me at first and told me I must stay with her always. When I said I should have to go home because Enderby was not my home any more, she sulked and avoided me for several days.

I was with Damaris a great deal. She wanted me to be there. Her face had grown very thin and there were dark circles under her eyes caused by the pain she suffered.

She never talked of it, but she had reverted to the incapacitation of her youth before she had roused herself to look after Jeremy and me. I knew she tried to exert herself, for she was very anxious about Sabrina and the relationship between the child and her father. I think she regarded them both as two children who needed her care and guidance, but she was too ill, too racked by pain, too tired to give them the attention they needed.

She did not talk of the incident on the ice nor of the future. She did seem to find a great pleasure in talking of the past, of her trip to Paris when she had rescued me. It was as though we relived that time together from the moment when Jeanne came into the cellar with her tray of violets bringing Damaris with her.

"Violets have always been my favorite flower ever since," she said.

Sometimes Jeremy would come in and sit silently watching her. She meant everything to him. She had brought him out of the slough of despond. She had shown him that there was happiness—great happiness—in the world for him as well as for everyone else.

Priscilla was very worried about her. "She's going downhill," she said. "She's worse than she was all those years ago. Then she was younger. That last miscarriage drained her of all her strength. It's as though she can't fight this anymore."

"She has a great spirit," I replied. "She will fight with all her might, if only for the sake of Jeremy and Sabrina."

"Ah," went on Priscilla, "he can't forgive the child. Every time he looks at her he thinks that it is her fault. She can see it in his eyes."

"Poor Sabrina."

"She is a wayward child. She's Carlotta all over again. You used to be able to deal with Sabrina, Clarissa, but she seems to have turned against you now."

"She must be made to feel that all this is not her fault."

"But it *is*. She has logic enough to see that. If she hadn't disobeyed orders and gone skating, Damaris would be well today. The child might have been safely born. Whichever way you look at it, it comes back to Sabrina."

"She's only a child. It's making things so much worse by enlarging on her guilt."

Priscilla lifted her shoulders helplessly. "And my mother is very worried about my father. I think he'll be lucky to get through the winter. And if anything happens to him . . . that would just about finish Arabella. I think, dear, that it would be wise for you not to come this Christmas. It would be too much for them at Eversleigh, and at Enderby it wouldn't be easy. I shall be busy in both places, it seems."

"I'll come in the spring," I said. "Everything will be different then."

My words were sadly prophetic.

We spent that Christmas at Clavering in the traditional way, with plenty of card parties thrown in.

On Christmas morning, among my presents was a long,

narrow case of dark-green velvet, and when I opened it I disclosed a necklace of glittering diamonds and emeralds.

Lance watched me as I took it out.

"Lance!" I cried. "You!"

"Who else? Don't tell me you are in the habit of receiving such gifts from others?"

"It's quite beautiful," I said, and I immediately thought of the cost and those unpaid bills about which Lance was so nonchalant.

"Put it on," he commanded.

I did so. It transformed me.

"Let's have a look at you," he said. "Ah, I knew it. It brings out the green in your eyes."

"But, Lance, it's terribly expensive."

"Only the best will do for you, my darling," he answered promptly.

"You shouldn't . . ." I wanted to say that I should have been more pleased with something which had cost less, but I couldn't of course.

"A bit of luck at the tables," he said.

"You should keep your winnings to set against your losses."

"Losses! Don't talk of losses. It's a word I don't much like."

"Nevertheless it exists . . ." I stopped. There I was, lecturing him again. Perhaps this anxiety over his gambling was making a shrew of me. I went on, "Lance, I love it. It's beautiful and it is wonderful of you to give me such a present."

I wore the necklace that evening. It looked magnificent with a white brocade gown.

Jeanne fingered it almost lovingly when I put it on. "It's the most beautiful necklace I ever saw," she said. "Sir Lance knows what is elegant. You would think he was. . . ."

"A Frenchman," I added. "I'm glad you approve of my husband, Jeanne."

"I do not like that others like him too much."

She was referring to Aimée. Would she never get over her dislike of my half sister? "She has a beautiful brooch give her." Her lips were pursed in disapproval because it was Lance who had given her the brooch.

"It is Christmas, Jeanne. A time for giving."

Jeanne continued to express her disapproval as she brought out the bezoar ring from its case and gave it to me to slip on my finger. She had treated it with great respect since she had heard it belonged to a queen.

She could not take her eyes from the necklace.

"It is beautiful," she said. "Think what it stands for. It is worth a flower shop in the Rue St. Honoré."

"Worth a flower shop!"

"I mean if it were sold. . . . You could buy a flower shop in the heart of Paris for what that's worth."

"Oh, Jeanne," I said reproachfully, "you make me feel as though I'm walking round with a flower shop round my neck."

I was to remember that conversation later.

It was a strange Christmas without the family and I was rather glad when it was over. There was far too much gambling, and my thoughts were at Enderby with Damaris and Sabrina.

It was a harsh winter. We stayed in London, where the weather was slightly less rigorous, but even there frozen snow remained piled high against the houses, and we were unable to go out.

The thaw set in at the end of February, and at the beginning of March I received a letter from Priscilla.

"I didn't want you to risk the roads," she wrote, "but I do think you should come down as soon as you can manage it. Damaris is worse. The rheumatism seems to have affected her heart. I think you ought to come, dear. She longs to see you, but she would not let you know for fear you might risk the roads, and she did not want that."

I showed the letter to Lance. He was loath to leave London now. He had had several invitations to people's houses and I knew that he was looking forward to them. Moreover, his presence was required on the country estate. On the other hand, he did not care for me to make the journey alone.

I said, "I shall be all right. I must go because there is an urgency in Priscilla's letter. I shall have the grooms with me."

"I'll come with you," he said.

I was pleased that he wished to do so, and then I wondered what I would find at Enderby. Damaris was clearly very ill indeed. If she were to die—and I had an overwhelming premonition—I must think of Sabrina, and I knew that I could handle whatever was awaiting me better if I were alone.

When Lance was there Sabrina held aloof. There was some absurd but passionate resentment in her jealous little heart, and it was directed against Lance solely because she believed he came first with me.

I said, "I don't know what I'm going to find there. It will be depressing, I am sure. Sabrina is a very unhappy child at this time. Lance, I do believe I can handle this best alone."

He understood at once. Perhaps he was relieved. Morbid situations did not appeal to him. He liked everything to be pleasant. "As you wish," he said. "But if you want me to go with you, you only have to say so."

"I know," I said gratefully. "And thank you, Lance."

Jeanne insisted on coming with me. I should need her, she said. And I was glad of her company. "And Sir Lance," she went on, "he will stay behind?"

"I have told him that is best."

She shook her head. "He should go with you. You should not leave him alone with . . ."

She did not continue and I did not ask her to.

So on the last day of March I set out for Enderby.

Although I had known that Damaris was seriously ill, I was unprepared for what I found.

It was indeed a house of mourning. Damaris was dead when I arrived. Her heart had been weakened during the first attack of rheumatic fever when she was young and this return of the disease had been too much for her.

When I stepped into the house I had the feeling that it was content, because this was its natural state. Happiness, gaiety, merriment did not rest comfortably at Enderby. The house had become alive again; it had come into its own—evil, menacing, haunted by tragedies of the past.

In a small room on the first floor stood the coffin. The room was darkened, for the curtains had been drawn across the windows. Lying there in the light of two candles, looking young and beautiful, with the lines of pain wiped from her face, lay Damaris. She wore a white cap of fine Brussels lace and I could just see the top of the shift in which they had laid her out, with lace at its neck. She looked so peaceful there, remote from all the harassments of life. Damaris was at rest; but what of those whom she had left behind?

Jeremy was a man who had lost his way and despaired of ever finding it again. He looked like a ghost. Smith told me that he neither ate or slept. He did not seem able to realize that she had gone.

"I dunno," said Smith. "When she came it changed everything. She was an angel, that's what she was. And now she's gone to the angels ... if you believe in that sort of thing. They'd have done better to let her stay. Angels could do without her. Mr. Jeremy can't. She's gone. That means everything will change back. I don't know, Miss Clarissa. I don't know at all. There's the little nipper. What's to become of her?"

"We'll sort something out, Smith," I said. "Never fear."

Sabrina had not come to greet me as she had in the old days. I asked Nanny Curlew where she was.

"Nobody can do anything with that child these days," she told me. "She's shut right in on herself. Doesn't seem to want anybody."

I found her at last. She was in one of the attics sitting under an old table pretending to read.

"Hello, Sabrina," I said. "Did you know I was coming?"

"Yes," she answered, and looked down at her book.

I crawled under the table and, sitting beside her, put my arm about her.

"I thought you'd be glad to see me. Aren't you?"

"I don't mind."

I started to get out from under the table, but she made a half move toward me. "She's dead now," she said.

I went back and sat close to her.

"Yes," I said.

"I haven't got a mother now."

"Dear Sabrina, you have us all. You have your grandparents ... your great-grandparents ... and here am I."

"They all think I killed her."

"They don't."

"They don't *say* it but they *mean* it. And I did, didn't I? It was because she pulled me out of the frozen pond."

"That was an accident, Sabrina."

"I made it an accident, and Papa hates me."

"Of course he doesn't."

"Why do you say that when you know he does? Why do people always tell lies? We ought to tell the truth."

"Of course we should, and we do. Your father does not hate you."

"You tell lies," she said. "You needn't. I don't mind if he hates me. I hate him too."

I put my arm round her and held her fast. I kept saying, "Sabrina, Sabrina, my dear little Sabrina."

Suddenly I felt her clinging to me. I thought she was going

to cry, and I knew it would be good for her if she did. But she didn't. Instead she said in a small voice, "Stay here, Clarissa."

I stroked her hair. "I'll look after you, Sabrina," I said.

After that she did not avoid me, and I felt I had made progress.

I went to the Dower House. Poor Priscilla was weighed down with grief. Damaris had been her favorite daughter. I don't think she ever understood my mother. Carlotta had, throughout her life, been exotic and dramatic. But Damaris had been the quiet and affectionate home lover, the daughter every woman wants—kind, generous, unselfish in the extreme, the one who gives all she has to give without thought of self-gratification. Dear, loving, simple Damaris was no more; she had gone, leaving behind so many who mourned for her, whose lives had become poorer without her, people who needed her.

There was gloom at Eversleigh. Carleton was confined to bed and Arabella was in a state of acute anxiety because of his health. The death of Damaris was a blow which she was not strong enough to sustain at this time.

It was indeed a house of mourning.

It was an April day, a week after her death, when Damaris was buried in the graveyard attached to Eversleigh Church, where generations of Eversleighs had been laid to rest.

I shall never forget the dismal tolling of the bell as the pallbearers carried the coffin into the church. I kept Sabrina's hand in mine; she was very quiet and her beautiful eyes were enormous in her pale face.

When we stood round the grave and listened to the sound of the clods of earth falling on the coffin, the child shrank close to me, and I put an arm about her to comfort her. She turned away from the gaping grave and buried her face in my skirts.

I dared not look at Jeremy, who was like a man in a dream. I saw that Smith was close beside him, and I was grateful to Smith. He had looked after Jeremy in the past and would do so now.

Back at the house we partook of some refreshment—ham, beef, and little pies, with mulled wine. In the great hall the company was assembled—a quiet, sad company. They talked of Damaris' many virtues. It is the custom at funerals to praise the deceased's accomplishments and gifts, but in the case of Damaris the compliments were deserved.

How we should miss her! This house would not be the same

again. I realized that it was her presence which had dispersed that air of menace.

Jeanne had said it was not a happy house; now it seemed to me that it was haunted by malevolent ghosts.

The guests had departed and silence fell on the house. Jeremy went to the room he had shared with Damaris and shut himself in with his grief.

I suggested to Sabrina that we walk round the gardens for an hour and she agreed to come with me. She was silent for a while and then she began to talk about the funeral.

"My mama is down there in that big hole in that box," she said. "It was a nice box . . . with shiny woods and a lot of gold on it."

"Brass," I said.

"Gold's better than brass. But you can't bury gold, can you? It costs too much. The gravestones look like old women . . . men too . . . wrapped in gray cloaks."

"Yes," I agreed. "A little."

"When it's night they stop being stones and turn into people."

"Who told you that?"

"I heard them talking."

She meant the servants. I knew they gossiped together, and several of them were sure Enderby was haunted.

"And," went on Sabrina, "the graves open and dead people come out of their coffins."

"That's nonsense."

"They dance on the graves, and if anybody goes there when they're dancing they catch them . . . and won't let them go. They take their hearts and everything and keep them for themselves. Then they're alive again and the other one is dead."

"Where on earth did you hear such gruesome tales?"

"I won't tell."

"You made them up."

"Perhaps."

"Sabrina," I said, "it's nice to be with you. The two of us together. Do you think so?"

"It would be if . . ."

"If what?"

"Just if," she said.

I fancied the old Sabrina was returning. She laughed a little. I thought, She's getting over it. She's only a child, really.

214

I stayed for three weeks in that house of mourning, and during that time the sadness did not diminish. Jeremy nursed his grief. He was the sort of man who concentrates his main affection on one person, and that person had been Damaris. His wife had been the center of his life, and his love for her, his need of her, were so intense that nothing else could encroach on them. His wife would always come first, and although he would have been fond of his children, they would always have taken second place in his affections; and he was a stern disciplinarian. He had wanted a son and Damaris had always hoped to give him one. When she had died he had lost his will to live, and his was not the temperament to allow him to adjust to a new set of circumstances. Nor did he make any effort to do so. And because Sabrina's wayward, thoughtless act had brought about the tragedy, he remembered it whenever he saw her. I knew it would be well for Sabrina to keep out of his way. She knew it too, poor child, and robbed of her mother, whom she had deeply loved, found no one to whom she could turn but myself and Nanny Curlew.

I should have gone back to London, but I did not feel I could leave Sabrina in this unhappy state. So I stayed on and spent as much time as possible with her, and I was rewarded by occasional glimpses of the child she used to be.

Then came the night when she was missing.

Nanny Curlew came to me in great distress.

"I went to her room," she said. "She was getting ready for bed. I heard her saying her prayers. I saw her into bed and told her you might be along to tell her a story."

"I did go in," I answered, "but she seemed sleepy, so I tucked her in and kissed her good-night."

"The minx," said Nanny Curlew. "She must have got up and gone off somewhere."

"Whatever for?"

"You can never know with Miss. But she's up to something. You can be sure."

"We must find her, Nanny, and bring her back to bed. I expect she's in the attic. She likes hiding up there."

"I'll go up right away and look, Miss Clarissa."

"I'll come with you," I said.

We were dismayed to find she was not in the attic. We searched through the house. No one had seen her. Nanny Curlew and I looked anxiously at each other.

"She must have gone out," I said. "Why . . . and where?"

"She's been strange lately. She's upset about her mother . . . and there's her father. She seems frightened of him and keeps saying she hates him."

"Poor, poor little Sabrina. We must find her quickly, Nanny."

We hurried back to her room. Her slippers were gone and so was her dressing gown, but the rest of her clothes were there.

"She can't go far," I said. "She's not dressed for going out. Oh, where can she have gone."

I tried to think of her favorite places. The stables was one. We went there together. There was no sign of her. Her pony was there, so she had not taken him. That was a relief. The thought of her going out at night on her pony was terrifying.

As we came out of the stables, Damon ran up to us. The old dog was essentially Jeremy's, and slunk about mournfully these days as though aware of the tragedy which had befallen the household, but he was constantly in Sabrina's company.

I called to him, "Damon! Damon! Where is she? Where is Sabrina?"

He gave a little bark and looked at me with limpid sorrowing eyes.

"Find her for us, Damon," I said. "Please, Damon, find Sabrina."

The dog wagged his tail, looked up at us and whimpered. Then he turned and started trotting toward the house.

I followed him in disappointment. I was sure Sabrina was not there.

As we neared the house Smith appeared.

"Hi, Damon," he cried. "I was looking for you, boy."

Then he saw us.

"Oh, Smith," I cried, "we can't find Sabrina."

Smith looked grave. "Not in her bed, then?"

"No. We've searched the house. We think she must have gone out. I can't think why and I can't think where. Have you any idea?"

There was a special bond between Smith and Sabrina, as there had been between myself and the man. He was the kind who have little time for adults but a great deal more to spare for children. I had discovered that; so had Sabrina.

"Poor mite," he said. "This is a hard time for her. The mistress . . . going. The master as he is . . ."

"I'm worried, Smith. So is Nanny. Where could she have got to?"

He said after a moment, "Damon will take us to her. He'll know where the little missee is. Come on, boy."

Damon was pricking up his ears. He stood very still, as though testing the air, and then he started trotting away from the house. He stopped and looked back at us.

"He's asking us to follow him," said Smith.

I cried out, "Good Damon. Take us to Sabrina, Damon."

He started to trot in the direction of the church. He paused by the lych-gate which led into the graveyard. Smith opened it and we all went through.

I knew then that Sabrina had gone to her mother's grave.

I saw her first. She was kneeling and her arms were spread out over the earth.

"Sabrina!" I cried. "Oh . . . Sabrina."

She did not move, and for a moment a terrible fear ran through me. I ran to her, and kneeling beside her, turned her body to face me. She was deathly pale and her eyes were wide.

"Clarissa," she said and threw herself at me. I held her tightly. She was shivering.

"Nobody came," she said. "The graves didn't open. I waited . . . and it was just the same."

"We must get her to bed quickly," I said. "She's shivering with the cold."

Smith picked her up in his strong arms.

"So you left your bed, miss," began Nanny Curlew.

I put a hand on her arm. "Don't scold . . . now," I whispered.

Sabrina reached for my hand, and I took it and kissed it. Nanny Curlew said, "We'll soon have you safe in bed."

Damon jumped up, barking.

"Good dog, Damon," I said. "Damon brought us to you, Sabrina. Let's get going quickly. It's all right. I'm going to look after you now."

"Always?" asked Sabrina.

"Always," I said firmly.

Smith carried her back and we put her to bed. She lay shivering while Nanny Curlew warmed up some broth and I wrapped her in blankets.

She said, "Stay with me, Clarissa." So I lay down beside her, holding her tightly in my arms.

I hoped she would sleep but she could not. She drank the broth and nestled close to me, holding onto my hand tightly as though she feared I was going to run away.

"Clarissa," she said.

"Darling, try to sleep. You can tell me tomorrow."

She was silent for a while, then she said my name again.

"What is it?" I asked gently.

"They don't come out."

"Who?"

"Dead people in graves."

"No," I said. "They're at peace. They have finished with the world. They don't want to come back."

"My mama would want to. She would want to come back for me."

"She would want you to be happy here."

"I want to go with her. I wanted one of them to come out and take my heart and make me dead so that I could get into the grave with my mother."

"Oh, Sabrina," I said, "you couldn't do that. You have to live your life here and make it happy."

"I won't be now, because . . . I killed her."

"That's nonsense."

"I did. I did. I went skating and she came and saved me and it killed her."

"No. It's not like that at all. She was ill long ago, before you were born. She was just ill again."

"But she wouldn't have been if she hadn't got cold on the ice."

"Listen, Sabrina, we are going to forget all that. It's over. It is what your mother would want."

"My papa won't forget about it."

"Things like that happen sometimes. They can't be helped. When they are over, there is nothing to be done but forget them. You're going to forget, Sabrina. I will make you forget."

"But . . ."

"Listen. You went on the ice when you were forbidden to do so. You fell in, and your mother saved you. That was what she wanted. She was ill for a while. Then she was better. Then she was ill again."

"Was she better?" asked Sabrina.

"Of course she was," I lied. "She was ill before and she had the same illness again."

"My papa . . ."

"He loved your mother dearly. He is hurt and wounded, and when people are hurt, they like to blame people. It's wrong . . . but it's human. So be gentle with him . . . and stop blaming yourself."

"You say nice things, Clarissa."

218

"I say what's true."

She was comforted and lay beside me, holding my hand tightly. I stayed with her until she slept. Then I crept quietly away.

The next day I saw Jeremy. He did not want to see me. He didn't want to see anybody. But I insisted.

I was very shocked by his haggard looks but more, perhaps, by the bitterness of his mouth. Smith had said, "He's gone right back, Miss Clarissa, right back to what he was before he went to France and brought you home."

He had been a bitter, angry man in those days, railing against fate, living the life of a recluse. Was that what he was going to return to?

"Jeremy," I said, "I'm sorry to disturb you, but I want to talk to you. It's about Sabrina."

He frowned as though the very mention of her name was distasteful to him.

"We have to remember how young she is," I went on. "She is only seven years old."

He nodded, a little impatient with me, I thought, for reminding him of an obvious fact.

"Children are very impressionable, and this tragedy is having an effect on her."

"I should hope it is," he retorted. "She should be made to realize what her wickedness has brought about."

"Jeremy, it was the thoughtless act of a child!"

"She had been told skating was dangerous and warned not to go."

"But danger appeals to children, don't you see."

"And Damaris went after her and gave her life for that child."

"It was not quite like that, Jeremy."

"I cannot see how else it happened."

I realized it was hopeless to try to make him see a different point of view, so I decided to come straight to the point.

"I want to take Sabrina back with me."

I was astonished by his reaction, for I had thought that in view of the effect Sabrina had on him, he would not hesitate for a moment to let her go.

"This is her home," he said.

"But I thought a little stay with Lance and me . . ."

"Where she will doubtless be pampered and made to feel something of a heroine. . . ."

"I do think she needs a little special care at the moment."

"What she needs is to understand what she has done. She must be made to realize that her disobedience has cost her mother's life."

"Oh, no, Jeremy! She is filled with remorse. Last night she went to her mother's grave. She had some childish notion of joining her mother. Don't you see how deeply hurt she is? She needs nursing back to normality. She needs love and security. Damaris would have understood."

The mention of her name seemed to unnerve him. He clenched his fists and turned away. When he spoke his voice sounded strangled.

"Damaris is . . . dead . . . because of this child's wanton action. She needs discipline. She is utterly selfish. She will stay here in her home. Thank you for offering, Clarissa. You have been a good girl. Damaris loved you dearly. But Sabrina has some wickedness in her and it has to be restrained. I can see trouble for her if she is not watched. She is to stay here. I want her to understand fully this terrible thing she has done."

"Jeremy," I said, "you were always kind to me. You were like a father to me. You and Damaris . . . I'll never forget . . ."

I could see I was stirring up his emotions, and because he had lost Damaris, they could only bring out more bitterness.

He said firmly, "The answer is that Sabrina stays here. She has that good Curlew woman to look after her, and this is her home."

"For a brief visit then," I pleaded.

"Perhaps later. When she shows some contrition."

I cried out in protest, "Don't you see? She is becoming obsessed by this feeling of guilt. It's doing something to her. Jeremy, she's little more than a baby."

He said, "My mind is made up."

I knew from the past that when Jeremy spoke in that way it was final.

After I had left, Sabrina's face haunted me for a long time.

"Soon you will come and see me," I had said when we parted, and she had just looked at me reproachfully. I was sure she thought that I was deserting her, and I trembled to think how she would fare in that brooding house of mourning. I was sure it was the worst possible thing that she should be left there. I relied on Smith and Nanny Curlew, and I had a word with them before I left.

It was in a very sad mood that I arrived back in London. Lance greeted me with pleasure. He was very happy to see me back, he said. He had had some good play and was the richer by several thousands. I could not be elated by the news, for if he was playing for high stakes, I felt sure there would in time be some disastrous results.

Aimée welcomed me affectionately and it was pleasant to see little Jean-Louis again. In spite of the ever-present apprehension caused by Lance's gambling, I could have been very happy if I could only have brought Sabrina with me.

Lance noticed that I was preoccupied and soon I was telling him all about it.

"If only I could have brought her with me, I would have been so relieved. I am sure I could make her into a normal child if I had her for a while."

"You are a little worker of miracles," he said lightly, and I felt a stab of disappointment, for I realized he was not really concerned about Sabrina. He would always be kind; he would put no obstacles in the way of my taking her as my own child if ever I was able to do so, and she could have a home with us and be treated as a member of the family; but at the same time he did not care deeply what became of her. There was a natural carelessness about him, an insouciance, and it applied to everything that touched him . . . except gambling.

In one way it was an asset, for it enabled him to make light of his troubles. When I considered how nearly the South Sea Bubble had ruined him, I was amazed at his reaction. I only learned later about this and how he had sailed along very near the verge of bankruptcy. He owed money all round but he had continued to live in an extravagant style. That was Lance.

Perhaps it was through Sabrina that I began to feel a vague dissatisfaction with my marriage. I would not at first admit it. I had the kindest and most indulgent of husbands. I tried not to see the superficiality of our way of life. Now I began to feel that there was no depth in it. It was only a vague feeling, for my thoughts were so taken up with the plight of Sabrina.

Every day I thought of her and I wished that I had asked Smith or Nanny Curlew to write and let me know what was happening. Neither of them, I imagined, would be very good correspondents. I might have asked Priscilla, but she was very occupied at this time, deeply concerned about the health of her parents.

I could talk to Jeanne about Sabrina. Jeanne understood.

"Poor mite," she said. "It's wicked to make her feel like a murderess. Men . . . I don't know. They have no sense, if you ask me. It is very *méchant* of this Monsieur Jeremy. He is no good father to that child."

"Oh, Jeanne," I said, "how I wish that I had brought her with me."

"She will grow up hating, that one. She will grow up with a . . . how you say . . . *un dent* . . . against the world."

"A grudge," I said. "Yes, I think you are right, Jeanne, and I do worry about her."

"Life is hard for some," added Jeanne, shaking her head. "For others easy. Madame Aimée has come out of it very well. She knows how to make a home for herself, that one does. Sharp as a wagon of *singes*."

Jeanne always grew more French when she was disturbed, so I knew that she, too, was worried about Sabrina.

"I could never like 'er," she finished, on her favorite theme of Aimée. "But at least I could talk to her."

"Dear Jeanne," I said to her one day, "I don't know what I should do without you."

"Never fret, little one," she answered, "you will never have to. The wild horse would not drag me from you."

I waited news from Eversleigh. Priscilla wrote now and then, but her letters were mainly concerned with Carleton and Arabella. I gathered she was spending a great deal of time at Eversleigh Court and was thinking of sending for her brother, Carl. She did say that she saw little of Jeremy. "He is so sad," she added, "and I do not think he wants to see anybody."

So my anxieties about Sabrina were not set at rest.

I was telling myself that I must go again to Enderby when I received the letter from Priscilla. It was a great shock.

"My dear Clarissa," she wrote, "there has been a terrible tragedy here. . . ."

The words danced before my eyes and for a few moments I found it impossible to read on because I was terrified to read that something had happened to Sabrina.

But it was not Sabrina, though it was going to affect her deeply.

We think it was an accident. They found his clothes on the beach. He had told Smith he was going to swim. His horse was tethered nearby. He had ridden down to the sea, and

222

there was no sign of him. There seems no end to this tragedy. Poor Jeremy, life was worthless for him without Damaris. I never knew anyone to be more devoted or to rely more on another person. We fear he is drowned. It is the only answer.

If you came to us now it would be so helpful. There is so much to see to, and with things as they are at Eversleigh, I find it hard to see to everything. I want to talk to you, Clarissa, about everything . . .

I sat there for some minutes with the letter in my hand. I could imagine it. Poor, desolate Jeremy who could endure it no more, deliberately riding down to the beach and swimming out to sea with no intention of coming back.

Had it happened like that, or had it been an accident?

Who could be sure? Perhaps Jeremy did not want us to be sure. Perhaps it was a secret he wished to carry with him to the grave.

Lance immediately showed concern when I read him the letter, but even then I could not help wondering whether he was thinking of last night's play.

I said, "I want to go, Lance. I want to leave at once. There is a cry for help here. They need me."

"Of course you must go, darling, I'll come with you."

He didn't want to go, of course. How he would hate that house of gloom! It didn't suit his mood at all. But it was the duty of a good husband to accompany his wife on such occasions and therefore he would do it with a good grace.

But I did not want him to make such a sacrifice and I did not really want him with me. I felt that this was too important a matter for anyone but myself. I sensed his relief when I insisted on going alone, although he displayed only concern for my safety.

Aimée said she would look after the household while I was away.

"That she will!" commented Jeanne. "She would like to be mistress of this household, mark my words."

So I went, taking my dear, faithful Jeanne with me.

It was indeed a house of gloom. Smith was there to greet me, shaking his head sadly.

"Times have changed, Miss Clarissa," he said. "Forgive me. I should say 'my lady,' I know."

"Miss Clarissa will do very well, Smith," I answered, "just as it used to be in the old days."

"They've brought him in, miss. He was washed up with the tide. One of the fishermen found him early yesterday morning."

"I'm glad he was brought home," I said.

"Yes. His funeral will be at the end of the week."

"Two funerals in such a short time. And Sabrina . . .?"

"It's hard to say," he replied. "You'll see."

"Where is she?"

He lifted his shoulders. "She went off. Since it happened she's been going off all day and staying away. She drives poor Nanny Curlew crazy."

"Does she know I'm coming?"

"Oh, yes. She was told."

"Was she pleased?"

"She didn't say, Miss Clarissa."

I understood. She guessed I would be arriving some time this day and she had decided to stay away to show me that my coming meant nothing very special to her.

I felt depressed and uneasy.

I stood in the hall looking up at the minstrels' gallery. The haunted hall, where a tragedy had happened years ago. The house had never been rid of tragedy. The things that had happened here had shown that. Perhaps they will sell the house, I thought, now that Jeremy and Damaris are both dead.

As I stood looking up at the gallery my eyes were attracted by a movement there and something told me that Sabrina was up there watching me.

I said, "I'll go to my room."

"It's all ready for you," Smith told me.

I went up past the gallery, not looking that way, and on to my room. There would be a great deal to decide. This time I must succeed in taking Sabrina back with me.

The door of my room was quietly opened.

"Come in, Sabrina," I said without looking round.

She came in. "How did you know?" she asked.

"Guesswork. You wanted to see me as soon as I arrived. You could have come down. You would have seen me better than from the gallery."

"How did you know I was there?"

"The evidence of these eyes."

"I was hidden."

"You moved."

She laughed suddenly, and there was the old mischievous Sabrina.

I turned and held out my arms. She hesitated for a moment and then ran into them.

"Oh, Sabrina ... dear Sabrina ... I am so glad to see you!"

"You like him better, though."

"Who?"

"Uncle Lance, of course."

"He's my husband. People want to live with their husbands, you know. I wanted to take you back with me, but your father did not wish it."

"He's dead," she said. "I'm glad."

"Hush, Sabrina."

"Why hush? Aren't people supposed to tell the truth?"

"Yes, but you shouldn't hate anyone."

"But I do and it's a lie to say I don't. He's lying in his coffin in that room Mama was in. I went in there and put my tongue out at him."

"Oh ... Sabrina!"

"Why do you keep looking like that and saying 'Sabrina'? I like being an orphan. It's better than it was before."

"Everything will be different now I'm here, Sabrina."

"Why?" she asked.

"Because there are two of us."

"I don't mind there being one of us."

I could see that a great deal of harm had been done. I longed to see the return of the carefree if rather willful child who had been so affectionate before the fatal accident on the pond. Then I felt confident that I alone could give her the help she needed.

Smith told me that the funeral would be very quiet. Most people thought that Jeremy's death was not accidental, but there was a possibility that he had gotten into difficulties when swimming. I tried to believe that this was so because that was what he had wanted people to think.

He was laid beside Damaris, which was where I knew he had wanted to be. Sabrina stood beside me during the service and when we were at the graveside. She allowed me to hold her hand, and I think she was pleased that I did so. There were times when I thought she was almost ready to break down and cling to me.

Poor child, she had been deeply wounded, but now there was a chance to save her from her wretchedness, and I was going to do that.

I talked to Leigh and Priscilla after the funeral and told

them that I wanted to take Sabrina back with me. They were delighted. Neither of them wanted to have the care of a child—certainly not such a one as Sabrina. Priscilla had been overcome with grief by the death of Damaris, Leigh told me, and the fact that her parents were ailing and were clearly not long for this world was an added blow to her.

"I want to take her away for a while," said Leigh, "but she won't leave her parents. In time, perhaps . . ."

Later Priscilla said to me, "Do you think you can undertake the care of Sabrina, Clarissa? It is rather a responsibility. It won't be easy."

"I know it won't. But I think I understand her and can look after her. I want to get her to put all that has happened behind her. I want her to stop brooding on it."

Leigh nodded. "She will have money in due course," he said. "Jeremy left everything to Damaris—with the exception of an annuity to Smith—so it will go to Sabrina, I suppose. I think Enderby should be sold."

"Yes," I said emphatically.

"Do you think Lance will agree to have Sabrina living with you?"

"I am sure he will."

"He's a good husband. I'm happy for you, Clarissa, in that. Damaris always used to say how contented she was to see you in a happy marriage. There was that affair in your youth— that poor boy who was transported."

"Oh, yes, yes," I said quickly, "but that was long ago."

I did not want to think of Dickon. He had been coming more and more into my thoughts lately, and I had often tried to visualize what sort of life he might be living in Virginia.

When I told Sabrina that she was coming to live with me she said in an offhand way, "Am I?"

"You needn't, you know, if you don't want to."

"I'll think about it," she said.

I was surprised and a little hurt, because I had thought she would be so pleased, for I knew it was what she wanted. She had been so badly hurt that the only way she could find a little balm to lay on her wounds was in hurting others—even those whom, in her heart, she cared for.

"You must decide quickly," I said. "Preparations will have to be made, and I have to get back soon."

She shrugged her shoulders.

"All right, then," I said. "You can stay here. I daresay you could go and live with your grandmother."

"I'll come," she said ungraciously.

I spoke to Smith. He was very unhappy. His life had been with Jeremy for so long, but he was brave and philosophical. He said, "He would never have settled down without her. The difference she made in his life was just staggering. I know. I was with him. I remember her first coming—right from that time she changed him. He couldn't have gone on without her. It's best . . . the way it's happened. Best for the nipper in a way too. If you take her, you'll bring her back to what she ought to be. I know you can do it, Miss Clarissa. . . ."

He himself would go and live in a little cottage by the sea. He'd take Damon with him. "He'll be able to run about on the beach and I'll have the sound of the sea with me always. I'll like that."

So when I left Eversleigh I took Sabrina with me.

Mysterious Disappearance

It was a strange and uneasy year which followed. My life seemed to be dominated by Sabrina. She was difficult sometimes—determined, it seemed, not to forget her wounds; they had gone very deep. I knew this because she often had nightmares and would cry out in her sleep. I had her in a room next to the one I shared with Lance, and I became as mothers are with their babies and heard her slightest cry.

Then I would slip out of bed and go to her. It was usually some nightmare. She would be skating on a pond, or she would be getting into a grave because she had given her life to one of the people who had risen from the dead. Every disturbance was due to that experience.

I would hold her tightly to me and whisper words of comfort and when she clung to me I knew how she relied on me and how necessary it was for me to lead her away from that which had affected her so deeply; and it seemed to me during those nocturnal sessions that I could do it and I only.

Nanny Curlew had come with us. She was good with Sabrina—kind and firm—and she was pleased to come because she looked on Sabrina as her special charge and she could join her cousin, Nanny Goswell. Jean-Louis was Nanny Goswell's special delight, and he was growing into a charming little boy. He was cheerful and good-tempered, bright and intelligent. "My little man," Nanny Goswell called him.

The two nannies would sit together, one knitting, one tatting endlessly, and discuss Miss Sabrina and "my little man." I thought it was good to have children in the nursery.

I did not need Jeanne to point out to me that there was a certain camaraderie between Lance and Aimée. They both had that intense interest in gambling; and my aversion to it meant that I did not share in the most important factor in my husband's life. Sometimes I wondered whether I should make an attempt to be interested in it. Then I realized how foolish that would be. I did not know the state of his affairs; he never discussed them with me, and if I enquired, he courteously dodged the issue. But I could not believe that he had successfully avoided financial embarrassment—and if he had, there must come a time when it caught up with him. I would be ready then to rescue him, but I did not intend to dissipate my fortune meanwhile.

I was, I found, thinking more and more frequently of Dickon, and as the time passed I suppose I built up an idealized picture of him. I liked to contemplate what would have happened if he had not been caught and transported. Suppose we had married. I looked longingly into a life of blissful content.

But I had married Lance. I loved Lance, of course. He possessed great charm and outstanding good looks. He was the most considerate of persons. But I often felt that there was a shadowy element there. Did I really know Lance?

This was foolish dreaming. There was too much reality all around me for me to waste myself in unsubstantial dreams, picturing what might have been.

My great-grandfather died peacefully in his bed that autumn, and about two months later Arabella followed him. I went with Lance and Sabrina to the funeral.

"There have been so many funerals in this family lately," said Priscilla sadly.

She was quiet and restrained, not easy to talk to. Leigh said he was making arrangements to take her away for a while. They would do a kind of Grand Tour of Europe, which would help to make a bridge between the past and the present. When they returned they might live at Eversleigh Court, as, before she died, it was what Arabella had suggested. Enderby should be sold.

"That will complete the change," said Leigh.

Sabrina and I went to see Smith in his cottage. He was managing very well, looking after himself, and Damon was there to keep him company.

"Poor old fellow," said Smith, "he's getting old, like I am."

He had acquired another dog—little more than a puppy. "He'll be a standby when poor old Damon's gone," he went on. "Couldn't bear to be without a dog."

Sabrina enjoyed playing with the puppy. She seemed more like a child than she had for a long time.

"You're doing a fine job with the nipper," said Smith. "It wasn't right of the master to treat her as he did. I told him so.

He'd take it from me. But it made no difference. He was that wounded . . . like a dog maimed in a trap. He just had to shut himself in. Oh, I knew him well. But you're the one to look after Miss Sabrina. You'll do it. There's good in her—if you can find it."

I felt comforted talking to that wise old man.

But during the months that followed, sometimes I despaired of Sabrina. There were times when she seemed determined to make trouble. We were all patient with her. Nanny Curlew was used to her, but Nanny Goswell was critical, comparing her with her "good little man," who, young as he was, commented Nanny Goswell, had more respect for other people's feelings than Madame Sabrina had. Nanny Curlew explained to her cousin that Sabrina had suffered through an unfortunate incident and that she must be given special care.

As for Aimée, she came to the nursery somewhat infrequently and seemed perfectly happy that her son should remain in Nanny Goswell's care. She ignored Sabrina until the incident of the cards.

Sabrina had a scrapbook in which she delighted. I was pleased to see her so interested in something, and she and I would discuss together where the pictures she collected should be stuck in. We would spend happy times together matching one color with another and fitting them in. She collected all the prints we could find, together with old songs and ballads and cuttings from the papers. Many happy hours were spent with the glue pot beside the open book; and sometimes I would say, "Let's look at the scrapbook," and she always eagerly agreed.

We were having a dinner party, one of those which did not make me very happy, for there would be play of course, and I knew that the stakes would be high. I sometimes wondered whether Lance would gamble with the house itself.

On these occasions Lance was always a little abstracted. He was perfectly charming, but it was quite clear that his thoughts were not with me.

I said to him as we dressed, "I am a little worried about Aimée."

Was it my fancy or did he seem suddenly alert?

"Whatever for?" he asked quickly. "She seems happy enough."

"Does she gamble for heavy stakes?"

He laughed. "Oh, it's gambling again, is it? Well, I'll say . . . moderate."

"Does she win?"

"She's naturally lucky. But not always, of course."

"Did she pay you back what she borrowed from you . . . to start her off?"

"Oh, yes. She soon did that. I'd say that she had far more than usual luck. At one time she was very fortunate indeed!"

Yes, I thought, and had a quick vision of her slipping a card from her petticoat pocket to those she was holding.

He laughed. "She has some notion of making enough to set up a house for herself and Jean-Louis. I have told her that her home is here as long as she wants it. I could say no more for your half sister."

"Thank you, Lance. You are very good to me—and Aimée."

He came over and kissed me. I saw his reflection in the glass—elegant, graceful, like someone playing a part on a stage. He could be trusted always to do what was correct in the etiquette of good manners.

"My dear, it is you who are good to me."

"I believe you would do a lot to make me happy, Lance."

"I'd be glad of the opportunity."

"Except one thing. You would never give up gambling for me."

"Leopards can't change their spots, my darling, and gamblers can't give up the game."

"I thought not," I said.

"I know you have never liked it," he went on, "but I couldn't give it up if I tried. It's a spell that was laid on me at birth. When I was eight I would bet with stable boys on a couple of beetles trundling along the ground. It's innate, its irredeemable. I'd do it for you if I could, but I couldn't. I wouldn't be myself."

"I understand, Lance."

"And you'll forgive me for it?" He took my chin in his hands and smiled at me.

"And you'll forgive me for being a bore and constantly nagging you about it."

"I know it is only your concern for my welfare, and bless you, my darling, I'm grateful for that."

He looked so handsome and rueful that I felt ashamed of my vague dissatisfaction and my suspicions, my vague regrets for Dickon.

Dinner was lively as usual, and immediately afterward they went to the card room to play. I went in with them, as was my custom, in order to see them settled before I slipped away to bed. The cards were on the tables and the guests were seating themselves before them. I watched Aimée. I had never been able to see her at a card table without wondering. There was now an avid, excited look in her eyes which I had noticed so often in Lance's.

There was a sudden cry of amazement. I swung round. Lance was holding a pack of cards in his hands and trying to separate them. Someone called out from one of the other tables, "They're stuck together."

There was consternation. The cards were kept in a drawer in this room. The whole household knew of this.

Even as I stood there I understood.

"What the devil . . ." Lance was saying, as near angry as he could possibly show himself to be. "What mischief is this?"

"Are they all the same?" I asked.

"It appears so."

"Yes, they are," said one of the guests.

"These are the same," pointed out another.

Lance cried out to one of the servants in a voice I had never heard before, "Bring more cards."

Fortunately there were plenty of cards in the house and these were immediately brought out and the game began.

As I came out of the room I saw a flash of white on the staircase. I went up to Sabrina's room. She was lying on her bed with the bedclothes about her face. I went over to her and pulled them back. Her eyes were fast shut in pretended sleep.

"It's no use, Sabrina," I said. "I know you're awake. I saw you on the stairs."

She opened her eyes and looked at me. She was trying to suppress her laughter.

"It wasn't really very funny," I said.

"It was," she retorted defiantly.

"They were very angry."

"Was he?"

"Very."

She looked satisfied.

"Sabrina . . . why?"

She was silent, smiling.

"You mustn't do things to hurt people," I said.

"I didn't. I did it because you don't want them to play cards. They couldn't if they were all stuck together. What'll *he* do?"

"He may speak to you."

That made her laugh again. "I don't care for him."

"You should."

"Why?"

"Because you're living in his house and he's fond of you."

"He's not fond of me. He's not fond of anyone. He's fond of cards."

I sat by her bed thoughtfully. I wondered if I was ever going to change Sabrina. Suddenly she was out of bed and clambering onto my lap.

"Clarissa, you're not cross with me. Say you're not. I did it for you. You don't like these cards . . . so I did it for you."

"Oh, Sabrina, I wish you hadn't."

"He's angry," she said, her face against my hair. "P'raps he'll send me away. Come with me, Clarissa. Let's go away. Far away. Let's run away."

"Of course he won't want you to go. He'll forgive you."

"I don't want him to."

"Now, Sabrina, please. . . ."

"Tell me a story."

I hesitated. Then I began a story which had a strong moral in it.

I sat with her until she slept. Then I crept away. It was late when Lance came up. I couldn't tell from his expression whether it had been successful play, for although he might be elated by a big win, he was never depressed by losses.

Imperturbability when things were not good was for him the essence of good manners, and that was a code he followed unswervingly.

He did not mention the incident of the cards, so I did. He burst out laughing.

"I suppose it was that minx Sabrina, up to her tricks," he said—and that was all.

I loved him dearly then. He was incapable of rancor, and the anger he had felt at the time of discovery had completely passed. He had dismissed the matter from his mind.

It was after she had had breakfast next morning that Sabrina came down for her riding lesson, looking adorable in a brown riding habit and a cocked hat to match. She looked triumphant and aggressive and clearly expected to be punished for her behavior of the previous night.

Lance was in the hall when she appeared. I saw her face change. She was a little apprehensive, I knew, by her air of bravado.

Lance said, "Hello, Sabrina. Just off on your charger, eh?"

"Yes, I am," she said quickly.

"Don't drive him too hard."

That was all. She was bewildered. He had said nothing about the cards incident. I guessed he had forgotten it. Sabrina was too surprised to hide her disappointment. I thought then that the best way to treat her outbreaks was to make them seem trivial.

She was still thoughtful when she came back from her ride. I followed her up to the nursery. Aimée was there, paying a rare visit to Jean-Louis. Nanny Goswell was expounding her little man's virtues; Nanny Curlew was mending a dress which Sabrina had torn; and Jeanne was there putting away some newly laundered clothes.

Aimée looked distastefully at Sabrina and said, "Oh, there she is, I was talking of you. You're a wicked girl. You ought to be whipped."

Sabrina's eyes sparkled. She hated Aimée, and I think that after the quiet reception of her action by Lance she was ready to delight in conflict.

"You wouldn't dare," she said.

"Wouldn't I? I'd have you beaten till you cried for mercy. I'd send you to bed and make you stay there. You're a bad, wicked girl trying to make trouble. Sticking the cards together like that. Why did you do that? To upset everyone. Everyone thought you were the naughtiest girl they had ever come across."

I wanted to intervene, but I didn't, for I felt Sabrina needed to know what effect her actions had on people.

"I would have come straight up to you and given you what you deserve," went on Aimée. "You're an ungrateful little beast. You have been given a home here . . ."

I did stop that. I didn't want Sabrina developing new resentments. I said, "Sabrina is very sorry. She won't do such a thing again."

"I might," said Sabrina, looking hard at Aimée.

I took off her cocked hat and ruffled her hair. "No, you wouldn't," I said. "Get changed, dear. We should be at our lessons."

I was teaching Sabrina myself at first. We had decided that she should have a governess later on.

Nanny Curlew had taken Sabrina's arm and was drawing her through to the bedroom.

"You'll have trouble with that child, Clarissa," said Aimée to me.

"I'll manage," I replied.

"She ought to be grateful. She's been given a home."

"I don't want her to think on those lines," I said quickly. "I want her to regard this as her rightful home . . . where she belongs."

"You spoil her. What she did last night was really venomous."

"It was done in the spirit of mischief."

Nanny Goswell said, "Nanny Curlew has punished her. She is to have no strawberry preserve today."

"No strawberry preserve!" muttered Aimée. "What a punishment. It's encouraging her to do it all over again."

I did not want to argue with Aimée so I went out. Jeanne came with me.

"And who is she to talk about Sabrina being given a home, eh? Tell me that. What of Madame Aimée, eh? A nice figure she'd cut if this house wasn't offering open welcome to her."

I was silent and did not reprove her. She was only saying what I thought myself.

Later in the day I went with Sabrina walking in the woods. I was wondering how to explain to her that she would be far happier if she did not fight against people. I did not refer to the cards incident. I felt we had had enough of that, but I wanted to explain to her that she must try to help people rather than upset them.

She was so happy running about gathering bluebells. They were a lovely misty blue under the trees. Summer was on the way.

"We'll have picnics in the woods when the warm weather comes," I said. "You'd like that, wouldn't you, Sabrina?"

"Yes, I would," she said.

Then we started playing a game naming the things we should put in a picnic hamper and then testing each other's memory by remembering them in the right order. Sabrina loved such games, and she put so much enthusiasm into them that she invariably was the winner. She was laughing as she corrected me for leaving out something, and in that moment she was a normal, happy child.

We came to the dene hole. This was one of the artificially excavated prehistoric pits which are found in Kent and Essex. It must have been about three-quarters of a mile or so from the house. Sabrina had always been fascinated by it, and I had made her swear not to go too near it. Remembering her exploit on the ice, she did promise, and I did not think she would break her word to me. But her footsteps always seemed to lead her to it and she would stand a little way back regarding it with awe.

"Why did they make it?" she asked.

"We don't know. It goes back too far in time. It might have been somewhere to hide from enemies. They were always fighting in those days. Or it may have been to store their food."

"But how did they get down there?"

"They must have had some means."

"Like Jacob's ladder."

"It may have been."

"How deep is it?"

"Very deep, they say. I don't think anyone has ever been down there."

Then Sabrina did what she always did; she picked up a stone and threw it down the hole. She stood listening, entranced. The fact that there was no sound as it reached the bottom gave credence to the story that it was bottomless.

"It goes right down and down to the center of the earth," said Sabrina.

"So be careful and promise me not to go too near."

She nodded and skipped away.

The weeks passed peacefully, and I believed that the incident of the cards had had a good effect on Sabrina. The only one who had been angry was Aimée, and she did not care enough about her to want to upset her.

She spent a great deal of time with me and seemed to have lost some of her resentment toward Lance. I thought she was growing to like him. She thought Jean-Louis was a silly baby and Nanny Goswell sillier still to dote on him as she did. She was fond of Nanny Curlew, who was quite immune to her wiles, and Sabrina respected her for that.

That she was growing even closer to me there was no doubt.

She learned her lessons with me and was bright and eager to learn. She did not want a governess and was anxious to show me that I could teach her far better than anyone else could. All she wanted was for me to be with her as much as possible; then she was happy.

There were only infrequent lapses now—little flashes of mischief, such as shutting Jean-Louis in the pantry, whither she had lured him with promises of procuring some pigeon pie for him. When we were all frantically searching for him she revealed what she had done, and we found Jean-Louis fast asleep on the floor, after having partaken too freely of pigeon pie.

"He likes food so much,"she said demurely, "that I thought it would be kind to shut him in with lots of it."

"He might have gorged himself sick," said Nanny Goswell indignantly.

"Then that would have been a good lesson for him," said Sabrina severely.

"It's someone else that wants to learn a lesson," retorted Nanny Goswell.

Nanny Curlew said some punishment must be inflicted, and Sabrina was sent to bed. I went up at that time when she should be going to sleep to find her reading a book.

"I like being sent to bed," she said complacently.

I tried to explain how worried we had all been about Jean-Louis, and she flung her arms about my neck and said she hadn't meant to worry *me*—only old Aunt Aimée. "She ought to worry," she said. "She takes Lance away from you with those silly old cards."

There was no doubt of her love for me; as for myself, she supplied that need in my nature for the child my marriage so far had failed to produce.

There was another occasion—a card party once more. We had dined, and just as our guests were about to go into the card room there was a sound on the stairs and there stood Sabrina. She had dressed herself in one of my more elaborate gowns, which hung loose about her and trailed on the floor. That was not all; she had touched her cheeks with carmine, her face was thickly powdered and she had placed a patch on her chin. She was wearing my emerald necklace, brooch and bezoar ring.

"Sabrina!" I cried.

"I thought I would like to join the card party," she said.

Lance roared with laughter. "Come along then, Sabrina," he said. "What will you play? We thought of faro for this evening."

"As you wish," said Sabrina languidly.

Nanny Curlew appeared on the stairs. "Oh, Miss Mischief," she muttered.

"Take Sabrina up," I said. "She thought she would join us, but it is a little late for her."

"I'm not tired," said Sabrina eagerly.

Nanny Curlew had her firmly by the hand and was dragging her away.

"What a charming creature," drawled one of the ladies.

"She is Clarissa's cousin," explained Lance. "She provides us with amusement. Now for the game. Shall we truly turn to faro tonight?"

When they were settled I went up to the nursery. Sabrina, robbed of her finery and in her own nightdress, looked subdued. I think that she thought for once that her little effort had failed.

I washed the cosmetics from her smooth young skin and I couldn't help laughing when I thought of the figure she had cut.

She laughed with me.

"You liked it, didn't you?" she said. "Did I look very funny?"

"It was wrong of you to come down like that . . . but yes, you did look funny."

"Lance liked it," she said.

I could see that he was making headway in her affections, and as he did so without making the slightest effort, it said a lot for his charm.

Once again I disturbed a scene in the nursery and once again Aimée was there. The nannies were talking about last night's incident.

"There she was, the minx," Nanny Curlew was saying, "all fine feathers—patched and powdered. I never saw the like."

Sabrina stood by, listening appreciatively.

"And not only that," put in Jeanne. "She was in milady's best emeralds and that ring of hers. All sparkling and glittering . . ."

"She must have looked a funny sight," said Nanny Goswell.

"She looked ridiculous," said Aimée. "This should be put a stop to. If I had my way . . ."

Sabrina surreptitiously put out her tongue and looked in Aimée's direction.

"All those jewels," mused Jeanne. "Worth a mint of money, they say. Why, you could buy a flower shop in the heart of Paris for what they're worth."

Aimée said, "Ah, hello, Clarissa. We were talking about last night."

"Sabrina felt like dressing up," I said.

"Where did she find that jewelry? You must be rather careless with it."

"Not usually. I was going to wear it last night but changed my mind at the last minute. It was in my jewel box."

"On the dressing table," piped up Sabrina. "I knew where to get it."

Aimée lifted her shoulders in a gesture of helpless resignation. I said nothing.

I did not want to discuss Sabrina with Aimée, so I turned to go, and as she followed me out she said in a sibilant whisper, "Something will have to be done about that child. She'll grow up into a . . . monster."

I looked back, hoping Sabrina had not heard. She did not appear to, she was listening to Jeanne, whose hands had gone to the Jean-Baptiste she wore under her blouse. She was murmuring, "All those fine jewels. *Mon Dieu*, she might have lost some of them. And there's enough here to buy a flower shop in the heart of Paris."

A few months had passed and the summer was nearly over. It was September and the leaves were turning to bronze, but most of them were still on the trees and it was a pleasure to walk through the woods. When I came in I was thinking that very soon we should be leaving the country for London. When the season started, that was where Lance wanted to be. He would find some excuse for returning there, and as the management of the country estates was in good hands, he could do this with ease.

There were card parties in the country, but there were even more opportunities for gambling for large stakes in London. He liked to go to the clubs and play, and it was in London that he had his circle of reckless friends.

I was determined to make the most of the days while they were still warm and I could ride or walk through those lovely leafy lanes and watch the coming of autumn, with its mists and fruits and silvery cobwebs, which suddenly seemed to be draped everywhere.

I remember distinctly coming in from my ride with Sabrina. She was quite a good little horsewoman now. Gone were the leading reins, and she had discarded her pony for a small mare which Lance had given her. She loved the mare more dearly and was growing more and more fond of Lance. She liked his indifference to her waywardness, and I think she was a little fascinated by his handsome looks and elegant way of dressing.

"He's my cousin," she said once with a certain satisfaction. "Of course not a real one—only because you're married to him."

Sabrina found it difficult to be indifferent to anyone. It seemed that for her there could only be fierce loves and fiercer hates. I was very glad that Lance was beginning to be included in the former.

So we came in that day little suspecting that anything unusual had happened. There was a dinner party that night and I went to my room to prepare myself. Jeanne was usually there laying out my things, but on this day she was absent and nothing had been prepared.

I rang the bell and one of the servants came to answer my call.

"Will you please find Jeanne and tell her that I am waiting," I said.

She went off in search of her.

That in itself was strange, for at such times Jeanne always assumed an air of importance and bustled about my room long before it was time for me to dress.

Jeanne did not come. In due course the servant appeared, rather breathless and concerned.

"Please, milady, I can't fine Jeanne. She don't seem to be in the house."

This was growing very strange. Had she gone out somewhere and forgotten the time? That must be the explanation. She never went very far. Sometimes she would take a walk in the woods to gather herbs, for she liked to make a few medicinal and cosmetic concoctions and was fond of remarking that everything of worth came out of the earth. It was an old saying which had caught her fancy.

At any moment I expected her to come bursting in breathlessly.

But no such thing happened. The minutes ticked away and still Jeanne did not return.

I had decided to wear a dress of cream-colored brocade, thinking that my emeralds would go well with it. I went to the cupboard and brought out the dress. Then I went to my jewel case. To my consternation it was empty. The emerald necklace and brooch had gone, together with the bezoar ring.

This was very strange. I could not understand it, and now I was beginning to feel alarmed.

I went to Jeanne's room. There was an emptiness there. The bed was neatly made, but there was no sign of Jeanne. I went to the cupboard. It was empty. Her best black gown, which she liked to put on in the evenings, was gone. There was nothing at all there. I opened the drawers in the chest near the window. Every one of them was empty.

Jeanne had gone!

It was impossible. There must be some explanation. As if she would have gone away like that! As if she would disappear without telling me! But where was she?

I began to look frantically around for a note. There was none.

I went back to my room and pulled the bell rope. The little maid appeared again.

I said firmly, "Find Jeanne. Let everyone look for her. Her bedroom is empty. Her clothes have gone."

The maid stared at me openmouthed.

"We must find her," I said.

But we could not fine Jeanne. She was not in the house; no one had seen her go out, yet everything she possessed had gone.

I had to dress. The party must go on however disturbed I was.

I put away the brocade dress. I did not want to look into that empty jewel case. There must be some explanation about the disappearance of my jewels. There was one solution, but I refused to believe it, although the logical sequence was beginning to force itself into my mind.

I put on a gown of scarlet, rather flamboyant, but as Lance had assured me, in excellent taste . . . a dress which required no embellishment.

I was desperately uneasy. I was worried. I was frantic. I was fond of Jeanne—more fond than I had realized. I would not believe what, on the face of it, was the only logical answer.

Aimée came in while I was dressing. She was quivering with excitement; her eyes looked luminous and unnaturally large. There was a high color in her cheeks.

"Where is Jeanne?" she asked. "I wanted to tell her . . . Isn't she here?"

"I can't find her. I think she must have been called away."

"Called away! Who would call her away, and would she go without telling you?"

"I can't understand it, Aimée. I am very worried."

"Disappeared," murmured Aimée. "It can't be. She was comfortable here. Why should she go away?"

I shook my head, and a sharp look came into Aimée's eyes. "Is . . . is anything missing?" she asked.

I was silent. I did not want to tell her about the jewelry. I should have to do so in time . . . but not yet. I kept telling myself that Jeanne would be back. There must be a simple explanation of her disappearance.

"Because if there is . . ." went on Aimée.

"What are you talking about?"

"It's obvious, isn't it? She was always talking about a flower shop in Paris. That was her great aim in life."

"You can't think that Jeanne . . . Oh, it's quite impossible. She has been with me so long. She looked after me in Paris . . ."

"She always longed to be back there. That I know. That flower shop in Paris was what she dreamed of. One of her own. It's what she always wanted."

"As if she would go without telling me! I don't believe she would ever have gone. She was so happy to have her home with us."

"She was by no means sentimental. Hard as nails, I'd say. That's how they are brought up in the streets of Paris."

"She was not hard. She was so good to me when I needed help."

Aimée nodded. "Well, who knows? Perhaps she'll come back. Has she taken some of her clothes with her?"

"All," I said.

"Oh, dear. Then it really seems . . ."

Lance came in while we were talking.

"What's happened?" he asked. "Everyone seems to be whispering together."

I said, "Jeanne has disappeared."

"Disappeared? How? When?"

"That's what I'd like to know. She's gone—that's all."

"Jeanne! I can't believe it."

I nodded. "It seems to be true."

"I really think we ought to see if anything is missing," said Aimée.

"I don't believe Jeanne would ever take anything that did not belong to her," I began.

"You wouldn't believe she'd go off without saying a word," retorted Aimée. "I think you ought to look round and see what valuables are missing. Jewels, most likely, as they would be easy to carry."

I felt myself trembling as Aimée went to my jewel case on the dressing table and opened it. She looked at me with wide-open eyes. "Did you have anything in it? It's empty now."

I said reluctantly. "I think my emeralds were in it . . . and the bezoar ring."

"No!" She almost let the case fall from her hands as she stared from me to Lance.

"You've put them somewhere else . . ." she said breathlessly.

I shook my head.

"Oh, yes, you must have," cried Lance. "They're somewhere in this room." He refused to accept the implication, as I did. He was silent for a few seconds, then he burst out, "Gad, you don't think that she . . ."

"It appears so," said Aimée. "She seems to have walked out with your emeralds, Clarissa. Who would have believed it, and yet she was always saying they'd buy a flower shop in the heart of Paris."

"That's absurd," I said emphatically. "It really is quite ridiculous."

"I expect they'll turn up," said Lance. "All of them . . . Jeanne and the jewels."

"They won't," contradicted Aimée firmly. "I know her type. She's typical of the back streets of Paris. Hard as nails and sharp as broken glass. That's what they are . . . looking for chances and never missing them when they come. It would not surprise me if she were already on the boat crossing to France. She'll get her ambition . . ."

I shook my head miserably and Lance came to me and put an arm about me.

Nothing was done about Jeanne that night. I would not allow anyone to say that she had run away; I believed she would come back and there was some explanation.

The party went on; the gambling took place. I was too upset to do anything but retire to my room.

I was still awake when Lance came up. For once I was not interested in whether he had won or lost at the tables. My thoughts were all for Jeanne. I kept seeing her in her various moods: often sharp and astringent of tongue, trying to hide that innate sentimentality in her caustic comments, and at heart good and kind. I would never forget what she had saved me from when I was young and helpless.

And now to find that she was a thief. . . .

I just would not believe that.

I talked about her to Lance, for I could not sleep, and he, understanding how I felt, did not sleep either.

He said gently that there was only one explanation, and we must accept it. Jeanne had decided to leave us. Perhaps all those years she had been hankering for her native France. She had seen the valuable jewelry and she had calculated what it would be worth.

"The temptation was too strong for her," said Lance. "Poor Jeanne, she could not resist it."

Lance thought he understood. He knew a great deal about irresistible temptations.

The next day he sent a man to Dover and Southhampton to discover if there was any sign of Jeanne trying to escape to France. It was impossible to find any information about her.

But as the weeks began to pass, even I began to believe that there could be no other explanation. Every time Jeanne had picked up my jewelry—as she had been in the habit of doing since Lance had given me the emeralds—she had seen through it the flower shop of her dreams.

It seemed that every way I looked at it, this must be the case. The temptation had been too strong for her, and she had left me to own a flower shop in the heart of Paris.

Then I had never really known her. She could not be the woman I had always believed her to be.

It was a heartbreaking discovery. What had I known of Jeanne? What did I know of anybody?

Discovery in a Shop Window

It was only during the next weeks that I realized how very much Jeanne had meant to me. She had been the mother-figure in my early, impressionable days, and in spite of all the evidence, something within me refused to accept the fact that she had run away in order to steal my jewelry and buy a flower shop. She had looked after me since I was more or less a baby with my parents in Paris, and when ill fortune had overtaken me she had cared for me. Then she had come to England to find me. Oh, no, I would not believe that Jeanne was a common thief.

There was some explanation. There must be.

"What?" asked Aimée.

As for Lance, he shrugged his shoulders. He did not want to dwell on the matter. It was a blow, losing the jewelry, he agreed, but when his winnings warranted it, he would buy more for me. It was no use crying over what was done was his motto.

Jeanne had gone, and there was no way we could find her without a great deal of trouble and expense. Besides, what if we did? Should we take the flower shop away from her?

No, let her keep it, said Lance. He had a grudging admiration for one who could devise such a plan and carry it out. If his luck held, he would buy me bigger and better emeralds.

He was ready to forget Jeanne. He almost wished her well of her ill-gotten gains. He did not understand that her action had wounded me far more deeply than the loss of the jewels. His indifference about the important things in life exasperated me—especially when I compared it with his intense passion for gambling.

It was three or four weeks after Jeanne's disappearance and we were back in London. The season had begun, and although we did not go often to court, it was necessary to do so now and then. The new King was reckoned to be a boor, and it was always the King and Queen who set the mode of the court. This King had no Queen—or rather he had put her away years ago on account of her suspected intrigue with Count Königsmarck. His German mistresses reigned in her place, and on account of their lack of charm, as well as their rapaciousness, they were not very popular. So there was no great desire to go to court which was not in fact the center of polite society. Queen Anne had called George the "German boor," and apparently the description still fitted him.

Lance said he selected his friends and companions from people who were considered inferior—lacking wit, dignity and good breeding. "He feels more at home with them than he does with English gentlefolk. He lacks dignity of mind and manners."

But Lance admitted that in some respects he served the country well, for although he was a good soldier, he believed that prosperity rested in peace, and he would therefore do his best to preserve it.

"George is better for the country than the Stuart would have been," was Lance's verdict. "Though with a Stuart we might have had someone who looked more like a king. Still it is actions that count, and we'll get by with George—and at least his mistresses provide some amusement."

He was right there. They did. They were both elderly and ugly, which perhaps says something for his fidelity. The fact that they did not speak English did not add to their popularity. They might have had the grace to try to learn the language of the country which was giving them so much, commented Lance.

He came in one day to tell us he had seen Mademoiselle Kielmansegge riding near the palace in her carriage. The people were shouting abuse at her as she rumbled past until she put her head out of the window and said in her own brand of English, "Why, you people, why you hate us? We only come for your goods." That amused the crowd, especially when someone shouted, "Yes, and for our chattels too!" And they followed the coach to the palace, shouting after it.

I went on brooding about Jeanne's disappearance and trying to reconcile it with what I knew of her. I just could not. In spite of all the evidence against her, I was sure that one day I must learn the explanation.

Aimée and I were going to Gracechurch Street to buy some material for the children's clothes. It was rarely that Aimée accompanied me on these expeditions; she was usually content for me to choose for Jean-Louis. The two nannies loved to seize on materials and make them into clothes, for they were both considerable seamstresses. I was thinking sadly as we jolted along of how often Jeanne had accompanied me on these missions.

As we came into the heart of the city Aimée said to me, "Clarissa, I want to tell you something."

I turned to her, surprised by her downcast look. "Yes?" I said.

She hesitated. "It's my mother," she began. "She . . . she's here . . . in England."

"Aimée! That must be wonderful for you."

"Yes," she replied. "She is a widow now. Her husband died. I thought she was settled for the rest of her life. Hers is a similar story to mine. Alas, her husband died with debts. My mother is very strict about such things. She always said that a debt was an *affaire d'honneur,* which must be settled at all costs."

"That's right, of course."

"When her husband died she had enough to cover his debts—and little more."

"So she is very poor."

Aimée lifted her shoulders in a typical French gesture. "She has . . . a little . . . a very little. I feel sad that I cannot look after her as I would wish. I did not have your luck at the time of the Bubble. If I had—"

"Where is your mother staying? Is she in London?"

"She is staying at the King's Head, close by St. Paul's, but she will not be able to remain there. I do not know what she plans. But she wanted so much to see me."

"You must ask her to come and stay with us."

I felt uneasy. I was very much aware that this was my father's mistress. It had been a little shock for me to discover I had a half sister, but to meet the woman who had shared my father with my mother was somehow distasteful to me.

I turned to Aimée. I had never seen her look so anxious. I pressed her hand. "But of course she must come," I said. "She must stay with us until she decides what she is going to do."

"I thought I would speak to you . . . before Lance."

"But of course. Lance will raise no objections, I assure you."

"He is the kindest man in the world," said Aimée emphatically, "and sometimes, Clarissa, I think you are the luckiest woman."

"I know I am fortunate. Lance is good to me."

"He is so easygoing . . . always wanting to make people happy. There are not many husbands like Lance, Clarissa."

"I am sure you are right. When will you see your mother?"

Aimée gulped. "Well . . . knowing that we should be shopping this morning, I told her. She wants to meet you. She will be at the mercer's shop. She said that if you did not want to meet her for any reason, I could give her a sign and she would slip away."

"I hope you told her that was an absurd suggestion."

"I did, knowing how kind you have always been to me."

"I shall look forward to meeting her. Oh, Aimée, you must be very happy that she is here."

"It is hard to be separated from one's family."

I could scarcely wait to get to the shop in Gracechurch Street, and as we stepped from the carriage and the mercer came out to hand us in he said, "There is a lady . . . Madame Legrand . . . who is waiting to see you."

As we stepped down into the shop a woman rose from the stool on which she had been sitting. She was of medium height, with quantities of red hair; she was quietly but very elegantly dressed in light navy, with a touch of delicate pink in the frilly fichu which was all that lightened the severity of her gown. But she wore a large blue hat with an ostrich feather tinged with pink at the edges. Her appearance was distinguished because of its contrast between something bordering on austerity and the extreme femininity in the fichu and the feather in the hat.

She looked at me with an expression of wonder and awe.

"So," she said, "you are Clarissa."

Aimée said, "This is my mother, Clarissa. She has been longing to see you."

Madame Legrand cast her eyes down. She murmured, "Forgive me. It is a moment of emotion." She spoke very little English, I discovered, and what she did was peppered with French words. "You are . . . a little . . . like him . . . I can see him in Aimée. He was the one never forgotten."

"Clarissa has said that you must come and stay with us," said Aimée.

Tears filled the Frenchwoman's eyes. "Oh, it is so . . . *gentil* . . . so good . . . so kind. I do not know if I may . . ."

"Oh you must," I insisted. "You must stay with us while you are in England. I am sure you will want to be near Aimée."

"Ah . . . my little one. It has been hard, this parting."

Again that lifting of the shoulders. "But what can be done? You see, there was my 'usband."

"Of course," I said, "the parting with Aimée must have been very sad."

She broke into French then. "It was right for her. You understand . . . a mother's heart. A mother must not shut her eyes to the blessings that can come to her children. She must not say, 'Ah, but I want them with me.' No, not if it is better for them to leave her. She must do what is best for them."

She was inclined to be garrulous in her own language, and although I was very interested in what she had to say, I did not think the mercer's shop was the place in which to say it.

I suggested that we make our purchases and then go to a coffeehouse, where we could talk in comfort, and this we did.

Madame Legrand, whose name was Giselle, explained to me in French, for she realized I could understand that language.

Her husband had died. Oh, that had been a dire tragedy. She had thought herself well provided for. She had planned that she would send for Aimée and the little boy, her grandson. It was hard to think of herself as La Grand'mère, but she was proud that she was one. They were to have lived together in comfort.

"A woman clings to her family, Clarissa. I may call you so? You and my daughter are sisters . . . but perhaps I should not say this. Your father . . . the father of you both . . . was such a man to adore. Having met him, it had to be whatever he wished." She spread her hands. "And this is what he wished."

As we sipped our chocolate in the cozy atmosphere of the coffeehouse, Madame Legrand talked. She was certainly never at a loss for words.

She talked about the past and her relationship with my father. "So tall, so handsome, so all that a man should be. Oh, it was wrong, it was sin, they would say. I have had to do a million penances for my lord. But I would do it all again . . . oh, yes, I would. There was never one like him." So vividly did she talk of him that she made me see him again. She recalled little habits of his which I had forgotten till that moment: his manner of raising one eyebrow when he listened to something he did not believe; his way of taking off his hat suddenly and tossing it in the air; the way he touched his right ear when he was concentrating on something. Recalling these gestures, she brought his memory back more clearly than it had been for many years.

"What a man!" she said. "Never one like him. But he was never a man for one woman. Ah . . . if he had been. . . . I did not see him so much after your mother came to France. I remember it well. She was said to be the most beautiful woman in Paris. It was no wonder that milord wanted her.

"He talked to me about you. 'That adorable daughter of mine,' he used to say. Oh, he was fond of you. He was fond of Aimée too. He would have been a good father if he could have settled down to one. . . ."

I grew quite emotional listening. I was back in that big *hôtel* which had been our home in Paris. I was lying in my little bed there longing for a visit from my mother in one of her exquisite gowns. I was completely bemused by her dazzlingly beautiful looks—and when he was with her, those had been the great occasions.

Madame Legrand touched me gently on the arm. "Oh, I see I have carried you back through the years. . . ."

When we were ready to go I said she must come back with us. She demurred. No, no, it would be too *difficile,* she being as she was . . . but with no regrets. Anyone who had known my lord would have understood that he had to have his needs gratified, and there were few women who could resist him. No, she would not come. She would content herself with having seen her daughter. Ah, but she would like a glimpse of her little grandson. Just once to see him, to say, "Ah, that is my little one, who has made my Aimée so happy." Just that and then . . . adieu.

"What will you do then?" I asked.

Again she lifted her shoulders. "I shall go back. There is work I can do. Perhaps be a housekeeper, eh? Am I not skilled in the work of the household, Aimée? It is best to forget the past and make the future."

"Dear Maman, you have only just come," said Aimée.

"At least come and stay with us for a while," I said.

"I could not. But you are so kind. I understand you have your husband. He will not wish me to impose. You have been good to Aimée and for that I thank you with all my heart. But for me . . . I shall go back to France. I will find some way of keeping myself. I am clever with my hands. I am a seamstress of some quality, am I not, Aimée? Oh, how I should love to make up that beautiful silk you have bought for my little one. But no matter."

"I am going to insist that you come and stay with us for a while," I said. "You must get to know your grandson. Besides, Aimée will be most upset if you go away just as soon as you have come."

She cast down her eyes and shook her head.

Aimée took her hand. "Please, Maman," she said.

Madame Legrand hesitated and then said, "Very well. For a little stay. A little rest before I go away. A little time with my daughter and my grandson."

"You are very welcome," I told her.

Aimée said eagerly, "Let us go back to your inn. You can settle there and come right away."

"Oh ... no ... no ... Give me today. Tomorrow I will come."

"Then let it be so," said Aimée. "Clarissa, may I have the carriage tomorrow and come and collect my mother?"

"But of course. And I will come too. We'll bring the children. Jean-Louis and Sabrina will love that."

Madame Legrand covered her face with her hands.

"You are too good," she murmured. "And I am too ... too happy."

So it was arranged.

So Aimée's mother came to stay with us in Albemarle Street. Lance welcomed her with his usual charm. "Strange," he said, "we lost one member of the household and have acquired a new one."

"Lance," I said earnestly, "you don't mind her being here?"

"Mind! Of course not."

"I could do nothing else but invite her. She is, after all, my sister's mother."

"Such complicated relationships," he murmured. "It all comes of your having such a colorful personality for a father."

"I'm sorry it happened that way."

"It's the way of the world," he said, putting a light kiss on my cheek.

Madame Legrand proved to be quite an asset to the household. She was voluble in her gratitude and at the same time determined to make herself useful. Like her daughter, she had a wonderful way with clothes. She could make them and wear them so that the simplest looked elegant. She could dress the hair and apply the right amount of cosmetic to the face; she could make a dress to show off the advantages of one's figure. She was good with the children, who were both a little fascinated by her strange accent, and her gesticulating conversation was a source of wonder to them both. Even Sabrina was at first impressed by her.

She did a great deal for me. She asked if she could dress my hair. She was sure she could show it off to better advantage. She understood I had had a French maid. Aimée had told her that the woman had turned out to be a thief and had upset us all by running away with valuable jewelry.

"I still can't believe it," I said. "I thought I knew Jeanne."

"Aimée tells me that she came from the slums of Paris."

"Oh, it is a long story, but I owed her a good deal. I will never really believe what everyone says is the only answer to her disappearance."

"Ah, people are strange," mused Madame Legrand. "They are good in one way . . . bad in another . . . but if the bad is there, or the good, it will break out sometime, and then some part of the nature is revealed."

She altered my clothes. "A little taken in here . . . you see . . . and we show off that pretty little waist. A little lower here, to show the white throat and just a little beginning of the bosom, eh? And a full skirt . . . sweeping out from the waist. I will make a dress for you and you will be so beautiful. . . . Yes, let me make it for you, dear Clarissa, to show you how happy I am to be here."

Sometimes she talked of going away. We persuaded her to wait a while. A whole month passed and she was still with us.

I knew she wanted to stay and would be desolate if she had to leave us. She was devoted to her grandson, and he would sit on her lap and listen to stories about France—how the children collected snails after a rainy day and put them in a basket to take to the kitchens to be cooked and served with garlic; how they picked the grapes and danced on great tubs of them; how they put slippers by the fire on Christmas Eve, when presents were put into them and opened on Christmas morning.

Sabrina listened too; she was clearly a little fascinated by Madame Legrand.

Then came the day when I knew for sure that I was pregnant. I was delighted. For the first time I ceased to think of Jeanne. The incident was now fading into the past, but I was still not convinced that what appeared so obvious was true.

I did think, however, how excited she would have been at the prospect of my becoming a mother. It was something she had always wanted.

Lance was delighted. I had rarely seen him so enthusiastic about anything except gambling. A child at last! It was wonderful news. I could see that he was planning for a boy. I wondered whether he would take a gamble on it, and it would not have surprised me in the least if he did. As for myself, I would be content with either sex. All I wanted was my own child.

Aimée said, "My mother is so delighted. She loves babies. The only thing that saddens her is that she will not be here to see the child born."

"Perhaps we can persuade her to stay till then."

"Clarissa, would you really! You would have a hard task persuading her, because she feels she is imposing."

"Oh, what nonsense! This is a big household. Besides, look what she does for me. She is never idle, and now that Jeanne has gone . . ."

"You still think about her, don't you, Clarissa?"

"She was a true friend . . . I always thought."

"Alas, that you can be so mistaken in people."

It was at length agreed that Aimée's mother should stay until the baby was born.

"I am sure you will be useful," I told her, to make her feel she was not imposing on our hospitality.

"Well, if there is anything I can do to help, so gladly will I do it."

My great pleasure was planning for the baby and talking of it with Lance. I think he lost a little of his desire to gamble, even, in contemplating the arrival of the baby.

"Perhaps we shall have a big family after all, Clarissa, eh?" he said.

"I should like ten children," I replied.

Lance laughed. "Let's get one first, to begin with."

Those were happy days. Often I found myself thinking how much Jeanne would have enjoyed this. Then I would remember and disbelief would sweep over me.

I was constantly shopping during those first two months after my baby's conception. I bought laces and ribbons and soft white materials. I would take the carriage and go into the heart of the city. There I would leave the carriage and do my shopping, telling the coachman where to pick me up.

Sometimes I was accompanied by Aimée or her mother; on occasions I took Sabrina. She enjoyed it, but I was always on tenterhooks that something might catch her fancy and she would slip away. I was terrified thinking of what might become of Sabrina. So I only took her when there was someone else with me.

I found that I enjoyed being alone; then I could wander where I wished as long as I remembered where to meet the carriage.

I loved to wend my way among the street vendors—past stalls full of apples and tarts, past the men selling hot gingerbread, or watercress, or doormats, past the chair menders repairing chairs on the cobbles.

Usually, different traders kept to certain streets. There were fishmongers in Fish Street Hill, booksellers in Little Britain, and barbers everywhere, for wigs were constantly worn by all and sundry and they needed frequent curling and powdering. I loved to see the man they called the Flying Barber who hurried through the streets calling to those who wanted a shave. He carried his hot water and razors with him and did his work there in the street under the eyes of the passersby.

Nowhere in the world could there have been scenes of greater interest and vitality. At least so it seemed to me, who had been bred in the country.

I felt stimulated by moving among those people, and the fact that I must cling tightly to my purse only added to the excitement of the adventure.

I was passing the jeweler's shop which always had a fascination for me because I loved to see those sparkling gems displayed on dark velvet. There were bars across the window, and I always wondered how soundly the jeweler slept in the gabled rooms above his shop.

I paused, and it immediately caught my eye. I stopped and stared. Lying there in the center of the shop window was my bezoar ring.

It could not be mine. But could it be? Mine had had an unusual setting. After all, it had been a royal ring—according to legend. I could have sworn that that was my ring.

On impulse I went into the shop. As I stepped down, a bell tinkled to warn the shopkeeper that someone had come in.

He rose from the counter.

"Good day to you, my lady," he said.

I returned his greeting. "You have a bezoar ring in the window," I said.

"Oh, yes. You recognized it for a bezoar, did you? They are not very common."

"I know. May I see it?"

"With pleasure. Allow me." He brought it out of the window and I took it in my hand. I saw the initial inside. It was identical with the one Lord Hessenfield had given me.

"I had one—exactly like this," I said.

He shook his head. "I would say this is unique. I have seen other bezoar rings. At one time kings and queens all had them—but those of lesser rank too. This is a special one. It belonged to Queen Elizabeth, who bestowed it on a courtier. You see the initial *E* inside."

I was sure now. I turned it over and asked the price. I was surprised at its value.

I said, "May I ask how this came into your possession?"

"Why, yes, indeed. I bought it as I do so many of my pieces. Most of them are not new, as you know. When something goes back into time it increases its value. So it is with this. I bought it from a French lady."

My heart sank. It seemed as though Jeanne's guilt was being proved.

I said, "I have reason to believe that this ring was once mine. It was stolen."

"Oh, my dear lady, I do not deal in stolen goods."

"I am sure you would not knowingly . . . but if someone comes into your shop and tries to sell you something, how are you to know how it was come by?"

He looked apprehensive.

"She was a very respectable lady. She had some fine emeralds too, which I bought."

"May I see the emeralds?"

"A necklace and a brooch," he murmured, frowning.

"Yes," I said. "That is right. Please let me see them."

"They were sold some weeks ago. A lady and a gentleman came in and he bought them for her."

"Tell me about the woman who sold them to you."

"She was French. She said she had to leave England in a hurry. She was going to catch the Dover coach. She had to return to France unexpectedly, and being short of money temporarily until she could settle her French estates, she was disposing of some of her jewelry."

Oh, Jeanne, I thought, how could you?

I didn't want to hear any more. I asked if he would deliver the bezoar ring to Albemarle Street, where he would be paid for it.

He promised to do so.

Menace in the Forest

Lance was very interested to hear that I had found the bezoar ring and that the jeweler's story had confirmed the fact that Jeanne had sold them and gone to France.

"She should have waited until she got over there," said Lance. "She might have been caught disposing of them in London. But I suppose she didn't like carrying them on her person. Although, of course, the money would be equally tempting to a thief. Anyway, I'm glad you have your ring back."

"I'm delighted to have found it. It's rather a special one, having been in the Hessenfield family for generations. Our baby shall have it."

"It will be a long time before he can wear it," said Lance.

"*She* shall have it in good time," I retorted.

Lance laughed. "All right, darling," he said, "I shan't grudge you your girl any more than you will grudge me my boy. I bet if it is a girl it will turn out to be exactly what I want, and if a boy, just your desire."

"That is the sort of bet you can always make with certainty," I said.

I was indeed happy during those early days of my pregnancy. It was only now and then, when I thought of Jeanne, that the shadow would fall, and every time I looked at the bezoar ring I imagined her going boldly into that shop with the tale she had prepared about hurrying to France and needing the money urgently.

Sabrina was not sure whether she wanted a baby or not. Sometimes she talked about it excitedly and what she would do when it came. She would teach it to ride and tell it the stories I used to tell her, she decided.

"It will be a long time before the baby is able to ride," I warned her.

"Oh, you can't start too young," said Sabrina with an air of wisdom.

Then at times she was jealous of it. "I believe you like this baby more than you like me. And it's not here yet."

"I love you both."

"But you can't love two people the same."

"Oh, yes, you can."

"No. You have to love one more, and this one is your own."

"So are you, Sabrina."

"But I wasn't born yours."

"It makes no difference."

"I wish this one wasn't coming. I know it will be silly . . . sillier than Jean-Louis."

"He's not silly."

"And I don't like her either."

"Who is that?"

"His grandmother. I don't like her."

"I thought you liked to listen to her."

"Not anymore." She brought her face close to mine. "I don't like her because she doesn't like me."

"Of course she likes you."

"And she doesn't like the new one either."

"You're not telling the truth, Sabrina."

"It is the truth. I know it."

"She didn't say so."

"She *looks* it. I don't like her. I don't like Aimée, and I don't like Jean-Louis."

"Oh, you are in a disliking mood."

"Uncle Lance likes Aimée, though."

"Of course he does. We all do—except you, of course."

"He likes her—kind of special." She hunched her shoulders and looked mysterious.

"Who told you?"

"I saw them."

"What do you mean?"

"I saw them talking."

"Why shouldn't they talk?"

"I saw them. I know. He likes her and she likes him . . . a lot."

It was silly to listen to Sabrina. She told wild stories, and if she saw that she had caught my attention her stories would become wilder. All she was doing was calling attention to herself, for she had an idea that now the baby was coming she was being set aside.

I tried to be extra loving to her. She responded, but the suspicious jealousy was there and I felt it growing.

After the first two months of pregnancy I began to feel quite ill. Aimée soothed me. It had been the same with her, she told me. She had been wretchedly ill during the first months. But it had passed. What was that tisane Jeanne had made? She thought she remembered. She would ask her mother, for she was sure she would know. She believed it was a well-known remedy in France for morning sickness.

Madame Legrand was only too delighted to make the tisane. She wasn't sure that it was the same as Jeanne's, but there was a recipe in her family which had been handed down for generations, and if she could lay her hands on the right herbs she would make it for me.

She did, and I felt worse after it. I thought it didn't agree with me.

"That can't be," said Aimée. "It often makes you worse for a time and then cures you. You see."

Madame Legrand was disappointed. She had believed it to be a certain remedy. She immediately prepared another, and I felt considerably better after taking it.

"I think we have hit on the right thing," said Madame Legrand. "The first one was too strong."

Lance was deeply concerned. "You'll have to rest more, Clarissa," he said. "There's no help for it."

I did not ride, but I did like walking. Lance said we should go to the country, which would be so much better for me. I supposed it would be, but I missed my walks through the teeming streets of London.

However, we went to the country, and Lance said he thought I should stay there until the child was born. He would have to be in London some of the time, of course, but he would accompany me and stay with me for a few weeks.

So we went to the country. Madame Legrand declared herself delighted with Clavering Hall.

"It is beautiful," she said. "The old English country house! Never would I wish to leave it."

"You're welcome to stay as long as you like," Lance told her in his generous way.

"Your husband is reckless man," she told me with a smile. "Listen to what he say to me! Why, you might be hating me in a few months' time."

"I am sure, Madame Legrand, I could never hate you, however much I tried," said Lance.

"Oh, he is a charmer," she replied.

I did not feel any better in the country in spite of the tisanes which Madame Legrand continued to make for me.

I remember one occasion when Sabrina was with me. She used to come and sit on my bed when I felt it necessary to be there.

"You see what a lot of trouble this baby is causing," she said. "You have to rest in bed because of it. You never had to rest in bed because of me."

"Oh, dear, Sabrina," I replied, "don't be jealous of this little baby. You're going to love it as much as I do when it comes."

"I am going to hate it," she told me cheerfully.

One of the servants brought in the tisane on a tray, and as soon as we were alone Sabrina picked it up and sipped it.

"Ooo, it's nasty. Why are things to do you good always nasty?"

"Perhaps we imagine they're nasty."

Sabrina pondered that. "Nice things do you good sometimes. You're wearing your ring. That's the one Jeanne stole. It's rather a funny ring. It belonged to a queen."

"That's right."

"Granny Priscilla told me about it. Kings and queens had them because people were trying to poison them, and if you put the ring in the drink the poison goes into the ring."

"Something like that."

She had the ring from my finger and with a laugh dropped it into the tisane.

"Let's see what happens," she said.

"Nothing will happen. That was not poison."

Sabrina's eyes grew round. "Suppose it was. Then we'd see it go into the ring."

She held it up to the light. "I can't *see* anything," she said.

Nanny Curlew came in. "Time for bed, Miss Sabrina. What are you doing?"

"She's testing my ring, Nanny. My bezoar ring."

"Whatever next!"

"I can see it going in!" cried Sabrina.

"What nonsense! You can't see anything."

"I can. I can."

I took it from her. The ring and the liquid were quite unchanged. I picked out the ring. "Now it's wet," I said, "and I really don't fancy drinking that now."

"I'll get another one made for you, my lady," said Nanny Curlew.

260

Sabrina put her arms round my neck. "Don't get killed," she begged.

I laughed. "Dear Sabrina, I have no intention of doing so."

Nanny Curlew brought a towel and wiped the ring, which I slipped onto my finger, and Sabrina went off with her.

A little while later Madame Legrand came into the room with another tisane.

"Nanny Curlew explained," she said. "She tells me Mademoiselle Sabrina have too much imagination. She look for poison with your ring in the tisane."

I laughed. "Sabrina likes drama."

"And to be the center of it, eh? I know that one."

I had noticed that one of the young men who came to Lance's gambling parties was interested in Aimée. Not that other men had not been, but with Eddy Moreton it was different. He was a tall, rather gangling young man, with very fair hair, pale-blue eyes, a rather prominent nose and a weak chin. He was an inveterate gambler, and I had heard that he once won fifty thousand pounds in one night at the gambling tables in one of the London clubs and lost it before the week was out. He was the younger son of a rich father, but he had quickly got through his inheritance, and the rest of the family frowned on his activities. All the same he was a likable person, always good-natured, happy-go-lucky, and always ready to take a gamble.

I mentioned him to Aimée, for I had always thought it would be a good idea for her to settle down and marry. She was young, attractive, and she needed someone who would be a father to Jean-Louis.

"I like Eddy," she said, "but he has nothing but his winnings. If I had had your luck with the Bubble, I wouldn't have to consider these things. As it is . . . what would we live on?"

"I believe he is fond of you, and if you loved him. . . ."

"You can't live on love, sister."

All the same, I think she liked Eddy. She certainly led him to believe she did.

He came to dine with us in the country. This was significant, because during dinner the conversation turned to my bezoar ring.

I think it was Madame Legrand who brought it up. She was always present at our dinner parties, and sometimes would join the players. Lance had told me that she had good luck.

"It might have been beginner's luck," he added, "for she has not played very much before."

They were talking about the past, and somehow the subject of the Borgias came up.

"It was easy in the old days," said Eddy, "if you wanted to get rid of people you didn't want around. You asked them to dine and ... hey, presto ... they partook of the delicious dish of—what shall we say? Lampreys? Sucking pig? It didn't matter which, for that took care of them. Those people developed poison to a fine art. No taste. No smell. Nothing suspicious, therefore."

"It is why they had the bezoar rings," put in Madame Legrand. "Clarissa has one. Do you wear it today, Clarissa? You do. Oh, then you are safe."

Everyone laughed.

"You know what it is?" I said. "It's formed in the stomachs of certain animals. It absorbs poison. That's why Queen Elizabeth had one. Quite a number of monarchs had them in the past."

Everyone was enormously interested, and the ring was passed round the table.

"It was stolen by that unscrupulous maid of Clarissa's," said Lance. "She found it by a miracle. Tell them about it, Clarissa."

So I told how I had seen the ring in a shop window.

"A chance in a million," said Eddy, awestruck.

"What a pity that you did not bet on my finding it!" I said.

They laughed and the ring was handed back to me.

The tables were set up in the usual manner, and after seeing them all settled I went upstairs. Madame Legrand accompanied me.

"They will play into the early hours of the morning," she said. "I wish that Aimée had not such a taste for this gambling."

"It's a pity," I agreed. "They win, then they lose. It all seems such a waste of time."

"And dear Lance, he has this love of the gamble, has he not?"

I nodded ruefully, and she lifted her shoulders, kissed me and said good night.

Lance came up eventually. I was half asleep. He came in, went to the dressing table, and went out again. Now I was fully awake, wondering what this meant.

Shortly afterward he came back.

He was in a rather sober mood, so I guessed that his losses must have been great to have that effect on him.

"Is everything all right, Lance?" I asked.

He was silent for a few moments, and I sat up in bed to look at him more closely.

"Don't worry," he said. "Just a bit of bad luck. I think we drank too much wine at dinner . . . and we were drinking afterward. Drink makes you do foolish things."

"Have your losses been so great, then? Tell me. What have you lost?"

"Let me explain," he said. "I want you to see it as it happened. We were all very merry . . . as I said, the wine . . . and we played poker. The stakes were getting rather high when Eddy said he was finished. He could bet no more, for if he lost he would be so deeply in debt that he would never get out of it."

"It seems he has come to his sense at last."

"No. He couldn't bear to stop, so he staked the diamond pin in his cravat. I won it. He was wearing a signet ring with the family's crest engraved on it. Heavy, solid gold, of some value. He wanted to throw it against some possession of mine, and suddenly he said, 'That ring we saw at dinner. That's what I want. We'll play for that.' I said, 'No. That's Clarissa's ring.' He shouted, 'What's hers is yours. Come on, I want to play for the bezoar ring.' I told him the bezoar ring was priceless. I said, 'It's worth more than your signet ring, Eddy, and you know it.'

"He said, 'All right. My country house for the bezoar ring.' Everyone had become excited because of the unusual stakes. We were urged on. Someone said Eddy was crazy. A house for a ring! Aimée was sitting beside Eddy, urging him on. She loves a gamble, that girl . . ."

Lance's eyes were shining, the excitement still with him.

"So you gambled with my ring," I said.

"Yes," he answered soberly.

"And you lost."

He was silent.

"Lance," I cried, "are you telling me that my bezoar ring has gone to Eddy Moreton!"

He looked shamefaced. "I'll get it back," he said.

It was rarely that I was angry with Lance, but I was then. I had always deplored his reckless gambling, but that he should have risked something which was mine filled me with rage. I was as furious as I had been on that occasion when he had used my money to buy shares in the South Sea Company without consulting me. I was tired, and this was the last straw.

"How dare you!" I cried. "It's tantamount to stealing. What right have you? Risk your own goods if you want to be so foolish . . . but leave mine alone."

"I will find another ring, I promise you. I will get you that one back. Clarissa, I'm sorry. It was wrong of me. But you must try to imagine what it was like down there. The excitement of it . . . the different type of bet. It was momentarily . . . irresistible."

"It's despicable," I said.

"Oh, Clarissa," he murmured. He came to the bed and tried to put his arms about me. I pushed him aside.

"I am tired of your incessant gambling," I said. "I don't know the state of your affairs, but it wouldn't surprise me if they're in a bad state. You are so foolish . . . like a child who can't say no, even when it comes to taking what is not yours. I do not forget what you did with my money in the South Sea Company."

"And look what I made for you."

"You did not make it. I made it by my good sense in putting an end to the gamble. I forgave you that, but this is too much. The ring was my special property."

"You did not seem to care so much when you lost it before."

"I cared deeply."

"That was because Jeanne stole it."

"You are as bad as Jeanne. You have stolen it, too. I see no difference in you. She at least had the sense to steal it for a sensible purpose. You . . . just satisfy your lust for gambling."

"Clarissa, I swear I'll get it back."

"Yes," I retorted. "Stake the house against it—all you possess. You might lose that too. Stake me, perhaps. Please go away now. I'm tired and I want to be alone."

He tried once more to cajole me, sitting on the bed, looking at me with wistful appeal, bringing out all his considerable charm, but I wanted him to know how deeply upset I was and that I no longer accepted this gambling when he so wantonly risked what was mine. I could not and would not forgive him for taking my bezoar ring.

Lance had always hated trouble and escaped from it as soon as possible, and when he saw that I was adamant, he did that now.

He sadly rose from the bed and opened the door of the

powder closet. He would go there and spend the night on that uncomfortable couch, hoping that I would soften toward him.

I stayed in bed next day, for I was feeling unwell. My condition, together with last night's shock, had upset me so much that I felt too ill to get up. Moreover, I wanted to shut myself away, to consider Lance and my feelings for him.

I loved him in a way. His charm was undeniable. He was always gracious and kind, and very popular in society, and there had been many an occasion when I had felt proud to be his wife. And yet sometimes—and this was particularly when the gambling fever was on him—I felt I did not know him. I thought of Elvira. How deeply did his feelings ever go? He must have been fond of her, albeit in a lighthearted way. Why had he not married her? I suppose because she would not have been a suitable wife, so their relationship had been a casual one. I *was* a suitable wife. Why? Because I came from a good family background—or because I had a fortune? Had that been the reason?

I was thinking now of Dickon. Our relationship had been strong and firm in spite of the fact that everything was against it. It had been young and innocent and beautiful even though the feud between our families was as fierce as that between the Montagues and Capulets. I wandered back to the old familiar theme. What would have happened to us if Dickon had not been sent away, and I dreamed of an ideal.

It was then that I felt that life had cheated me.

Sabrina came to see me. She was always uneasy when I was not well. It was touching to see how much I meant to her. I believe I stood for security, and that was what Sabrina, in common with most children, wanted most in life.

She climbed onto the bed and studied me closely.

"You're ill," she said. "It's that silly baby."

"People often feel slightly less well when they are going to have babies."

"Silly to have them then," she said scornfully.

She studied me again. "You look a bit angry too," she commented.

"I'm not angry."

"You look sad and angry and ill."

"Whatever else you are, Sabrina," I said, "you're frank. I'm all right, though."

She said, "I don't want you to die."

"Die? Who says I'm going to die?"

"Nobody says it. They only think it."

"What on earth do you mean?"

She put her arms round my neck and held me tightly. "Let's go away from here. You and me . . . We can take the little baby with us. I'll look after it. I'd like there to be just the three of us. No Aimée. No Jean-Louis. No *her*."

"And no Lance?" I asked.

"Oh, he'd rather stay with them . . . now."

"What do you mean?"

"He likes her, you know."

"Who?"

"Aimée," she replied with conviction. "He likes her better than you."

"I don't think he does."

She nodded vigorously.

One of the servants came in with a dish of chocolate. It was steaming hot and smelt delicious.

Sabrina looked at it suspiciously. "Where is the ring?" she asked.

"The ring?"

"Your bezoar ring."

"I haven't got it anymore," I told her.

"Has it been . . . stolen again?"

"In a way."

Her eyes were round, and on impulse I said, "Lance gambled with it and lost it."

"It's yours," she cried. "It's wicked to take it." I was silent, and she suddenly clung to me, her eyes round as saucers.

"Oh, Clarissa," she said fiercely, "you mustn't die. You mustn't."

"What are you talking about? You are a funny girl, Sabrina."

"I don't know," she said in a small voice. "I know I'm frightened . . . a bit."

I held her tightly to me for a moment. Then I said, "What about a game of I Spy?"

"All right," she answered, brightening.

As we played I thought what a strange child she was, and how dear to me, as I knew I was to her. There was an intimacy between us. It had been there from her birth. She was more than a cousin; she was like my own child. I loved her dearly. I loved her strangeness, her waywardness, her love of the dramatic, and what seemed like a determination to create it when it was not there—all that made up Sabrina.

*　　*　　*

Sabrina was now caught up in an intrigue of her own imagining, and it concerned Lance, Aimée and myself.

It was difficult for me to know how much to suspect, or how much had been planted in my mind by my own observations or by Sabrina's suggestions.

Sabrina wanted me to herself. She was ready to accept the new baby, but she wanted us to be alone. She resented the others, and now Lance more than any. She saw him as the real barrier, and with characteristic determination, she was doing her best to remove that barrier.

She had made up her mind that Aimée and Lance were the enemies and that Madame Legrand was their ally. In her mind she with myself stood against them. As Lance was my husband, she thought there should be another woman, for she was very knowledgeable about such matters, having listened avidly to servants' gossip. Sometimes I wondered whether the servants were gossiping about Lance and Aimée.

Eddy Moreton was still paying attention to Aimée. He had a small house not far from Clavering Hall. His family's ancestral home was in the Midlands, but he hadn't a chance of inheriting that. Aimée did not exactly encourage him. I think my sister was far too practical to enter into a marriage which would bring her no financial advantage.

Sabrina watched them cautiously. I wondered whether anyone would notice her absorption, but the manner in which she sought to protect me was touching.

Sometimes in life there appears to be a special bond between people; it is almost as though their lives are entwined and therefore they are of the utmost significance to each other. I often thought of that afterward.

She was now having a deep effect on me. She was sowing seeds of suspicion in my mind. She was creating in me an atmosphere which at one time I told myself had grown entirely out of her imagination, and yet at the same time I was not sure that this was so. Sometimes I wondered whether she had an extra sense, at others I dismissed her insinuations as childish nonsense. She was possessive and she wanted me for herself; moreover, she had an insatiable desire for drama. Her great interest now was to protect me from some impending evil, and whether she actually sensed it or built it up out of jealousy of Lance, I could not be sure.

I often thought of the bezoar ring, and I wondered if it had more magical qualities than those assigned to it. Through it I had learned of Jeanne's frailty, and I would have sworn her loyalty was unshakable and perhaps the most important emotion in her life. And through it the fact that Lance would stop at nothing in his mad passion for gambling had shown itself.

Sabrina's study of Lance and Aimée was becoming noticeable. She was very watchful. I was sure they would notice and I told her so.

She said cryptically, "I have to watch them. How would I know what they will be doing next if I don't?"

She was firmly convinced that Lance and Aimée were lovers. There had been a case in the village when one of the farm laborers had come home suddenly and caught his wife in bed with another man—one of his fellow workers. He had strangled him and later been hanged for murder. Everyone talked of it for weeks, and Sabrina, of course, listened with the utmost interest.

One day when she was sitting by my bed—I had stayed there, having felt ill in the morning—she narrowed her eyes and said, "Perhaps you are being poisoned."

"My dear Sabrina, what notions you get! Who would want to poison me?"

"Some," she said darkly. "They put things in people's food."

"Who?"

"People who want to get rid of someone. The Borgias were always doing it."

"But we have no Borgias in this house, darling."

"It's not only them. Other people do it too. Kings and queens used to have tasters, just to make sure their food wasn't going to poison them."

"Who told you that?"

"It comes in history. You ought to have a taster. I'll be your taster."

"Then if there was poison, you'd take it."

"I'd save you, and that is what tasters are for."

"Dear Sabrina, it is sweet of you, but really I don't think I need a taster."

"You're going to have one," she said firmly.

That evening when my meal was served she insisted on being with me and tasted everything before I ate it. She enjoyed it, being rather fond of food.

My tisane came up, and when one of the servants brought it to my bed, Sabrina looked at it suspiciously.

"Do you remember how we used to put the ring in it?" she asked.

"You did," I reminded her.

Her eyes grew round with horror. "You haven't got the ring anymore. Perhaps they took it away from you because . . . because . . ."

"Sabrina, my ring was lost in a gamble."

She narrowed her eyes. "I don't believe it," she said. "It was stolen because it was taking the poison out of your food."

She picked up the tisane and took a gulp. She grimaced. I went to take it from her, and in doing so I spilt it over the counterpane.

I laughed at her. "Oh, Sabrina," I said, "I do love you."

She flung her arms about me.

"I'm going to keep you," she told me. "We're going to catch the murderers, and they'll be hanged like poor old George Carey who was hanged because he killed his wife's lover. I wouldn't have hanged him, but I would anyone who hurt you."

"Dearest Sabrina, always remember that there is a special bond between you and me. Promise me you'll never forget that, and won't be jealous if there is someone else I love besides you."

"I'll remember, but I might be jealous."

This ten-year-old girl was half child, half woman; at times she seemed merely her age and at others much wiser than she could possibly be. She was passionately interested in everything that went on around her. She listened unashamedly at doors; she watched people and followed them. The act of spy-protector was one after her own heart. Once she said she saw Lance and Aimée kissing, and when I pressed her, admitted that they had just stood close together talking. If anything did not happen as she wanted it to, she tried to make it do so, and sometimes imagined it had. She did not exactly set out to tell lies, but her imagination ran away with her. When I said that she must not say they had been kissing if they had not been, she replied, "Well, they might have been when I wasn't looking." That was her reasoning. She was obsessed with the idea of saving my life.

So when next day she was ill, I was not sure whether the illness was . . . well, not exactly faked, but whether her strong imagination had willed her into sickness because she so wanted to prove her point about the tisane.

I went up to see her at once. She was lying very still, her

269

eyes raised to the ceiling. I was concerned as I knelt by the bed; then I saw the smile of satisfaction steal across her face.

"Sabrina," I whispered, "you're pretending."

"I did feel sick," she said. "I had cramping stomach pains."

She had heard that was a symptom of poisoning, I realized at once. "Where?" I asked.

She hesitated for a moment and then placed her hands on her stomach.

"Sabrina," I said, "are you sure you didn't imagine it?"

She shook her head vigorously. "It's what happens to tasters," she whispered. Her eyes grew round with excitement. "Last night I tasted the tisane," she said. "Just one sip was enough." She threw up her hands dramatically.

I pretended to laugh, but a terrible uneasiness persisted. "You're romancing," I said.

"I'd die for you, Clarissa," she said fiercely.

"No, you won't," I retorted sharply. "You're going to live for me."

"Oh, all right," she said almost grudgingly.

"Now, what about getting dressed and coming for a stroll in the wood. Be ready in half an hour."

"Can I have my breakfast first? I'm starving."

I laughed and, bending, kissed her.

We walked through the woods to the dene hole.

"Do be careful, Sabrina," I said. "If ever you come to the woods alone, don't go too near."

"All right. I won't. I don't care about the old dene hole now anyway.

I could see that she thought our domestic drama was far more interesting than the dene hole.

A few days later I was seated in the garden on the wooden seat close to the shrubbery when Sabrina came out and sat beside me. She looked both secretive and triumphant, so that I knew something she considered important had happened.

"Well?" I asked.

"I've found something. I think it could be an important clue."

"Well, tell me."

"You'll think I was wrong to do this. Promise you won't."

"How can I until I know what it is?"

"I've been watching them. . . ."

"Who?"

"Oh, you know. Lance and Aimée. I'll catch them—then

270

we'll know for sure. But this is even better. Her door was open when I went past, so I looked in. She was sitting at her dressing table, and I saw her take something out of a drawer. She kept looking at it, and I wondered what it was."

"You were a long time passing," I said. "How did you manage to see so much?"

"Well, I stopped a little while."

"And spied on her."

"I *am* a sort of spy. That's my job. I discover things. But you wait and see what I've found. I waited until she had gone out and then I went to her room. I saw where she had put this thing she was looking at. You know the secret drawer. You have to take out one drawer and there's another drawer behind it. That is where she had put it ... in the secret drawer—so it must have been a secret. So I went in and found ... Guess."

"You tell me."

She put her hand in her pocket and when she withdrew it she was holding something in the palm of her hand. It was the bezoar ring.

I was so startled to see it that I gasped. She watched me with satisfaction.

"He gave it to *her*. He gave her *your* ring."

"No—he lost it at the tables."

"That was what he told you," Sabrina spoke scornfully. "She wanted it. She said, 'Get me the bezoar ring and I'll be yours.' So he just gave it to her."

I shook my head, but of course I half believed what she was telling.

I sat staring at the ring. I was wretchedly unhappy, for I felt in that moment that there was more than a pinch of reality in Sabrina's wild imaginings.

She was watching me intently. "They took it away," she said darkly, "because it was taking the poison out of the tisane."

I laughed, a little unconvincingly. I didn't want her to know that I was worried. I think that at times Sabrina herself did not believe in these accusations. It was a game to her, like charades and I Spy. She had always loved treasure hunts and games of detection.

"You won't need a taster now," she said. "You have the ring."

I said thoughtfully, "I think the best thing you can do is take it back and put it where you found it."

She was astounded, and I went on slowly, playing her game, "It is best for them not to know that we know where it is."

She nodded darkly.

I sat still, watching her speed across the grass to the house.

Was it possible? I asked myself. Was he in love with my sister? It was feasible enough. She was attractive and she shared that all-consuming passion. They were together a great deal. She was often invited to accompany him to gambling parties. I was left out because people knew I did not care to play. How often had I heard them laughing together or growing excited as they discussed the manner of some past play!

Was it so absurd? Was I willfully blind to what was happening about me? Did I need the awareness and the possessive love of a child to make the picture clear to me?

After that I seemed to become conscious of a certain menace all about me. At times I thought it must be due to my condition. Women had strange fancies at such times. Sabrina had planted suspicion in my mind—and it grew.

There was Lance. What did I know of Lance? He was in a way a secret person, and this was all the more alarming because he showed no signs of secrecy. He appeared to be lighthearted in all ways, reckless, even careless, but always kind ... avoiding trouble or any form of unpleasantness. How could he be capable of intrigue, of plots to be rid of me—for that was what it amounted to. I looked for motive. He had been both passionate and tender—a lover and a friend, but I had always known that his real passion was for gambling, and it had made a barrier between us. I had made it clear that I thought his gambling foolish—and there was Aimée, pretty enough and very elegant, with a love of gambling which almost equaled his own. They were together a great deal. . . . There was one other dark thought, I guessed that there were debts, and they might be enormous ones. Lance was constantly staving off his creditors. If I died my fortune would be his ... except the Hessenfield inheritance, which had so rapidly increased at the time of the South Sea Bubble. But Aimée would have that, because my money was to go to her, and hers to me, in the event of either one of us dying.

So there was a motive.

I wondered about the extent of Lance's debts, but he would

never tell me. He would always shrug the matter aside if I raised it, as though debt were a natural sequence in the life of a gentleman. Then it occurred to me that he might be in dire financial straits, in which case my death would be a necessity to him. It would give him escape from his creditors and at the same time give him Aimée, if it was true he was in love with her. How could I be sure? He was charming to her, but he was charming to everyone, and it was his nature to pretend that people were of the greatest importance to him. My death might even mean to him escape from a debtors' prison—and marriage with Aimée.

No, I could not believe it. There were times when my doubts seemed to have grown out of the wildest imaginings and to be quite absurd.

Oh, Sabrina, I thought, I am as bad as you are!

I found a certain pleasure in escaping to the woods, which I loved. I found them enchanting and different every day. I liked to watch the leaves change and to listen to the birds' song. There was peace there, and when I was among the trees everything seemed natural and normal, and my doubts faded away.

Of course, I would say to myself, it must have been Eddy who gave the bezoar ring to Aimée. She had been intrigued by it from the time she had first seen it, and knowing how I felt about it, she did not want me to know that it was in her possession. She probably felt she ought to hand it back to me, and I could understand that she wanted it for herself. As for the suggestion that she and Lance were lovers, it was too ridiculous to stand up to credulity. He was my devoted husband; and I did not believe that he had ever been unfaithful to me either in thought or deed.

So I went to the woods in the late afternoon of each day; that was when Sabrina was having her riding lesson and that was something she would not willingly give up. She was learning to jump now and was very excited about it.

I had returned from the woods that afternoon and was resting, as was my custom, when I heard Madame Legrand in the corridor outside my room talking excitedly to Aimée.

I rose and looked out.

"Has something happened?" I asked.

"Oh, dear," said Madame Legrand, raising her hands and looking extremely annoyed with herself. "Now I have awakened you, which is *méchante* of me. Oh, but the 'eart it go pit-pat, pit-pat. I think it burst from the bosom."

273

"Maman had a shock near the common," Aimée explained. "There were Gypsies there a day or so ago. One of them was lurking in the bushes. He called out to her as she passed . . . something about telling her fortune."

"He look . . . evil," said Madame Legrand. "I begin to run . . ."

"And he ran after her, or so she thought," went on Aimée. "Poor Maman, rest a while, and I will bring you one of your tisanes."

"And now we have return and disturb poor Clarissa. See to her, Aimée. I will go to my room. Clarissa, you must forgive."

"Oh, it was nothing," I assured her. "I wasn't asleep. I'm so sorry you've had a fright."

"Maman is nervous by nature," whispered Aimée, "but she will be recovered in half an hour."

I went back to bed, and shortly afterward Sabrina came in to tell me how high her horse had jumped and how Job, the groom who was teaching her, had said he had never had as good a pupil as she was.

She was so proud of her achievements that she could think of nothing else and was not even very interested when I told her how Madame Legrand had been frightened by a Gypsy.

It was a few days later when I took my usual walk in the woods. My favorite spot was a little clearing among the trees. There was an old oak there under which I liked to sit. From there I could just glimpse the dene hole between the trees. I would sit there and wonder about it and imagine for what it had been used in prehistoric days. I would dream, too, of my baby, who had now become alive to me. I could feel its movements and I longed above everything to hold it in my arms.

I knew that to have a child of my own would be the greatest happiness I could hope for.

There was something strange about that afternoon. Was it a premonition? I wondered afterwards; but from the moment I had entered the woods I had been aware of something . . . I was not sure what. It was a certain uneasiness. I had felt it before . . . in Enderby particularly . . . as though I were being watched, that I was menaced in some way. The servants had said it was the ghost in Enderby, but were there ghosts in the woods?

Little sounds made me start: a crackle in the undergrowth, the displacement of a stone, a sudden rustling. It was probably a squirrel getting his hoard ready for the winter; perhaps a rabbit or a weasel or a stoat scuttling through the foliage; the breeze making moaning sounds as it moved among the branches of the trees. They were the natural sounds of the wood, which, but for the unusual nature of my mood, would have gone unnoticed.

When I came to the clearing the strangeness passed and peace descended upon me. I sat there under the oak, thinking of my baby. This time next year you'll be here, my little one, I thought. And how I longed for the waiting to be over.

And then . . . there it was again. I was not alone. I knew it.

I turned my head sharply. I thought I saw a dark shadow darting among the trees . . . scarcely a human being . . . a shape.

I sat very still, peering into the wood. I could see nothing.

I had imagined it, of course. I turned away. And then . . . there it was again . . . the sound of a footfall, the eerie certainty that something was menacing me . . . something evil.

I must get back to the house. To do so I had to go through the woods, and suddenly I was afraid of what might be lurking there. There was no other way, though. It was absurd to be afraid of those familiar trees which I loved.

I had let my imagination run on. Sabrina, I thought, you are responsible for this!

I was getting a little cumbersome and not able to get nimbly to my feet, and as I attempted to do so, there was a movement from behind. I turned. Something struck me on the back of my head. I had fallen to the ground. I was not sure what happened then. I think I must have lost consciousness for a moment or so before a terrible realization came sweeping over me that Sabrina had been right. Someone wanted me out of the way, and here I was in the woods, alone and helpless.

It could only have been for a few seconds that I had lost consciousness. I was aware now that I was being dragged across the grass. I could smell the scent of earth; the grass brushed my hands. I had returned from blankness to horror and a fearful understanding of what was happening to me.

I was being dragged toward the dene hole.

I could not see who my assailant was. It appeared to be a dark-cloaked figure . . . man or woman. I was not sure. I was lying facedown on the ground and I could not see who was looming over me. I could feel my head beginning to throb and I knew that death was staring me in the face.

Sabrina . . . oh, Sabrina . . . I was thinking. You were right after all.

I had stepped into a nightmare. I was going to be taken to the dark pit, and then . . . I should disappear.

Suddenly I heard a voice! "Clarissa! Clarissa!"

Everything seemed to stand still—time itself. But the voice I heard was that of Sabrina. I thought I must be dreaming. It was the last moments of consciousness before death took me, and it was significant that it should be Sabrina of whom I was thinking.

Sudden silence. What had happened? I knew I was still above the earth—vaguely I could see the light, I could smell and feel the grass beneath me.

I tried to rise. I heard Sabrina's voice again. "Stop. Stop. What are you doing to Clarissa?"

Then she was close to me, kneeling over me. I could see her face hazily through the mists which seemed to be settling over my eyes.

"Clarissa . . . oh, dear, dear Clarissa. Are you all right? You're not dead, are you?"

"Sabrina!"

"Yes, I came. Buttermilk was in a bad mood today. He wouldn't jump. Job said, 'Leave him. He's touchy today.' So I did, and I came here to find you . . . and talk. Then I heard you call out, and I saw . . . I saw . . ."

"What did you see?" I was fighting the desire to slip back into unconsciousness. "Sabrina . . . Sabrina—what did you see?"

"Someone . . . was pulling you across the grass."

"Who was it? Who?"

I was waiting for her to tell me. It seemed like a very long pause. I was praying, I think. O God, let it not have been Lance.

"I don't know. It was the disguise. A long cloak and a hood over its face. It could have been anyone."

"Oh, Sabrina, whoever it was was going to kill me. I felt the strangeness as I came into the woods today . . . something evil . . . lurking there."

"Yes," said Sabrina, "yes. I ought to get you back to the house. Can you walk?"

"I think so."

"We ought to get someone to carry you. I can't go away and leave you, though. *It* might come back."

I was sitting up, leaning against her, and she had her arm protectively round me.

"Oh, Sabrina," I said, "it was . . . horrible."

"It was attempted murder," she answered. "If I hadn't been here they would have killed you."

"You saved my life. I am sure of it. I know what it was going to do. Take me to the dene hole." Sabrina was shivering.

"I knew I had to save you," she said. "I knew it."

We clung together for a moment. Then I said, "We must get back. If whatever it is comes back—"

"I'd kill it," said Sabrina.

"Help me up."

She did. My head was swimming and I could feel the large bump on my head. I felt I was going to faint.

Then I thought with alarm of my baby. I felt it move within me and for a moment I felt exultant. I had greatly feared it might have suffered from the assault.

Sabrina put her arm round me and, although she was only a girl of ten, I felt safe and secure with her beside me.

I took a few tottering steps toward the trees.

"It's not really far," said Sabrina. "Can you do it, dear Clarissa?"

I said I could and I would.

As we came within sight of the house I saw Lance. He was on his way to the stables. When he saw us he stopped and stared.

"Clarissa! Sabrina! What's happened?" he cried. He had run to us, and as I looked at his kindly handsome face, so full of concern, I was ashamed of myself for thinking for a moment that he could wish me harm, let alone do me any.

I said, "I was attacked in the woods."

"Good God! Are you all right?"

"I'm very shaken . . . and I can feel a bump on my head. Sabrina has saved my life."

It was as though a radiance had settled on Sabrina. She smiled and nodded. Then she said excitedly, "Something told me to go into the woods and save Clarissa. I came just in time. I saw this man . . . or whatever it was . . . all dressed in a cloak like a monk's . . . and there was Clarissa on the ground. It was dragging her along to the dene hole."

"What are you talking about?" demanded Lance.

"It's true," I said. "Someone did attack me. It didn't seem like robbery. I *was* being dragged across the ground, and I can only think it was to the dene hole."

277

"It sounds mad. But let's get you in." He picked me up in his arms, and the tenderness in his face touched me deeply.

As we entered the hall Madame Legrand was coming down the stairs.

She stopped suddenly at the sight of me and murmured, "*Mon Dieu.*"

Lance said, "Clarissa has been attacked in the woods. Let's get her to bed."

He went on up the stairs, Sabrina still at his heels, with Madame Legrand joining her.

"Attack, you say? What is this attack? This dear child . . . is she well? The little *bébé* . . ."

"Everything is all right, I think," said Lance. "I'll have the woods scoured to see what prowlers are about. Everyone must be warned." We had reached our bedroom, and he laid me gently on the bed. "I shall get the doctor," he said. "I think that's wisest."

Madame Legrand said, "I will nurse her. I will see that she is well again. No harm must come to this little baby."

Sabrina said, "*I'm* staying with her."

"No . . . no . . ." murmured Madame Legrand, "she must rest. It is best for her to be quiet."

Sabrina insisted stubbornly, "I shall stay."

I smiled at my little defender. "I should like Sabrina to sit by my bed," I said.

Madame Legrand started to protest and Lance said, "If that is what you want, Clarissa . . ."

Sabrina smiled complacently.

Nanny Curlew had come in. She had heard what had happened. It always astonished me how quickly news traveled. She said a hot, sweet dish of tea was what was wanted and she was brewing one immediately. I had had a nasty shock and that would help until the doctor came.

Lance went off to send someone for the doctor. Then he came and sat by my bed. Sabrina sat on the other side. When the tea came she took it from Nanny Curlew and tasted it.

"It is not for you, miss," said Nanny Curlew.

"I know," retorted Sabrina, "but I'm the taster."

I wanted to tell her how she comforted me, how happy I was to have her with me. It was to her I turned before I did to Lance, and that was significant. I could not feel suspicious of him as he sat there at my bedside looking so anxious and tender, and yet . . . lurking at the back of my mind there were still a few doubts and fears.

Those shapely white hands of his, with the Clavering crest on the signet ring he wore on his little finger . . . were they the hands which had dragged me along? I kept thinking how much he would have gained by my death. He had had plenty of time to discard the monk's robe . . . perhaps leave it somewhere in the woods . . . and then appear sauntering casually toward the stables.

And so I turned to Sabrina . . . the only one of whose fidelity I could be absolutely sure.

The doctor arrived. He shook his head gravely. It was a nasty blow I had had on the back of my head. My arms and legs were grazed too, but fortunately the baby appeared to be unharmed by the adventure. As for myself, I was very shocked—perhaps more than I realized just now. I must rest for several days and take nourishment. If I did so, he believed I would be myself in a week or so.

The news spread. Madame Legrand had been chased by a Gypsy and now I had actually been attacked in the woods. The next day Aimée came running in from the woods in a breathless state. She had been chased by a figure in a dark cloak with a concealing hood which hid the face. She had been terrified and had just managed to reach the edge of the woods before the apparition caught up with her. As she came into the open her pursuer disappeared.

"It is some madman disguising himself with the hood and cloak," declared Lance. "I'll set people to watch in the woods. He has to be caught."

This he did, but the apparition seemed to have learned that he was being looked for and made no appearances.

I recovered quickly. Sabrina was constantly with me, and I began to be glad of what had happened because of the change it had wrought in her. She had never forgotten that it was her disobedience which had cost her mother her life. Now she had saved mine and felt she had expiated her sin. Through her a life had been lost; now, through her, one had been saved.

I loved to have her near me, tasting my food, as she insisted on doing. She was now even talking about the baby and admiring the clothes which were being prepared for the child.

I found that I had lost a garnet brooch during my adventure. It wasn't very valuable but was precious to me because Damaris had given it to me long ago.

I told Sabrina. I said, "The clasp was weak, and when I was dragged along the ground it must have come undone."

"I'll find it for you," said Sabrina, confident in her powers to do everything she set her hand to.

"It's lost forever, I daresay. Don't go into the woods alone."

She was silent, nodding her head.

It was two days later, when I was having my afternoon rest, when she burst in on me.

That she was excited was obvious. Her hands were grubby and she looked as if she had been digging up the earth.

"Oh. Clarissa, what do you think I've found!"

"My brooch?"

She shook her head, and for once even Sabrina was at a loss for words. Then she said slowly, "Look. I found it near the dene hole. It's Jeanne's Jean-Baptiste."

I stared down at the little plaque with the chain attached. Soil was sticking to it. As I took it and held it, memories of Jeanne came flooding back, of her showing me this when I was a child, her Jean-Baptiste, which had been put about her neck when she was born and which she must wear until the day she died.

I felt sick. And it had been found near the dene hole.

Thoughts crowded into my mind. I was there again . . . lying on the ground . . . I was being dragged along with obvious intent. Someone had planned to throw me down the dene hole. Could it have been that Jeanne had met the same murderer and that there had been no one to rescue her?

But no. Her clothes had gone. My jewels had gone and only the bezoar ring had been recovered.

Wild thoughts were racing through my head.

Lance said the dene hole must be searched. No one, as far as he knew, had ever been down there before, but that was no reason why someone should not go down now.

All the men in the estate were with him. They all knew of Jeanne's disappearance, and now that this ornament had been found near the dene hole, it seemed significant. For I could testify, and so could others, that Jeanne had taken off her Jean-Baptiste only to wash, and she had always said that she would wear it till she died.

Several men volunteered to go down the dene hole. Stakes were brought, with a thick rope ladder. There was excitement throughout the community and everyone was talking about the prowler in the woods. They were certain that Jeanne had been his victim.

I remember that afternoon well. It was hot—the beginning

280

of July—and in the woods practically the entire neighborhood had gathered. Lance had said I must not be there. In any case, the doctor's orders were that I should rest every afternoon. Sabrina stayed with me, although I knew she was longing to be in the woods.

At length Lance came to my room. His face was pale and for once very serious.

"Poor Jeanne," he said. "We misjudged her. She's hardly recognizable . . . but her clothes are down there and her old cloth bag . . . do you remember? The one she brought with her from France."

I covered my face with my hands. I could not bear to look at Lance nor Sabrina.

Jeanne—dear, good, misjudged Jeanne, how could we ever have thought she was a thief? We should have known.

"It's a mystery," said Lance. "The jewelry was missing. What can it mean?"

Aimée had come into the room.

"I heard you come in, Lance," she said.

He told her that Jeanne's body had been found.

"In the dene hole!" Aimée was almost disbelieving.

Lance nodded.

"It must have been this Gypsy . . . or prowler . . . all that time ago . . ."

Lance was silent."

I said, "There is the loss of the jewelry to explain. What could that have to do with Jeanne's being attacked in the woods?"

"That," said Lance, "we shall have to find out."

"But . . . how?" asked Aimée.

"Well, someone sold the jewelry to the London jeweler from whom Clarissa bought the bezoar ring."

"Oh, yes, I see," said Aimée slowly.

"We'll get to the bottom of it in time," said Lance. "At least poor Jeanne has been exonerated. Poor girl . . . to die like that . . . and to be blamed for stealing . . ."

"Dear Jeanne," I said, "I never really believed it of her. At least some good has come out of this attack on me."

"I shall go up to London at once," said Lance. "I'll call on that jeweler."

There was no talk of anything but the fate which had befallen Jeanne. In the village, in the servants' hall, it was discussed endlessly. Most people declared that they had always known Jeanne was honest and that there was something decidedly odd about her disappearance—which was not true of course, as most of them had stated at the time of Jeanne's disappearance that you never could be sure of foreigners.

After a few days Lance came back from London. It was a stormy evening when he returned and he had had a difficult journey from London because of the weather. He had seen the jeweler and questioned him. The man had repeated his story about a Frenchwoman coming in with the jewelry and the tale she had told about leaving England in a hurry. Did he think he would know her if he saw her again? He was sure of it.

More enquiries were being made, said Lance, and they would go on until the mystery was solved.

The next morning Madame Legrand and Aimée were missing.

"It began to seem rather obvious," said Lance, "from the time we found Jeanne's body. A Frenchwoman selling the jewelry could very likely be Madame Legrand or Aimée."

"Yes," I pondered, "but what has that to do with the death of Jeanne?"

Lance thought that when she had disappeared, they might have had the idea that they could steal the jewelry and make it appear that Jeanne had taken it—which it did.

"They are obviously running away now," he said. "You can depend upon it, they will try to get to France. I'm going to get them back, because there is a lot of explaining to be done. They might try to make for Dover. On the other hand, that would take time. How would they get to Dover? The horses are all in the stables . . . besides, Madame Legrand cannot ride. I am sure they will take one of our little boats and try to get along the coast in it . . . to Dover possibly, where they can take ship for the Continent. I'm going to get down there and see what I can find out."

I watched him ride away. Sabrina was with me. She looked pleased; although she said nothing she was reminding me by her very expression that she had always known there was something wrong with both Aimée and her mother.

All through that day I waited. It was late evening when Lance came back, bringing Aimée with him. She seemed more dead than alive and unaware of what was happening to her. We got her to bed and the doctor was sent for. She was like someone in a trance.

While we were waiting for the doctor Lance explained to me. In desperation they must have taken one of the boats and attempted to get along the coast, as he had thought they would. The sea was rough and their craft very frail, and they could make no headway. They were washed back to the shore again and again, but when Lance found them they had been carried out to sea. He watched them, contemplating how he could best get out to them. He saw their boat capsize and the two women washed overboard.

He saw that they were in danger of drowning. Madame Legrand went under, but he managed to save Aimée.

One or two of the grooms were with him, but they could not save Madame Legrand although they made several attempts. Aimée was half-drowned, but when Lance applied artificial respiration she survived. He thought the best thing was to get her back to the house, and here they were.

Aimée recovered in a day or so. She was deeply shocked and very frightened, but I think there was a certain relief that she could tell the truth. This she did, throwing herself on our mercy.

She was wicked—she was a cheat and a liar—but she begged our forgiveness and said that if we could possibly give her another chance she would go back to France and try to earn her living there as a dressmaker, which was what she should have stayed in France to do all the time.

I was sorry for Aimée. She was quite different now from the girl I had known first at Hessenfield Castle and later here in my home. She was very fearful of the future; she was subdued, almost cringing in her terror.

She seemed to be afraid of Lance, and turned her pleading eyes on me as though begging me to save her from her deserts.

When we heard the whole story, Lance and I decided we must not blame her too much, for she had been under the influence of her dominating mother. She had done what she had done because she had always obeyed her mother without question, and it had not occurred to her that she could do otherwise.

The truth as Aimée told it to us—and I do not think she was lying for there was no point in doing so now—was as follows.

Giselle Legrand was in fact Germaine Blanc, who had lived as a servant in the *hôtel*. Because Germaine was in the household and saw my father frequently, she could give such

283

an accurate account of his habits and talk of him so knowledgeably. When he and my mother had died almost at the same time, because of what was believed to be some sort of plague, Germaine had seized her opportunity. She had stolen my father's watch and ring. It must have been easy to pilfer from his dead body. He had realized that he was suffering from some fatal illness and had written a letter to his brother about my mother and me. But as he did not mention our names—he had already mentioned us to his brother—it was easy for Germaine to say that the letter was given to her by my father and concerned her and her child.

Germaine had always been a clever woman. She had waited for the right moment to act, realizing, of course, that it might never come. But when it did she would be ready and she was. When Aimée grew up and there was easy traffic between France and England because the war was over, she had decided to send her to Lord Hessenfield. My father had had a reputation as a philanderer, and Carlotta, my mother, had been one of his many mistresses. It was logical to assume that Germaine might have been another. Who was to know that she had been a servant in the household? Shrewd and good-looking as she was, she had become the mistress of a bookseller on the Left Bank, and when the Hessenfield household had broken up, she went to live with him. The plan had been growing in her mind for some time, and she thought it would provide very well for her daughter's future. When that was established, she might decide to join her—which was really how it worked out. Aimée was to present herself to the living Lord Hessenfield as his brother's daughter, and one who, according to the letter, was to have a share in the estate.

"I did not want to do it," Aimée kept assuring us. "But I was afraid of my mother . . . I always have been. So I came, and it was easy at first . . . and I liked the life. It was so much better than what I had had to do in Paris. I really made myself believe it was true . . . I *was* your half sister, Clarissa. It all seemed to fit . . . and it could have happened just like that. Only it didn't. You were so kind to me . . . you and Lance . . . I could have been happy and forgotten it was all a fraud if she hadn't come here."

She shivered and covered her face with her hands at this point. "You see," she said so quietly that we could scarcely hear, "Jeanne knew her. She recognized her at once. She was about to come into the house, and there . . . in the garden, was Jeanne. She took one look at my mother and said, 'Why, if it isn't Germaine Blanc. What are you doing here?' My mother hadn't thought of Jeanne. I had forgotten to mention her. How she cursed me for that. And when she came face to face with her, she turned and ran into the woods. She allowed herself to be caught by Jeanne . . . there."

I felt overcome with horror. I was beginning to see exactly what had happened.

"Jeanne said, 'What are you up to, Germaine Blanc? No good, I'll swear, if you are anything like you used to be.' My mother then went for her. I don't know whether Jeanne was dead before she threw her down the dene hole. But that was the end of Jeanne. I was terrified and horrified. I really was. I could see Jeanne could ruin everything for us, but I didn't want to kill her. I would never have done that. You must believe me, Clarissa . . . Lance . . . I was there, but I didn't do it. I had no hand in *that*. I never wanted to be a party to . . . murder."

"I understand," I said. "I do, I do."

"My mother said we must make it look as though she had run away, taking things with her. I did show her where her clothes were. And the jewelry—yes, I did that. But I had to, Clarissa. I had to do what she told me."

"And then your mother sold the jewelry to a London jeweler," said Lance. "That was a mistake."

"Yes, she needed money. It was for that reason."

"And," I said, "she was going to kill me."

"She always made plans. She said she had to get what she wanted from life. She wasn't born lucky. That's what she always said. She had to make her own way. None of these plans ever really brought her what she wanted. She wanted to be lady's maid to Lady Hessenfield, and when she might have got it, Lady Hessenfield died. Then the bookseller was going to marry her, and he died. I think that made her determined to succeed with this bigger plan."

"And why did she want to kill me . . . to send me down the dene hole with Jeanne?"

"So that the money you had from Lord Hessenfield, which had grown so much would come to me. Then she wanted a grand marriage for me . . ." Aimée flushed.

Good heavens! I thought. She was planning that Lance should be Aimée's husband. So Sabrina's suspicions were true.

Aimée said quickly, "She thought if I had your fortune it

285

would be easy for me to find a rich husband." She broke down and began to cry pathetically. "What can become of me now?" she sobbed. "Let me go back to France, please. I'll work there. Perhaps . . ."

Lance and I talked a great deal about Aimée.

"She stole the jewelry because her mother insisted that she should," said Lance. "She acted the part of your half sister for the same reason. She would have done none of these things on her own."

"And yet she cheated at cards," I told him. "I saw her. I know she needed money badly, but it is no excuse really. She has my bezoar ring."

Lance looked startled. "Why, Eddy must have given it to her."

"It seems the only answer," I said. "Sabrina discovered it. You know, she has established herself as my guardian angel or my watchdog."

"Bless the child," said Lance fervently.

"Lance." I turned to him earnestly. "I'm almost glad this happened. Sabrina saved my life. There is no doubt of that now. It was what she needed. I wonder if she would ever have got over that unfortunate incident on the ice without this."

Lance took my face in his hands. "It was a risky price to pay for the lesson." And then suddenly that veneer of graceful manners dropped from him. He held me to him; he was intense and briefly allowed his fears to show. I loved him for that, and I was more than ever ashamed for having doubted him.

"And what of Aimée?" I asked.

"It's for you to decide," he told me. "Poor girl. She shouldn't be charged with murder. An accessory, perhaps . . . but in extenuating circumstances. No—I think Aimée will get by if she is free of her dominating mother. The Hessenfield money is all yours now . . . if she has any left. We can send her back to France and set her up as a dressmaker there. Perhaps that would be the best thing that can happen to her. As far as robbery is concerned—we should have to bring a charge against her, and I am sure you would not want to do that."

I agreed that I would not.

I talked it over with her. She was very grateful.

"It might have been so different," she said, "if my husband had lived. I would have stayed in the north. Jeanne would never have seen my mother."

"But it didn't work out that way, and I think you are honest enough not to have been truly happy in such deception."

"Honest?" she said with a wry laugh. "You caught me cheating once, and there is the bezoar ring . . ."

"Yes," I said, "what about the bezoar ring?"

"My mother wanted you to lose it because she was trying to poison you with her tisanes. She hated Sabrina, for she was arousing suspicions. 'How does that child know so much?' she was always saying. 'Has she second sight?' She was sure the ring had magical properties and she wanted you to lose it, so she hit on the idea of letting Eddy win it from Lance. I'm weak, Clarissa. I'm not worthy of your regard. I helped her again. I put him up to it . . . and I helped him win that night."

"You mean . . ."

"You saw me do it once. He won the ring . . . through me. I saw to it that he had the right card. He was fond of me, Eddy was," she added wistfully.

She brought the ring back to me and I slipped it on my finger, glad to have it back. It was part of my Hessenfield inheritance.

The problem of Aimée was solved for us. Eddy asked her to marry him. He knew that Aimée was not what she had pretended to be; he knew that her mother had murdered Jeanne and that Aimée had played her part in this, but he believed she was repentant and under his influence could regain her self-respect. He genuinely loved her.

He sold his house and decided they would be better right away, so he bought a farm in the Midlands and declared that he would give up gambling and they would make a life together.

There was the question of Jean-Louis. He had grown up in our nurseries; Nanny Goswell was the one he loved best. What should happen to Jean-Louis?

Aimée had never been a maternal type, and she told me she wanted a complete break with the past. Jean-Louis was in a state of misery when he heard he was to leave us and go with his mother and her new husband. He followed Nanny Goswell round and would not let her out of his sight. He cried at night and had nightmares. In the morning he would not get up from his bed and used to cling to the bedposts. Once he hid himself in the attics, and we thought he was lost.

At last we came to the conclusion that he should stay with

us . . . for a while at least. There was no disguising Aimée's relief. As for Jean-Louis, he was beside himself with joy.

So Jean-Louis stayed with us when Aimée left.

In spite of everything that had gone before, my baby was born at the appointed time. She was strong and healthy from the start, and I had never been so happy in my life as I was when I held her in my arms—my very own child. I called her Zipporah, and from the moment of her coming she changed the household. She was a contented baby and only cried when she was hungry or tired. She bestowed her smiles on everyone indiscriminately and never failed to charm them all. Lance adored her, and it was clear that she had a special feeling for him. As for Jean-Louis, he would stand at her cradle and gaze at her in wonder. He would rattle a case of beans for her pleasure over and over again; he would put colored rings into a little sack and get them all out again, as though it were the most interesting occupation in the world, just because that was what Zipporah wanted to do.

I think his devotion to her had something to do with his desire to establish himself as part of our household. In any case, his devotion to Zipporah amused us all except her. She took it for granted.

Nor did it diminish as the years began to pass.

The Seed-Pearl Stole

We came to that period when my daughter was ten years old—a lovely child and a joy to us all. To my regret there had been no more children. Lance did not seem to mind. He was well content with his daughter. She looked rather like him—tall, fair-haired, with intensely blue eyes—but it was her smile which was so enchanting.

I suppose I could have been said to have settled down. I was happy—not perhaps ecstatically so, as I had been with Dickon, but I had come to believe that my feelings then had been partly due to youth and my first and sudden encounter with romance. Lance had been a good husband to me—always kind and tender, but perhaps never as close as I had felt myself to be with Dickon, even though we spent but a few days together. Lance had his secrets—for he was really a very secretive man—and I always believed they were between us. I had often felt that his gambling was my rival and that this passion for it would always exceed that which he felt for me. I used to think that he would gamble us all away if the challenge was strong enough. It was a foolish thought, and yet I was sure there was some truth in it.

This discontent with my marriage was only vague. In my sober moments I reproached myself for reaching out for the impossible . . . as perhaps most people do when it would be so much wiser to accept and enjoy what they have. They dream up an ideal . . . an impossible dream . . . and spend their lives unappreciative of what they have because it does not exactly fit the dream.

Lance was often in financial difficulties. In fact, he lived constantly on the verge of them. No sooner had he won than he would risk all he had gained. It would always be like that, I knew, and I must accept it, because it was his nature. But, as I said, it set a barrier between us. He would never admit defeat. If ever I asked him how he fared, it would always have been wonderful. I was shut out of his gambling life, and as that meant more to him than anything, I could not be very close.

Then, of course, there was Sabrina. She had grown into a beautiful young woman, bearing a strong resemblance to her aunt Carlotta, who had caused such consternation in the family. But she was not like Carlotta in other respects. She was determined, strong-willed, vivacious and adventurous. Carlotta, it was true, had been all these; but in Sabrina the dominating trait was to care for the weak.

She had begun, I suppose, by caring for me, and the bond between us had not lessened with the years. She looked after me, protected me, watched over me, just as she had in those old days when she had suspected—rightly—that my life was in danger.

I was of special importance to her because she had saved my life, and that had brought about a change in her. For I do believe that had she not done what she did for me on that day in the woods, she would have gone on remembering that fatal day on the ice when she had disobeyed orders and her action had been the indirect cause of her mother's death.

I was fond of Lance and Jean-Louis, and Zipporah was my own precious child, but between Sabrina and myself there was such an intensity of feeling that nothing could rival it. She knew it and she was content that it should be so. The jealousy of her early childhood had disappeared. She was serene and confident and, what gave me great pleasure, contented.

Ours was a happy household up to that time. It was as though we had all come to terms with each other. Nanny Curlew stayed with us even though Sabrina was at this time a young woman of nineteen and certainly not in need of a nurse. But, with Nanny Goswell, she presided over Zipporah's needs, and the two nannies made themselves useful in a hundred ways, so that we could not imagine our household without them.

We spent the time between Clavering Hall and Albemarle Street, paying occasional visits to Eversleigh, which seemed so different now. Priscilla and Leigh were at the big house, Eversleigh Court; Uncle Carl remained with the army; Enderby had been sold, and the Dower House was empty. Change was inevitable, but everything was so different there from the old days. As for myself, I was now in my thirties and no longer young.

I had thought that Sabrina would marry early and was

rather surprised that she had reached the age of nineteen without doing so. That she was very attractive there could be no doubt, and there had been several young men who had wanted to marry her, and among them more than one would have been a very desirable husband, but although she enjoyed their admiration and regard, she had no wish to marry them.

It was soon after her nineteenth birthday that Lance gave me the stole. It was a beautiful thing, trimmed with lace and thousands of tiny seed pearls. Being silver-gray, it toned with everything and was very useful to wear round my shoulders at some of the evening parties we attended. It was elegant in the extreme but at the same time very outstanding. People never failed to admire it when I wore it; if I did not do so, many enquired what I had done with my beautiful seed-pearl stole.

There was one man whom we met frequently in society. I disliked him intensely from the moment I set eyes on him. He was big, of florid complexion, with fleshly indulgence written all over his face. He ate heartily, drank heavily and was reputed to have a voracious sexual appetite. His name was Sir Ralph Lowell, but he was generally known as Sir Rake, a name in which he delighted. He had what I can only call a "familiar"—a pale-faced mean man, as tall as himself but about half the width. This was Sir Basil Blaydon. Sir Basil was ill-favored rather in expression than features. He had very small pale-blue eyes which seemed to dart everywhere, noting the disabilities of everyone, and a thin, curved mouth which seemed to express delight in them.

I used to say to Lance, "Why do we have Lowell and Blaydon? We could well do without them."

"My dear," said Lance, "Lowell is one of the most reckless gamblers I ever knew."

"Even more so than yourself?" I asked.

Lance smiled with his imperturbable good humor. "I am cautious in comparison. No, we have to include Lowell. He would come in any case. I have known him appear uninvited now and then."

"Well, I don't like him in the house—or that man who comes with him."

"Oh, Blaydon just walks in his shadow. Just ignore the two of them since you don't like them."

And whenever I mentioned my abhorrence of these two men Lance always turned my objections aside with a light remark, which was so much more effective than a protest would have been.

So we continued to endure Sir Rake.

I was a little dismayed when his son, Reginald, became friendly with Sabrina. Reggie, as he was known, was a poor creature, as different from his father as it was possible to be. He was a tall, gangling youth, with pale eyes and skin, and he was clearly cowed by his father, who seemed to despise him. He limped slightly because of a fall when he was a baby. His mother had died as the result of a miscarriage when she was trying to produce another of the sons Sir Rake desperately wanted. So the only son he had was Reggie.

It was perhaps typical of Sabrina that she should be interested in Reggie. Sabrina wanted to look after people—manage their affairs, care for them—and to do this she must find someone in need of care.

Poor Reggie, slightly crippled, cowed by his father and dismissed as of little importance by most people, fitted the role perfectly.

I am sure that at first it was pity with Sabrina. Other young women had little desire for his company; she would show them all that she, the most sought-after among them, was willing to pay some attention to poor Reggie.

She would seek him out. At first the poor young man was bewildered, and then he would look for her, and if she did not appear he would be wretched; when she did come his eyes would light up with such adoration that I began to be alarmed.

They would chat together, and she even persuaded him to dance with her. He did this clumsily because of his disability, but she always looked as though she was enjoying the dance, and I heard her tell him once that there was no one she would rather be with.

I talked to Lance about it. He shrugged his shoulders. It was unwise, he said, to interfere in the affairs of the young.

"Could she marry him?" I persisted.

"If they agreed to it, of course."

"I mean, would it be wise? Reggie is dependent on his father . . . and as for Sabrina's going into that household . . . it makes me shudder to think of it."

Lance's thoughts were elsewhere. He said lightly. "These matters work themselves out."

It was at times like this that I felt irritated with him and disappointed. Dickon, I felt sure, would have understood my fears. At least he would have given his attention to them.

I decided to speak to Sabrina.

"Do you think it wise to give so much of your attention to Reggie Lowell?" I asked.

"I like Reggie," she answered. "And I think he likes me."

"I'm sure of it," I said. "That's the trouble. He likes you too much. I think he's in love with you."

She nodded, smiling gently.

"But, Sabrina," I went on. "I know you feel sorry for him, but is it right to lead him on to think—"

"To think what?"

"Well, that you might marry him."

"Why shouldn't he think it?"

"But you wouldn't."

"Why not?"

"Oh, Sabrina, do you really mean you're in love with him?"

She hesitated, and I went on triumphantly. "There, you see. You're sorry for him. I know that. I know you well. But that is not enough."

"Enough? He needs someone to look after him, to show him that he would be all right if he would forget about not being so."

"Dear Sabrina, what you are doing is giving him the wrong impression."

"I am not," she said firmly.

"Do you mean to say you would marry him?"

"I might."

"Sabrina! There are so many . . . you could have almost anybody."

"I don't want anybody. I want to help Reggie."

I was disturbed, and then I began to think that perhaps she was right. Reggie needed her, and Sabrina was the kind of girl who needed to be needed. It may have gone back to that incident on the ice and her father's dislike for her. I had thought when she had saved my life we had wiped that out forever, but perhaps some dramatic incidents made such an effect on the mind that they are indelible.

I saw that Lance was right. Matters must take their course.

And how was I to know what a dramatic and tragic course this would take?

Sabrina came to me in the garden where I was gathering roses. It was a lovely summer's day. I could hear the voices of Zipporah and Jean-Louis in the paddock. They were riding there, as they often did, and Jean-Louis was teaching her to jump the hedge which separated the paddock from the home field.

I snipped my roses contentedly, picking the best blooms and thinking what a beautiful afternoon it was. I heard the buzzing of the bees that were marauding the lavender growing in profusion round the pond, where now and then I saw the flash of the goldfish which Zipporah called her own because she liked to feed them. The smell of the lavender was sweet, there were white butteflies on the purple buddleia, and it was an afternoon for contentment—so I thought.

Sabrina was standing beside me. She looked cool in a green linen gown and a big shady hat—cool, beautiful and sure of herself.

"Clarissa, I wanted you to be the first to know."

I turned to look at her. There was a smile on her face and her lovely eyes were looking past me as though into the future.

My heart sank. I was afraid of what she was going to tell me.

"Yes," she said, "you've guessed. I'm going to marry Reggie."

"Sabrina!"

"You don't approve, I know. Dear Clarissa, I promise you that it will be all right."

"Do you . . . love him?"

Again that momentary hesitation. "But of course," she said at length, almost irritably.

She looked so beautiful standing there—and so young that I felt she had not yet come to womanhood. When she did she would be a vibrant, passionate woman. There must be some man who would awaken her—but it was not Reggie. I knew that she would marry him for pity, and that was no good reason for a woman like Sabrina to plan for her future happiness.

"Have you thought of this *very* seriously?"

"Of course," she said, again with that touch of irritability which suggested to me that she was far from sure.

"Perhaps if you waited a little . . ."

"Waited? Who wants to wait? I shall soon be twenty years of age. Most people are married when they are as old as that. Oh, Clarissa, I want to make up for all that he has suffered. He has been through so much with that dreadful father of his."

"He will be your father-in-law—think of that."

"One does not marry for the sake of a father-in-law."

294

"No, but you would doubtless come into contact with him often."

"We should not. I should see to that. I will take Reggie far away. We would visit rarely . . . just for convention's sake. His father has not been very good for him. In fact, it is his father who has made him what he is . . . timid, uncertain . . . a little afraid of life."

"Do you really want to marry a man like that?"

"I want to marry Reggie. I can help him."

"Sabrina, you should be a wife, not a . . . reformer."

"You are being a little difficult, darling. It is not like you. You have always understood and helped me. Oh, don't you see what parents can do to their children? When they are young they feel things so deeply."

I could see the past in her eyes. I remembered vividly that time when Jeremy had come to her and let her know that he hated her for what she had done to her mother.

She was right. Parents' actions could be very significant for impressionable children. She remembered still, and she saw that Reggie was one who had not had the good fortune to fall into the hands of someone who was as sympathetic as I had been. I loved her so much because she cared for others, and passionately I wanted her to find the happiness she deserved.

I think I could have become reconciled to the marriage if there had just been Reggie. It was the thought of the family connection with Sir Rake which appalled me. I had hated the way in which his eyes dwelt on all women—including myself. He had an air of assessing them and speculating as to how he could get them into his bed. I was sure that he lived up to his reputation.

But Sabrina was determined, and none could be more so when she had made up her mind to be.

When I told Lance he was only mildly interested. He was going to his club and was already thinking of the night's play ahead.

I did discuss the matter with Nanny Curlew, who regarded Sabrina as her own child.

Nanny Curlew said, "Well, we wanted a good match for her, but if she really loves this young man, I'm agreeable."

Nanny Curlew obviously had not heard the evil rumors concerning Sir Rake.

They had decided not to announce the engagement just yet, for which I was thankful. I did see Sir Ralph on one or two occasions. He came to us in Albemarle Street for a night's play. Reggie did not accompany him. Sabrina was present, and when I saw Sir Ralph's eyes following her, assessing her in his lewd way, I was deeply disturbed, and it occurred to me that Reggie had probably told his father of his proposed marriage, which would account for Sir Ralph's interest.

Then came the day when she was to visit the Lowell's town house. A note had been delivered to her from Sir Ralph.

He wrote:

> My dear daughter-to-be,
>
> I cannot express the delight I felt when I heard from my son that you had agreed to marry him. I have always admired you so much and there is no one I would rather welcome into the family.
>
> I want Reginald to bring you to see me, so that the three of us can have a little talk together. He will call for you at eight of the clock tomorrow evening. Just a family affair, one might say. Then we can plan how we shall make the announcement.
>
> So humor me in this. There is so much I wish to say to you.
>
> From one whose joy it will be to become
>
> > Your father,
> > Ralph Lowell

"He sounds as though he is pleased," I said when Sabrina showed me the note.

"I think the stories about him have been highly exaggerated," replied Sabrina.

"I thought he was unkind to Reggie."

"Quite a lot of fathers are," she retorted with feeling.

She would judge for herself and for the occasion she would wear a very lovely gown in pink silk, cut from the waist to show a petticoat very finely embroidered beneath. The bodice was tight-fitting and rather low cut and she looked exquisite in it.

I said, "You need something to cover your shoulders." I went to a drawer and brought out the seed pearl-decorated stole. I draped it round her shoulders. The silver-gray of the stole and the delicacy of the pearls enhanced her gown. I had never seen the stole look as beautiful as it did on her that night.

She was full of confidence in the future. She was going to

marry Reggie and make him a happy man; and this night she would face his father.

At precisely eight o'clock the carriage arrived. A footman knocked at the door. Sabrina was waiting. From an upper window I saw her get into the carriage and drive away. Not for a moment did it occur to me that the happenings of this night would affect us all so bitterly.

Lance was at the club, and I was trying not to picture him at the card table, that intense look on his face as he gambled away . . . heaven knew what.

I preferred not to think of him. Instead I was thinking of Sabrina, about to marry and go away from us. So it happened. One day Zipporah's turn would come. It was heartbreaking to lose those one had loved and cherished through their childhood, when one had been the most important person in their lives. But there must come the time when it was necessary to slip back and hand over the loved one to a husband.

Zipporah was young yet, but I was already beginning to wonder how much longer I should keep even her with me.

I should be rejoicing in Sabrina's happiness . . . if happiness it was. She was like a nun dedicated to a mission. She was marrying for pity. However, I must accept the fact that it was what she wanted; and when she had set her mind on something, she would never diverge from it.

I settled down to read. It must have been nearly two hours after the carriage had left when she came back. She was wrapped in an old cloak which she had certainly not been wearing when she left the house. She came into my bedroom, and as she threw off the cloak I saw that her bodice was ripped open and her skirt was torn; there was a bruise on her neck, and her face was the color of parchment.

"Sabrina!" I cried.

She flung herself into my arms. She was sobbing and I could not quiet her.

"Clarissa . . . oh, Clarissa," she murmured. "It was dreadful . . . dreadful . . . He's dead. I didn't do it. I swear I didn't do it. It . . . it happened."

"Sabrina, my dearest, try to be calm. Tell me what happened."

"It was . . . that man . . ."

"You mean . . . Sir Ralph . . ."

She nodded. "It was terrible, Clarissa. I fought him, and I was getting exhausted. I couldn't hold him off . . . he seemed so strong. I kicked . . . I screamed. . . . I fought with all my might, and then . . . Oh, Clarissa, I didn't do it. It wasn't my fault. It . . . it just happened . . ."

I went to the cupboard where Lance kept his brandy. I poured out a little and gave it to her. Her teeth were chattering so that she could not drink and her hands were shaking so that she could not hold the goblet.

"Now tell me, Sabrina. Tell me right from the beginning."

She sat staring ahead as though she were still living in the nightmare. "When I got into the carriage," she said, "Reggie was not there."

"I saw you go and I thought it was strange that he had not gotten out to help you into the carriage."

"I didn't think much of it until I arrived at the house. A housekeeper was there, but there was no sign of Reggie. She said that Sir Ralph was waiting for me, and she took me up to a room. She knocked on the door. There was no answer. Then she opened the door and I went in. It was a bedroom. There was a four-poster bed . . . I thought the housekeeper had made a mistake and I was about to say so when the door shut behind me and I was suddenly seized. It was that man . . . oh, Clarissa, how can I tell you? I was so frightened. He was so strong . . . and he was holding me."

"My dear child, this is terrible. I should never have let you go alone. I thought Reggie was taking you."

"So did I. But that man had planned it. He was waiting for me. It was awful. He said he had always wanted me. He said it would be in the family, and there should be love between father and daughter. . . . I tried to get away. I went to the window. I think I would have jumped out if I could. But he was there behind me. He had taken off the robe he was wearing. He was *naked,* Clarissa. It was . . . horrible. He pulled me down on the bed. He tore my bodice and my skirt . . ."

Again she turned to me, and hid her face against me as though to shut out that terrible scene.

"He said I was a vixen . . . but he liked vixens. He said there was more excitement when the girl was unwilling. He said horrible things . . . and he was leering at me all the time, licking his lips . . . his horrible flabby blue lips. I fought hard, Clarissa, but he was stronger than I was, and I was afraid that he was going to win." She shuddered and shut her eyes tightly. "He was cursing me . . . and laughing at me . . . and tearing at my clothes and then suddenly I felt his grip loosen. I had my hand over his mouth; shutting off those

horrible lips . . . I could not bear the sight of them. And then
. . . he wasn't holding me anymore. His face had gone blue
and he was breathing in a noisy way. I was able to push him
away from me . . . and he rolled off the bed and lay very still
on the floor. His breathing had stopped and his eyes were
wide open . . . staring. For a moment I couldn't understand
what had happened. Then I knew . . . He was dead."

"You came back home. That was all there was to do."

"But him . . . Clarissa. I left him there. I found this cloak.
Perhaps it is his. I had to have something to cover myself
with. I took it without thinking. I ran out of the house. I saw
a chairman going by and he brought me here. I had just
enough money to pay him, which was still in my girdle
reticule. Oh, Clarissa, what will happen?"

"Nothing. You have done nothing wrong. It was his own
fault. You are not responsible for his death. But are you sure
he is dead? He might have fallen into a faint—or something
like that."

"He was not breathing. I was sure of it. Clarissa, I was so
frightened. I just ran. . . ."

I soothed her. "Let me get you out of these things. I'll take
you to your bed. I'll get something for you to drink, something that will soothe you. Nanny Curlew will know what is
best."

She clung to me. "I could only think of you," she said. "How
to get to you—how to be safe."

I was deeply moved. It was as though she were part of
myself. I wanted it to be like that always, throughout our
lives. I believed that only death could come between us.

I spent a sleepless night. I lay with Sabrina until Nanny
Curlew's potion had had its effect and she fell into a peaceful
sleep.

When Lance came in late he was flushed with success
because he had had a winning night. I was still sitting up. It
was no use going to bed, for I knew I should not sleep. I kept
wondering what the outcome of this would be. If Sir Ralph
was indeed dead there would be an enquiry, and Sabrina's
name would be mentioned as the woman who was with him
when he died. There might well be malicious gossip. There
were always those ready to damn reputations.

This was where Sabrina's pity had led her.

Lance was amazed to find me sitting up. I quickly told him
what had happened.

"The swine!" he cried. "By god, if he really is dead, that's no loss to the world."

"But what of Sabrina?"

He was thoughtful. Lance was a man who understood every facet of the social scene, and I could see that he was thinking exactly as I was. There would be many to say that Sabrina had gone willingly to the house; some might say she had been Sir Ralph's mistress and that her proposed marriage with Reggie was to make an easier situation for them. Sabrina would be notorious.

Lance and I talked for a long time, and finally Lance said he knew how to handle the matter, and this should be fairly easy as long as no one knew that Sabrina had been the woman who was present when Sir Ralph died. As so many women had been connected with him—many of them courtesans who would have visited him for a night—there might be no involved enquiry into the identity of his companion. That was providing it could be proved that he had died of heart failure which was clearly brought on by intense excitement.

I said, "There was a letter from him to her asking her to call."

"We must destroy it," said Lance.

"I'll get it at once." I knew she had left it lying on her dressing table, for I had seen it there—without noticing it very much—when I had helped her to bed. I went quietly to her room. She was sleeping deeply. I picked up the letter and took it back to Lance.

He held it in the flame of a candle. We were both silent as the blue flame curled upward.

"Now," said Lance, "if no one saw her, there is no evidence that she was there. No one would suspect a girl who was to marry his own son."

"Would they not?" I asked. "Those who knew him might think he had found the idea of making love to his daughter-in-law rather piquant."

"It won't occur to them . . . unless the housekeeper who took her in recognized her."

"Wait a minute!" I cried. "What of the coachmen? He sent his coach for her. They would have seen her."

Lance looked abashed. "I'll see the coachmen," he said at length. "I'll make it worth their while to forget they called here and took her back."

"Lance . . . is that wise?"

"It's necessary," he added.

"Oh, Lance, I'm so glad you are here to help."

He looked at me tenderly. "That's my mission in life—to serve you," he said.

I was so grateful to him. He had always been so good and kind; in real trouble he was always there beside me.

Sabrina woke much calmer next day. She had always been logical, and she saw at once that she was in no way to blame for what had happened. Lance and I told her that the best way out of the trouble was to keep quiet. The only people we had to fear were the housekeeper and the coachmen.

Had the housekeeper seen her clearly, could she say?

"I hardly think so. It was dark and the house was not well lighted. She quickly took me up to Sir Ralph's bedroom. We were only a minute or so in each other's company."

"We'll risk the housekeeper," said Lance.

Sir Basil Blaydon called that morning. He was clearly shaken. Lance was at home when he called for which I was grateful.

He burst out at once, "Have you heard the news? Ralph is dead. He died last night. They say there was some woman with him. It was apoplexy, they think. I always told him that if he continued at the pace he was going it would happen one day."

"By gad!" cried Lance. "What an end! Who was with him at the time?"

"There seems to be some doubt about that. The housekeeper says she let a woman in but she didn't see her very clearly. She didn't hear her name. She just knew that he was expecting someone and she took her up."

Sir Basil was clearly upset. He had walked in Sir Ralph's shadow for so long, he could not imagine life without him.

As soon as he had gone Lance went out. When he came back he was smiling.

"I've seen the coachmen," he said. "I've made it worth their while to forget they called at this house to pick up a young woman. They will say they picked her up from some other point. At the top of Dover Street, I suggested. Anywhere to stop attention directed to this house. There's nothing to fear now. They will not think of looking for his companion here."

How thankful I was for Lance!

The entire circle of our acquaintances were talking about Sir Ralph's sudden death. There were a few smirks of complacency, for many had said he would meet his death in that way. A man could not go on indefinitely practicing the excesses he did without one day succumbing to exhaustion.

The great curiosity was to find the woman.

Then came the blow. I had not missed the seed-pearl stole and had forgotten that I had lent it to Sabrina on that night. Of course she had been wearing it when she left the house, and she had come back without it.

It was found in the chamber of death. It was unusual, even unique, and many people knew to whom it belonged.

That was how the scandal started.

The identity of the woman was discovered, and who else could it be but the owner of the seed-pearl stole—Clarissa Clavering?

Lance was appalled. Sabrina was horrified. She said she would confess at once. Lance stopped that.

It was a tricky situation. Suppose someone discovered that Sir Ralph had not died by accident! We must keep very quiet. In the meantime Lance endeavored to find another stole like the one he had bought before. There was not another like it to be found. He would have to have one made—speedily, he said—and he wanted me to appear in it.

There was another factor. One of the coachmen whom Lance had bribed to keep quiet decided to talk when Sir Basil Blaydon promised a larger sum than Lance had given him. He told Sir Basil that he had come to our house in Albemarle Street and had picked up the lady in the seed-pearl stole. She had gone willingly to Sir Ralph's residence, where he had been waiting for her.

The whispers grew to a rumble. Everywhere they were talking. The mystery was solved, and the general opinion was that the woman in the case was Lance Clavering's wife.

Sabrina was beside herself with grief. "People must be told," she said. "I went because he was to be my father-in-law. Surely that will be easily understood."

"No one would believe it," I told her. "No, it is better for them to suspect me than you. You have your life before you. You are young. We do not want scandal clinging to you. However false it is proved to be, there will always be some who insist that it is true. Lance knows the truth. That is all that matters."

Lance came in with a new stole. "Now," he said, "it only remains for you to appear wearing it."

"What if the stole-maker talks . . . as the coachman has?" I asked.

"We must risk that," said Lance.

"Oh, Lance, you take too many risks!"

The news was soon being circulated. The stole-maker had lost no time in spreading the news that she had made another stole for Lance which was an exact replica of the one found in Sir Ralph's bedroom.

Lance came in looking pale and very serious. I had never seen him look like that before. His eyes were glittering, his lips tightly set together.

He said, "I've called Blaydon out."

"What do you mean?" I cried.

"He insulted you. He insulted me. He said you were Lowell's mistress. There were several people there and . . . I challenged him. We are meeting in Hyde Park tomorrow morning."

"No, *no*, Lance!"

"It has to be. I couldn't stand by and let him insult you."

How like him that was. He would always obey the rules of society. To him it was the only gracious way of living. He would risk his life because he considered it was the only honorable thing to do.

"What does it matter what they say of me?" I cried. "You and I know it is untrue."

Lance's reply was, "I shall be meeting him tomorrow morning at dawn."

"And if he kills you. . . ."

"Luck is always on my side."

"And if you kill him?"

"I shall aim for his legs. It'll teach him a lesson if I put a bullet through one of them. He'd recover, and perhaps regret he said what he did."

"Lance . . . stop this. It's not worth it."

"It is worth it to me," he said, and there was that about the set of his lips which told me he would not diverge from his purpose.

I whispered. "What is it to be?"

"Pistols," he said.

"Please don't do it, Lance," I pleaded. "Let's leave London. Let them say what they will. What does it matter to us? We know the truth. It's agreed that Sir Ralph was responsible for his own death. No one is accused of foul play. It is so easy. Let us slip away. Scandals die down."

"No," he said firmly. "I shall defend your honor. It is the only thing I can do in the circumstances."

"It is not. There are other things. It is a silly code that doesn't fit in with reality."

"It means something to me, Clarissa. Leave this in my hands. I will make him repent. He shall eat his words. I will not have your name sullied."

There was no persuading him.

I did not tell Sabrina. She would have been frantic with remorse. I kept from her the fact that both the stole-maker and the coachman had talked. She did not go out, for which I was thankful. She had not seen Reggie either. I was sure she could not bear to think of him now, for he would surely remind her of that terrible scene with his father.

I did not sleep all night. I wanted to go with Lance to the park, but he would not allow that.

"You must not be there," he said. "I'll be back with you soon. Then, I promise you, we'll leave London. We'll go to the country and take Sabrina with us. We'll take Zipporah and Jean-Louis and forget this nightmare."

It was dawn when he left the house in the company of Jack Etherington, a friend of long standing, who was to act as his second.

I sat at the window, waiting . . . waiting . . .

I was there when they carried him in. He was bleeding profusely from a wound in his side. I scarcely recognized him. He looked so unlike the jaunty man I had known, with the insouciant smile, who had never really taken life seriously.

He had to take it seriously now for I feared he was about to leave it.

"I've sent someone for a doctor," said Jack Etherington. "We'd better get him to bed."

The moments seemed to drag interminably. Lance was looking at me, trying to speak. I bent my head down so that I could hear him.

He said, "It was the only way. Understand, Clarissa. I was too slow. He got me first."

"The doctor will come," I told him. "You'll be better then."

He smiled, and as he did so I saw the blood on his lips, and that frightened me more than seeing him lying there.

The doctor came. He shook his head gravely. The bullet was too deeply embedded. He could not remove it. Besides, Lance had lost too much blood.

There was no hope and there could only be an hour or two left to him.

So Lance, the gallant gentleman, the exquisite dandy, the inveterate gambler, was dying, and his death was typical of the way he had lived. It made me bitterly angry to think of how he had thrown his life away . . . uselessly, unnecessarily. But that was Lance.

I heard Jack Etherington say that Blaydon was preparing to get out of the country quickly. That could only mean that he knew he had killed Lance.

Lance lingered for a few hours, and during that time he was lucid and talked to me a little. I told him to preserve his breath, but it seemed to comfort him to talk.

"Oh, Clarissa, my Clarissa," he said. "I loved you always, you know. Still, it wasn't what we looked for . . . not quite, was it? There were shadows between us. I was the gambler. I couldn't stop. I wanted to . . . for you. I know how you hated it. But I went on . . . and on. It was between us, wasn't it . . . the barrier . . . There'll be debts, Clarissa. I would have paid them . . . in time . . . out of winnings."

Later he said, "For you there was Dickon. You never forgot him, did you? I knew he was there. A shadowy ghost in our house . . . at our table . . . in our bedchamber. Those were the shadows between, Clarissa. But it was good . . . all the same, it was good."

I kissed his lips and his brow. He smiled faintly.

I bent over him and said quietly, "Lance, it was wonderful." And he closed his eyes and passed away.

The Return

It was nearly ten years since Lance had died. I was completely shattered by his death; so was Sabrina. I saw the old fear in her eyes which I had detected all those years ago when Damaris had died.

"What is it about me?" she cried to me. "Why am I fated to bring disaster? There was my mother. I was indirectly responsible for her death. And now . . . Lance. If I had not thought of marrying Reggie, I should never have gone to that house that night. I should not have left the stole behind, and Lance would be alive this day."

"It is not your fault that things happened the way they did," I insisted.

"But why me? Why should I be the one every time to bring disaster and death?"

"You saved my life. Don't forget that. I never shall."

"Oh, Clarissa, I'm so unhappy. There is a terrible guilt on me."

"No," I cried. "You must not feel this. Be sensible, Sabrina."

The task of bringing her out of that terrible gloom was mine, just as it had been all those years ago, and I felt more than ever that our lives were inextricably woven. I was closer to her even than to my beloved daughter Zipporah.

Zipporah was soft and feminine and yet, strangely enough, more equipped to take care of herself than Sabrina was . . . She had her friendship with Jean-Louis and I think, in her heart, was fonder of him than of anyone else.

Sabrina did not marry Reggie. After that dreadful night she could not bear to be with him. It reminded her too much. Poor Reggie was heartbroken. He went abroad to some members of his family—in Sweden, I think. But Sabrina had done something for him, I was sure. She had restored a certain confidence to him, but perhaps that was partly due to the fact that his father, of whom he had been in such obvious awe, was dead. However, hè went out of our lives. I sold the house in Albemarle Street and we settled in the country. I decided we would live there quietly, away from the social scene, although after the manner of such affairs, the scandal of Sir Ralph's death was soon forgotten.

During those ten years Priscilla and Leigh had died and Uncle Carl had come home to take over the management of the Eversleigh estates. Occasionally I went to see him, but it was a sad business now that Arabella, Carleton, Priscilla and Leigh were no longer there.

The old generation passed on; the new ones were coming up. I myself was now forty-three years old, and Sabrina herself was thirty. People were amazed that she had never married. Such a beautiful young woman, they said of her. She had had her admirers, of course, but I was sure that contemplating marriage brought back to her too vividly that scene in the bedroom, and always she shied away from it.

We were together so much, it seemed as though we knew each other's thoughts, and what we wanted now was to live in peaceful security in the country. It suited us, and we did not miss the house in Albemarle Street. We threw ourselves into the life of the country; we entertained and were entertained by people we knew who were not always those we had known in Lance's day. There was no gambling at our house— except the occasional game of whist, which was played merely for amusement. I had a stillroom and interested myself in the garden, particularly growing herbs. It was the sort of life I had been brought up to in Eversleigh, and although I was not ecstatically happy, I was serene and at peace.

I was delighted to see the bond between my daughter and Jean-Louis grow stronger with the years. It was taken for granted that they would marry in due course. They were eager to do so, but Jean-Louis wanted to be sure he could afford to keep a wife first. Jean-Louis was very independent. He knew the story of his mother's deception, of course, and I think that made him more determined than ever to stand on his own feet. He had always had a great interest in the estate, and before Lance's death had learned a good deal about it from Tom Staples, who was Lance's very excellent manager. When Lance died, Tom had managed for us with Jean-Louis' help; and when Tom died, I offered the job to Jean-Louis, and he accepted it with alacrity. As there was a pleasant house that went with the job, he would now have a home of his own.

That was what he had been waiting for. I knew that he and Zipporah would now marry.

They were happy months before the wedding. Zipporah, Sabrina and I spent long hours refurnishing the manager's house. It was good to see my daughter so happy, and I had no doubt that she had chosen the right man, one whom she had known and loved through her childhood. They had had the same interests, the same upbringing. I did not see how the marriage could fail.

I wished that Lance could have been there to see our daughter's happiness.

It was the beginning of the year 1745. I had said Zipporah should have waited for the summer. "June is the month for weddings," I added.

She had opened those lovely violet-colored eyes very wide and said, "Dear Mother, what does the time matter!"

She was right, of course; so the wedding was to be at the beginning of March.

"Spring will be in the air," Zipporah reminded me.

I thought how wonderful it was to be young and in love and about to be married to the man of one's choice. My thoughts went back to Dickon, and once again I was wondering what my life would have been like if I had married him.

It was absurd to go on dreaming after thirty years. Even if he returned, he would find a middle-aged woman, and I asked myself if he would love me in the autumn of my life as he had in the spring.

The day before the wedding arrived. The house was full of the bustle of preparation; the smell of roasting meats and baking pies and all sorts of preparations filled the house. The guests began to arrive. Zipporah had wanted a traditional wedding, with blue and green ribbons and sprigs of rosemary.

I was taken back all those years to the day I had married Lance. I remembered the haunting uncertainties which had beset me and how, when I had stood at the altar with Lance, it had seemed as though Dickon was at my side, watching reproachfully.

Soon Sabrina and I would be alone. It would be strangely quiet without Zipporah and Jean-Louis. I should miss my daughter's bright presence greatly. But she would not be far away, and I should see her often. And Sabrina and I would be together. I was always uneasy about Sabrina nowadays. I thought she should marry and have children. That would have been the life for her.

I wondered often whether she regretted not marrying. She took solitary rides. I wondered then did she brood on all that marriage might have offered; was she beginning to think of her life as wasted? Now that Zipporah was getting married, did I detect a certain wistfulness in her eyes?

I was thinking about Sabrina when I heard her calling me.

I wondered why she did not come to my room, so I went to the top of the staircase, and there in the hall was Sabrina and beside her was a man.

I went down the stairs. There was something about him which seemed familiar.

I cried, "Can it be . . . ?"

He turned to me and smiled. His eyes, I noticed, were of the same intense blue that I remembered.

"Yes," he said, "it is. And you are Clarissa."

"Dickon!" I whispered, unbelieving.

"Returned to the home of his fathers," he said. Then he took my face in his hands and looked into my face.

I was immediately apprehensive. I had aged considerably and could not bear much resemblance to the girl he had known all those years ago. There were shadows under my eyes and lines which had not been there when he had last seen me.

And him? He had changed too. He was no longer the boy I had known. His lean, spare figure, his deeply bronzed face, the hair which was not so plentiful as it had been and flecks of white in it. But the eyes were as brightly blue as ever and they burned with an intensity of feeling which I felt must match my own.

Sabrina was saying, "I found him looking at the house. He has come to see you. He went to Eversleigh, and Carl told him where to come to find you. When he saw me, he thought I was you."

"Yes," he said, "I thought I recognized you."

"There must be a family resemblance. After all, we are cousins."

"I am so delighted to have found you."

We were tongue-tied. I suppose after all the emotion we had shared and the passage of years that was inevitable.

"You have come in time to dance at my daughter's wedding," I said.

"Yes, Sabrina told me."

They smiled at each other, and I felt pleased because they liked one another. "This is wonderful," he said.

And so it was. Dickon was back.

I suppose what happened was inevitable. I should have seen it coming. When he had gone away I had been an innocent girl, very young. Sabrina had only just been born. When he came back he found an aging woman, one whose own daughter was just married. He would have been thinking of that young girl all through the years. She would be ageless in his imagination. Surely he could not have expected me to have remained as I was before he went away. Perhaps he had forgotten the passing of time. He would have expected a certain maturity, of course. Perhaps he thought to find me looking like Sabrina.

Zipporah and Jean-Louis had left for the house on the estate. They were absorbed in each other. The guests departed. Dickon stayed with us. I had an idea that this would be a spring like no other.

I loved Dickon. I always had, and not even time and space could change my love for him. He had begun as an ideal and he continued so. As he talked to us I caught glimpses of the old Dickon, the Dickon whom I had loved all those years ago and who had continued to haunt my life in the years between.

I knew that he had felt the same. I knew that he had come back for me.

We talked a great deal about his life in Virginia. He made us see the forests of pine and oak and maple; he talked vividly of the plantations to which he had been assigned. He had found a certain consolation for exile in hard work.

"I used to count the hours, the days, the weeks, the years," he told us. "Always there was the dream of coming home."

He had worked with cotton, and finding it interesting, had worked hard. He was given promotion; his master appreciated him and added to his responsibilities as the years passed. In time it was not like captivity at all.

"If I had not wanted to come home so badly, I might have become reconciled," he said.

The climate was benign; he had been free to ride when he wished to. He loved to see the animals—the elk, red and gray foxes, muskrats and martens, mink and weasels; he loved the opossums and often saw black bears in the Appalachians. He used to fish in Chesapeake Bay for sturgeon and trout as well as cod and Spanish mackerel.

In time he had been taken into his master's house and treated as one of the family.

"You never married," said Sabrina.

"No . . . but there was a daughter of the house. She was a widow with a young son. She reminded me of you, Clarissa. When her father died I took over the management of the place. We might have married . . . but always I had this dream of coming home."

Those were happy days. I felt uplifted. He had come home for me, and all the years when I had thought of him, he had been thinking of me.

I looked at my face in the mirror and wondered how different I was from that young girl. I had aged considerably. But so had he. Who does not in thirty years? We were mellowed, mature now . . . but that should be no barrier to understanding.

I thought, He will ask me to marry him. It is the happy ending to our story. "And so they lived happily ever after." How often had I read that line to the children. It always satisfied them. So it should. It was the only satisfying ending.

Those evenings in the twilight were the most precious moments of the day.

Sabrina was always with us. I insisted, although sometimes I think she avoided us. I wanted it to be known that Sabrina would always be with me. I knew Dickon would understand that. He always included her in the conversation, and if we went riding, Sabrina would be there.

He told us how, when his term was over, he had felt impelled to stay until he had earned enough money to come back. He had felt an obligation to stay until the widow's son was old enough to take over. Moreover, he did not know what had happened to his family's estates, and he had wondered whether, after the debacle of the rebellion in 1715, they had been confiscated. He had ascertained that they had not and that a distant relative had been looking after his interests while he was away, so he had a considerable estate in the north.

"I am a free and independent man now," he assured us.

A week or more passed. Dickon had said nothing to me. Sometimes we went for long walks together and occasionally he would go alone. Once I saw him returning with Sabrina. When I asked if she had enjoyed the walk she told me she had and that she had met Dickon by chance.

Sabrina had changed. She looked younger than her thirty years; there was a new bloom on her cheeks. I had become used to her, but it was as though her beauty struck me afresh.

I should have known. I should have seen it. Heaven knew, it was obvious enough. But I had to hear them before I accepted it. I had been living in a false world of my own making. It was not real. I should have seen it.

I was coming downstairs and they were in the hall. They had just come in. I was about to turn the corner of the staircase, which would have brought me into view when I heard her say, "Oh, Dickon, be careful. What are we going to do?"

He said, "Clarissa will understand."

I stood there, holding the banister, listening. It was almost as though I knew what they were going to say before they said it.

"All those years she has never forgotten. She waited for this, you know. I know her well . . . none better. She loves you, Dickon. She always has."

"I love her too. I always shall. But, Sabrina, I love you . . . differently. Clarissa is a memory from the past. You are here . . . the present. Oh, my beautiful Sabrina . . ."

I turned and went quietly back to my room.

Fool! I thought. Didn't you see it? Didn't you know? You are an old woman, and he has been dreaming of a young one. You have lived your life. He came back to you . . . for a dream . . . and he found Sabrina.

That it should be Sabrina was a twist of the knife in my wound.

Could I see them happy together while I myself would be longing for all Sabrina had?

How could I bear to lose them both!

They acted well. They attempted to disguise their feelings for each other, but it was becoming more and more obvious. But perhaps it seemed so because I knew.

Sometimes the desire came to me to do nothing . . . to wait. How could he ask Sabrina to marry him when I was there? This was the reason for his hesitation, for the haunted shadows in his eyes.

I struggled with myself. It was not easy. I had waited so long, dreamed too much. I could not give him up. Perhaps he would realize that. I could not see him married to Sabrina. How could I live near them and see them together, and yet how could I bear to lose them both?

You have your daughter, I told myself—Zipporah, who would live nearby and always welcome me to her home. I had my interests here.

No, I could not bear it.

I wrestled with myself. I knew what I ought to do, but how hard it was!

I awoke one morning with a strong resolve in my heart. I was going to be unhappy whatever happened. It was inevitable that I should be. I loved Dickon. I wanted Dickon. I wanted to start a new life with him. I wanted Sabrina too; we had been together so long. What could I do?

I could see only one way. It was hard, but I took it.

I told Sabrina I must talk to her. She came to me uneasily, and I said, "Sabrina, I am in great difficulty. It's about Dickon."

Her eyes opened wide and I could see the excitement in them.

"You know how I have always thought of him, dreamed of him."

"Yes," she said quietly, "I know."

"But things don't always turn out as one thinks they would. It's a mistake really to expect to be able to take up things where you left them off years ago."

She was looking at me disbelievingly.

"Do you mean . . ." She gulped a little. "Do you mean that you don't . . . care for him in the same way?"

I lowered my eyes. I dared not look at her and tell this blatant lie, which was what I must do.

"I am fond of him. He has grown into a fine man . . . but I have grown used to my freedom. I want things to go on as they have been. I want to stay mistress of myself."

"I understand, Clarissa."

"I thought you would. But how can I let him know? . . ."

"He will understand, I'm sure."

She was wanting to leave me, to go to him, to tell him what I had said.

I stood up. She was beside me. She flung her arms about me.

"Oh, I do love you, Clarissa," she said.

* * *

How happy they were! Sabrina had changed. She seemed to have flung off every one of those inhibitions which had plagued her from childhood. She was in love, and because she was no longer very young she loved with a great intensity. Dickon adored her. That was obvious. He was a little worried because he was some thirteen years her senior.

"What is age?" I asked. "You are ideal for each other."

My seemingly delighted attitude at the way things had turned out was a perpetual joy to them. They kept looking at me as though they were grateful and so delighted just because I did not want to marry Dickon.

I would smile brightly to hide the fact that I was broken-hearted. It was no mean feat, and I was rather proud of myself. It was only when I was alone in my bedroom that I allowed the mask to drop and sometimes wept a little in the darkness of the night.

The end of a dream!

There was nothing left of it now. I must settle down, and perhaps when Zipporah's children began to arrive I should find some solace in them.

Sabrina and Dickon were married quietly at the village church, and then left with him for the north.

It was one night in the July of that year when Charles Edward Stuart landed in one of the small Western Islands of Scotland with only seven men and a few hundred muskets and broadswords, and the money lent to him by the King of France. He had come to wrest the crown from our King George the Second and claim it for himself. It was like a pattern to me. It was when the Prince's father had come that Dickon had been involved and sent to Virginia. Now Dickon was back, and here was the son come to fight for what he considered to be his right.

Everyone was talking about the new insurrection. We had had thirty peaceful years, with little mention of Jacobites, but this seemed a serious threat.

Proclamations were issued. Rewards were offered for the capture of Charles Edward Stuart. In Scotland they called him Bonnie Prince Charlie because he was said to be young and handsome.

When visitors came to Clavering they talked of nothing but the Jacobites.

"It seems," said one of our guests, "that we might be getting the Stuarts back."

"Feckless family!" said another. "We're better off with German George."

People were not taking the rising very seriously, however. Many of them remembered what they called "the Fifteen," referring to the year 1715, when this Prince's father had come to Scotland in the hope of gaining the throne. Nothing had come of that. What were the Prince's Highland supporters, compared with the trained English Army?

There was some consternation when Sir John Cope was beaten at Prestonpans and Charles Edward started to march south and actually reached Derby.

Everyone now knows the outcome of that adventure and how the Duke of Cumberland marched to join the main army and so catch the Prince in a pincer movement. They knew that he could have reached London and that he might have succeeded had he not been persuaded to return to Scotland and fight the decisive battle there.

He was back in the north in December.

I heard from Sabrina. She was in distress. Dickon was a Jacobite at heart, and she knew that she could not stop his joining the Prince. "I reminded him," she wrote, "of what had happened before. He said that a man must fight for what he believed in, and that the throne belonged by rights to the Stuarts.

"Dear Clarissa, he is with them now, and I am desolate and full of fears. I have been so happy since I knew that you no longer cared for him, and now he has gone away. I don't know when I shall hear from him again. I am here in the north, far away from you. If only I could be near you I could bear it better. I play with the idea of leaving and coming to you. But I must be here . . . for when he comes back."

It shared her anxieties. I waited avidly for news.

It was April before it came—a lovely spring day, with the birds singing wildly with the joy of greeting summer and the buds bursting open on the trees and shrubs. Spring in the air and fear in my heart.

I heard of the terrible battle of Cullodon and prayed that Dickon might be safe. I wanted him to be happy; I wanted Sabrina to be happy.

The tales of the terrible slaughter shocked me. I shuddered at the name of the "Butcher" Cumberland. "No quarter," he had said. "None shall be spared. We will finish the rebels once and for all."

There was no news from Sabrina.

I prayed that he might be returned to her now. She knew I was anxious. Surely she would let me know.

No news . . . and the days were stretching on. May had come.

"This will be the end of the Jacobites," people said. "This is the final defeat."

"Cumberland was right to be so harsh," said others. "They have to be shown that these rebellions must stop."

"No man should treat his fellowmen as Cumberland has treated those who fell into his hands," said others.

Talk of the atrocities was rife. I could not bear to listen.

And still there was no news.

I wrote to Sabrina, "Let me know what is happening. I am frantic with anxiety."

I waited. Each day I watched. Surely something must have happened to explain Sabrina's silence.

May is the most beautiful of months, I had always thought until this May. I shall never forget it . . . the long warm days and the whole of nature rejoicing, and in my heart a feeling of dread that was almost a premonition.

It was the middle of the month and I was in the deepest despair when she came.

She walked into the house as though she were in a dream. In fact, I thought *I* was dreaming when I saw her. So often had I pictured her coming home to me . . . that it seemed like part of another dream.

"Sabrina," I whispered.

I saw her face then, pale and tragic, and I knew.

She ran to me and my arms were about her, holding her fast, rejoicing in the midst of my fears because she had come home to me.

We clung together without speaking for some minutes; then I drew away and said, "Dickon . . . Is he . . . ?"

She nodded. "He died . . . from his wounds at Cullodon."

"Oh . . . Sabrina . . ."

She could not speak. She could only cling to me as though begging for comfort. I said to her, "Do you remember when we did our lessons together? There was one thing we discussed, and I often think of it. It was what one of the Roman poets—Terence, I think—wrote. It was: 'The life of man is as when you play with dice; if that which you chiefly want to throw does not fall, you must by skill make use of what has fallen by chance.' Everything depends on the drop of the dice, but once it has fallen, there can be no going back. We must do the best we can with what is left to us."

She nodded; and in comforting her, I could comfort myself.

Later we talked. All through the day and night we talked. "He would go, Clarissa. I tried to stop him. I reminded him of what had happened before. But he had to go. He was a Jacobite, and nothing could make him forget that."

I thought, He forgot it once when he helped me to escape. And a great pride filled my heart at that moment.

"I begged him," she went on. "I pleaded with him, but he could not stop himself. He had to go. I understood at last. He was so certain that Charles Edward would succeed. And he did at first, but it was hopeless against the English armies. And Cumberland was determined that there should not be another Jacobite rebellion. The slaughter . . . oh, Clarissa, I could not describe it."

"You were there?"

"I followed him. I could not let him go. I was nearby, waiting. I wanted to join him when the battle was over. He was wounded badly, but some of his men brought him in from the battlefield. Thank God, at least he died with me beside him."

"Sabrina, my dear child, how you must have suffered!"

"Yes, I have suffered. I never really found complete happiness. You didn't entirely deceive me, Clarissa. You loved him, didn't you?"

"It's over," I said. "Dickon is lost to us both now."

"He spoke of you when he was dying. I think his mind had gone back to that time when you were young. He kept saying your name over and over again."

I could scarcely bear it. Nor could she; but as she told me of his last hours we wept, mingling our tears.

But she is back with me now. We are together, as something tells me we were always meant to be.

And yesterday she called in the doctor. She did not let me know that she had done so, and when I was told by one of the maids that the doctor had been there, I was filled with a terrible apprehension.

I ran to her bedroom. She greeted me with a smile. I looked

at her intently. There was no mistaking the radiance in her face.

"I was hoping it was true," she said. "I did not want to tell you until I was sure. But now I know. Oh, Clarissa, I am going to have a child. . . . Dickon's child."

I was trembling with a joy I had not known since the day Dickon came back, for now I knew he was going to live on . . . for both of us.